REVARY

ABIGAIL LINHARDT

Revary and all productions of the work, including but not limited to audiobooks, ebooks, and print, are copyright © 2025 by Abigail Linhardt. All rights reserved.

A SpaceDragon Creations book. First publication date April 14th, 2025 by SpaceDragon Creations.

This book is a work of fiction. Names, characters, places, and incidents either are the product of the author's imagination or are used fictitiously. Any resemblance to actual persons, living or dead, events, cultures, or locales is entirely coincidental.

No part of this book or its audio production may be reproduced in any form or by any electronic or mechanical means, including information storage and retrieval systems, without written permission from the author, except for the use of brief quotations in a book review. For more information, email spacedragoncreations@gmail.com or visit www.abigaillinhardt.com

Edited by J.H. Fleming. Cover art and design by Caroline Léger.

Paperback ISBN: 978-1-957175-24-9

Hardback ISBN: 978-1-957175-25-6

Ebook ISBN: 978-1-957175-10-2

Acknowledgments

A very hardy and meaningful thank you to my editor J.H. Fleming who tore this thing apart and made me make it better. I know working with me isn't the easiest thing and I appreciate all your comments, constructive criticism, and help.

I'd also like to actually thank the people who encouraged me to finish this book for the billionth time. I didn't want to, but you said you wanted to read it so I hope you enjoy it.

For David. Scout ahead.

CONTENTS

PROLOGUE
A CELESTIAL WARNING

P rince Gwen aimed his bow with one eye, holding his breath. He watched the chieftain of the norcan flee. The big, humanoid, green-skinned brute had been shouting through his tusk-like teeth not moments ago, hurling insults at Gwen. Now his horde ran from Gwen's warriors. He watched as the norcan's black flowing main of hair moved like a silken flag in the wind as he rode away on the back of its giant warg. He waited until it flitted to the right, giving him a clear shot of the norcan's left shoulder.

The arrow hissed through the air, bolting past the horde to strike the leader deep in his shoulder. Prince Gwen saw the norcan chieftain stagger, but continue his retreat into the hills. Gwen's keen eyes tracked him until the entirety of the horde vanished and the hoofbeats of their massive black horses and giant wargs faded. Once he was sure they wouldn't turn, he collapsed onto his bow, using it as a staff to hold himself up. He held his middle where one of the monsters had touched him with one of their long-bladed swords.

Removing his hand, he checked the wound. More than deep, the cut was jagged. It wouldn't heal clean and would leave an ugly scar. But a scar was worth saving the outer village of Arimathia. It was one of the smaller villages of his kingdom of Calimorden, but they all deserved his protection from the invading norcan.

"Your Highness!" the gruff yet feminine voice of his life-long trainer and mentor shouted behind him. She galloped up on a white mare, golden armor flashing in the setting sun. "I told you the Watch had this sorted. The norcan are vicious, not to be faced alone."

"I'm not alone," Gwen said with a smile. He straightened up and wiped his long blue-black hair out of his sweaty face. "You are here. And as you said, so is the Watch." He glanced around. They were here. Somewhere. Somehow he'd ridden out ahead, farther than he'd thought. "Elenor, the kingdom and its villages are under my protection. The norcan are getting fiercer. Bolder. This village is outside the immediate watch of Calimorden, but they shouldn't venture this close to the main city. We must be cautious with the norcan this close."

"Highness," Elenor sighed, sheathing her own longsword, "under your protection does not mean you must be amongst the battles. You have men to send under your banner into such frays."

Behind Elenor, a village girl smiled at Prince Gwen and leaned against the well. Her brown hair and sun-touched skin appealed greatly to him.

"I like to take in the appreciation of the villagers," he replied to Elenor with a grin. "Besides, no one likes a king who rules from the top of a hill. Calimorden is steward to the entire Surface Plane. The other Planes are none of my concern. But when the people of the Surface need my help—"

As if on queue, a shadow passed over the sun. Gwen glanced up as the peasant girl approached him. She held a flower in her hand. The thing that had overtaken the sun was a huge, round, floating kingdom: The Arcane Plane. Miles long, when the Arcane Plane crossed over the sun, it blotted it out for hours.

"Those Arcane devils," Elenor grumbled. "At least they never can be bothered to come to the Surface Plane."

Gwen didn't take his eyes away from the floating kingdom. The Arcane Plane hovered in the clouds above the Surface Plane, filled with winged beings who had learned to harness Arcane magic into power, weaponry, and machines.

"You're right, though," Gwen consoled his mentor. "They never come to the Surface Plane, and the only way for you to see them is if you find the gate guardian. Which is more trouble for you than it's worth, so I don't see what you have to be so upset about."

"They despise us. That's enough for me," Elenor quipped. "Think they are better than us here on the Surface." When she saw the village girl, she bowed quickly to her prince and moved aside to let him bask in the young woman's praise and pining.

The girl held the flower out to Gwen. "Thank you, Your Highness," she said with a blush. "The norcan have never attacked Arimathia in my lifetime. I'm glad you were here to protect us."

Gwen took the flower graciously. "They seem to be moving closer to the city. And the warriors in the north have been coming down their mountains as well. Any trouble from the northern barbarians?"

The girl shook her head. Then she looked up at the Arcane Plane. "If only we had their magic."

"We do fine with our own," Gwen replied. "Take some pride in the Surface."

The girl turned her wide hazel eyes back to Gwen. "Calimorden doesn't need such magic."

The prince took her praise personally. Taking her hand, he kissed it lightly. "All seems well now. I am afraid I have been wounded and must return to my mother with news of Arimathia. She has guests for me to meet this evening."

A sad look took hold of the girl's face as he turned to leave. She tried to keep her hand in his as long as she could. Once he was free of her, he remounted his horse and waved a farewell to the villagers. They were a few paces out with his small army when he finally asked Elenor, "Where *did* the Watch go?"

She glanced at him from under her golden helmet. "You didn't see them?"

He shook his head. "I happened to be riding past when the raiding horde came. The villagers followed my lead and took up arms to fight them off. I rode ahead of the Watch, I am afraid."

"That explains the wound, then," Elenor said with a disapproving scowl.

"I didn't intend to get wounded," Gwen replied, smiling, knowing full well what she thought.

"Of course," Elenor sighed. "A freshly-wrapped wound will make you look strong in front of our visitors from the Celestial Plane."

A bit of Gwen's spirit dropped at hearing this. "So they did come."

Mithra and Magnah, the king and queen—sun and moon

—from the Celestial Plane had not made an appearance on the Surface Plane in perhaps a hundred years. Not in Gwen's lifetime, nor that of his mother's, Queen Zephyr.

"It can't be good news, then," Gwen sighed, steadying himself to ease the pain of his wound.

Elenor shrugged and smiled with a single raised brow. "Could be. They have more beautiful daughters than they know what to do with. Perhaps they want a Surface prince for one of them."

Gwen had never seen a star, the offspring of the sun and moon, but he firmly believed they had to be beautiful, considering the glory they gave the night sky. He smiled. He'd believe that was why Mithra and Magnah came to visit the Surface Plane. Anything else that drove the sun and moon to leave the sky would be too terrible to imagine.

"The norcan are on the move," he said quietly so no one else overheard them. "Something could be very wrong. But I will choose to believe they are here for diplomacy."

Elenor kept her eyes trained ahead. "I hope you are right."

THE DOORS TO THE APOTHECARY SLAMMED OPENED, banging into the stone walls on either side. Gwen didn't jump, sitting on the raised table, shirtless. The poor old gnomish apothecary, however, started, pulling hard on the stitches he administered to the prince's side. Gwen hissed in pain, then he glared at his mother and her dramatic entrance.

"I should have known you hurt yourself," Queen Zephyr spat, fingers arching in fury at her side. "Mithra and Magnah are here. In the throne room. Waiting. What have you done?"

"My duty," Gwen replied, raising his arms as the tiny apothecary wrapped his middle. "The norcan raided Arimathia."

"Where?" Queen Zephyr asked. She looked genuinely confused.

Gwen rolled his eyes. "A village not two miles from our city's borders."

Zephyr scoffed and shook her head. "Those monsters never come that close to the city. The Watch would have seen them. Stopped them. But no matter," she said over Gwen as he was about to reply. She handed him the silver circlet he wore around his head to mark him as a prince during public meetings. "Come as you are. Perhaps the humiliation will teach you to stray from the halls when you know guests are coming."

Smirking, Gwen slipped his navy-blue shirt over his body and left the laces undone so his chest, still shiny with sweat, could be seen. Elenor rolled her eyes, helmet under one arm as she followed him out.

Gwen had to lean on his mentor as they climbed up from the stony basement of the palace. She took his arm and walked him into the throne room. The resplendent hall radiated sunlight in a warm, gentle glow. A single white ray of moonlight cut through it from time to time.

Mithra stood seven feet tall in elegant robes made of liquid gold that continuously ran from his shoulders. His long white hair and beard glittered with sunlight. A crown of spikes made from sunlight flashed around his head. It was from him that the sunlight filled the white hall. Beside him, just as regal and tall, stood Magnah, the moon. Her skin glittered blue, dusted over with star shards. Her eyes were piercing white orbs. She looked grave.

Mithra bowed and smiled kindly at the prince. "Fresh from the battlefield, human prince?" he asked with a twinkle in his eye.

"As you see," Gwen replied, moving to lead them into the council chambers in the cloisters behind the thrones. "It is my duty to protect my kingdom, and I do it with pride."

"Good man," Mithra boomed, clasping Gwen's shoulders between his glowing hands. "It is time for men of courage to rise up, I fear."

"To put it lightly," Magnah added in a hallow, echoing voice. She took a seat made of thick oak next to her husband.

The council chambers were a set of round rooms, throne-like chairs lining the circular walls. Windows let the natural light in, but with the sun within, the light beamed out. The walls and floor were made of white stone, and golden filigree decorated the corners and ceilings.

"I don't know what you mean," Zephyr said stiffly, gathering her ample skirts in her hand before she sat as well. She pointed for Gwen to sit next to her. He did.

"Don't you?" Magnah asked, raising her chin high. "Have you not seen the movements of the creatures of the Surface Plane?"

"Like the norcan?" Gwen asked. "And the warriors coming down from the mountains."

"Barbarians, you mean," Zephyr quipped.

Mithra stopped his reply by stroking his beard to think before he spoke. "No Plane is so divided than the Surface," he said sadly. "So many creatures, and yet you fight amongst yourselves."

"The norcan feast on flesh," Zephyr cut in. She spat to the side. "Even their own. The barbarians are mindless brutes, raiding whenever they wish. They have overtaken the eastern sea, cutting off trade for Calimorden and the west."

"I care not," Magnah cut in. "Queen Zephyr, something I have not seen in many ages of our world has shown itself in the dark corners of the WyldWood and Sylvan Murk, where the fae creatures gather."

Gwen leaned forward, elbows to his knees. "What have you seen, Majesty?"

Mithra and Magnah shared a worried glance. "A darkness," Mithra said, turning grave for the first time. "While not all darkness is a harbinger for evil, like the sorceress here on your own Plane, it can be a warning. Knowing that the mountain people have moved and that the norcan also sense danger, I have to wonder."

"What do they know?" Zephyr said. She tapped her long nails hard against the arm of her chair, her other hand going to her lips.

"They have their own shaman," Mithra reminded her. "They may be a terrible people, but they hear the Golden Tree. Perhaps it has spoken to them." He watched Zephyr fiddle with the elegant scarf hanging under her crown.

"You were not yet in existence when Malice came to our world," Magnah said, "but you no doubt have heard of the entity."

Gwen frowned. "Malice?"

"A powerful entity from the Other World," Mithra said. "One that can change the very weave of reality in our world. Can take our people from here and put them into its world. It can travel the Planes without the permission of the gate guardians."

"A Planes Strider," Gwen whispered. "I thought they were good. They are heroes in our world's history."

Magnah nodded her glowing head. "This is another entity. A wayfaring darkness. The Planes Striders are heroes. Saviors from the Other World. They were the only one who could defeat Malice. We tried, but we are weak to its power. Where Planes Striders are creators, Malice was a destroyer."

Gwen's heart beat fast and his wound throbbed. "And you think this Malice has come again?"

Mithra shook his head. "Not Malice. Malice was a servant of a much greater foe. The maker of the darkness. No servant has come. We believe Umbra the Unmaker is here at last. It is a destroyer of worlds, devouring life as it moves across existence."

"And it's here?" Gwen asked, standing up. "How do we call a Planes Strider to aid us? Where are they?"

Mithra smiled at the prince's passion. "Not in our world, young prince. They must be summoned."

"How?" Gwen pressed.

The sun and moon shared another glance. Zephyr cut in. "We don't need Planes Striders, Gwen. Calimorden is formidable. We have stood against battles and wars that have raged for a decade. Calimorden is our strength in the west. There is nothing we cannot defeat."

Magnah's head dropped. "I warned you, Mithra my love. She will not hear us. Just as those winged fools in the Arcane Plane would not heed our warning."

Zephyr stood. "I will not be spoken about thusly in my own council chamber." She strode to the door, tossing it open. "You may go, my Celestial friends."

With a final glance, Mithra stood, gathering his molten robes in his hand, taking his wife's hand in the other, and gracefully walking out the door. Gwen watched them go.

"Why are you not heeding their words even a little?" he asked once they were gone.

Zephyr groaned loudly, pushing past her son. "They think they can control us through fear. They sit above us in the Celestial Plane, seeing things we do not. Things we never can."

"Are you saying they're lying?" Gwen asked, jogging to catch up with her. They marched quickly through the palace halls back toward the cellar doors that would lead them to the massive underground network beneath the castle.

His mother steeled her face. "No. I know they speak the truth."

"Then why?"

"Because they see us as weak. Lesser than they, since we are but Surface Plane dwellers. The celestial beings of the stars have always behaved like that."

Gwen didn't think Mithra and Magnah had come off that way. They'd seemed genuinely concerned. And afraid. "I want to take what they said to heart," he said. "Let me go out and find a way to summon one of these Planes Striders."

Zephyr moaned. She lifted the cellar door with a grunt and pulled him down after her. "I have already taken the steps necessary to protect our land from this Umbra. But I see it is closer than I thought."

She wound her way through the cobblestone tunnels, following tiny torches dotting every few yards.

"Where are we going?" Gwen asked. "What do you mean, it's close?"

"I cannot explain it to you, my son," she whispered. Her voice cracked a little. She swallowed hard and stopped before a door with many locks. She fumbled with the keys, opening the locks one by one.

Gwen sensed a change in his mother then. Her brow glistened with sweat, her hands shook, and her breathing was audible now. "Mother," he said, standing close to her and taking her shoulder firmly in his hand. "You have nothing to fear. I will protect Calimorden from any threat. Even something as mysterious as this Umbra. Let me go out and see it for myself."

"You don't know what you would face," Zephyr hissed.

"I don't care," Gwen shot back. "Did this entity have something to do with the Watch vanishing? With the mountain warriors moving?"

Zephyr finished with the last lock and put her hand on the door. "I believe so. Umbra takes us, but we do not just vanish. There is a way in which its plans unfold." With a grunt, she shoved open the doors.

Gwen took a staggering step back, shielding his face from the sudden bright red light that exploded out from the open door. In the center of the room, a swirling vortex of orange and red rotated before his eyes, blinding him. He felt Zephyr grab his wrist and pull him in. Something akin to the sound of a raging fire, the roar of a hundred beasts, and the screaming of tortured souls shot out the minute they got close to the portal, deafening him.

"But there are ways to remain safe," Zephyr shouted over the sound. "It has given me a way."

Hot wind pulsed out from the vortex, tossing Gwen's hair into his face and whipping it away again. He squinted into the vortex, fear spilling out from it into him. "It? Umbra? The very thing Mithra warned us about? What do you..." He trailed off. What was her plan? He tried to pull away, but she held fast.

"Gwen," Zephyr sobbed, tears filling her eyes now. "The

way in which Umbra takes a creature is dark and terrible. I cannot see it happen to you."

He tugged on her grip again, digging his heels into the stone floor as she marched closer to the vortex. "Let me go. I'll find the Planes Strider. I will save Calimorden. It already took the Watch, Mother. It's here. Let me save my kingdom!"

She flung her other hand around and took hold of him hard with both hands. "This is a portal to the Nether Plane."

"That cursed hell," Gwen panted, his eyes flicking to the terrors that would lie just beyond the vortex.

"Umbra has taken it," Zephyr went on. "Let it have the Nether elves, the vampires, and monsters of the lower plane. But it cannot take the Surface Plane. I will not let it. Umbra will leave Calimorden if I give to it willingly."

Now he understood. With a cry, he jerked against her grasp. She sensed his movement and leapt at him, tackling him to the ground.

"Don't make this harder on me, Gwen!" Zephyr cried, pinning him hard. He shoved against her.

"Let me go," he grunted. "I'll find aid. We don't have to give in."

Zephyr growled and dug her hand hard into Gwen's wound. He screamed as she ripped it open anew and tore at his sides. The pain made his eyes roll and he stopped his cry. He half-passed out from the pain. Satisfied, Zephyr stood, hauling him up with her. She panted as she dragged him to the vortex.

"This is for Calimorden, Gwen," she whispered. "This way, Umbra will not touch us. The kingdom will be safe." She lifted him, grunting. "I love you."

"Mother," Gwen said, coming to a little. He grabbed her shoulders, stopping his fall into the vortex. "Don't give in. It took the Watch. It's attacking the norcan. It's already here on the Surface. Let me fight!"

She pried his hands off. "I know. But with subjugation, a conquered people may be rewarded. Umbra may show me mercy." She shoved him, but he clung on.

"Don't, Mother!" he cried. The pull from the Nether finally grasped him. Fiery tendrils slithered out, taking hold of his legs. He grunted, pulling against the vortex. "No one who bends a knee in fear is rewarded!" he shouted.

Finally, she got his fingers open. She grasped his wrists, all that held him to the Surface Plane.

"Please," he whispered.

"I love you."

She let go.

"Mother!" Gwen cried one last time before the vortex swallowed him up and everything went dark.

CHAPTER 1
CELESTE

Celeste's eyes darted over the map in a panic, looking for the weaknesses she must have missed when building the defensive wall of her stronghold. "Send all the elven sorcerers up north!" she cried. "Take an army of footmen to the northwest and follow that up with the knights and priests to the northeast. Where are my catapults?"

An explosion from the south alerted her as cries rang out from the left and the sound of crackling fire erupted louder. "Where are my workers? Send them to fix that! We cannot let the enemy behind our walls." She should call for aid. "Dark Star, do you hear me?" she asked the leader of the army who had allied with her. No answer came in her ear. Where were her allies?

The army moved out as instructed as she looked around in a panic to find the civilians who could put out the blaze.

"They're destroying our village!" the lord mayor cried out again from the town hall.

"Defend yourselves!" Celeste cried, calling all workers to take up an axe and act as a militia. That would only work for a little while; she had to find a way to save her people if Dark Star would not come to her aid.

"The army is under attack!" an elf called out to her from a distance.

She looked up to see the elven army being slaughtered by undead warriors from the north. Something wasn't right. The elf cast fire on the undead, but he didn't die. Why wouldn't he die?

"No!" she cried. "Save the elven forest before the undead take it." It would take several minutes for the knight army to reach the elves in time. It would never work. And her ally was gone. She eyed the burning undead. He still lived. The flames should have made him fall by now. Something wasn't right. There was only one thing left to do.

She'd have to invoke the ancient words. Forbidden magic. The only way to ensure her elves would not be killed was to commit the ultimate sin. She had to make them immortal. Besides, the leader of the invading army had made a mockery of her the other day in court. He'd tried to laugh it off, saying he didn't mean it, but the emotional damage had been done. Dare she stoop to such a low level?

The flaming undead killed her last elf.

The cries of her villagers deafened her as she stalled, hand poised to make the spell. Her city was lost. Her army was only safe for now. All she had left was the elven forest. She could not let it fall to the undead. She was the last defense between the poison of the necromancer and the young, new kingdom just beyond her borders.

"Love never dies." She whispered the incantation as her fingers moved, spelling out the words. A chorus rang out and cymbals clanged in her headphones. A white light shot up around her army and engulfed it in little twinkles and stars.

"Cheat enabled," it read in her chat bar. Her immortal fighters laid waste to the undead horde.

She waited for the repercussions of her actions.

"What the hell?" Justin shouted from behind the computer monitor that was back to back with hers.

Celeste's basement came back into focus as she looked up from the screen. A blue banner scrolled over her screen declaring victory as the others burst into an argument. She sat on one side of a table in her mom's basement. The linoleum floor made it cold and the white lights glared above. It had that musty smell some basements had when they were older than time. The boys—Kiyoshi, Justin, and Oran—came over to her house to use the faster internet. Her best friend, Stella, had high speed internet and so played from the comfort of her own bedroom.

Justin leapt up, almost overturning the table. She gasped, stifling a giggle.

"Celeste, you cheated," Justin spat.

"I couldn't lose to you," she protested, smiling weakly still. "And let's be honest. Guys, did you see his undead Chaos Warrior?"

Oran, the quiet one of the group who wore only black and had shaggy black hair, gently shook his head. "I was too busy fighting off Stella."

Celeste waited a moment. So Stella *was* still online. She hadn't abandoned Celeste after all. She'd have to go and talk to her about it, though. Online or not, she'd left her to fight Justin and Kiyoshi on her own. "I swear your undead warrior was not dying, Justin," Celeste went on. "He was burning for ten seconds and had almost no hit points left. What the hell?"

Justin pushed his glasses up his thin nose and shrugged. "Luck? The undead have more hit points than you think. That's not the point, though."

"You did kind of screw Oran and me over, too, Celeste," Kiyoshi put in. "Automatic win for you is a loss for us."

This gave Celeste pause. She glanced between Kiyoshi and Oran's sad blue eyes. She sighed. "All right, fine, I shouldn't have cheated. But can we please find someone else to play with us? Three against two is hardly fair."

"What else do you cheat in?" Justin snapped, crossing his arms. He glared hard at her. "What about when we play *Runes and Empires*? Do you fudge your rolls? You got a natural twenty last game. Was that cheating?"

Celeste scoffed indignantly at this accusation. "No, Justin, I roll in the community dice tray. You can see my dice."

Unconvinced, Justin shook his head. "I think you should take the loss."

"Stella left me!" Celeste blurted. "I was all alone. What was I supposed to do?"

Oran and Kiyoshi gave each other quick glances. "She was hiding in the forest. She had a base camp there," Oran said softly. "I found her and was trying to get around her."

"But did she attack you?"

Oran shook his head, ducking it down between his shoulders in shame.

"See? It was one versus three," Celeste shot. "She always stands back like that, waiting for me to go in and start the fight, then comes in later and cleans up." She growled, planting her fists into her hips.

"Tell you what," Kiyoshi said gently. He was always the peacekeeper. "We'll re-roll for opponents and do one versus one. No teams."

This sounded like a plan. Celeste smiled. "I like that."

"And cheaters lose instantly," Justin quipped, still glaring.

"Instantly," Celeste agreed, eyeing him. She wanted to ask him if he'd cheated before she did. But not in front of the other guys. He'd just get defensive.

Kiyoshi bent over the table and drew up a quick bracket. "There. This is who we'll play and winner moves on. Easy, right?"

Celeste took a quick glance and nodded. "I'll tell Stella. What will you guys do?"

"Library," Oran and Kiyoshi said together. "We'll use their internet while you're gone," Kiyoshi said. "Since it's me versus Oran." He smiled.

"Why don't you just hop into GameSpeak and tell Stella?" Justin asked. He leaned against the basement's support pillar like he was not about to go anywhere.

Celeste got a weird feeling in her stomach. "I want to chat with her, anyway." *That okay with you?* she added in her mind.

Kiyoshi gave Justin a weird look, shrugged when Justin flicked his head toward the stairs, and led Oran out after they gathered up their laptops. Celeste stood frozen to the spot. Justin had given Kiyoshi some kind of signal. And now they were alone.

Oh, great, Celeste thought. Justin was going to ask her out. Again.

"So, Celeste," Justin started. He leaned onto his palms on the table and looked up at her through his golden-colored fringe. The sun that came through the window well glinted off his glasses. "Our senior year starts soon. There's a special occasion that comes with that that I think would be a good jumping off point for us."

"Justin, wait," she said, holding up her hand. She glanced at the victory banner still waving on her screen. "We've had this conversation before. My answer is still the same."

A little annoyance flashed over Justin's face before he dropped his head. "Fine. Think about it, though."

I already have, she thought.

"I could help you find your place in this world," he went on, pushing himself up off the table. "You're always saying you don't know who you are, what you should be, what you should do. I know who I am. Let me lead you to who you can be." He reached his hand over the monitor and Celeste took an instinctual step back. Justin stopped. "Fine," he repeated.

He grabbed his things, tossed them into his backpack, and marched to the stairs. "*Runes and Empires* this weekend? We have a dungeon crawl to get through."

"I like the dungeon crawls," she replied, hoping the change in subject would lighten his spirits.

He shrugged. "Jake doesn't want to play over GameSpeak since he moved away. So we're down a barbarian and tank." He sighed. "I'll start to look for a replacement."

Celeste nodded. Jake was just the first casualty. He was a year ahead of them and had already headed off to college. These kinds of departures were what Celeste was afraid of more than anything.

Justin vanished up the steps, taking them a stomp at a time. Celeste winced with every step. She waited, counting to thirty before ascending the steps herself, hoping Justin would be gone. She ran past her mother preparing dinner in the kitchen and stopped to look at herself in the hallway mirror before heading out the front door. She ran her fingers through her blonde hair and leaned in close to examine the day's old mascara around her green eyes. She pinched her nose, wishing she had a more slender nose like Stella. Stella was like a Greek statue: willowy, alabaster skin with a straight, small nose. She died her hair neon pink and black and wore thick, black eyeliner every day, but Celeste was jealous of her lithe frame.

"I'm going to Stella's!" she called to her mom before flying out the front door. She trotted down the street in the late midwestern afternoon sun. She went a few houses down and then crossed. The unkept front yard told her that Stella's dad had not been out to take care of it in some time. He must have been working nights again at the factory at the edge of town.

She hopped up the steps, knocked once, then entered, knowing Stella was probably busy online. The inside of the house looked just about as unkempt as the outside. Not dirty —just not neat. She ignored it and took the stairs two at a time to Stella's room. Some kind of loud, metal music pulsed from inside. Celeste pushed open the door, wincing. Stella, with her black, chain-laden pants, sat at her computer, headphones on and mic flipped down. Celeste looked around for the boombox that blasted the music and switched it off.

Stella whirled around, glaring. "Oh, it's you. Cheater."

"Damn, Justin already get to you?" she asked, pulling up a purple dish chair to sit next to Stella. She looked over her shoulder to see her playing against someone she didn't know. "And for the record, I think he cheated first."

"Yeah?" Stella asked, eyes glued to the screen, clicking madly as she commanded her troops.

"I cast fire on one of his undead," she explained, "and he burned for ten seconds on four hit points and never died. Explain that."

"Damn it!" Stella exclaimed as a loss banner flashed red

over her screen. She pulled the headphones off and swiveled to face Celeste. She smiled at her best friend. "I wouldn't put it past him. Ever since he insisted on rolling behind the screen for *Runes and Empires*, I've been suspicious." She tapped her long black nails together. "I think we need to have a town meeting before this school year starts." She rolled her eyes. "Goodbye, summer."

Celeste nodded, blowing out hard through her lips. "Senior year. This is it. Guess we better figure out what we want to be when we grow up."

"Justin and Kiyoshi have already started to apply to universities," Stella mumbled. She licked her lips and cleared her throat. "Have you heard if Oran has?"

Celeste rolled her eyes. Stella was after Oran like Justin was after her. But, like her, Oran was not interested. "Stell, leave him alone. Stop pushing him to do what you want." She sighed. "Trust me, it's annoying."

"And Jake?" Stella asked like she was reading through a laundry list of things to talk about. "We don't have a tank in *Runes and Empires* now. We're vulnerable."

The choice of words hit Celeste hard. "Vulnerable," she repeated. "We should do something big before summer is over. Like LARPing again."

"LARPing?" Stella coughed, smiling like Celeste had made a joke. She cleared her throat when Celeste didn't break eye contact. "That would be a good bonding experience," she said more soberly. "We could pick up where we left off from last year. Continue the story of *Sun Age*. Get the others together again. Maybe doing it when school starts is a better idea. Something to look forward to, you know?"

Celeste nodded. "That's a good idea. But..."

Stella tilted her head, looking sympathetically at Celeste. "What is it?"

Celeste took a moment. "Stella, I'm afraid. I'm scared of senior year. I'm scared everyone will go in different directions after and that our party will be broken up. Put asunder. I'm not ready to lose everyone. This can't be the end."

"We will not," Stella said soothingly. She reached up and gently touched the ends of Celeste's hair, smiling sweetly. "We've all been friends since the football team crashed the first meeting of our TTRPG club in eighth grade. That bond is for life," she added seriously. "We're not going anywhere." Stella leaned forward and hugged Celeste. "I promise." After a moment, she added, "I'm sorry I abandoned you to Justin and Kiyoshi. I won't do it again. And don't worry. We'll all always be friends."

Celeste hugged her friend back. Of course she was being overly dramatic. Just because high school ended didn't mean everything else did. Sure, they had to pick universities to attend and no doubt everyone would go in different directions. But that didn't mean it was the end.

Right?

"We have to be strong," Celeste said, pulling back from the hug. "We have to stick together."

"Forever." Stella smiled. She pulled a necklace out from under her shirt. It was half a silver star.

Celeste returned the smile and pulled her half out. They leaned toward each other and placed the two halves together to make one six-pointed star. She felt lucky to have Stella as a best friend.

She leaned back and looked out the window at her house. From here, it looked so peaceful. Stella noticed her glance.

"Parents still fighting?" she asked.

"More than ever," Celeste sighed. "It just adds to the anxiety, you know? They won't help me, won't talk to me because they're too busy screaming at each other."

Stella pressed her lips to the side, thinking. "I guess we need our escapes more than normal, huh? But don't worry, I got you. Same as always."

"I know I can trust you and count on you," Celeste said. "You've always been there for me."

Stella beamed and nodded. "So. *Sun Age* and LARPing again?"

Celeste grinned mischievously. "The friends that LARP together, stay together."

CHAPTER 2
LANCE

L ance expelled his breath hard through his lips as he punched the heavy bag with all his might. Once, twice, three times fast. His long brown hair fell into his dark brown eyes and stuck to his face, but he ignored it. The classic rock blasting from the boombox to his left played his and his dad's favorite songs as sweat poured off his body. He imagined the bag was the star quarterback from the rival high school they'd be playing in their first game. The summer heat of Texas warmed his muscles, making him spry and agile. He ducked, pretending the other guy had thrown a punch, then rose in an uppercut that sent the bag flying.

"Whoa there, champ," Dad called from the other side of the garage. He stepped down the two small wooden stairs that descended from the garage door in the kitchen, where his mom was no doubt making dinner. "Save something for the start of the year."

Lance smiled at his dad and wiped the sweat from his brow. "I've got plenty, Dad. Make no mistake." He playfully jabbed at the bag, making it swing toward his dad. Dad caught it deftly and held it still while Lance laid in another several cross hooks and jabs.

"Maybe we should have put you into boxing instead of football," Dad laughed, grunting into the bag as Lance knocked him a pace back.

"That's my throwing arm is all." Lance smiled. He stopped, panting, and leaned against the weight bench behind him. "What's up? You just come out here to flatter me?"

Dad laughed and punched Lance's muscled arm with a grin. "Nah, I have a surprise for you." He reached over and turned off the boombox, throwing them into a weird, buzzing silence. "Today is a very special day."

Lance smiled hard, looking down at the ground. His cheeks reddened. Today was his eighteenth birthday, and Dad had been talking about it for a month. Lance thought Dad was more excited about it than he was. Still, turning eighteen meant a lot to him. It also meant growing up. And that was more terrifying than facing their rivals in the finals.

"I got you a little something," Dad beamed. Lance saw his eyes sparkle. Mom said he and his dad had the same mischievous grin. Dad sauntered over to the garage door number pad and pushed in the code. The door rattled and clanked as it rose up. "I hope you like it."

Lance winced in the late afternoon sun and looked out into the driveway. His heart leapt and his stomach dropped out. "No way," he crowed. "No way, Dad!"

Sitting in the driveway, gleaming and sparkling, was a huge, brand new white pickup truck. Lance leapt once and dashed out the door to the new vehicle. He circled it, taking in every detail he'd ever asked for. Sparkling rims, extended cab, long bed, a little bit of a lift, and tinted windows, among other things.

"There is no way this is for me," Lance laughed in hysterics. He turned to see Dad holding up a set of keys on a lanyard in the yellow and red of his high school.

"There sure is," Dad beamed. He shook the keys, enticing Lance to swipe them from his hands.

He did and ran to the driver's side door. The key slid in like it had been well-oiled. It crunched and clicked, opening the door. Lance leapt up into the truck and quickly plugged the key in. The engine turned over and purred in a deep, guttural rumble.

"Oh, it's beautiful," Lance sighed, running his hand over the dashboard.

"Glad you think so," Dad grunted, hauling himself up into the passenger seat, "because you're taking me to the game." He flipped his hands up to show two tickets to the local baseball team.

Lance smiled so hard he could hardly see. "I'm sweating and gross."

"It's Texas, it's summer." Dad shrugged. "We're all going to be sweating and gross at the game. C'mon, let's go."

"Oh, hell yeah." Lance pushed on the break, loving how smoothly it went down, then shifted into reverse. The car turned and moved at his slightest touch. Smiling still, Lance turned around and drove them out into the bigger city and to the stadium.

Hours later, satisfied from hotdogs, lemonade, and their team actually winning, the two came back late into the night. They talked energetically about the game and Lance once again thanked Dad for the day they'd had.

"Well," Dad sighed as they made the last turn onto their street, "you're growing up, and this time next year..." He trailed off and shook his head. "Aw, look at me. Getting emotional. I love you, son. And I want you to know..." He trailed off again, frowning and looking ahead.

"What?" Lance asked, feeling the mood shift to cautious. He followed his dad's gaze and saw what he looked at. "Why is there a red Mustang in our driveway?" he asked.

"God damn it," Dad growled. "How? Why is she...?" He couldn't finish a sentence. "I bet your mother's home, too." This made him growl. Almost snarl.

"Dad, what's going on?" Lance asked. His heart raced. He was always good at picking up on people's mood shifts, and this one had him almost panicking. His dad was almost enraged.

Dad cursed like Lance had never heard him curse before and threw the belt buckle off so hard it hit the window. The glass cracked.

"Dad, what the hell?" Lance shouted.

"Park the damn car, Lance," Dad snapped.

Dad rarely used that tone. It struck Lance to his core, made him feel like he was in trouble, that he'd done something wrong. His nose tingled but he put a stop to the rising emotion then.

"Dad?" he asked again, but Dad silenced him by slamming the door shut. Fear shot through Lance as he watched his father march into the house, hands in angry fists.

Shaking, he got out and followed. He clutched the keys in

his hand, all his senses on hyper alert. Just as he reached the closed front door (Dad had slammed it behind him), shouting erupted from the inside. Lance froze for just a moment. Then, courage overcoming him, he threw the door open, wondering if his parents were in danger. The living room, just inside the front door, was a war zone.

Mom screamed at Dad just as he'd appeared and another woman—tall, pretty, blonde, and leggy—stood off to the side, arms crossed in a red leather jacket that matched the Mustang. Her sharp eyes darted to Lance when he entered.

"You have a kid, Nick?" the woman shouted, jaw dropping.

"Oh, did he not tell you that, either?" Mom snapped.

Lance understood in a millisecond, but he dared not believe it. His mind went completely and utterly blank. A shiver ran down his spine and over his arms, making his hair stand on end. The room seemed suddenly cold and dark.

"Dad, who is this?" Lance asked in a small voice.

"This is his side whore!" Mom shouted.

The word felt like a slap in Lance's face.

"I bet you didn't know your dad was a cheating pig, did you, hun?"

Lance looked to his dad. The entire day flashed before his eyes. The last week. Then month. There were no signs Dad had been cheating. Not one. Lance wracked his brain. His gut twisted and he felt sick. Bile rose in his throat. What had he done wrong to make his dad lie to this woman who didn't even know he had a son? His throat tightened and he couldn't speak.

"Mom, what?" he choked out.

"I can explain," Dad cut in. "Lorena, listen to me."

"Explain?" the other woman barked a laugh. "Are you

even in sports marketing? Is that true? What else is a lie, Nick?"

"Wait," Lance begged. "How did this happen?"

Mom and the other woman glared daggers at one another.

"I came over to surprise Nick—your father." The woman almost choked on the word. "Kid, I'm sorry. I didn't know."

"And I answered the door," Mom finished.

"You were never supposed to meet," Dad interjected.

"No shit, Nick!" the woman spat.

Mom looked like she wanted to punch Dad. She rushed to a shelf filled with decorative glass objects.

"You. God. Damn. Pig!" Mom shouted, throwing an item from the shelf of glass objects with every word. Dad ducked and they all missed him. But the last one, a small green vase, crashed over Lance's head.

The shattered glass rained down over him. The shock of the blow made him cry out and he blinked rapidly as he stumbled back. Something hot trickled down his head and into his eye, stinging it.

"Shit, Lorena!" Dad snapped.

"You okay, kid?" the other woman asked, genuine concern on her face.

"Don't talk to him, Therese," Dad commanded. "Lance, go into the kitchen before you get blood on the carpet."

Dazed and shaken, Lance pushed himself up from where he'd slumped against the wall and marched into the kitchen. His legs shook. He gripped the countertop to steady himself. His brain now spun in addition to the illness he felt in his gut. His ears rang.

Behind him, the shouting continued. Another thing crashed and he winced away from the violence. He ran a rag under the water in the kitchen sink and pressed it to his bleeding scalp. Then he glared out the window at his new white truck and tried to drown out the screaming. Tears threatened to fill his eyes, but he shoved them back down, letting rage rise instead.

Eventually, the screaming and fighting moved out into the front yard. Lance hid in his bedroom and put headphones on, opening up a game on his computer. He'd ignore them for as long as he could.

He started a game of *Elderforge* and concentrated on his own tiny kingdom. He checked his crops to make sure they were growing and harvested some. Then he trained a few more troops before looking for a match, finding another kingdom to go to war with. His dad thought the game was stupid, but right now Lance didn't care.

He turned up the volume when Mom's shriek cut through the headphones, deafening him. By now all the neighbors had to be out watching the commotion. They'd come by later, ask if he was okay, whisper among themselves, say they knew it all along. He blinked angrily and a single tear ran down his cheek. Frustrated, he wiped hard at it and focused on the game. He'd found a match and was at war now.

It felt like mere seconds had gone by when suddenly red and blue lights flashed over his bedroom walls. His heart thudded in his throat as he spun out of his chair to look out the window. The cops were there. Someone must have called them. He moved to his bedroom window and looked out over the front yard. They hadn't handcuffed anyone, and the woman, Therese, stood with her car between her and his parents. He watched the silent movements until exhaustion finally overcame him. There was nothing he could do, and the grownups were just screaming and yelling more. The cops stood by, hands on their hips. They weren't paid enough for this.

He lay down in his bed, still dressed, and waited until sleep took him.

A FEW DAYS LATER, MOM KNOCKED ON HIS DOOR AND came in before he could pause the game he was playing. She gently removed his headphones and sat on his bed, facing him.

"Lance, I'm really sorry about everything," Mom whispered. She'd been speaking more and more softly since Dad had left.

It wasn't her fault, but he hadn't been able to speak since that night. He just looked up sadly at her from where he sat, willing her to just go on without his prompting.

"Dad's here to get some of his things," she whispered. "I want..." She choked but then cleared her throat. "I want you to go see him. We might not see him again for a long time."

Christmas? New Year's? High school graduation? What was a long time? Lance nodded, not knowing.

"Go on. He's waiting for you." She stood up, gently took his face in her hands, and kissed the top of his head. "Then come see me. We need to discuss a few things."

Lance waited until she was gone from his room before he stood up and descended the stairs into the living room. Dad stood there, backpack on and a bag in his other hand. He looked pathetic, Lance thought.

"Hey, kiddo," Dad sighed. "Look—"

"I don't want to hear it," Lance cut in, shocking himself.

The snap in his voice took him off guard. He wanted to shout at his dad. Ask him how he could do that to Mom. But he didn't trust his voice as a quivering sigh rose in his chest.

"I hear you," Dad mumbled. "I don't blame you. Listen, though, please. You're the man of the house now, understood? Take care of your mom. That's your job. Make sure she helps you apply to universities. Don't let her convince you to go to UT, okay? Go where you want. Or wherever the scouts take you."

"Dad, stop," Lance grumbled, not trusting his voice still. "Just get out, okay?" He stopped there. His throat was so tight he couldn't even swallow.

Slowly, Dad nodded and looked away. "Okay, son. I love you."

Lance's brow snapped down into a glare. He didn't believe that. Not when he didn't exist in the fantasy his dad had with this other woman. Seeing the visceral reaction, Dad nodded and backed away. In a minute, he was gone. Lance didn't see him go, his brain all white noise. Before he knew it, his mother was at his side.

"We're moving in with my sister," she whispered, rubbing his arm affectionately.

"Which one?" Lance asked.

"Beth, the adopted one. The mother to your cousin Alice."

"Aunt Beth?" Lance burst out. "Mom, that's up north. That's a whole different state." He couldn't keep the fear and whining tone out of his voice. But he didn't care. "For how long?"

Mom bit her bottom lip. "Until I find work up there."

His gut dropped out from under him. That wasn't what he meant. "A job? We're moving for good? You're uprooting my entire life. This is my last year. What about football?" The struggle to not give in to the hysterics strained his muscles.

Mom gently took his hand and raised her brows. "Calm down, Lance. You'll try out when we find a school. Nothing will change."

"My friends are here," he protested. "Why do we have to run away?"

"It's not running," Mom snapped in her own defense. She blinked and shook her head. "We need a new start. Some-where out of here." She gripped his shoulders. "Texas will still be here if you want to come back. But for now, we need to get away." She smiled weakly. "Text Alice. You guys are friends. You play that game online all the time."

Him and his cousin Alice being semi-close over the internet didn't lessen the blow. He wanted to argue, to rage. To beg Mom to let him stay. But he knew it was useless.

With the weight of his crumbling world crushing him, Lance nodded in defeat.

CHAPTER 3
PARTY MEMBERS

Celeste set everything out the night before, from her light makeup down to her shoes. She chose specific earrings to match her medallion necklace and an unassuming band t-shirt with jeans. Standing back, she looked into the long mirror hanging on the inside of her closet door.

"Low-key," she whispered. "First day of the rest of my life."

Once downstairs, the family ran through its routine of shouting matches, arguments, her brothers fighting over a certain piece of toast, and the other ritualistic behaviors of a family that couldn't wait to get out of each other's way. Unlike her, everyone else was glad school had started up again.

On the bus, she collapsed next to Oran, whose face was set in a deep pout. He was more decked out in black and accessories this time because it was the first day of school.

"You look cheerier than usual," Celeste said.

Oran glared at her, but only half-seriously. "Justin was in the chat room last night asking for you." He was so slumped in his seat that he looked up at her. "I told him he was being too pushy with you."

"What did he say?" she asked, taking out her algebra book to get a head start on the foreign signs and symbols that would dictate her mood from now until Christmas.

Oran shifted uncomfortably. "Wanted to know if you'd told any of us where you wanted to apply to college. If you were working this , and where."

Celeste pulled a confused and exhausted face. "Good grief. Why is he so obsessed with me working and filling out applications? I don't even know what I want to major in. He needs to focus on himself."

"He has," Oran moaned. "He's been done planning his future for some time. He's trying to get Kiyoshi's life ordered now, too, but his mom wants him to spend a year back in Japan with her family. So then Justin started in on me. Wish you were there to lighten the load, you know?"

The sun blinked behind the neighborhood trees rapidly as the bus pulled out onto the main street to head toward the high school.

"What was it you wanted to study, anyway?" Celeste asked. "I never asked because I wasn't sure you would after..." She stopped herself, her face burning. "I'm so sorry, Oran. I've known you for years. I know you want to go to college. I shouldn't have assumed you weren't."

He gave her a gracious look that softened his usually guarded eyes. "I was thinking maybe somewhere for game design."

Celeste gasped, grabbing Oran's bony shoulders. With an excited squeal, she shook him hard, then hugged him. "That'd be awesome! Some of the biggest game developers are in California, though. It's the home of *Elderforge*."

Oran smiled shyly but broadly. "Yeah. My senior project is that PC game I've been working on. Figured if I can make it actually happen, maybe I could use it to get a scholarship. Or it would at least look good on an application."

"Oh, hell yeah it would," she said. She sat back, smiling wildly. "I bet Justin shut up when you told him that, huh? Does anyone else know about your game?"

He looked away shyly, dipping his head down into his shoulders to hide. "Last time I told someone—with that battle system I was making?—the titans destroyed everything. I still don't know how they found out."

The memory came back to Celeste in red, vivid detail. The football team—whom they called the titans—had appeared one day in the classroom they'd booked for their gaming club. Oran was right: how they'd known where they were or that they were testing out Oran's new system was still a mystery. They'd destroyed everything he'd typed up and had smashed his laptop. Only a handful of them had suffered consequences, and Oran had had to save up for months to buy a new laptop.

"I cannot believe the beldam didn't believe you when you told her what happened," she said in reference to the principal.

"It was Friday," Oran reminded her. "They had a game. Couldn't get the royal football team in trouble."

"Ugh," Celeste moaned. "Those guys are insufferable." She sighed, seeing the school come around the corner. "I'll catch you in whatever class we have together."

Oran nodded. Celeste saw him physically brace himself for the coming storm of high school seniors and the new torments they'd lay into him. Oran had been bullied most of his life, but it had gotten worse in eighth grade. The last four years had been a nightmare. She wished she knew how to stop it, especially with what he'd been going through recently.

She hopped off the bus and watched him head through the far north door before gathering her own courage to walk through the doors for the last first time.

LANCE FULLY EXPECTED TO MAKE THE FOOTBALL team. The week before, in tryouts, he had blown the coaches away. Mom had been very supportive and said things like, "I knew it, I knew you'd make it," and had taken him out for dinner. Lance had plans to meet his cousin Alice as soon as possible and try to integrate himself into the school's hierarchy. But it hadn't been hard. Once anyone knew he was on the football team, they pretty much wanted to be his friend. It should have made him feel happy and relieved. But it felt fake.

He walked, not living too far away in their new house, and not wanting to park his brand new truck in a parking lot full of wild drivers. It was only September, but it was already colder than he was used to in Texas. And the sky was gloomy, dark. No clouds could even be deciphered among the slate of gray above. He stopped when the bus passed him and parked to let the kids out. He watched them, wondering if any of them would end up being a friend. In the sea of colorful clothing, a single black mass exited and quickly made its way to the the side door that led to the gym. He watched the boy hurry, head down. A flash of silver on his face told Lance he had a ring in his nose. He liked the weird, shorter boy almost at once. That kind of person was genuine. Interested, he half-followed him through the side door and down the hall. Before he could catch up with the boy, a hand flew out of a hall opposite some lockers and dragged the boy down it. Lance trotted to keep up. A gaggle of boys in the school's white and blue surrounded the black-clad boy. Lance froze as the familiar scene of bullying ensued.

One boy—Lance remembered his name to be Thomas, and he was the captain—made fun of the boy's nose ring and made a mad grab for it. The weird boy dodged, but was quickly pinned to the wall. His wide, dark blue eyes found Lance. Realizing he'd be ostracized if the team saw him coming to the weird kid's aid, he walked on, head down.

His stomach knotted. How much of a coward was he?

CELESTE STOOD IN THE MIDDLE OF THE HALL, READING her schedule. She had a few classes with her friends, but found they were mostly spread out. She was just losing hope when she looked up and saw a girl with colorful dreadlocks wearing a *Runes and Empires* t-shirt. She smiled at the girl and said shyly, "I like your shirt."

The girl looked up from her own schedule and said, "I like yours. Love that band." She marched to Celeste, hand out. "I'm Alice. How come I don't know you?"

"Big school," Celeste replied. "You don't happen to play, do you?"

"No," Alice sighed, falling in step with Celeste. "I just wear the shirt so the bullies know to target me."

Celeste frowned and looked up at the girl.

"Kidding," Alice giggled. "I love the game. Haven't had a group in months, though. I don't suppose you need a new party member, do you?"

Celeste beamed. "Do you play tanks?"

"Almost exclusively," Alice said. She skipped once, showing her excitement. "I have a barbarian princess I've been dying to play, if you're interested."

The door to her classroom appeared on their right. Celeste stopped outside it and faced Alice. "We'd love to have you. I can introduce you to the others after school, if you'd like."

Alice beamed and grinned so hard her white teeth showed. "Before we go in," she said, stepping between Celeste and the door. "Would it be cool with your game master if I brought someone else?"

Not sure what Justin would think, Celeste shrugged.

"My cousin just moved to town," Alice explained, "after a really messy divorce between his parents, and he really needs a friend. He hasn't played *Runes and Empires* before, but he'd love to learn. I know he would."

To Celeste, the more the merrier. She didn't mind at all. "I'll talk to the guys," she said with a smile. "I'd love to have you both."

Alice's smile lit up her face. "Thanks." She quickly produced a bright pink sticky note and scribbled her online name down. "Find me online with this name in GameSpeak. You on *Elderforge*?"

Celeste smiled and took the note, nodding.

Alice grinned one last time and turned and entered the classroom.

Celeste braced herself for English class. Ms. Vanders, the old crow who taught easily the most interesting class in school, made it the absolute worst. Shakespeare was on the list of books they needed and she knew Ms. Vanders had the talent to make every single senior in her class hate Shakespeare for the rest of their lives. Teachers were good like that.

When she sat down, someone else occupied the crow's seat at the front of class. A man, maybe late thirties, with dirty blond hair in a messy pony tale and wearing an old brown cardigan that was too big for his thin shoulders, lounged in the chair with his feet up on the desk. His leather shoes were old and worn. Curious, Celeste stared at him as Alice slid into the desk next to her.

"Ms. Vanders sure looks different," Alice laughed quietly, taking out her reader.

"Anything is better than her," Celeste groaned.

"Really?" the man asked, dropping his feet to the floor and looking the girls in the eyes. He wore round glasses, which they hadn't seen before because he'd been holding a huge book, covering his face. "I thought substitutes were the worst." He stood up, stretched, and looked out over the class. "I'm Alexander Granger, and I'll be your substitute today for English among other classes today. At least for some of you."

The class snickered and a few of them immediately started to horse around, making noise and chatting.

"I thought we'd start today off with a pop quiz." He smiled, opening the desk and pulling out a stack of papers. "Ms. Vanders kindly left behind instructions for me." He pushed his glasses up his nose and read a clipboard with a slight frown. "Phone bucket?" he read out loud.

The class moaned.

"Over there," Alice said, smiling deviously and pointing to a bookcase near the whiteboard.

The teacher smiled at her and wrote something down on his clipboard.

"Oh, you're one of those," Celeste said, teasing. "So I'll come and study at your house, then?"

"Absolutely," Alice beamed.

The container went around and students grudgingly dropped their phones into the bucket. When it got to Celeste, she passed it on, since her parents still had her phone from a previous grounding. Mr. Granger looked at her, clearly assuming she'd hidden it.

"I'm grounded," she mumbled. "Don't have my phone."

He narrowed his eyes at her, marked something on his clipboard, and went to the stack of papers on his desk. After handing them out, and an agonizing thirty minutes of silence in which the class did their best to fill out the answers, he perched on the edge of the desk.

"We will check them together as it's a syllabus quiz," he said. He cleared his throat and read the first question out loud. "What are the three plays on the syllabus you should be reading this semester?"

Alice's hand shot up. Before he called on her, she recited, "*A Midsummer Night's Dream, Much Ado About Nothing,* and *MacBeth.*"

Mr. Granger stared at Alice, half amused and half curious. "Mhm," he mumbled. "Question two—"

"Every paper must be formatted in MLA and printed out," Alice interrupted, nearly bursting at the seams with keeping the other answers inside her as her hand flew up into the air again.

Mr. Granger clicked his tongue. "Mr. Kent," he said, calling on a student in the back who had been whispering to his gaggle of friends. "Answer to question twelve?"

Celeste moaned as Alice shot her hand up again.

The boy in the back stammered and looked at his quiz. "Uh, Jennifer Snell?"

The girl next to him, Jennifer Snell, glared at him.

"Ms. Snell," Mr. Granger asked, checking the girl's quiz, "what is wrong with Mr. Kent's answer?"

The girl glared at the boy. "It's my name."

"And what does that mean?" Mr. Granger asked.

Celeste checked question twelve. It was a throwaway question to help students get a few points on the quiz: What is your name? She laughed out loud and turned to look at the boy who had clearly cheated.

"You see, Mr. Kent," Mr. Granger said, crossing his arms and leaning against the desk, "sometimes, cheating doesn't harm you. If the question was, 'What is Lady MacBeth trying to wash off her hands?' and you cheat to write the answer that it's blood, you still get that knowledge. You have to write the word 'blood,' and you most likely will remember that for the rest of your life. But if the questions are more personal, about you and who you are, you cannot cheat." He smiled. "Lest you look the fool."

The class laughed at this. The boy sank into his chair, glaring at the substitute. Part of Celeste loved what the substitute had done, but the other part felt bad for the kid, being humiliated in class like that.

Mr. Granger looked up at the clock. "The bell's about to ring, but I'll see some of you in history. If you have any questions, don't hesitate to inquire."

AT LUNCH, LANCE GAZED ABSENTMINDEDLY OUT THE window, thinking about the boy he'd left to the bullies. He'd liked the boy's weird sense of fashion and had wanted to talk to him, but had stopped when the team had shown up. He wished he'd been a bit braver.

Someone slammed their tray next to him with a loud, "Hey, cuz!"

Lance jumped, almost choking on his pizza to see his cousin Alice slide up the table next to him. Alice was a tall, pretty, Black girl with long hair in colorful dreadlocks. Her smile beamed brightly down at Lance as he calmed down.

"Shit, gave me a heart attack," he coughed.

"My pleasure," Alice giggled. "How you been? Saw you made the team. That's good." Her smile turned sympathetic. "Sorry we had to meet under these circumstances. But I'm so glad you're here!" She turned and almost bowled him over with a big hug. "Now I can introduce you to all the games you should be playing."

"Not the table top games, please," Lance moaned, prying her arms off him. "Those things are so...nerdy. *Elderforge* was bad enough."

Alice raised a brow, smirking hard with the right side of her lips. "Nerdy? What? You're crazy. Just be glad I'm inviting you. And I met someone who needs players. So you'll come and participate and you'll like it. She was really nice, too."

Lance shook his head but smiled. When he looked up, he found the band kids circling around the weird kid in black from before. The kid shrank away into a corner between the huge lunchroom window and the wall outside. He looked terrified. Lance knew the look of a group of kids circling prey. Remembering his cowardice from before, something in Lance snapped.

"Hold on, Alice." He stood and strode to the exit door, throwing it open with all his might.

The band kids jumped and backed away. Then they glared at him, waiting for him to say something.

"You that new player on the football team?" one of them asked. "Good arm, coach says."

"Yeah, whatever," Lance spat. He placed himself between the boy and the band kids. "Stop picking on this kid and get out of here."

The one who'd spoken scoffed and smirked. "Uh, do you know who this is? He's our regular prey. You don't need to worry about him. You'll get your chance to torture him." When Lance didn't move, the band kid raised his hands and backed away. He laughed nervously. "I get it. You want him to yourself. C'mon, guys."

Lance glared after them, watching them go. He turned back to the boy in black. His backpack had been upturned and all this textbooks, pens, a sketchbook, some CDs, and a few other things spilled all over the ground. Lance knelt down and started to pick them up.

"You just ruined your chances of being cool," the boy said, his voice thick.

Lance looked up. The boy had a black eye and he quickly tried to hide it behind his long bangs. "I'm, uh, sorry I didn't step in before. I'm Lance."

"Oran," the boy said, wiping his eyes. Lance offered him the textbooks. "Thanks. So you're new? Football? Why'd you help me, then?"

Lance stood up, easily head and shoulders taller than Oran, and picked up his backpack from the ground. "I've never been into bullying people. My dad used to tell me only the weak bullied others." He stopped then, not wanting to think about things his dad used to say.

"Pretty common pastime here," Oran said. His tone came more easily now and he dropped his shoulders from their defensive hunch.

Lance picked up the last item on the ground: a tiny figure he almost hadn't seen. It was a wizard or some kind of similar thing. It held a staff in one hand and a ball of fire in the other. He recognized it from the games Alice was always begging him to play.

"You play those board games?" he asked, handing it to Oran.

Oran blushed a little. "Yeah." His blue eyes ignited. "If you're okay with not having those dicks as friends, you could hang out with us. We need a new player for *Runes and Empires*. And we play *Elderforge* almost every night."

"I love *Elderforge*," Lance interjected. Oran was not the kind of person he usually hung out with, but his first impression had been right: he was genuine.

"We also play *Runes and Empires*." Oran held up his wizard. "I play a magic class, but we need some beef if you're okay with playing a tank or a strong fighter."

"Something beefy for you to hide behind while you sling your spells?" Lance asked, a smile creeping onto his face. "Yeah, I can do that. I don't know shit about those games, though. You guys will make fun of me."

"No, we won't," Oran sputtered quickly.

Lance smiled. "Relax, I can take it. I'd love to meet your friends."

It turned out Lance had a few classes with Oran. By the end of the afternoon, he decided he really liked the strange boy.

"Hey," he said, when they were getting ready to part ways at the end of the day. "I'd like to come and play if you guys are cool with someone like me invading your space."

Oran smiled through his black eye. "A guy like you is just what we need." He glanced around. "I haven't had a dirty look since lunch and I think it's thanks to you."

At this, Lance felt a small ember glow in his chest. "You sure you wouldn't mind? I'd hate to...intrude."

Oran's blue eyes rounded a little. "*You're* nervous about integrating with *us*?"

Lance half-shrugged and nodded.

Oran shook his shaggy head. "You'll raise our cool points to max level. Don't worry about us. We're more worried about sullying your cool guy reputation."

Not knowing what to say to that, Lance waved to Oran and they parted ways. Yes, he was nervous about injecting himself into a tight-knit group of friends, but he also really didn't want to be alone right now.

CHAPTER 4
RUNES AND EMPIRES

After school that Friday, Celeste met with the group in the parking lot, half-hoping Justin had driven his SUV to school so they could all take it back to her house for a short session in their table top campaign. A new kind of session zero to introduce the new players. Oran would be hiding, though: the varsity football and soccer teams were both out throwing and kicking balls around in the parking lot when the group gathered to leave. He tended to avoid them as best he could.

When Celeste met with Justin, Stella, Kiyoshi, and Alice, they were discussing the bizarre substitute teacher they had all run into at some time during the week.

"He's a bully," Justin said, spinning his keys on his thumb. "Embarrassing students like he did is unacceptable."

"He was making a point," Alice said, scanning the group of athletes, looking for someone.

"You just think he's cute," Justin snapped.

Alice smirked. "Ha! He's not my type. Trust me. But maybe he's yours?"

Justin glared at her, face reddening.

"What are you looking for?" Celeste asked, diffusing the tension.

"That guy I told you about, my cousin," Alice said. "I don't know if you have a class with him, but I wanted you all to meet him."

Despondent, Celeste looked at the heard of meatheaded football guys. If Alice had told her the guy she wanted to bring in was an athlete, she would have come up with a reason to say no.

A black form shrank away from the herd of athletes as they converged in one place all of a sudden. "Oh, no," Celeste moaned, taking a step toward the group. "Oran. It's like they were waiting for him."

"Should we do something?" Kiyoshi asked, joining her.

Celeste looked back at Justin. He shook his head and crossed his arms. "I'm keeping my nose clean this year," he said.

Alice rolled her eyes, pushed off the car, and marched toward the herd of athletes. Celeste followed at a cautious trot behind her. She ran over a million scenarios in her head of what could go wrong, each one more terrible than the last. Before they reached the group, a tall boy in a football jersey over jeans cut through the crowd to Oran.

"All right, back off," the boy snarled. "This one's mine this year." He reached down, grabbing Oran by his backpack, and dragged him out of the center of the herd. He pulled him to a huge white truck.

Once they were away from the heard, Celeste ran to the

boy and Oran. "Hey!" she shouted. "I'll get a teacher if you—"

"Celeste, relax," Alice said. "This is Lance, my cousin. Lance, Celeste."

Everyone quickly and awkwardly introduced themselves after a moment of silence and uneasy staring into each other's faces.

The boy, Lance, had released Oran and ruffled his hair in what Celeste could only assume was a friendly way. Oran mumbled a thanks.

"Oh," Celeste stammered, looking up at the guy, at Alice, at Oran, then back at the guy.

A cascade of honey brown hair tumbled down to his sharp jawline. Radiant dark brown eyes looked down at the shorter people.

"You didn't tell them about me. Am I a secret friend, Oran?" the guy asked, opening the door to his truck and tossing his backpack in.

"You've been helping Oran?" Celeste asked to clarify.

"Yeah." Lance nodded, smiling.

Lance was tall. His broad shoulders wore the jersey very well. The jeans hugged his legs, contouring muscles Celeste didn't even know a human could have. And he was brave enough to hang out with Oran?

"Holy Galahad," she breathed, her eyes captivated by the face above her.

"Uh, no. The name's Lance," he said, reaching out and shaking her hand.

His fingers were long and strong around her hand. Her cheeks flushed.

"These are your friends, Alice?" Lance asked.

"Lancelot," Celeste sighed.

"Just Lance," Alice corrected her, patting her shoulder and pretending to wipe saliva off her chin. "Well, when Celeste here revisits planet Earth, she can invite you to their gaming session this afternoon. I think she is totally fine with you playing with them."

"You're not joining?" Lance asked.

Alice shook her head. "Not tonight. I have a girls' night out with my mom and your mom." She rolled her eyes, but smiled. "Should be fun. And you're in good hands."

Oran nodded, eyes locked on Lance.

Celeste suddenly blinked and looked at Alice. "Yes, *Runes and Empires* tonight." Then she looked back at Lance. Why had her breath stopped in her lungs? "You play barbarians?" Could he actually be into the same games as her? Life was not that nice.

Oran's worried face went from Celeste's clearly enchanted gaze to Lance's chiseled jaw and back again. "We'll see you at your house, Celeste." He grabbed Lance's hand and marched him back to his truck.

"Holy shit," Stella droned when they rejoined the group again. "Did you see that guy? I have never seen so much sex crammed inside one football jersey before."

"Gross," Alice laughed.

"Ugh, you girls are worse than most boys," Justin gagged. "Celeste was thunderstruck for sure. Why? He's a meathead. Our kind don't mix. Didn't you say last year that they all have head injuries and won't make it past thirty-six?"

Celeste faced her friends, walking backward and smiling. "I was just looking. Being friends with anyone who looks like a real life version of Sir Galahad can't be that bad."

"It sure can be," Justin moaned.

They all piled into his SUV while Alice departed in her

own car and drove for Celeste's house and some much needed TTRPG time.

As they drove past the tree-lined streets, Celeste watched the woods flash past and imagined Lance galloping through them on a white horse. She sighed, fogging up the window.

LANCE GRIPPED THE WHEEL OF HIS TRUCK HARD AS HE drove himself and Oran down the neighborhood streets. Celeste had looked at him like he was a god incarnate. It had been extremely adorable, he thought.

"So that's the girl who gets you all together?" he asked Oran.

Oran gave Lance a sidelong glance. "Yeah. We all knew her from various things and kind of came together in freshman year. She got us all into *Elderforge*, but we all played *Runes and Empires* before."

"What do I need to know about this game?" Lance asked.

"Just watch out for Justin," Oran advised. "He likes to try to force you to follow certain storylines, but just do whatever you want. You'll narrate whatever you want your character to do."

Still confused, Lance nodded. Up ahead, he spotted the address on the mailbox he had been given for Celeste's house. A green Porsche was already parked on the street outside her house.

"Who the hell?" Lance asked, admiring the expensive car.

"Ugh," Oran moaned. "The Troll King. A player who joins us whenever he feels like it. He's more of a LARPer, but joins us for *Runes and Empires* every now and then."

Lance parked his truck and spotted Justin's SUV pull up into the driveway ahead of them. He grabbed his things and followed Oran out. The others from the SUV piled out and approached the Porsche, too. A boy about Lance's age got out, tossing his glossy black hair out of his deep brown eyes.

"What do you want, Troll?" Stella groaned.

"That's Garzier, king of trolls, to you, witch," the boy replied.

Celeste made a disgusted sound. "No, it's Zain Halabi, you idiot. No *Sun Age* names outside the park. You know that."

"*Sun Age*?" Lance asked. "What's that?"

Justin sighed and rolled his eyes, shoving past Lance to walk into the house.

Oran explained, "It's the LARPing—live action roll playing—game we play sometimes."

"Wow," Lance mused. "A lot of games."

"We have a lot of reality to escape," Stella supplied with a wink.

"And lots to get to," the troll king said with a devious smile. "We have a dungeon to crawl, do we not?"

Justin nodded. "Yeah, let's get going."

ONCE INSIDE, LANCE FOLLOWED CELESTE DOWN TO her basement. She'd decorated the small space with glittering lights, a fake fireplace, and a few scarves strewn up on the walls to mimic medieval banners. The space was lit up by the lights and the setting sun blazing through the window wells. Little sparkling flecks of dust coasted about lazily in the beams of light. The basement smelled like dust, books, and a little of mildew. Somehow, Lance loved it.

In the center rested an old, dented, solid wood dining room table. It was covered in battle mats, dice, trays, figures, and stacks of books and papers. Celeste quickly ran forward and gathered up a few leftover wrappers and an empty can of soda, her face turning red. She glanced at Lance and smiled sheepishly before tossing the trash into a bin. He smiled inwardly, realizing she had been embarrassed in his presence. He was liking her more and more.

Celeste quickly gave Lance the rundown on everyone's name and what they played while they all stood around. He nodded to each one as she went into some detail for each of her friends. It was obvious they were a close group. He suddenly felt awkward.

"I think we should start with getting the newbie involved," Justin said, taking his seat at the head of the table behind a screen.

"We have to write up his character sheet first," Oran interjected.

"We can role-play until you're ready," Kiyoshi suggested, taking a seat at the table. The others joined him and Oran motioned for Lance to sit next to him. "That should give you some time."

Justin winced dramatically. "I'm not sure about that. We need Oran in the game."

Lance caught Oran give Justin a quick glare. "It'll take us five minutes. Besides, my character was harvesting for herbs. So let him do that for the morning and the rest of you start."

Justin frowned disappointedly at Oran, both his palms pressed down into the table.

"Let him harvest the herbs," Stella said, leaning close to

Oran. She playfully nudged him with her arm, but he ignored her.

"Fine. Do whatever you want," Justin huffed.

"Thank you." Oran pulled up his bag and took out a piece of paper. He handed it to Lance. "Character sheet. Now, since we're down a tank, would you mind being something beefy?"

Lance caught Celeste looking over the table at him, her wide eyes fixed on him. Was she holding her breath? "Yeah, that's cool," he said quickly. He picked up a player's handbook and flipped it around, looking at the pictures. He spotted a huge, muscled man wielding an ax. The man had long black hair flying around him like the mane of a lion. "This guy looks cool."

"Ah, yes," Garzier the troll king said. "A huge, meathead of a brute. Just right for you."

Lance ignored him.

"Perfect," Oran beamed, shooting Garzier a quick glare. "Barbarian. Now let's roll your stats."

The numbers threw Lance off. He'd thought the game would involve rolling dice, but didn't know he needed to divide by percentages, taking half his cunning points and adding them to this or that. Oran, fortunately, made it sound easy, and he did most of the work for Lance. Justin rolled his eyes and scoffed every time Lance asked a question, so he figured he better keep his questions to a minimum. He tried to listen to what they called the role-play, too, to try to understand. It sounded like they narrated what their characters were doing.

One time, he got too wrapped up in a conversation Kiyoshi and Celeste were having. Justin, though he was liking Justin less and less, was a great narrator. Oran had to tap him three times to draw his attention back.

Finally, they were done. Oran helped Lance find a backstory for his barbarian, and soon Lance found himself getting nervous about playing his character.

"The morning was growing old," Justin said once everyone was ready, "and Ashlore had finished gathering his herbs. Terra and Bane have interrogated the innkeeper and—"

"Hey," Kiyoshi cut in, "don't narrate for us. We wanted to role-play this."

Justin glared at Kiyoshi for the interruption. "Fine. Do what you want."

Kiyoshi cleared his throat. "Welcome back, Ashlore," he said to Oran. "After some persuading, we found out the mysterious disappearances are happening up by an old farm in the north."

"I came in to town from the northern road," Oran said in a hissing, deeper voice than his own. Lance smiled. "I saw the dead crops one night. There was a scarecrow among them, but nothing else of note."

"Can I make a lore check?" Celeste suddenly piped up. "Terra comes from a rather witchy background. She might know something."

"You can't make a lore check every time someone brings up something mysterious," Justin moaned.

"I can, too," Celeste countered. She looked crestfallen. "Why not?"

"Ugh, fine!" Justin gestured wildly with his hand. "Roll."

Smiling, Celeste took up her dice and rolled them into the tray in the middle of the table. "Yes! Four successes and I'm trained in lore."

"High roll," the troll king noted, tapping his chin. "How fortunate."

Lance noted how Justin looked annoyed.

"You know," Justin said, putting on the guise of thinking hard. "You roll high a lot. Like I said before. Celeste, I think you should let me roll for you from now on."

"Agreed," the troll king put in.

"Come on, Justin," Oran said. "She rolled right here. We all saw it."

"Yeah, but think about how many high rolls she gets," Justin countered.

"Wait, hold on," Lance interjected. "Are you saying she's cheating?"

"I'm not!" Celeste protested.

"No, I know," Lance said. "You can't cheat a dice roll like that, Justin." He caught Celeste blush again out of the corner of his eye.

Justin dropped his mouth open. "Is this why you cheat, Celeste? To impress this meathead?"

"Justin!" Kiyoshi admonished.

"That's what I thought," the troll mumbled, looking away from the others.

But Lance took the insult on the chin. He let it hit him, then roll off. "I'm already impressed, Justin. Let's just let her roll this session and then if you still feel like she's cheating—somehow—then we can talk about it. As a group."

Even the troll hummed in thought at this. "You have to admit, Justin, her stats are high. Maybe— What's your name, barbarian?" he asked Lance.

"Galtor Whitestorm," Lance answered proudly. "I hail from the icy mountains of Northrex and have come to free my people in the middle lands."

"Oh, very cool," Celeste cooed.

"You haven't met yet!" Justin roared. "He's not even in the tavern yet."

"Ah, c'mon," Kiyoshi sighed. "Just roll with it, Justin."

"Barbarian scum!" Garzier snapped. "It was your people who destroyed my village and killed my family."

"Only by the orders of those who enslaved us," Lance shot back, loving the sudden gameplay. "I have come to redeem my people and free them from the grasp of the darkness that permeates my mountain even now."

"Wow," Celeste breathed. "That's good."

Lance smiled, now feeling his own cheeks turning a bit red.

"Hmm," the troll king hummed. "I'll need some convincing, but I'm open to the idea of a warrior seeking redemption."

Justin deflated, annoyed.

Oran put in, "I found the warrior while I was out gathering herbs. He, uh..." He looked up at Lance. "He was wounded and came to me for aid."

"Yeah," Lance agreed. "I ran away in the middle of battle and was wounded during my escape. Even now my father fights to free our people from the hold of the darkness, and I have come to seek a way to redemption."

Stella raised one brow, smiling gently. "You picked this up pretty quick, jock-boy. I'm impressed."

Lance grinned proudly. He had to admit, it was fun. And with Oran's help, he'd been able to slide right in.

"We welcome you, warrior," Celeste said, bowing her head. "Well met and good fortune be upon you."

"In that case," Kiyoshi said tentatively, "shall I tell you about my investigation?"

The group played in this manner for some time. Lance

lost track of time, wrapped up in the story and the eventual combat. Oran had to help him with the first few encounters since he didn't know what strength modifiers were or any of the rest of it, but after a few hours, he had the idea down and could roll for himself. Justin continued to question Celeste's rolls except when she failed a roll. They made their way through a forest and soon came to the edge of the farmland mentioned several hours before.

"But I think we'll stop here," Justin said, pushing his glasses up his nose. "The next part is too long to do in an hour."

"That was great," Kiyoshi sighed. "Experience, please."

"And don't be stingy," Celeste said with a smile.

After more calculations and additions for the experience points they'd acquired, the group began to pack up.

"So, this weekend?" Celeste asked. "School is back in session, and we always play *Sun Age* when school starts again."

"*Sun Age?*" Lance asked. "Remind me what that is again."

"Our live action role playing campaign," Celeste said. "It's not as involved as it sounds. You should come! We play in the nature preserve behind the big cornfield. Off the highway. Oran can show you."

Lance glanced down at Oran, who nodded enthusiastically. "You'd be great."

A little excited at being included, Lance dipped his head in agreement. "Count me in, then."

CHAPTER 5
SUN AGE

"It's so weird seeing you nervous," Oran said with a smirk as Lance drove his truck into the nature park's lot that Saturday morning. "You don't seem like the nervous type."

Lance loosened his fingers on the steering wheel, stretching them. He surveyed the parking lot before them. It was pretty full. "How many people play this game?"

Oran shrugged. "A couple dozen? It's not just our school that does it either. We have members from other schools, too. I don't know them all by name. Not their real names, anyway." He examined Lance again. "You are nervous."

"I am not. It's just a game, right?"

Oran made a noise that said that wasn't entirely true. "Celeste takes it pretty seriously."

Lance glanced sideways at Oran. "You like her a lot?" Oran's reply would dictate exactly how much he used this afternoon to flirt with Celeste.

"We're good friends," he said. "Have been for a while. She was the only one who called when my dad…died."

Lance turned to face Oran. "I'm so sorry. I didn't know."

Oran bit his lip, looking shy again. "I don't talk about it much. To anyone. No one asks really, either."

Lance didn't pry, but the way Oran looked told him this was something recent, and that there was more to it than his dad simply passing away. Something had happened. His heart went out to Oran then. Rather than prying, he decided that he'd just be there for Oran, like he wished someone would be there for him.

Oran smiled weakly. "I think she sees me as a friend. But, uh…" He laughed now, genuinely happy. "It's pretty clear she has a few thoughts about you."

Lance clenched his jaw. He'd thought the way she lost all normal functions when meeting him had been adorable. He loved her green eyes and the way they'd darted around the parking lot that afternoon, desperate for something to distract her. When she blushed, her cheeks and the very tip of her nose turned red.

He put the truck in park and got out, moving to the bed to carry his and Oran's things. Lance saw through Oran's smiles, though. He clearly had some feelings for Celeste, but wasn't going to mention it. This put Lance in a tough place. He liked Celeste and wanted to flirt and see where it went, but he didn't want to jeopardize his new friendship with Oran.

"I have that effect on girls," he said as humbly as he could. "It doesn't mean anything. I think she likes you. You guys have clearly been dancing around one another for years. You should make a move."

Oran paled and stopped in his tracks, dark blue eyes looking up at him. He looked terrified.

"Or don't," Lance offered. "If you ever do, though, I'll be your wingman."

Oran lowered his head and plowed toward the group, but Lance caught him smiling.

The group ahead, packs on backs and in various states of dress up, looked like a confused theatre cast. Some squinted and looked around and others poured over a map of the park near an old payphone. Lance noted the phone and almost laughed. He saw fewer and fewer of them these days.

"Relic of a simpler time," Oran said when he caught Lance looking at the phone.

"Relic?" Lance asked. "It's 2007. It's not that old."

Oran rolled his eyes and grinned. They integrated with the group around the phone and park map.

"What's going on?" Oran asked. "Why are we all standing around like we're lost?"

"That whole area back there," Justin pointed west, "is all dug up. The trees are gone and the river feeding the lake is dammed."

"We're damned," Celeste sighed, looking crestfallen. "All of it?"

She led the way into the park to a smaller wooded area with a clearing. The tents were set up here and a few other people milled about.

"What's going on?" Lance asked, dropping their things outside the main tent Kiyoshi had set up in a small clearing of the wooded area.

Members of every clan began to speak at once, drowning out Celeste as she tried to speak up. It sounded like a lot of the clans' main base areas had been destroyed in some new construction. Lance saw Celeste desperately trying to get everyone to calm down. He nudged Oran.

"Okay, shut up," Oran said, using his authoritative voice. Celeste sighed in relief when everyone quieted down.

Lance realized Oran probably only ever had the courage to take command during the game. Somewhere he knew he couldn't fail. This would be the perfect time for him to make a move on Celeste.

"The humans and barbarians will be closer to us all from now on. If what Justin said is true, their place was mauled," Oran finished. "We just have to share less space. It's not a big deal."

"Besides," Celeste said, "the size of *Sun Age* isn't determined by the acreage we play on."

"No, it's the size of our hearts," Stella mocked, fluttering her eyelashes.

Lance grimaced at her. Oran had said Stella was Celeste's best friend. He hadn't found a reason to like her yet, and now liked her less.

Celeste surveyed the land quickly. "Okay, here's what we'll do. We'll call the dug-up part the Nether Plane. Try to stay away from it since it could actually be dangerous. We'll say that's where the dark elves are from, but they left when a certain ruination came to their land."

"Oooh," Alice cooed, smiling. "Intriguing!"

"Like back story," Lance said, using a term Oran had taught him while making his *Runes and Empires* character.

Celeste blushed. "Okay, everyone, please gather around."

All the clans were present, including everyone's least favorite clan: the trolls, led by their snobbish leader, Troll King Garzier. His clan wore horns great and small, tusks, and long claws. Garzier's horns were long, twisted, and black.

"Ah, Garzier, I was hoping your clan would be joining us today," Celeste said with little effort to hide her distaste.

"I don't need to join your council to be a part of this game," Garzier said in a thick accent he'd made up for his character. "*Sun Age* is open to everyone. Those are your words." He stamped his troll staff into the ground for emphasis. All of his troll minions grunted and stamped their staves in agreement, making a terrific racket.

"You talk about the game at school," Justin added. "You blow the whole idea of its mystery and secrecy. You can't be on the council if you don't abide by the rules."

"We're not allowed to talk about the game at school?" Lance asked.

Justin rolled his eyes, but Celeste replied, "We don't use our game names in school. Well," she glared at the troll king, "we're not supposed to, but Zain here does."

"Garzier to you, human rogue," Zain snarled. The Troll King arched his brow at Lance. "What would your football mates say if they knew you were here with us?" he sneered.

Stella smirked. "For once, your status as school jerk works against you, troll. Who would listen to you?"

"Okay, enough," Alice said, laying her hand on her sword. "Arguing among us is stupid. Celeste, go on. What should we do?"

But Zain had verbalized one of Lance's only fears. The team should follow his example, mimicking him, since he was the new quarterback. But video games, table top games, and other similar hobbies was where they drew the line. If the team isolated him, he wouldn't know what to do. He'd never been without a built-in friend group. His confidence came from the sport. He quickly met Celeste's eyes. She seemed to be waiting for him to answer.

"Well, uh," he stammered, "I'll follow the rules, won't I? No one will know."

"Coward," the troll king scoffed.

"Okay, listen," Celeste sighed, looking around again. "Why doesn't the troll clan take the bridge area by the creek —er, river. Whatever it is. Is that acceptable?"

"Most acceptable," Garzier the troll king said. "trolls like bridges." He ordered his minion trolls to gather everything up and they all marched down to the little river.

Lance loved watching her take command; her quick prob-lem-solving and her creativity were attractive. He saw why Oran liked her. She was strong.

She'd never go out with a guy like him.

"All right!" Celeste called out so the departing clans could hear. "You have thirty minutes to settle. Remember, your workers can set up your camps while we play. Check in with Kiyoshi when you finish projects, though." She took a walkie-talkie off her belt and said into it, "Stalls, stores, and inns, are you ready?"

"Almost," came Justin's voice over the device. "One merchant has changed into a healer, if that's all right."

"Kiyoshi, you got that?" Celeste said into the device.

"Uh huh," came his hurried reply. "Adding it to the map now. It's Devin, isn't it? He said he wanted to be a healer instead. He didn't like his role in the scenario they had put together."

"Yup," Justin replied. "Okay, I'm putting the finishing touches on the castle, and we'll be ready to go."

"Stand by for story time," Celeste said into the device.

Lance marched out with Alice to their designated base. The sun reached its peak and had mysteriously cooled down, as if taking pity on the gamers. A few clouds rolled in and a light wind had come in from the west. They passed Kiyoshi's mom, Mrs. Kagami, who volunteered to watch out for the gamers. She had a satellite radio and first aid kits for all the areas. She stayed just far enough away in a camper to give the kids space. She waved to Lance as they marched into the woods.

"Excited?" Alice asked when they stood with the rest of their clan.

Lance half-nodded. "I'm afraid I'll mess something up."

"I've done this before." Alice shook her head. "Very hard to mess up. Just have fun. Lean into your manly urges and hit stuff with your sword."

He laughed, knowing she meant well.

"Welcome to *Sun Age* and the first session of the joined clans," Kiyoshi's voice came over the radios. "This campaign is the largest team-up we've ever seen. This is your story: While mining deep in the caves of *Sun Age*, the barbarians unearthed the scroll of the Elder Ones. Unable to read it but knowing full well its power, they have sought out someone who can translate the script. This must be kept a secret, for what the scroll contains is an ancient, mystical power unknown to all present clans. The seal on the scroll appears to be of either elven or magic make, but the script is yet unknown. Some say the scroll leads to a vast treasure, igniting the trolls' hunger. Others say it opens portals to lands yet unknown. All clans want to claim the scroll for themselves. It must be taken from the barbarians and translated before more is known. Deciding as the finders of the scroll that it belongs to them, the barbarians are just as prepared to defend their right to it as the other clans are to take it."

The barbarians listened with rapt attention. Lance couldn't help but let himself be pulled into the game. A few of them smiled at him and Alice as she was the new queen of their clan.

"But something is not right with the townsfolk near Lord Justin's keep," Kiyoshi went on. "Is it magic? Is it sorcery? As you try to find the scroll and learn its secrets, you must find allies and become strong enough to withstand the trials that will no doubt plague your quest. Those within your own clan may well become the enemy."

"And now, clans of *Sun Age*," Celeste's voice said into the device, "once you have your costumes on, we shall begin!"

CELESTE GATHERED UP A SMALL BAND OF RANGERS IN dark green and brown garb to take with her to scout out the barbarians. They couldn't get close, but they saw Alice outside the caves with another warrior practicing their sparring. There was no sign of the new prince.

"Perhaps he is already out finding a man who can translate the scroll," Celeste said quietly to her companions. "Let us not start a fight so near the camp. Perhaps in town, we may find out more. To the meadow."

She and her companions moved quieter than snakes in the grass as they sprinted away toward the village. They had not gone a few paces when the snuffling and grunting of trolls could be heard. In the clearing ahead, two trolls had captured a dark elf using their magical spells to block his. They had tied his wrists and were using their evil power to take his magic to empower themselves more. This would only be temporary, but with his magic gone, the elf could be killed if the trolls wished it.

"Glutinous, power-hungry fiends!" one of the human rangers hissed under his breath. "I care not for the elves, but to steal power is darker still than they."

Celeste peeked out again.

One of the trolls snarled, "Let's kill him now!"

The other said, "No, we can take him for the sacrifice to Ooglasloh. The gods demand sacrifice!"

The trolls were about to depart with their living sacrifice when Oran leapt from the bushes and called out, "You cannot move, troll fiend!"

He swung his magic staff to protect his back from the magic attack the other troll prepared to cast. The spell backfired from Oran's staff and hit the troll in his face. Both trolls lay stunned on the ground. For a moment, Oran stood in the sun, his white wig glinting in the glow and his robes settling dramatically around him as he made sure his enemies were not moving. Celeste smiled at his bravery. She felt as though a magic butterfly had appeared in her stomach from watching him fight.

"Come, my brother," Oran said, pulling the other dark elf up from the ground. "We must teach you how to block unfriendly spells."

The elves departed deeper into the woods, leaving the path to the village open. Celeste motioned to her companions and they quietly sprinted into the safe boundaries of the village.

"Sometimes I want to know how to steal magic like the trolls do," one ranger said as they passed the very few village homes and stalls trading goods.

"What?" Celeste gasped. "Those animals are evil. And stealing magic is to steal the essence of that creature's soul. It is a vile thing."

The human ranger sighed. "Yes, but think how much stronger we could be with that power!"

"Think not of it," Celeste said in a final tone. She walked up to a woman by the stream in the middle of washing her clothes. "Pardon me, good lady," she said. "I am a ranger from the west and was wondering if you have heard any mutterings of a scroll near this village?"

The woman wrung her clothes out and piled them up in a basket. "There have only been mutterings here because trolls have been seen passing by." The woman stopped and looked around nervously.

"They do not come into the village?" Celeste asked.

"We leave them alone and they do not bother us. However, they have been harassing travelers who use the bridge beyond our borders."

Set back near the border of the village was Justin's castle (just a large, green camping tent, but they pretended otherwise). In the window, she could see him looking out, staring at her. She flipped her hood up to hide her face and led her companions back into the shade and protection of the woods. Something about the nervous woman stuck with her. And Justin's uncanny gaze made her uneasy. She took her companions out of the tiny village, moving closer to the barbarian caves.

The small band soon made their way deep into the forest, close to the west end they could no longer enter. The wind wafted up again. Celeste took her hair down from its leather ties to let her scalp breathe. The heat was managing to slip through the clouds and make the moist ground soggy and the air uncomfortably hot.

"Not a sign of anyone else," her companion muttered. "We're far off course by now, my lady."

"Shh!" she hissed suddenly, swooping her hood back over her hair and crouching down in the foliage. Movement came from the right. Someone walked with no care, as if they feared nothing. The clinking of animal bones and teeth reached the Humans. Celeste pricked her ears up. The boots tread softly, despite the strong stride. She motioned for her companions to fit arrows to their bows and she did as well with slow, careful movements.

Into the clearing stepped the strong barbarian figure of Alice. The rangers hunkered down closer to the bush. Alice would not be an easy enemy to escape from if they were seen. She looked swift and strong, and her eyes showed her cunning nature. Behind her approached two solemn barbarians robed in cotton and skins: shamans.

"My lady," one of them said, "the hiding place of the scroll is in danger from the elves. Their battle with the trolls has brought them close to it."

Celeste grinned over at her companions. They could easily follow the shamans back to the scroll. The barbarians only had weak magic, and the rangers were more than a match for them there. The shamans could fight with their short swords, but the rangers could outmaneuver them.

"There is something else, my lady," the other priest said. He hesitated when Alice snapped her warning glance to his eyes. "The trolls have surrounded the prince's location and he is unaware of it as of yet. They will move in at any moment."

Alice let out a screech of anger. The sound rang all through the woods.

"To the caves, you fools!" she cried, unsheathing her sword. "Bring me the warriors!"

The barbarians dashed through the woods, leaping over logs and bramble in their haste. Celeste stood up only to see

Justin rise a few yards away. He was smirking in triumph as well.

"This is great news for the humans," he said to her. He held out his gloved hand to her. The red leather was embroidered in gold and looked expensive. "Come with me and we can take the scroll together."

Celeste held her head up just a little higher. "Is there no honor in us humans? The prince does not deserve to be taken by the trolls. Perhaps if we rescue him, he may reveal the location of the scroll. We could treat with the barbarians. We need allies in this fight. We don't know what dark magic is seeking this scroll, but I have felt it."

Justin's noble face fell into a sad glare. "No, Celeste, say it isn't so. The magic folk have been spreading a rumor that the great Celeste has fallen prey to the barbarian man's charms."

"Heed not the words of that Dark Star Sorceress at this time!" cried one of the rangers. "Her spirit has not been of good character this last fortnight."

"Hold your tongue when addressing a lord, rogue!" Justin snapped back.

"Peace!" Celeste called. "Justin, you and the other nobles of your village do as you see best and leave me and my rangers in peace. I agree," she added when he opened his mouth to speak again, "that as humans, we must stay together and protect each other. Now, depart and leave us to our hunt if you have any nobility and honor left to you."

With a swish of his gold and red cloak, Justin departed into the woods, calling for his fellow nobles to follow him to the stream for their attack on the magic folk. Celeste thanked her companion for his aid and they went on into the woods, watching for barbarians.

They had stopped and rested, climbed a tall oak to see far beyond to the east, and headed on when they were sure of their direction. The wind once again blew and with it came a foul odor. The rangers clapped their hands over their noses and let out groans of disgust.

"Smells like piles of sunbaked roadkill," the ranger gagged.

"Days old, too," Celeste said. "That must have been the unsavory message Oran was speaking of before."

"Let's get out of here," the rangers suggested.

Celeste halted. She turned to the west and dropped her hand. Had someone just called her name?

"Come, my lady. Not that way," her ranger insisted.

Still, she watched. No, she hadn't been wrong. Someone called to her. Not with a voice. Not by her name, but without words. Like someone yearned for her to notice them. She felt like eyes were on her.

"Don't you hear that?" she asked her companions. "That calling. Can you feel it?"

Confused, the rangers exchanged glances, not sure how they were supposed to reply.

"The call of a million dead deer," one said trying to lighten the mood. "Come on, the smell is killing me."

But Celeste walked away from them in the opposite direction. Something over there was in trouble and it needed help. Someone shouted to her. The feeling in her stomach made her steps quicken and her heart race.

"We have to go!" she called. "They need us!"

Just as she yelled these words back to her rangers, her foot pushed through the air. The ground disappeared under her and she pitched forward. She gasped and splatted belly-first onto a muddy ravine wall. Throwing her hands out in front of her, she tried to stop slipping down the side, but the force of her dash careened her down the muddy slope. She slipped to the left and right as she sledded down the mud on her front, tearing and ruining her clothes. The end of the ravine was covered in gravel and if she didn't slow down, it was going to hurt a lot on impact. She managed to pitch herself over and onto her back and dug her heels into the ground, coming to a stop that relied entirely on her strength to hold her on the steep slope.

She coughed and panted, trying to catch her breath after the frightful scare. Her arms and legs trembled as she gasped for air. Her fingers squished into the gritty mud. Looking down, she saw the whole wall was mixed mud and mangled animals. Letting out a terrified and disgusted scream, she tried to crab crawl backward up the slope, but only slipped again. Steadying herself, she looked out over what had once been her kingdom. The trees were gone. The hills and the creek, also. All had been replaced by a massive mud hole. Was this the area the construction team had dug up? It had become some kind of nether world from her distant nightmares. Looking up, she took in a burned and blackened red sky. The sun, setting in the east, was orange and flickering. On the horizon behind her, black oozing masses trudged back and forth. A heartbroken, lifeless moaning sound came from them. Dead, burned black things thrust up out of the swamp. They were once trees. Single raindrops fell from the rumbling sky.

Something inside her told her to say the name of this nightmare place out loud. Naming it would make it real.

"The Nether?" she said, her lip trembling. The name came

to her as if she'd seen this place before. "I've fallen into the Nether Plane."

She spun on the spot. The cliff face was not the same one she'd fallen down before. This one was tall and rocky, made from black and red rock like she'd never seen before. She had been transported somewhere else entirely.

CHAPTER 6
THE NETHER PLANE

Planting her hands deeper into the black watery ooze, crunching small animal bones, Celeste pushed herself up to standing. Her feet sunk in to the muck up to her ankles. She expected the black water to seep into her cloth boots, but they had turned to real, tanned leather. Her leggings had changed to tougher material and her tunic and hood were now a stronger, thicker fabric. Checking her bow, she found the weight of the draw had changed and her arrows were sharp.

"I have fallen and hit my head," she reasoned even as her heart thudded in her chest. "I'm knocked out. I'm dreaming. I would dream myself into a ranger," she said quietly, afraid to disturb the surface of the swamp. "Low class, hardly any magic. Just like when I'm awake."

Touching her head, she realized she'd hit it on her fall into the ooze.

The more she looked around, the more she saw. Charred remains of long burned-out structures stood around her to one side and pyres smoldered in dilapidated heaps in various places. Some of these still had blackened skeletons tied to them. Farther out, the remains of a tall stone wall circled what must have been a city. The only thing not entirely destroyed was a many-turreted castle far off in the distance. Beyond all of this was a bleak mountain range outlined through the dense red fog. Coughing, she looked up. Above was something that looked like black clouds made of smoke. Red lightning ripped through them every second or so, sometimes silently, other times followed by a deep rumble.

Pulling lightly on her leg, Celeste managed to slip it out of the muck and take a step. The squelching sound caused a crow to caw in a gargling screech in the distance. It was unlike any crow she'd heard before. She chanced a glance over her shoulder. The crow tilted its head in her direction and rolled three purple eyes toward her. She gasped, cringing away from the monster.

This is the part where I figure out how I got here, she thought. She looked back up the way she'd fallen. There was no way to scale the muddy wall. But it didn't lead to the green, grassy forest she'd just been in. She couldn't see over the steep incline.

Think and walk, she ordered herself. *If this is a dream, I can't be hurt, right? I should move.*

She slogged on for several minutes until a bright, white flash across the top of the mountains got her attention. When she looked up and tried to focus on it, it vanished. She shook her head and walked on into what looked like the charred and rundown remains of a town square. Pillories, tall structures with nooses, and a few hanging cages with corpses inside came into view through the red smog.

"Oh, wow," she breathed, taking in the dead. The place

didn't look like a happy city. A basket of heads beside a chopping block confirmed it. "I need to leave," she said to a skeleton in one of the hanging cages. "This isn't a dream; it's a nightmare."

"Hey, you there! If you are not imprisoned by some invisible means, you need to leave before you're taken captive by the fell beasts. Get out of here while you're free."

She looked in the direction of the alarmed voice. Inside one of the cages, a young man near her age with long hair and ratty clothes squatted. He waved his hands at her again to shoo her away. When he did, she spotted a gold ring on his finger.

"You cannot stay here. You must leave," he urged her.

"Can I help you?" Celeste hollered toward him.

At her call, a rumbling crept over the mountain range and rolled across the sky. When the sound ran just above her, something huge and angry growled in the distance. Her eyes widened with alarm and she pressed her lips tightly together, looking toward where the growl had come from. She waited a moment before speaking again.

"I'll get you out," she said more quietly and sloshed over to the prisoner as quickly as she could. "What happened here?"

"You don't understand. You have to leave," he said, eyes round with fear. "Why did you come to the Nether Plane? No human walks free here. Especially not now."

Celeste peered at the lock in the dim light. It was a simple lock with a wide opening for a crude key.

"I can figure this out," she whispered and looked up at the prisoner hanging in his cage. "I'm a ranger, right?" she stammered a little when they locked eyes. "I know locks." Just as the words left her mouth, she had a pretty good guess on how to pick it.

The man's navy blue and gold-trimmed clothes looked regal closer up, but blood and mud covered them. He also wore a small circlet of gold around his head, showing his rank as royalty. His fair face was speckled with grime and tear tracks. Despite his situation, she thought he was strikingly good looking. Like a hero on the covers of *Runes and Empires*.

Not a bad nightmare, she thought to herself. *So long as all I wake up with is a concussion, I'm fine with that.*

"So, what happened here?" she repeated as she worked the lock.

The young man watched her work. "The Nether has never been a place of life and joy. But now, it's even worse. There was a flood of fire and a flood of water. The creatures of the Nether have been subjugated by the darkness that is taking over our land."

"Are you a prince?"

He cast his blue eyes down. "I was. There are no ranks among the souls in the Nether anymore."

"The Nether," she mumbled, frowning.

"That sound you hear is the guardian of the gate to the Nether Plane," the prince whispered. "He is like a warden, keeping all creatures down here while Umbra prepares them for its army. The guardian answers to very few. But keeping the Nether closed to the Surface Plane is perhaps the best thing right now."

Celeste smiled as a faint click sounded in the lock. One down. "Umbra? Who's that?"

"It is lord of this land now. The Nether was not its realm, but it came from the Other World and took it, seeing the natural evil in the creatures who dwelled here. It lives in a place made of smoke and shadow, they say, sleeping in a great castle made of flesh and bones. Umbra has sent its hellions to watch for Planes Striders from the Other World."

"Planes Striders?" Celeste asked. "Are they the heroes or something?"

The prince's eyes scanned the horizon skillfully. "That is how my mother used to tell it. My mother—the queen of a great kingdom that has brought prosperity to all on the Surface Plane—lost hope of seeing a Planes Strider." His voiced tilted in just as much hopelessness. "Umbra has not moved in my lifetime. I only know what my mother has told me of its reign: dark times, until a champion from the Other World, Umbra's world, comes and defeats it."

The last dial clicked. Celeste smiled in triumph. So that was what cracking a lock felt like in these games? She liked it.

"Other World?" Celeste asked. "I'm not sure I get it." She laughed a little, despite the situation. "Like human worlds? Are you human?" She held up her hands to help the prince down, seeing he had an injured leg.

"I am," he grunted. "Only the Surface Plane harbors humans. The other Planes are home to many other creatures. Now," he looked around the square, "I must find a weapon. I will not be helpless now I am free."

Celeste looked around. Corpses and weapons lay everywhere. "Pick one," she laughed darkly. "I don't think they need them."

"Not any weapon will do," the prince said, scanning the dead. They strode among the corpses for some time as he scrutinized the weapons.

"Aren't we in danger or something? Should we maybe hurry up a bit?" she asked.

"As long as you are silent, we have nothing to fear. The servants of Umbra need not know I am free of my cage."

Trying to breathe and slosh through the muck more quietly, she picked up a long, curved sword. "What about this one?"

"Nether elf sword." A look of disgust pulled on his handsome face. "I dare not use such a weapon."

She nodded half-heartedly, tossing the sword back. They moved stealthily toward the mountain range as they searched for a weapon not eaten away by rust or from a race the prince noted as vile.

"Tell me what you meant when you said Planes," Celeste said, turning over a soggy log with her foot.

The prince stalled and looked at her. "You don't know the Planes?"

She shook her head. "I'm from the Other World." She put air quotes around the phrase.

"Are you?" he asked, his caution turning to guarded fear.

"Yes?" she said, doubting herself. "I'm not from here, anyway. I fell into this place after following some kind of call. If that makes sense."

"If that is so, then you are either a servant of Umbra or..."

"A Planes Strider!" she said gleefully.

The prince moved to walk on and search, turning away from her. "This city is Zane'barren. The capital city of the Nether. The Nether Plane and Zane'barren are the realms of the Nether elves and other foul creatures. Above, through the gate, is the Surface Plane, my home."

"And then a sky plane?" Celeste asked.

"The Arcane Plane," the prince corrected. "A winged people who have harnessed magic and live in cities above us. We have no way of ascending to their realm, and they do not see the Surface as worthy of their time." He glowered a little, showing he also wasn't fond of the Arcane people.

"So you're a human prince," she reiterated. In her head, she made an image of him sitting on a gold throne, clean, commanding. "Fair, just, noble and all that?" she asked. "I've read about princes like that in stories."

They struggled quietly through the grime. "I tried to be such a prince. I was heir to my throne. I wanted to save my realm, but my mother…"

Interested, Celeste asked, "Was she an evil queen? A secret sorceress?"

The prince shrugged despondently. "She says there is no point in leading a hopeless people against an enemy we cannot begin to defeat. I don't know what was happening to my people. They vanished, turned to violence. I wanted to save them. I thought it was the kingly thing to do."

Celeste waited, but he didn't go on. "I know what you mean about hoping against all the odds. Where I'm from, I'm a little lost, too. I hate to see someone like you so hopeless."

She spotted a golden hilt with a blue gem jutting out of the grime. With silent glee, she hopped to it through the more solid ground. She expected it to be impossibly heavy, but it wasn't. As she pulled it out, she found it attached to a belt with another smaller sword.

"Hey," she called to him. "Here you go. This looks just like you."

Happy to see the light in his eyes as he beheld the sword, she tried not to eye him too much as he belted it on. He looked every part the prince now, aside from the grime and the shadowed eyes. She read hopelessness there.

"Tell me about these Planes Striders," she prompted. "As you said, I shouldn't be here. I—I don't know—magically

portaled here. I came here because I felt someone calling me."
And I fell, she reminded herself. *This is all a dream. A good one, though.*

The prince looked cautiously at her. Flatly, he said, "I dare not believe you."

"But I could be telling the truth," she said excitedly. "I know these kinds of places. There's magic, lore, big bad evil guys, and brave warriors. It's all I've ever wanted."

His face turned to slight disgust. "You seem overjoyed at our suffering."

"Oh, no, sorry," she quickly apologized. "I just mean, I think I can help you."

"If you are a Planes Strider," he said, and she was a little stung by his doubtful insinuation, "then you would have come here to aid us in our fight. My mother said there was once a Planes Strider here who met with the Eidolon who lives in the Astral Plane—far above this one, even above the Celestial Plane, where the stars live—and he tried to save us."

"And that Planes Strider failed?"

"He must have. Umbra is still here. Now some, like myself, hope and pray for another to come."

"But not your mother."

He eyed her up and down, frowning. He opened his mouth to ask her a question, but the screaming, feral roar of a huge cat-like creature cut him off. The thing soared through the air with a mighty leap and dove directly at the prince. He spun around and unsheathed the short sword from his side and the longer broadsword from his back all in one smooth motion.

The broadsword went up into the cat-monster's side and the prince used its own momentum to flip it over his head and kick it off his blade. Celeste ducked as it flew over her, nocking an arrow to her new bowstring. She was glad to find even though the weight had changed, she could still draw it with ease. She rose, aimed, and put an arrow through the creature's eye socket. It shrieked and reeled, giving them just enough time to turn and start to run.

"Whoa," she gasped. "I did it. That was like magic."

With each dashing step, more slime splashed onto Celeste's face and bones cracked underfoot. With the adrenaline pumping in her veins and the solid sound the arrow made going through the creature, it felt all too real. Her heart ached as her mind realized she was nowhere familiar and this was not cosplaying. Tears filled her eyes and mingled with the black water on her face, but she ran. She couldn't allow the fear to weaken her. Besides, this had to be a dream.

"Can we reach the mountains?" Celeste panted. They seemed closer than they had been before in the mist. Now the great peaks were visible and she could even see a path zigzagging up the side and over the top.

"If we run," the prince called between breaths. "But every bit of the Nether is inhabited."

A few steps more and a new enemy presented itself. From the dark waters rose the corpses of burned and mangled people. The ones with eyes still in their sockets fixated on them and began to pursue them in a loping gallop.

"Undead!" the prince called. "Shoot your way through them!"

Fluidly, Celeste pulled out arrow after arrow, firing quickly to make a path for them. It was harder to aim while running than she had ever imagined while playing her games. But in this world, she was a great shot. She hit two before they collided with the ranks of the dead. The prince used huge swipes of his broadsword to carve a space for them to pass through and kept running.

With the dead behind them as well as the creature, Celeste wanted to run faster, but her legs weakened and her lungs burned. She realized something like sulfur stifled the air.

A shadow passed over them, revealing hungry wyverns hunting from above.

"We can't make it!" Celeste gasped. She stopped and fired up at the small flyers, hitting one to her great satisfaction. It reeled and fell into the marsh, flailing frantically as it sank. Looking down, she saw the longer she stood, the deeper she sank as well.

"Don't stop!" the prince cried, taking her hand.

They ran again. One of the undead soldiers made a mighty leap and landed on the prince's shoulders. With its gruesome detached jaws, it sank its teeth deep into the side of his neck.

Stopping and bracing herself, Celeste swung at the corpse, dislodging it with a mighty hit of her bow. Then she shot the monster through its soggy eye, killing it. They only stumbled on for a few more yards before the prince collapsed. The skin around the bite turned a putrid gray. His eyes streamed and he grew cold quickly. Celeste tried to pull him up, but now they were both sinking into the marsh.

With the creature and the undead closing in, Celeste wondered—wished—she could do something. "Help!" she screamed to any living thing that might listen. "Someone help us!"

Just as the words left her mouth, a horn blasted through the mist and the heavy thumping of a dozen hooves answered her. Out of the darkness came a herd of armed female centaurs. One of the great creatures, clutching a ram's horn, galloped up to her. She was outfitted in armor with a large sword strapped to her side.

"We are pilgrims and have heard your cry," the centaur said. "Quickly, mount!"

To Celeste's surprise, the prince halted. "I will not mount a centaur. Fools who read the stars as if they were prophets."

Celeste reached up and took the warrior's hand, hoisting herself up onto her strong back. "Don't be stupid! Do it to save yourself!" she screamed.

Another centaur raced by and took the prince's hand, jerking him up against his will. They galloped away faster now and were safe on the solid ground of the mountain path in only a few moments.

Celeste threw a glance back and saw the corpses sink back into the mire and the cat creature turn back into the mist when the centaurs pulled too far ahead of it. Its one great yellow eye watched until it turned fully away.

"They can't go out of that muck?" Celeste asked, scared they'd leap out at any moment.

"The fell creatures cannot leave the city borders of Zane'barren. Not yet," the centaur said comfortingly. "The magic that binds them holds them there. But the journey up the mountain is just as dangerous. The spider-lizards of Mauth reside there, as well as the Nether elves. Any creature who lives so near the base is dangerous. We centaurs only make this pilgrimage on rare occasions to study the Nether beings when the stars demand it."

"Elves," she breathed. "Really? Wow."

Her surroundings would not let her ignore the reality of where she was. Her throat constricted while her heartbeat slammed against her chest until she became nearly unconscious from lack of breath. She gasped, the sulfuric air suffocating her until her vision went black. She pressed her hand into her chest and the impact of the situation finally hit her. She'd just been running for her life from undead and monsters. If this was a dream, it was all too real. She gasped and couldn't get a good breath into her lungs. She tipped and strong, feminine arms caught her as she blacked out.

CHAPTER 7
THE CENTAURS AND THE ELF

Celeste woke to a proper camp site and the herd of centaurs around her whispering. Around the camp, odd telescopes with basins of colorful liquid pointed up at the red sky surrounding them. A large fire burned in the middle where more centaurs cooked tangy-smelling food and poured tea into tankards. The prince sat beside her. He watched her as she came to.

"Hi," she groaned, pushing herself up. "I don't normally pass out like that. The air here is...thick."

The prince smiled kindly. "Nor I," he said pointing to the bandage around his neck. "Fortunately, you fell with much more grace than I."

Celeste allowed herself a small smile at his attempts to calm her. She was taken in by his sweetness. "Yeah," she agreed.

"I'm grateful I woke up at all," he said. "I have you to thank for that?"

The centaurs stopped talking and watched her now.

"No." Celeste laughed nervously. "They saved us." She pointed to them.

The leader shook her head. "We cannot take that credit. You called us. We all felt it. A ranger like yourself is connected by nature and the stars, as are we. Speaking to nature and her caregivers is natural for you. These are gifts of the rangers. It is perhaps by the design of the cosmos that we happened to make our pilgrimage when you called for aid. Or perhaps..." She tilted her head, making her thick, wild blonde hair shimmer. "Perhaps you called us by some other means?"

All of the centaurs nodded, looking at her eagerly.

Celeste hesitated, not sure where centaurs fell on the alignment scale on this world. She glanced at the prince. "Are you good guys or bad guys?"

The centaur scoffed and laughed heartily. "We are benevolent warriors, not like the norcan who would feast on their own if the right famine hit them. Your question is strange and makes me wonder if you are the one we've been waiting for. The stars have begun to vanish. This is an omen of great destruction, usually followed by a great champion." The centaur eyed Celeste again. "You are a curious one to be found below the Surface Plane."

"Oh, I'm not a champion," Celeste said quickly. "I don't do powerful magic or save burning villages. I have a hard time picking out what to wear to school on a regular basis. I can't even intervene when my parents are fighting."

The centaur looked hard at her. "I think you do not know who you are. You have decided what your purpose is and have made it your identity. But you have chosen incorrectly. That is what I saw in the stars."

Celeste stammered, frowning at the centaur. "What's that supposed to mean?"

The prince sighed heavily. "I thought she was a Planes Strider, too. It doesn't sound like she has much hope."

"Hey," Celeste shot at him. "I thought you said I could be this hero Planes Strider you needed. You seemed pretty eager earlier."

He shrugged pathetically. "I want to believe. They say if you have the spirit of a champion but do not test it, you are like a tarnished sword on display, not whetted by battle. A waste. If you are not, then I cannot save my kingdom." He picked up a tankard and drank from it. "It is better that I am here dying than above, watching my kingdom succumb."

Celeste shook her head in disbelief. "How can you be like that? You're a prince. Your job is to lead your people and protect them. Not give up."

He turned his eyes on her in the firelight. His face clouded over with fatigue. "My world is doomed. Why fight against that when it's simpler to wash away with the rest?"

All eyes around the fire were on her. She shrank a little, biting the inside of her cheek as she tried to come up with an answer. She wanted to be their champion, but what if she said she could be, then couldn't? And what did the centaur mean, saying she wasn't who she thought she was? The heat from the fire warmed her skin as she blushed. How real was this place?

Just then, a small stream of pebbles slid down the mountainside, alerting them all. The prince silently leapt to his feet and drew his short sword soundlessly. The centaur women bent their legs and quietly readied their weapons. All eyes went up.

"Spider-lizard?" the prince whispered, his muscles tensing.

The centaur sniffed the air quietly. "Yes and no. I smell its venom but I also smell..." She didn't finish her sentence. "If what I smell is there, then it can hear me."

Elves, Celeste thought.

More little pebbles hurried down and the centaur tracked the trail back up the mountain. Just outside the firelight, a small ledge protruded out where someone could crouch and wait just out of sight. Celeste took out her bow. The prince stealthily climbed onto a centaur's back without her consent, using her like a stepping stool. The creature glared over her shoulder at him, but held still. After a quiet count, the prince leapt up, took two quick steps up the rocky wall, and slashed at the top of the ledge.

A shriek rang out and a small black mass tumbled down, crashing by the fire.

"Nether elf!" the centaur cried, and two others surrounded it with axes.

Celeste aimed her bow, not sure if elves were good or bad.

"Show yourself!" she called to the winded bundle.

The elf, entirely wrapped in black, stood. He was short, but his limbs were strong. A black-gloved hand reached up to the hood and pulled it back defiantly. There before her stood a real elf. His white skin and white hair glimmered orange in the firelight. His eyes were solid black. He glared at his captors with malice.

"Nether elf," the prince addressed the short figure with disgust. "What were you doing spying on our camp?"

Looking into the elf's pure black eyes, Celeste was strongly reminded of Oran and his costumes.

The elf didn't move to reply or fight. He stood in a strong stance of defense, his fists clenched as if refusing to draw the twin blades on his back.

"Speak!" the centaur roared, poking him with the sharp

point on the top of her axe. "Never does your kind travel alone. Where are the others?"

Twitching around to face her, the elf bared his fangs and hissed through his teeth at her. All the other centaurs pointed their weapons at the elf. The prince took a step forward with his short sword poised. The elf didn't even flinch.

"Wait!" Celeste cried, raising her hands.

"For what?" the centaur asked. "This is a Nether elf. They are servants of that which caused the devastation you see before you. He will never admit it, but he's wounded. I think he's poisoned; I can smell it. We should strike now."

"Good riddance," the prince growled. "His people are treasure-hoarding killers. They've hidden in the mountains, bowing to Umbra. It is because of his people that Zane'barren was destroyed."

"Even before they were servants of Umbra, they terrorized the Surface Plane," the centaur added.

Around the elf's booted feet, a darker shadow grew; a dark purple poison dripped off of him.

Celeste pointed. "You're right. He's been hurt. Was it that spider-lizard thing?"

"We should finish him!" the centaur cried, raising her axe.

"I have no love for his kind," the prince whispered through gritted teeth. "My father's grave is witness to that."

The elf finally fell to his knees, his strength sapped. He held his side where the deadly stinger must have pierced him and from where the poison dripped.

Celeste moved to help him, but the prince stopped her, holding her back. "It could be a trick," he warned her. "They are vile like that. If he hurts you while you aided him, he'd be honored for slaying a Planes Strider."

"Planes Strider?" the elf whispered. He looked up, one

black eye peering through his white hair. Celeste spotted sweat dripping from his brow. He shook, but his eyes didn't show ill intent.

"He's hurt," she snapped, shoving past the prince. "Are you really willing to let him die just because he's a Nether elf?"

The prince and the centaur exchanged glances that told her yes.

Carefully, she approached him and knelt. "I'm going to help you, okay? I'm a ranger; I know some healing, right?" She thought back to *Runes and Empires* and remembered that the class did have a little bit of field aid knowledge. So she should. That was who she was in this world...right?

The elf guarded himself, shrinking away from her a little. She slowly reached out, taking his arm and helping him sit. When he did, she spotted the wound in his side. She looked up at her other companions. "Do not threaten him."

Submitting, the prince lowered his sword and stepped back, but kept an eye on her.

Celeste asked the elf, "Can I remove your cloak?"

Wordlessly, the elf unlatched it. He kept his black eyes on her and untucked his shirt. He tried to take his arm out of the sleeve but groaned, unable to do it. Celeste reached over and helped him with it. The wound on his side festered with a purple pus.

She pulled her satchel around and dug in it, finding some balm and bandages. She sighed in relief, glad to see what she needed inside. Then she moved to his side and gently wiped the wound before administering the balm. It smelled like lavender and something else she couldn't place. When she touched his skin, he didn't flinch. She looked up to see if he was in pain and found him grimacing but silent.

She suddenly knew what to do. It came to her quickly, like she'd always known how to clean a spider-lizard bite. It felt strange and exciting at the same time. She almost giggled.

Celeste cleaned out the poison and dressed the elf's wound. By the end of it all, his glare had changed to cautious curiosity. When Celeste stood to put away the medicines and left over bandaging in her leather pack, the elf's eyes followed her. When she walked back to the bedroll the centaurs had lain out for her, he rose and followed her. His eyes never left her.

"Are you a Planes Strider?" he asked. His voice was a husky tenor and cautious.

Celeste found herself checking the others' faces before answering. "I don't actually know," she confessed.

"Humans dwell on the Surface," he countered. "Are you from that Plane?"

She shook her head. "From somewhere else. I don't know how I got here." Her heart dropped. "Or how to get home."

He squinted at her hard, even leaning in a little. "You have to be a Planes Strider, then."

She blushed and smiled. "Thanks. I'd love to be the champion they are looking for. But if I am, aren't you supposed to stop me?"

"I do not kneel to Umbra," the elf said softly. "It is why I was banished."

"Oh?" the centaur asked, running her hand down the blade of a knife. "A lone Nether elf? So vulnerable."

"Stop it," Celeste moaned. "If he is, then it would be shameful to attack him, wouldn't it?"

The prince shook his head. "We need not show such honor when dealing with his kind."

Ignoring the prejudice, she asked the elf, "What do you mean, banished? Why?"

The elf cautiously glared at the others.

"I won't let them hurt you," Celeste promised. "Maybe if you tell me a little bit of your story, it will help me figure out if I am this Planes Strider."

"You must be," the elf insisted. "You are a human, but not a Surface dweller. You don't know where you came from. That is the way of them. When Umbra came to my home, I ran. I wanted my people to stand up to it, fight it off, when I saw what it did to them. We cannot see the stars, and they never descend to us in the Nether, so I wanted to venture above and find the champions they speak of in stories. Someone to save us. Anyone. Even a Surface dweller."

"You'd never accept our help," the prince cut in.

"I would," the elf snapped back. "I left to find help. When they discovered my plans, they drove me away with the sting of their blades, leaving me to die in the wilderness."

At this, the prince sat back, almost marveling at the bravery of the elf. Even the centaur's face fell.

"Such faith," the centaur said. "And from a Nether elf." She met Celeste's eyes. "Perhaps you *are* the Planes Strider. Maybe there is a way to know."

"How?" Celeste asked, excited.

"We do not know Planes Striders," she explained, "but they can know us. Who we are to ourselves. It is part of the power of a Planes Strider to know."

"What do you mean?" Celeste asked.

The centaur narrowed her eyes. "Where are you? What are our names?"

The pit of Celeste's stomach dropped. How the hell was

she supposed to know? She stammered, looking from each set of eyes to the other. The elf looked at her desperately.

"You know," he whispered in his husky tone. She decided then that she liked the short elf best. He had unwavering faith in her already. He wanted to save his people.

His faith in her made her feel even worse for not knowing. She tried to open her mind, make it blank, whatever she could do to let the magic or whatever had brought her here tell her what she needed to know.

The only thing she got in reply was a headache and a sudden wave of exhaustion.

"I'm sorry," she said. "I don't know." She asked the prince, "Will I understand more when I come to your kingdom?"

"That depends on you," he said. His eyes held a touch of melancholy now. "Our land is in danger, and only a Planes Strider can save it. The Planes Strider who can save us from Umbra is one who knows our world."

"Only one from the Other World can stop the darkness," the centaur said. "Being of this nature, Umbra knows this. Maybe in time, it will show us the truth."

Celeste collapsed back down. "I'll try to help."

"Any Planes Strider can do this task," the prince said. Celeste opened one eye to look up. "But you are perhaps the one who answered our call."

She stared into the flames, thinking of all the tales she'd read in her life. All the games she'd plotted and played. She knew hundreds of magic systems, had read a million stories of humble saviors who rose up to face the challenges forced on them. She always thought it'd be easier to face a dragon than an algebra final. "You have stories of Planes Striders. In my world, we have stories of princes and centaurs."

She relaxed a little then but glanced at the elf one more

time. He sat beside her, hope swimming in his black eyes. Then, a feeling rose in her. She knew where she was, knew the name of the world she'd landed in, and each of the creatures she'd met. Her mind spun as every name came to her like magic. She heard the names but couldn't say them. Every time she came close, it flitted away from her mind like a mouse teasing a cat.

"We must rest," the centaur said at length. "Let us sleep and discuss more once our minds have rested."

CHAPTER 8
THE NAMING

Celeste didn't know if sleep ever came to her at the foot of the mountains in Zane'barren. Instead, words and images of places she didn't know filled her head. Her stomached knotted with excitement until she felt sick. A pearly white light told her that she knew everything she needed to save this world, to not be afraid. It told her that she was called to this place.

"What place?" Celeste wondered, trying to dive deeper into sleep to hear the voice better.

"You know it," the voice said back. "Just say it. There is power in your words. I need you to name my world. A nameless world is vulnerable to the darkness."

Confused, she asked, "Doesn't it already have a name? And the prince, he does, too."

The pearly light formed into the shape of a boy about her age, wreathed in golden light. He wore a crown of glass on his head over pale hair. "Yes, but you have to know the name. Say any name."

"What if I guess the wrong one?"

The boy's face turned sad. "Celeste, you cannot guess. You know. Say it, please. Save my world. Time is running out for me."

Sadness quickly filled Celeste. She wanted to help him, but she didn't know the names as she slept. She thought she'd had them just moments ago, but didn't trust herself to speak them out loud. And what did they matter? She could just ask. But that didn't seem to be the right thing to do. Naming the places and characters had always been her job, and they usually just came to her. But now, she didn't want to be wrong. So she said nothing.

"Celeste," the boy whispered, "Umbra is coming for me. I am the heart that beats for this place. If I am taken, all will be lost. Please, arise and take up your role. Be who you are."

Who I am? she wondered. *I'm a freaked-out high school senior. That's all.*

"You're more than that," the boy whispered.

The dream began to fade and the light pulsing out from the glass crown dissipated into darkness.

THE PRINCE SHOOK CELESTE AWAKE GENTLY. "THE gate guardian is near; we hear his long strides. We must go if we are to catch him. The stars know when we'll see him again."

Celeste sat up, rubbing her eyes with the palms of her hands. The prince's blue-black hair glowed in the orange sun while he gathered up his things. "What do you mean about the gate, Gwen?" she asked. She gasped. She hadn't meant to say his name out loud.

The prince turned to face her, cautious optimism softening his features. Then he said, "The guardians *are* the gates. They roam their Planes, overseeing the creatures that live there. One is good and benevolent. he guards the Astral Plane. But the other—Amdusius, the great spider-lizard and keeper of the Nether—have a spirit of malice. But even he will bend to the will of a Planes Strider."

Assuming I am one, Celeste thought sadly to herself.

She got up and noticed the elf had packed up the things that the centaurs had given her, and loaded them up onto his back. His all-black eyes were still surrounded by a purple bruise.

"You don't have to do that," she said.

"Yes, I do," he replied flatly. "They may need proof as to who you are, but I have faith. You saved my life."

She couldn't stop the smile and light blush that came to her face. As they started their march, she wondered idly if she could act on her light attraction to the dark, mysterious elf. Just some harmless flirting? Would that be permissible? After all, this wasn't her world. What could the repercussions be? She glanced sideways at the Nether elf and let herself take in his lean, muscled legs and slender, pale neck.

Good grief, Celeste, she chided herself. *Stop looking at him like that.* She blushed in embarrassment and looked away.

They didn't have to go far before she felt the galloping gait of what could only be an eight-legged creature the size of a pickup truck. The creature spotted them from atop a rocky pathway. It stopped, silhouetted against the dying sun.

The keeper of the gate between the Nether and Surface Plane was a huge spider-lizard. His eight legs were taller than

Celeste and made of green lizard skin. Rising up from his spider legs was the unmistakable curving body of a lizard with four arms. At his side hung a massive sword that Celeste remembered was called a zweihander from all her medieval research. But this one was proportionate to the monster that held it. As they approached, Amdusius's forked tongue slipped in and out from behind malicious fangs.

"Who comes to me?" it hissed. Celeste swore he smiled evilly as it slowly descended to stand above them. When he spoke, it was as if thunder had been beckoned by his voice and the sky rumbled.

Celeste looked up at the rumbling.

"I do," she said timidly. "We are on a pilgrimage and need to return to the Surface," she echoed what the centaurs had said earlier, hoping that might help.

But the guardian's fang-filled smile only broadened. "You have one who belongs to the Nether," he said.

"Prince Gwen of Calimorden does not belong to the Nether," Celeste said. She stopped again, hearing herself name the kingdom. Was it the right name? What if it was the wrong name? She shouldn't have said it.

Amdusius considered her. "I am no friend to the Surface, but I have failed in my task of protecting the Nether. One greater than I has taken my Plane. All I can do now is keep the gate closed."

"Yes," Celeste said excitedly. "I'm here to stop that entity. One of your own," she motioned to the elf, "was sent to find me. I'm..." She hesitated, not sure if Amdusius would be on her side. Her voice became far less sure as she went on. "I'm a Planes Strider and I've been called to help save..." She stopped. No, she couldn't name the world. If she messed that up, something bad might happen.

"Are you?" Amdusius said, amused. He reached for his zweihander. Gwen, the elf, and the centaurs laid their hands on their weapons and Celeste took a step back. "This is the key to the Nether," Amdusius hissed, unsheathing the great sword and holding it flat in his palms. "If you are a Planes Strider, the one thing you can do is open the gates without my aid." He smirked, handing the monstrous blade to her. "Open it and you may pass."

Well, shit, Celeste thought, heaving the sword from his scaly hands. With a grunt, she turned the point down, setting it against a bit of a large bolder just under the ground. She held onto the first grip just above the blade but below the handle, since she couldn't reach it. She felt ridiculous.

Beside her, the elf furrowed his brow and nodded to her.

Okay, well, it's a key, so... Push in and turn? She grunted, shoving the sword down with all her might. To her surprise, it sank into the stone. She turned the zweihander into the stone like a key. Behind the sword and stone, a great red portal opened.

An exclamation went up from the whole party. Even Celeste cried out, leaping back from the sudden portal. Catching her breath, she stared into it. A swirling orange and red vortex waited for her.

Smiling, the elf pushed past Gwen and walked through, completely unafraid.

Gwen's mouth hung open in awe. "I must take you to my mother," he whispered. "She will see who you are and will have hope again."

The centaur leader looked down at Celeste with wide eyes. She didn't say anything as she stepped through.

"After you," Gwen said, bowing his head to her.

Celeste held her breath still and looked up at the spider-lizard. The monster hummed and nodded. He didn't speak. Still holding her breath, Celeste stepped through the portal and onto lush, green grass.

THE FARMLAND SURROUNDING THE CITY WAS LUSH and beautiful. The party appeared in a small mountain valley nestled between two far greater spines of peaks that angled outward. Celeste gasped as she took in the purple mountains, the ocean of soft grass waving around the bases, and the patches of homesteads. Yellow-thatched roofs caught the fresh morning sun, and a blue river fed several small streams that watered the homes. A few stray sheep, goats, and cows munched on the juicy grass. She spotted two mills, one run by a river wheel, the other slowly turning from the great sails catching the gentle breeze.

In the distance, beyond the pastoral homes, the city walls of Calimorden gently curved around the base of the tallest mountain. The city and the grand, many-turreted citadel that lorded over the land were hewn from the mountain that enthroned it. Calimorden glittered like a spear of ivory amidst emerald waves. The scent of wildflowers and fresh grass rose up on the cool wind that buffeted against Celeste's face.

"It's exactly how I dreamed," Celeste whispered. It was far better than the dark, red, muggy air of the Nether.

Before they went down the other side of the mountain, the pack of centaurs—all but their leader—bid them farewell and returned to the pilgrimage, calling out to the stars for guidance.

As they moved through the prairies, Celeste spotted

several creatures she thought she recognized. A large bird with feathers like fire soared over them and piped a tune to its hidden fellows. In a clearing to the left, a dazzling unicorn solemnly watched them pass. She wondered if all these were magical creatures like she'd read about. A small pack of adventurers stopped by a well, looking at a map and meeting her eyes as she passed. She recognized a ranger like her, a woman in white armor who towered over them all, a kind of wizard, and a talking dog. She suddenly wanted more than ever to save this world. Umbra be damned. He couldn't have this world, and Celeste would see to it.

Outside in the fields, a few workers could be seen. Fences lined every homestead, and each worker was armed and grave-looking.

Celeste asked Gwen, "Why does everyone look so tense?"

"These are defending against the norcan, barbarians, and other unpleasant raiders," Gwen said, with no effort to hide the malice in his voice. "And last I was here, an entire battalion of men went missing. Umbra is close, but my mother denies it."

"Norcan," she repeated testing the unfamiliar word.

"Base cousins of the humans, if you can call them that," the centaur murmured with distaste. "A vile race of green giants with manes of midnight black and jaws worthy of a wolf."

"Like orcs?" Celeste asked, thinking of *Elderforge*. But the others looked lost. "Never mind," she said.

The city around the castle thrived and looked exactly how Celeste had imagined every city she'd been queen of in their games. Cobbled roads led to all the shops, inns, and taverns, where musicians played lively melodies for coin and food. In the streets, the rural vendors sold their wares to the rich city-dwellers. Deeper into the center, a massive sparkling blue moat surrounded the white palace.

Only the prince, the Nether elf , and the centaur entered the palace walls. The guards, after getting over their initial shock of seeing the prince, allowed the elf through the gate at Gwen's behest. The prince led them through marble halls and golden rooms to a set of great doors. Soon they were outside the throne room, about to be announced.

"What am I supposed to say to your mother?" Celeste asked Gwen. "I mean, I'm not sure what I'm supposed to do."

"She will not be pleased to see me," Gwen reassured her. "But with you by my side, I hope she understands."

Celeste gently frowned. "Why won't she be happy to see you? You were in the Nether—not a great place by my standards. I'd be glad to see my son after he escaped such a place."

Gwen took a long, deep breath. "She sent me there."

Celeste gaped. Before she could reply, the doors opened and the small band followed their guards into a large circular throne room. The room matched the rest of the white and gold finery of the palace. Open windows that were nearly floor to ceiling lined the walls and looked out over the thriving kingdom of Calimorden. At the head of the room, a great golden throne waited, with an older but beautiful woman seated in its great depths. She tried to hold herself tall, but something weighed down on her, making her face wrinkle in worry.

"What darkness is this?" she called out through the room. "A Nether elf in my court, and my son back to haunt me?"

The prince held his head high. "You sacrificed me in fear, Mother, but I have come back. And I've brought a Planes Strider with me. It was she who saved me and opened the portal to this Plane."

Hearing the title, the queen gasped and rose from her seat, clutching her heart. "A Planes Strider? It cannot be. Planes Striders are lies whispered by my father at my bedside." She sat back down in despair. Her silver, hawk-like eyes shot up to Celeste through strands of chestnut hair. "You will not save us."

Celeste made an awkward curtsy in her tunic. "I suppose I'm here to help." But she didn't know how.

"There is little left to help," the queen said. Her eyes fixed on the prince again. "Planes Striders come from the Other World like Umbra."

Celeste tried to decipher what that might mean. "So, is this thing a Planes Strider, too, Queen Zephyr?" She stopped. She'd done it again. Named something without having known it before. She swallowed hard.

Queen Zephyr raised her brows. Then they fell into a skeptical glower again. "It is not a physical thing. It fills our people like an illness. Takes our lands into a void." She looked back down at Celeste. "How did you come here?"

Celeste shuffled her feet awkwardly and self-consciously crossed her arms. "Well, I was in the woods when I fell into the Nether and met your son. He wants to save his kingdom, and I'll do everything I can to help. But I need to know how."

"You speak like a fool," Zephyr spat. "So brave and ignorant. Planes Strider magic. I've seen what it does to people from your world. It destroys them slowly, changes them so grotesquely until they can no longer return to the Other World."

At this, Celeste paused. So Planes Striders did have some kind of power, even if she couldn't figure it out yet. But it changed them somehow? Of course magic came with a cost. So she wasn't all powerful.

"You may not believe in me, Queen Zephyr," Celeste said, "but Gwen does."

"As do I," the elf whispered darkly.

"Monster," the queen spat at the elf. "It was the Nether who fell first. With Zane'barren bending a knee to Umbra, I knew it would come for us next. It's already here. Soon, it will devour the Nether entirely, then the Surface. Already its servant prepares the way, moving amongst the stars."

"A servant of Umbra has reached the Celestial Plane?" Gwen cried. "Mother, why have you not stood up to this beast?"

"I gave Umbra *you*!" she shrieked. "With you in its grip, it should not have come to our Plane. That was the promise."

Celeste scoffed. "You trusted the word of some dark entity? What happens once it takes the Nether and the Surface? What's in the Celestial Plane that it wants?"

"The way to the Astral Plane," the elf whispered. "The Glass Throne where the Eidolon sits in the Golden Tree."

Celeste remembered the glass crown on the boy she'd seen in her dream. "He called me here," she said in awe. "I heard his voice." Excitement shot through her. "I saw him in my dream last night."

Before Queen Zephyr or Gwen could answer, the Nether elf let out a war cry and pulled two hidden blades from his black robes. At first, the others looked confused. The elf had reacted as if some danger had sprung up from the shadows. Outside, a great bell rang as if alerting the city to some danger. But then they heard it.

Following the elf's cry came a great roar the likes of which Celeste had never heard before. It rattled her inner ears and thrummed in her chest. Turning her eyes to the open windows of the throne room, she saw the huge, winged form of the only thing that could have made such a roar, simultaneously filling her with awe and terror at once.

"Dragon!" the centaur shrieked. She took her bow from her back and quickly aimed at the beast's fiery eyes.

The dragon was massive, its forelegs knotted with muscles, ending in long, black claws. Its gray scales were rough and firmly calloused. Horns and spikes decorated its back and head. Its nostrils flared and huffed, and Celeste smelled something she could only describe as burning or molten rock: a putrid smell.

White-clad guards flooded the throne room and the queen was quickly whisked away to safety. Gwen valiantly drew his sword and stood before Celeste. Archers appeared and began to shoot at the dragon's sensitive eyes.

"We must get you to safety," Gwen called to Celeste over the dragon's roars.

"Wait!" Celeste pulled away from him. *Planes Strider magic*, she thought to herself. Maybe it would work on the gray dragon?

The huge yellow eyes fixed on her and it spoke. "Your magic will not work on me, Planes Strider!"

Frightened that the beast knew her thoughts, Celeste ducked away with Gwen. The door was a good sprint away, but they had to chance it. The elf ran first, war-crying to the dragon to distract it. Celeste had not asked him to do this; he just did. The brave act rang in her heart. Then she made a dash for the exit, but not fast enough. The huge claw of the dragon burst into the room, slamming onto the floor, causing it to rift, crack, and finally crumble under Celeste, Gwen, and the elf. The centaur had moved closer to the dragon and attempted stabbing it with her massive ax.

Celeste tumbled and flipped on the broken marble floor,

her heels wheeling over her head as she did. With a sudden desperate grab, she managed to hold onto the floor as her legs and boots swung in the air above a pit she could not see the bottom of.

"Celeste!" Gwen called. "Hold on!" He bled badly from where a single claw had nicked him across his chest. The beast was so large that even the smallest hit caused what looked like a mortal wound.

Seeing her hanging there, the dragon reached in again, aiming at Celeste. In a black blur, the elf took up Gwen's broadsword, far too large for him, and held it out to ward off the dragon. He stood firmly between Celeste and the beast.

Her fingers seared with the pain of holding on, and the dragon's breath burned her lungs as she panted.

"I grant you a mercy, Celeste of our world," he said, bestowing the strange title on her. "Stay away. Go home."

With one more rumble of the tower room, her grasp slipped and she screamed as she held on with only one hand over the vast pit.

The elf heard her cry and threw aside the sword. He ran and fell to his knees, grasping her hand in his.

"Hold on!" he yelled over the commotion. "Climb! I can't hold you!"

She grunted and tried to heave herself up, but failed, sliding a little further down and pulling the elf with her. She looked up to meet his eyes for what she thought may be the last time. His black-lined eyes and his thick lashes reminded her of Oran. At last, she slipped from between his little fingers. She watched his horrified black eyes widen as she fell.

Somewhere above, Gwen called her name in desperation over the last roar of the gray dragon. The darkness took her.

CHAPTER 9
DISSENT AMONG FRIENDS

Celeste cried out as she landed hard against mud and rock. Creek water splashed up onto her face. She panted, her chest throbbing from the impact. Waiting for the pain to subside, the water trickled into her ears. Her eyes took a moment to adjust in the dark. The moon hung high overhead and the evening creatures sang their lullabies. In the distance, the city hummed and roared with night light. The clouds above were tinged orange from the city lights. A siren went off not too far away: the sounds of real life.

Above her, the constellation Draco glared down at her: a familiar sky.

Celeste stood and brushed her soft cotton leggings, feeling the cold air seeping through. They were no longer tanned leather. She looked around and recognized the familiar woods. It was night now. Where was everyone? Had they noticed she'd gone missing?

"The sun has gone down," she gasped. "I must have been gone for hours."

She stopped to think. It had been morning when they arrived. When she fell, it couldn't have been much later. But in that weird dream, or whatever it was, it had been night. It was as if time ran backward in the dream world. It only made sense that now night should settle in when the sun shone in Calimorden.

"No." Celeste sighed, lightly banging her head with her fist. "Don't think about that. At least not like that. Didn't happen. A dream." Her head pulsed in agony. She took a step to find her ankle had been sprained. Groaning, she sat back down.

Close by, the sound of panicked, screaming people crashed through the underbrush. About a dozen beams of light swung back and forth in the trees and all different voices called her name.

"I'm over here!" she called. "I think I hurt my ankle."

Alice, Stella, Oran, and Lance ran toward her, led by Justin. He dashed to her and fell to her side, throwing his woolen jacket over her. She was very quickly surrounded by lights and panicked voices. Kiyoshi arrived next with his wild-eyed mother and a first aid kit.

"Celeste!" Kiyoshi's mom breathed in relief. "Do you have any idea how scared everyone was for you? Are you hurt? We very nearly called the park rangers after you."

"I'm so sorry, everyone," she said. Tears rimmed her eyes as she saw the horrified looks on everyone's faces. Justin helped her up, putting his arm around her to help her stand.

"We were so worried," Alice said through a stuffy nose. "I was crying my eyes out for you." She had a coat on over her costume.

"What on earth were you doing?" Stella demanded. "We thought you were dead."

Celeste laughed at her overdramatic friend and hugged them both again. If they had been worried, wait until they heard about the dragon.

In the crowd, she quickly found Lance's relieved face, and near the back, a white-haired boy in black robes. She looked twice as her heart skipped to find Oran there. She pulled away from Justin enough to put one arm around her shy friend and hug him tightly.

Lance met her eyes over Oran's head. "We're all glad you're safe, Celeste," he said.

Justin swept Celeste away onto the walking trail that led to the campsite. Celeste watched as Lance faded back into the crowd, staying with Oran. Despite the cold, she felt a warm glow in her heart.

"Hey," Justin said, waving his hand in front of her face to get her attention. "Let's get you dried off and warm, okay?"

"To the camp," Kiyoshi's mom said. "And let's get you taken care of."

ALL CELESTE COULD DO SUNDAY NIGHT WAS THINK about the prince, the centaurs, and the Nether elf. She hardly slept and was sleep-deprived Monday morning. She had English class, which would make her morning so much more interesting, but it still couldn't drive away the adventure she'd had. Or dreamed she'd had. Part of her wanted desperately to tell someone about it, but another, far more scared part told her to wait. She didn't have a long time to think about it as she had work later that night at a little shop in the mall called Wanderer's Gold. It sold little trinkets like magical talismans, home decor that an aging hippie might like, and other such things. Work and real life would take her mind off the magical world she had fallen into. The week would pass slowly if all she could do was wait until the weekend again. Then she would go into the woods and try to find the portal.

Celeste opened her locker Wednesday morning to grab her dice bag before English. They were supposed to meet at a game shop in the mall after school for a session zero of a new campaign, one that Lance would be running. This made her excited but also nervous. Part of her wanted him to be a natural at it, but she feared how the others might react.

"Celeste," Oran called, jogging up to her. "Do you still have the master tome of narrative?"

She blushed. "That thing was a travesty." The tome in question had been a journal she'd kept in her early days of game management. She'd written notes about narrative structure, plot twists, how to handle when the players went off the rails—everything she'd learned in her first two years of dungeon mastering.

"Do you still have it?" Oran asked.

Embarrassed, she nodded. "But no one can see it."

Oran made a guilty face. "I kind of told Lance he could have it. He wants any tips he can get, and your notes were the first thing I thought of."

"Is he nervous?" she asked, a little too hopefully.

Oran nodded. "Wants to make a good first impression."

She smiled, biting her bottom lip, hiding behind her locker door. "You're a good friend to help him out, Oran." She closed her door. Oran's pale face looked even paler inside his great black hood. His eyes quickly flicked from her to over her shoulder, then back. "What is it?" she asked.

He stammered. "I was wondering if—if you want to, of course—if our characters could have a thing later in the campaign."

She tilted her head. "Huh?"

"So Jaxton, my wizard, lost his wife, right? And Sera, your fighter, has amnesia. What if our mid-story arc is we discover that Sera is his lost wife and—"

"They're from warring clans," she interrupted.

"Yeah," Oran said, getting excited. "Then, when they discover this, they have to fight past that and try to rekindle their love, thus bringing their clans together to face off against whatever big bad guy Lance has in store for us."

Celeste gasped, grabbing Oran by his shoulders. "She's a fighter in his army, so it would build crazy tension within her group of comrades. She'd be a traitor, but for love. Love she had before her military days. Oran, you are a genius!"

He smiled, setting his hand on top of hers. She let him stay there the two more seconds they had before the bell rang. She liked him so much, and was keenly aware he didn't remove her hand from his. But they'd been friends forever and she didn't want to jeopardize that.

"Well, I'm off to have Ms. Vanders ruin Shakespeare for me." Celeste smiled, taking her copy of *A Midsummer Night's Dream* out of her locker. "You?"

"Science, but Granger is subbing, so it should be interesting," he said. He took off down the hall.

English slogged on forever for Celeste. At first, she got interested when Ms. Vanders talked about how the lovers entered the woods and thus stepped into a world where fairies were real and the characters could act wildly. But then she droned on about how immoral the characters were and Celeste lost all interest. She looked at the cover. It showed the fairy queen in a beautiful forest: the forest where they left reality behind.

Will any forest work as a portal? she wondered. She had been in the woods when she'd fallen into that world. She wanted to get back, but didn't know how. Wouldn't she know if she was a Planes Strider? Maybe she wasn't a Planes Strider after all. She sighed. Why would she think she was the hero, come to save that world? That just made her sound pompous.

But... What if she could decide what role to play? She shook her head. It wasn't a game. At least, it didn't feel like a game. Grateful that Ms. Vanders had finally said something useful—about the woods being a portal—she zoned out, imagining that night as Lance would take over his first campaign, holding her very life in his hands. She sighed, smiling.

LANCE LOOKED OVER THE SCREEN HE HAD BETWEEN him and his players. Stella glared at him. Her and Oran's miniatures stood at the base of a colossal model castle she had made. It had many spikes and turrets rising up from it and was painted almost entirely black. Behind it, Stella's eyes shot sparks at him as she crossed her arms.

"Well?" she snapped.

"I'm not sure how rolls against other player characters should go," he confessed, catching Justin roll his eyes to his left. Oran looked at him with pleading eyes.

"You're the game master. You decide," Oran said. His

expression begged him not to let Stella roll to flirt with his character, though.

"We could always role play it instead." Stella smiled, tightening her arms and looking coyly over the table at Oran.

"This is embarrassing," Justin said. "Lance, let her roll and get it over with."

"But," Celeste cut in, clutching her character sheet, "what if she succeeds? Oran will have to make Jaxton flirt back with the witch."

"All this meta gaming." Justin sighed. "Let's talk more instead of actually playing, that's a good idea." He crossed his arms and scoffed at Lance. "Some table management."

Kiyoshi held up his hands. "All of our characters are in this war room of Stella's castle, right?"

Lance nodded, becoming more flustered as he tried to remember what was going to happen next, and what might happen if he let Stella proceed. Kiyoshi nodded to Celeste.

Celeste perked up. "I slam my fists on the table where the map is and say, 'Is the prince's life in danger or not?' I look at the witch, pleading with her to think of the kingdom. 'He's been taken by someone we thought we could trust, from inside his father's own council. We have only each other to lean on.' I look at the prince's champion. 'What can you tell me about the religious order on the edge of town?'"

Lance smiled, thanking Celeste with his eyes for remembering the mysterious order he'd mentioned an hour ago. "The prince's champion meets your eyes, concerned. 'They call me Deran, warrior. My father was the deacon of the order before I was born—"

"What the hell?" Stella interrupted, chucking her D20 across the game mat at Oran. She glared at Celeste.

The table went silent as Stella seethed.

"I was just trying to bring the game back," Celeste said cautiously. "Lance is new and I wanted to help us stay focused."

Stella turned her icy eyes on Lance. "Why didn't you just let me roll?"

Lance awkwardly tapped his pencil against his binder. "It didn't seem like the right thing to let happen. It takes away Jaxton's agency, don't you think? Basically forcing him to romance your character when Oran doesn't want to."

"It doesn't matter what he wants. Let the dice decide," Stella shot back.

"Lance said no," Celeste snapped. A different kind of silence fell then. "Why are you making this so hard?"

Justin dropped his face into his hands, Kiyoshi and Alice shared silent glances, and Oran shrank into his hoodie. Lance wasn't sure what to do. Not only was the game new to him, but so was the group he'd joined. He'd thought Celeste and Stella were best friends. Had he driven a wedge between them somehow? Did Stella notice his interest in Celeste and see him as trying to steal her away?

"Okay," he said slowly. He gathered his courage for his next words. "New table rule. Under no circumstance can one player character roll against another player character. No pickpocketing, no romancing, no attacks."

Justin raised his brow, judging Lance's decision. "Seems like an easy way out for the game master. Have some balls, Lance. Let the dice decide." He looked over at Celeste. "If I were game master, I'd let anything go. Leave it up to us to figure our way out."

"Then let's vote," Alice suggested. "Lance?"

It seemed like a safe option. "Okay, a vote. Who votes in favor of no rolls against player characters?"

Oran's hand shot up, and he raised his. Kiyoshi, Alice, and Celeste raised theirs.

Lance gave Justin a satisfied glance. "Five to two."

"Don't be so smug," Justin grumbled back, picking up his dice. "This isn't even how a session zero is supposed to go. We should have spent more time fleshing out our characters to avoid unwanted romances."

"Why does every campaign have to have romance in it, anyway?" Alice groaned.

"It's realistic," Lance tried. "Most people wouldn't go through things like this—adventuring, questing, risking their lives—without coming out with some kind of connection to the people they experienced those things with. We get to choose our roles, make characters that mean something to us. But we don't want to see them forced to go down a path we are strongly against."

"Then why won't you let me roll against him?" Stella moaned.

"Because it doesn't make sense for the story," Lance replied. He felt he tread on thin ice with the group. He was the outsider and he had made them all argue. He sighed and leaned back. Stella had a thing for Oran, that much was obvious. But the way Oran acted, he was not interested. He might even be a little scared. He wouldn't let his new friend suffer.

"Okay," he said with finality. "We got our character sheets written, right? Let's call it a day and plan another session for later."

"Quitting?" Justin sneered.

Lance had had enough. It was clear Justin and Stella did not want him there, that he'd somehow destroyed their friendships. He pressed his palms into the table and licked his lips to reply when he caught Celeste's face over the table. She looked worried he might say yes. He checked Oran beside him and he had the same look on his face. He took a deep breath.

"No, Justin, I'm not quitting," he said steadily. "I'm stopping before you all say something you regret."

"Don't do me any favors," Stella said.

"Wouldn't dream of it." Lance smiled. He gathered up his things, slid them into his backpack, leaving the game shop, Oran in tow.

LANCE WAITED UNTIL THEY WERE OUTSIDE AND AWAY from the other before asking, "You want to get some air before heading home?"

Oran glanced at his phone, then tucked it away without checking it. "Yeah, actually. Mom's working late again anyway."

Lance took Oran's things and tossed them in the back of his truck before driving out into the neighborhood. He wasn't sure where he as going; he just knew Oran needed some space. He drove around until he realized he was going in circles. He needed to stop. They ended up at the old playground behind the elementary school, sitting on the swings even though the chains creaked under Lance's weight. The cool wind rustled leaves across the empty basketball court. Lance focused on them as he contemplated what he was going to say.

"Sorry about Stella," Lance said after a while. "That got weird back there."

Oran kicked at the wood chips under his feet. "It's fine.

She does that sometimes." He paused, then added quietly, "Everything's weird now."

"Since your dad?"

Oran had mentioned in passing that day at the park that his dad had passed. Lance hadn't wanted to pry at the time, but now seemed like a good time.

Oran's hands tightened on the swing chains. "Yeah. Mom works all the time. The house is just...empty." He swallowed hard. "Sometimes I sit in his chair in the garage. Where he used to read. It still smells like his cigarettes."

Lance watched his friend's face carefully. "You can always come over, you know. Mom already thinks you're awesome because you actually laughed at her terrible joke that one time."

That got a small smile from Oran. "Thanks. It's just... I don't know. Sometimes I feel like I'm just taking up space. Like maybe it would have been better if—" He cut himself off, shaking his head.

"Hey." Lance made sure his voice was gentle but firm. "Don't finish that sentence. Look at me." He waited until Oran met his eyes. "You matter. To a lot of people. To me."

Oran looked away quickly, blinking hard. "You don't even really know me."

"I know enough. I know you're smart as hell. I know you make amazing characters. I know you're the only person who didn't treat me like an outsider trying to infiltrate your group." Lance smiled. "And I know you need to come over tomorrow and help me plan this campaign, because I have no idea what I'm doing."

"You're doing fine," Oran said, but he was smiling a little now too. "Though maybe fewer mysterious religious orders next time."

"Noted." Lance stood up, stretching. "Come on, I'm driving you home. And we're stopping for milkshakes first."

"You don't have to—"

"Nope, too late. I'm your ride now. Forever. Deal with it."

Lance spoke confidently but inside he was panicking. Had Oran really been about to say what he thought he was going to? *Don't give up,* Lance thought, wishing Oran could read his mind. He made up his mind then to watch out for Oran, no matter what.

As they walked to Lance's truck, Oran said quietly, "Thanks. For, you know. Everything."

Lance slung an arm around Oran's shoulders. "That's what friends are for. And hey, text me tonight if you want. Even if it's late. Even if it's just to talk about random campaign stuff."

"Yeah," Oran said. "Maybe I will."

Lance caught the slight tremor in his friend's voice and made a mental note to check in more often. Sometimes the smallest things could save someone—like knowing there was at least one person who would answer when you called.

CELESTE SAT ACROSS FROM JUSTIN AND STELLA. ALICE had run after Lance and Oran.

"Why are you trying to take him away from me?" Stella snapped at Celeste. "Are you jealous?"

Justin's brows went up. "Celeste doesn't have a thing for Oran. Do you?"

"No," Celeste moaned. "He's one of my oldest friends.

Stella, you're my best friend. I wouldn't do anything to hurt you, either. I just think Lance had a point."

"Lance," Justin growled, suddenly packing his things up. "That guy has been nothing but trouble. You two have only fought since he joined the group. Oran ignores me now. I've talked to Zain more than him so far this year."

Celeste leaned back in her chair. This was exactly what she had been afraid of with senior year. Everyone would break up. Go their separate ways. There had to be a way to keep everyone close. She eyed Stella. She could tell her about crossing over into the other world. But first, she had to be sure she had.

Making up her mind, she decided then to try and get back. Then she'd share her adventure with her friends, bring them close once again.

CHAPTER 10
HEART TO HEART

L ance checked the clock above the miniature display again to see how close to noon it had gotten in the last few seconds. Fifteen more minutes, then he could take his break and walk down the mall halls to that weird little store Celeste worked in. As far as he knew, he and Celeste were the only ones of their group that worked in the mall. So they could be alone.

"Master innkeeper, your finest room!" Alice called, entering the game store with a broad smile. She led Stella into the store, pulling her past a display of new cards.

"Ladies," Lance said from behind the counter, pushing aside the box of dice he'd been sorting. The kids who came into the game store never kept the dice in their neat, separated boxes. His constant task was sorting them back. "What are you playing today?"

"Nothing. Just visiting. What made you want to work in the game store?" Alice asked her cousin, leaning heavily onto the counter and looking around.

Lance half-shrugged. Alice didn't need to know that he wanted to work in the same vicinity as Celeste. "I needed a job since moving here," he said honestly. "And working here helps me understand you all better."

"Sure," Stella mumbled. "That's why you want to work in the mall just a few stores down from Celeste."

Lance tried to ignore her.

Alice studied the collection of boxed-up games behind him. The shelf boasted the best collection within a one hundred-mile radius easily. Customers could come in, pay to rent the game, and play it in one of the back rooms. Alice tapped her chin, reading the titles she'd run her eyes over a million times in the past four years.

"Oh, six o'clock," Stella mumbled, turning her back to the front of the store.

Lance glanced over her head to see Justin enter and scan the shop with a hunter's eye. Lance knew immediately he was searching for Celeste. He didn't look away fast enough before Justin saw him looking. He marched up to the counter.

"Have you seen Celeste today?" he asked. "I couldn't catch her at school."

"She's working," Lance replied. "Not everyone has the luxury of not working during the school year."

Justin smiled condescendingly at Lance. "If you see her, tell her I'll be in the food court."

"Why?" Alice asked for Lance.

Justin ignored her and left.

The three of them watched him leave.

"He's never going to give up," Stella said. "Why won't Celeste just date him until school's over? He's going to Crazyville, Alabama or something for college."

"He wants her to apply," Lance said. "Oran and I were playing arena in *Elderforge* and he hopped into the chat. Would not stop talking while we were trying to win a game full of trolls."

"Celeste's not applying to Alabama," Stella said, frowning. "She would have told me."

"Yeah, exactly," Lance replied. "Why's he so controlling over her? It's like..." He stopped. It was like Justin was obsessed with her. He reminded himself to not think defensively about Celeste. *Oran likes her, you idiot,* he chastised himself.

"And speaking of boys," Alice said, pretending to busy herself with the dice Lance was sorting.

Stella groaned and leaned backward in a weak attempt to remove herself from the situation.

"Why do you keep flirting with Oran?" Alice sounded like a judge about to sentence a prisoner to life in jail. "Why can't you just be his friend?"

"I can't help that the little freak is so cute." Stella shrugged far too casually for such a serious accusation. "It's fun. Everyone wants a little dangerous crush now and then."

The way she talked about Oran made Lance gape. "Freak? Fun?"

Stella glared at him. "What do you care?"

"Dangerous?" Alice laughed. "Have you met Oran? Guy's practically a marshmallow."

Stella scoffed in disgust and glared at Alice. "I just want to play with him a little. He gets all squirmy when I flirt with him. It's fun. And who appointed you his high guardian?"

"He's my friend," Lance shot back. "What is wrong with you?"

"Shut up, newbie." Now Stella glared like a viper. "You may be some tall hot guy with muscles, but you're a poser. This isn't your scene. I know you work here just to try to fit in with us. Why are you so obsessed with Oran?"

Lance stammered, more angry than anything else. "He needed help. I stepped up one day and he just kind of latched on to me."

"Oh, of course he did." Stella laughed dryly. "Because everyone just loves you, huh? Celeste's just smitten with the big football guy who happens to like role play, RPGs, and video games."

"Stella," Alice hissed, "cut it out. What's wrong with you?"

"Alice, it's fine," Lance said. He'd heard what she said. Lance had appeared in the eleventh hour of their high school lives. He'd gotten in the way of Oran. And apparently Celeste. Celeste was Stella's best friend and Oran was the object of her weird, twisted desire.

The clock hit noon.

"Donny," Lance called to a co-worker running a table for a group of kids. "Come help these guys get a room and a game. I'm on lunch."

LANCE JOGGED DOWN THE HALL, NOT WANTING TO lose more time to walking than he had to. The mall cop gave him a warning glance as he almost ran past him. He slowed to a power walk as he rounded the corner and smelled the store before he saw it. Mist floated out from a display of fountains and the smell of burning incense filled the opening.

He spotted Celeste cleaning out the little desk fountains on display. Justin was already hovering close to her, talking a million words a second.

"Oooh," a voice cooed behind him as he quietly entered. "That is a good aura."

He turned to find a woman, whom he guessed from her name tag was the owner. She closed her eyes and pulled her waist-length hair over one shoulder. "You have a pleasant spirit, young man. I'm Heather. I own the store."

"Uh, thanks," Lance said, a little embarrassed. "Nice store."

Heather smiled wistfully. "What you have come looking for is not for sale." She smiled genuinely. "But you're not buying, are you? No, you'd never do that to her."

A little taken by surprise by the woman, Lance stood awkwardly, fiddling with his own lanyard and name tag. When he looked up, he found Celeste watching him. Her eyes bulged just once as if to say, "Please come here," so he did.

"Oh, Lance, hi!" she said a little overly loud, cutting off whatever tirade Justin had been on.

Justin deflated, eyes going hard as he looked at Lance.

"Look at this statue we just got in," Celeste said, turning her back to Justin. "It made me think of you."

The statue in question was a shirtless, absolutely ripped primal warrior wearing a leopard skin and standing atop a a tiger corpse, raising his sword to the sky.

"Wow, thanks," he said honestly. He caught her blush and press her lips together. She was embarrassed.

"Anyway," Justin said, obviously annoyed, "we all have been noticing you've seemed a little off lately. Ever since last weekend's session in *Sun Age*."

"I did fall asleep in math on Tuesday." She shrugged. "But honestly—"

"No, that's just it," Justin said. "You were awake and Ms. Havisham was ready to kill you when you wouldn't answer. You stared right at her for about a minute."

A blush found its way to Celeste's cheeks. "So?"

"I'm concerned about your future," Justin said, putting his hand on Celeste's shoulder.

Lance wanted to knock his hand off her. Celeste wasn't Justin's to worry about. But she wasn't his to defend, either. Alice's words to Stella came back to him: just be her friend.

"You know you can tell us anything," he tried. "If something is going on... None of us have perfect lives." *And to be honest,* he thought, *the dynamics of this group of friends is toxic as hell.* He didn't know why they all still hung out together. It was clear they were drifting apart, but fought fiercely to remain together.

Just then, the troll king Garzier entered with two cronies at his sides, one carrying his backpack, the other struggling to hold three soft drinks in his chubby arms. Without his troll getup on, Garzier almost could have blended in with the athletes. He was tall, had angled features, and looked fit.

"What do you want, troll?" Celeste moaned.

Lance had quickly learned that Garzier never used his real name and insisted that no one else use it either. He wondered if the teachers at school knew his real name. That was one reason why the group disliked him: he took their sacred game, their magic, and escape, and used it everywhere. He put their stories on display for everyone at school. He was one of the reasons they were all criticized so much.

"We are here to purchase the needed ingredients for my ritual tonight," Garzier said smugly as he announced his intentions. "We shall need sage, a goblet, and three red candles if you have them, wench."

Celeste reluctantly showed the troll to the new herb rack. "Here. And the candles are under the table back there. Goblets behind the counter. I'll have to pull them out for you to look at. Plated in silver."

The troll king smiled and motioned for his slaves to help him pick out some sage bundles. "Very well then. Get to it, shop girl."

"Celeste," Celeste snapped. "You know my name, troll."

"Dare you speak to a king thus?" Garzier cried, raising his head up.

"Just because you live in the rich county doesn't make you better than everyone else," Lance cut in. His tone came out strong, but measured.

The troll king laughed. "Actually, it does. Have you seen my house?"

Justin quailed at the conflict, moving toward the front of the store. Lance noticed Celeste's eyes on him.

"I have." Lance smiled kindly. "Your rich oil dad's house, actually."

Garzier's face fell a little. "Wench," he shouted to Celeste, "my wares."

Lance sighed as she moved to the front of the store to ring up the troll king. His entire lunch break had been foiled. Now he'd have to try to talk to her at school, where the rest of the party would be watching his every move.

THAT MONDAY NIGHT, LANCE SAT ALONE IN HIS ROOM. His mother was working late and the house felt emptier than before. Quieter. Lonelier. He messed around on his computer for as long as he could before boredom overcame him. He began to think about his dad. What had his father been thinking when he'd met that woman for the first time? Did his mom mean nothing to him? Did *he* mean nothing?

Lance sighed sadly and flopped down on his bed. He picked up his phone and tried to think of someone to call. He hated when the darker thoughts intruded on his mind. But who would pick up? Would anyone want to listen to him whine about his issues? His friends back home had abandoned him, not sure how to handle his parents' divorce. He'd been alone for a while.

He flipped open his phone and scrolled to Oran's name, sending a quick text. He asked Oran to come over and bring his console so they could play games. Then he closed his phone and waited, begging his mind to not think about his dad. But the silence wasn't so kind.

He'd always thought his dad was strong and brave. But no brave man would hide an affair like that. Maybe Dad wasn't as strong as he'd thought.

Was *he* strong? He couldn't even tell a girl he liked her. But he'd stood up for Oran. Surely that had to count for something. But he did keep his new friends a secret from the team.

No, he wasn't brave.

Moments later, the doorbell rang and Oran stood outside, holding a huge box and smiling. "Brought some fighting games. Figured those might be more your speed."

"Anything to keep me from working on my English paper," Lance lied. He'd finished the paper days ago, but didn't want to admit it. He just needed the distraction.

A few minutes later, Oran had the console set up on the family room TV and handed Lance the second player controller. They sat together on the rug facing the TV and started up the fighting game. Oran taught Lance a few moves with one character before quickly and soundly kicking his ass. Lance took it in stride.

"Does Justin play this game?" he asked as he slid his thumb over the buttons as quickly as he could, moving his character across the 2D screen.

"Yeah." Oran sighed. "He whips my butt every time."

Understanding, Lance decided not to express his disappointment at losing so much. Oran probably needed a win. He played the same character over and over, getting used to their moves until he finally beat Oran once. He smiled triumphantly. When he glanced over at Oran, he noticed his dark blue eyes looked to be staring into a world a million realms away.

"You okay?" he asked, elbowing Oran gently. "You basically just stood there and let me win. Don't do that."

"Uh," Oran stammered. "I didn't mean to. It's just this character I picked... It's one my dad used to play a lot. He used to quote all the catchphrases, too."

Lance let the controller hang loose in his hands. "Hey, Oran, remember, I'm here if you ever want to talk. I mean, I get it. I'm no stranger to familial issues."

Oran looked up at Lance, cautiously biting his lower lip. "I... It's been almost six months since my dad..." He stopped and looked away.

In that moment, Lance realized what must have happened. Oran's dad hadn't died in some accident like he'd assumed. He swallowed hard and looked away, giving Oran some privacy.

"When I saw that lady in our house," he started, "I knew what had happened. I didn't want to believe it. It felt so unreal. How could it happen to me? I was scared."

"You? Scared?" Oran asked. "I can't imagine you scared."

Lance half-shrugged and nodded. He felt like he could be real with Oran. He wouldn't judge him. "I also feel guilty sometimes. I'm relieved they broke up. Things were tense before that. I don't think they ever actually loved each other. They just stayed together for me. I realized that after they split."

"You don't have to feel guilty about that," Oran whispered. He scooted closer to Lance and faced him, dropping the controller.

"But I do." Lance sighed. "I was the reason they prolonged their suffering."

"At least your dad thought about you."

Lance met Oran's large eyes, silent. This was the time to wait and let Oran speak.

Oran's eyes shone with sudden tears. "I don't think he thought about me. What it would do to me when he left."

"What he did was selfish," Lance tried.

"Don't say that," Oran begged, sniffling. He pulled his head down into his shoulders like he was trying to hide in his oversized hoodie. "He was hurting. He had nothing to live for."

Lance thought before he spoke next. "He loved you, Oran. I'm sure."

"Then why did he do that?"

Lance didn't know.

"Why did he leave me?" Oran buried his face in his hands, hiding his emotions.

Awkwardly, Lance gripped his own hands in his lap. He

wasn't sure Oran was the touchy type, so he held back on the hug he wanted to give him. He glanced at the screen where the characters waited, paused. "This was his favorite character?" he asked. "What else did he like? Did you guys do things together? Like video games? My dad and I loved going to sports games together, or car shows." He let out a single huff of air in a dry laugh. "He bought me my first remote-controlled car when I was six. I don't remember what it was, just that it was white. Ever since then, I've wanted white cars. He bought me my truck. White."

Oran sniffed, but didn't drop his hands. He said, "My dad loved old eighties fantasy movies. He made me watch them with him all the time." Finally, he dropped his hands. Tears stained his pale cheeks. He didn't meet Lance's eyes, staring into nothing. "We used to go to this drive-in movie theater he liked. They played a lot of old movies."

Oran smiled at some private memory.

"Lance," Oran said softly. He finally looked up. "I have thoughts... Thoughts I wonder if my dad had before he... Sometimes I think the world would be better off without me in it." He swallowed hard.

At this, Lance couldn't stop himself. He leaned over the small space that separated them and wrapped his arms around Oran's shoulders.

"Please don't ever think that," Lance begged. "I need you. You're my only friend."

A long silence fell as Oran let Lance embrace him. Oran didn't reply. Lance heard his own heart beating in his chest. He let go and gently touched the ends of Oran's shaggy black hair, resting his wrist on Oran's shoulder.

"You've really helped me the last few weeks," Lance confessed. "I'm glad I met you that day."

Oran smiled weakly, his eyes downcast. "Me too, Lance." He sighed heavily and looked up. "You can call me whenever you want. Day or night. If you ever need support."

"You, too." Lance locked eyes with Oran. "I mean it. Anytime. I want you in my world. Got it?"

Oran smiled and his cheeks colored slightly. "Okay," he said.

CHAPTER II
A CALL IN THE WOODS

Normally, Celeste looked forward to the weekend. After some stiff back and forth in their chat room, the party decided to cancel *Sun Age* for the coming weekend and spend time together in the old arcade at the mall instead. Celeste hadn't been there since eighth grade, and hoped the nostalgia and memories would draw them together again.

But first, she had a side quest that Thursday night.

Her father's boss and his wife had invited her family for dinner, and that meant dressing up. She knew the dinner was just an excuse for the boss to chat with her father. He'd been talking about a promotion for almost five years now, and this should be it. For some reason, Celeste doubted it. She saw it as her father's way of trying to convince her mom to stay with him. She'd been in denial too long about her parents' imminent separation. The dinner was just a reminder of all the ways her life was falling apart.

To smooth things over, she invited Stella over to help her

pick out a dress for the night. The private messages had been intense, but after some apologies and bringing up her fears about her parents' separation, Stella came over.

"Just wear the elf dress," Stella suggested from Celeste's bed across the room as Celeste stared dismally into her closet. "Oh, and the dice necklace. I love that one. You can pretend that it's a talisman and that you're rolling for luck all night."

The dress in question was a knee-length navy blue summer dress with silver laces on the back for flare. Celeste had made it herself for a cousin's wedding and had been dying for an excuse to wear it again. The fabric was heavy and flowed easily, hence the name the girls had given to it.

"My mom hates it. And she *hates* the dice necklace." Celeste sighed, holding the dress up to herself. It was her favorite, and any excuse to use it would be welcome. She always felt more positive and alive in the elf dress. It was a shame it was so low on her mother's expectations for a well-dressed daughter.

Stella stood, then planted herself in front of Celeste's computer and scrolled through her many social media threads while she waited.

"You are subscribed to a lot of things," Stella mused. "Fantasy pages, dance web sites, culture clubs, writer's blogs, and even some geology journals." She hummed, impressed. "Geez, what do you want to be when you grow up?" Stella laughed, adding herself to Celeste's top friends list.

Hearing the laugh, Celeste emerged from her closet, halfway dressed between two outfits. "Stell," she said carefully. "I am sorry about what happened the other day at the table."

"You already apologized."

"I know. I just wanted to do it in person." She cradled the

elf dress in her hands. "You're coming to the arcade this weekend, right? It'll be like old times."

Stella turned in the office chair to look Celeste up and down. "I love the red sweater with the green shoes," she said sarcastically.

Celeste smiled. That was the Stella she knew and loved. "I was thinking these yellow plaid leggings would be great." She giggled.

Stella faked vomiting. "No. Elf dress for sure." She reached over to Celeste's jewelry stand and pulled off the dice necklace, a sparkling green D20 on the end of a black string. She held it up. "Green and blue are so your colors."

Celeste sighed in defeat. "You'd never lead me wrong. Elf dress it is."

Delighted, Stella turned back to the computer.

Satisfied, Celeste began to hang up the rejected clothes and look for shoes to compliment the dress while Stella clacked away at the keyboard.

LANCE COULDN'T FOCUS ON THE SCREEN BEFORE HIM. He kept reliving the argument around the table. Kept seeing Celeste's face asking him to take charge, to make a choice, to save the game. Justin's condescending voice rang in his head, too.

"You're dead again," Oran said from the chair next to him.

"Huh?" Lance looked up. He and Oran had been taking turns in a first person shooter that recently came out. The game modes were fun, but only supported local team ups. "Oh, sorry. Here, you give it a go."

They swapped seats and Oran took the mouse and keyboard. He was about to click for a rematch when the group's chat room popped up with activity. Justin had written something.

Oran read it out loud. " 'So, Celeste, about the arcade this weekend. After a couple of hours, I wanna talk with you and tell you about the colleges I may be getting into. Maybe you can look at them, too. I hope you took that email I sent you seriously. I didn't mean to upset you. I just think it's time you started getting your head out of the clouds.' "

Lance and Oran shared a glance.

"Wrong chat, Justin," Alice typed, her message appearing under Justin's. "This is the group."

The chat froze for a minute, no one typing.

"Why does he do that?" Lance asked Oran. "He's so controlling."

"He's obsessed with her." Oran sighed. "He can't stand that she's not dedicated to her future like he is."

He understood. That was what he liked about Celeste. She lived in the moment, but overflowed with ideas and plans. She wanted to do so many things, and Justin tried to stifle that. Celeste was like a wild lioness. She'd thrive in the right environment, with the right support.

"I know it is," Justin's late reply said, popping up. "Frankly, the fact that none of you are as concerned about college applications as I am is very disheartening."

Lance wrapped his arms around Oran from behind, reaching for the keys. He typed, "Scouts at my next game. I think I'm set, thanks."

"Oh, hi, Lance!" Celeste's profile typed. "Didn't know you were on right now. What are you doing?"

"Playing *Unreal Tournament* with Oran," Oran typed

under Lance's user name. "Or at least, you're supposed to be," he said to Lance in good humor.

"Ugh, he's so clingy to you," Celeste's user name typed. "It's weird."

Lance watched the blood leave Oran's face. He knelt, making sure he'd read the chat right. "What the hell?" he murmured. "Oran, she doesn't mean it."

But Oran didn't reply. Lance heard him audibly swallow.

"He should give Stella a chance," Celeste's profile went on. "Maybe ask her out for Halloween. Lance, tell him. I think he wants to ask me, but I'm not going to say yes. Sister code and all that."

Lance reached over and closed the chat. Oran didn't move or say anything for a long time. The game timed them out due to inactivity. How could she say that? Had Oran been into Celeste harder than he'd thought? Is this what he'd done to his new best friend?

"This is my fault," he said. "I came into this group and just ruined everything. I didn't mean to, I swear." He waited, but Oran didn't move or speak. "What can I do?" He gently pulled Oran's hood off his head to see his face. He looked destroyed.

Lance stood. "You want to go home?"

Oran shook his head.

Lance scratched his head then ran his fingers through his hair. He hit some tangles and started to fiddle with getting them out so his hands had something to do. "Want to just sit with me while I get slaughtered online?"

His friend didn't reply, but moved over to the second seat, letting him take the wheel for the game. Lance sat down and cracked his knuckles.

"Right." He sighed with a gentle smile. "Let's get owned."

THE EVENING FOUND CELESTE SITTING AWKWARDLY around a stranger's table with her smiling parents and rambunctious brothers. Her father's boss had never had children.

"So, Celeste, what do you want to do when you graduate?" the boss's wife asked her with a weird, old lady kind of smile.

Everyone asked that of senior students. If she were paid for her patience every time that or a similar question was asked, she never would've had to apply for scholarships.

Before Celeste could answer, her father stepped in with, "She's very fond of interior design, right? We're very enthusiastic about the potential that will have, especially in this area." He met her eyes and smiled.

"Ah, yes, very promising," the boss said, sipping his wine like a connoisseur. "There will be good money in that field. And it has the potential for upward mobility. Plan on owning your own business?"

Celeste stared across the table at her father. She was not angry, but she was not amazed at his interjection, either. She knew how disappointed he was that she had not yet decided on a college or a career. *Why do I need to decide when everyone is deciding for me?* she thought.

"I like it well enough." She experimented with a meek smile. "I'm just eighteen. How am I supposed to know what to do with the rest of my life? I've hardly lived yet."

All the adults laughed at her kindly, like she was a child making a joke about things she didn't comprehend.

"When I was eighteen, I had a car and a fiancé," her father said, not even glancing at her stony mother.

"I made a lot of mistakes at eighteen," her mother mumbled, taking a quick bite.

"What's that?" the boss asked, frowning across the table.

Celeste's gut dropped out from underneath her. *Not here,* she begged. *Save the fights and jabs for behind our own walls.*

Even her brothers quieted down, nervously looking at her parents.

"Sometimes, we have to make sacrifices and not follow the ambitions we'd like to," her father went on awkwardly. "Life doesn't always turn out the way we want."

"Regret is normal," her mother added softly.

"Ah." The boss sighed, cutting into his expensive fish. "If I did what I liked, I wouldn't live in this house with that car." He pointed at Celeste with the fish on the end of the fork. "And your father is a great worker, too. Do you think he'd be able to support children in this economy with just any job?"

"I understand," Celeste said, her nerves twisting.

"I'm not sure you do," her mother said.

"Damn it, Carol!" her father shouted, pounding the table.

Before he could go on, her mother rose, grabbed the boys by their hands, and marched out of the dining room. Celeste almost puked up the bite she'd just taken. Her father sighed and dropped his face into his hands.

"I get it, James," the boss said, dabbing delicately at the corners of his mouth. "I really do."

"I'm sorry you had to see that," her father apologized, still hiding his face.

"You've made a lot of sacrifices for your family," the boss went on. He smiled at Celeste. She hoped he didn't see her utterly petrified expression. "Maybe we should talk about your position at the company. Look at what you've done for us."

"May I be excused?" Celeste blurted. "I want to go and see your property. It's very nice."

She got up from the table before she was excused and rushed out the door. She ran down the path that wound around the house until it ended in a gravel trail leading into the backyard. She ignored the pinches and stabs in her feet from the nice shoes she'd chosen and approached the white fence heading into the little woods serving as the hub of this wealthy neighborhood. Even in man's attempt to urbanize, they had taken pity on the twenty acres of trees and creek and let it be, building the houses around it. She wanted the peace and quiet of the woods, and these would do.

It wasn't so dark that she couldn't see where she went. She didn't know these woods, but ran anyway. She needed her heart pumping to remove all the toxins she'd just picked up. Muddy splashes gradually marred up her legs with forest grime and muck. When she reached a clearing not too far from a creek, she found some moss and flopped down. Her fingers dug in to the soft green and the earth gathered under her fingernails. She waited until her panting subsided then concentrated on the sounds around her. Simple night sounds filled her head. She breathed in the calming, rising evening chorus. One sound rose above the others. A high, melancholy howling. The sound echoed over the tops of the trees and water. It wasn't a wolf howl. It was far more beautiful.

She listened to the call, rolling the dice necklace between her fingers.

A branch snapped a few feet away. Leaping to her feet, she looked between the trees and caught sight of a man walking toward her. Their eyes met and he halted mid-step. She didn't recognize him at once in his old clothes. The worn t-shirt and jeans had thrown her off at first.

"Mr. Granger?" she called.

"That *is* you, Celeste," he said. "I wasn't sure at first." He walked up to her, a walking stick in one hand and a camera around his neck. He wore old jeans and a Guns N' Roses shirt. "What are you doing out here at this hour?"

"Hiding. I had a family dinner with my dad's boss."

"Ah." Granger sighed, eyeing her up and down. "Didn't go well?"

"I didn't know teachers did cool stuff," Celeste said, pointing to his camera and shutting down that conversation. "What are you looking for?"

Granger smiled wearily and studied the branches above. "I do cool stuff all the time, thank you very much. But you won't think so."

"Try me," she said, falling into step with him. "I do bird watching sometimes, you know. So I doubt anything you say will seem lame to me."

Just then, the melancholy howl echoed throughout the woods. Celeste spun around to look.

"I'm looking for him," Granger said. "And please, I know it's weird, but when we're not in the classroom, call me Alexander. Or Alex. Whichever. Lets me separate work from the outside world."

It *was* weird to Celeste. She'd been taught to respect authority her whole life. Especially school teachers. Not one had ever asked her to call them by their first name.

"What is making that sound?" she asked, following him as he picked his way through the bramble toward a quarry-turned-lake she had not seen before.

"I'll show you," he whispered in concentration as they broke through the trees.

The quarry below had once been a source for the old

mining town, but now water filled it and they could look down on it about thirty feet from the rocky cliff face. A few miles beyond the lake, she spotted the nature preserve where they played *Sun Age*. She could see the brown patch that had once been her ranger's fort and campground. It was far away, but visible. The memory of falling came back to her. Gwen's hand taking hers. The elf's wide black eyes. The dragon's claws.

"Wow, someone has a lot on her mind," Alexander mused, squinting as he aimed his camera into the quarry. He snapped a shot and held the screen out for Celeste to see. On the glowing visual, a plain-looking duck floated on the water below.

"Nice lens." Celeste looked down and saw it. "He's cute." Then, while she looked, the duck threw his head back and howled. The melancholy call erupted from him and echoed around the quarry, up to them, and then out over the woods. Celeste gasped.

"Exactly," Alexander said. "Not what you expected, was it?"

Celeste shook her head, grinning wildly. "I had no idea what could make that noise. But it's just a duck."

"Not just a duck," he corrected her. "This guy is called a loon. Just a common loon, though." A giggle was prompted by the name and he joined her. "Yes, crazy," he agreed. "But doesn't it make the sound better, knowing that he's just a duck? When something like that makes such a beautiful sound, you have to ask yourself, 'Why do you sing like that, duck?'"

"Sometimes I feel like a common duck." Celeste glanced over at her eccentric teacher. "Why is he calling like that?"

Alexander sat back against a rock and put his hands in his

pockets, studying the floating loon. He sighed. "He's saying to his mate, 'Where are you? Come to me.' He's waiting for her to call back."

The conversation suddenly took on a tragic and romantic turn. Wanting to see what would happen, Celeste took a few quick steps closer to the edge to look over. She lowered herself to the ground and onto her knees as if crouching might make her harder to detect while she spied. Her mind instantly made up a thousand tragic stories for the loon in the lake, each sadder than the last as he waited for his no doubt fated mate.

"Where is she?" she asked, her face screwed up in wonder.

Alexander didn't reply. He waited, and so did Celeste. The duck called again.

As the sound faded, she sighed. "That's my life. Calling and waiting." She regretted the dramatic words almost right away. Was her call as sad as the loon's? Did the loon even know if his mate, his purpose, was out there? If not, would he just call and call, waiting forever? "Maybe I shouldn't call. Maybe I should just get going."

Celeste relaxed back onto her knees when nothing answered the sad wail.

"Alone?" Alexander asked.

She shrugged sadly. "This world is too big. I don't know my place in it. What's my role? Am I on a solo mission, or is there a team out there for me?"

"Do you want to be alone?"

"No," she said more sadly and quickly than she meant to. "But that's the right thing to do, right? Not be co-dependent. Not drag other people along with you and make them regret going with you?"

Alexander tilted his head sympathetically. "Are we talking about you or the duck?"

"It could be me in a few years," she said. "Maybe it's better to do a solo mission."

"I doubt that," Alexander said with a playful shrug. "Humans aren't meant to be alone. Finding a mate can be what we need. But, Celeste, you have time. You may be alone now, but if you want company on your quest through life, you can find someone. That's what friends are for."

"How depressing. I've never really talked like this to an adult." She closed her eyes in frustration. More and more she had been speaking out of turn. "Not that you care, of course," she tried to recover. "Just thought you should understand my lack of authority in life in case I say something really dumb someday."

Alexander shrugged and smiled. "Some of us never get mentors or proper adult figures to look up to. My brothers and I didn't. But that's memoir-fodder." His tone came casually. He was honestly not judging her. This put her at great ease. "But there is a role out there for you," he said more gently this time. "You just have to find your place in this great big story called life. And try not to do it alone. You have friends; I know you do."

From out of the trees, a longer, louder wail came. The loon turned around on the lake and faced the woods again. He howled loudly in the other direction. A few breathless moments later, the second howl came. In the blink of an eye, a second loon flapped out of the woods and landed with an elegant splash next to her mate.

Celeste smiled. She pushed herself up and joined Alexander on the rock where he reviewed his images.

"So, what brings an elf maid such as yourself out here on this cool evening? You don't live around here, am I right?"

A short sigh escaped Celeste. She was angry at her parents, her dad's boss, and herself for not knowing what she ought to do at her age. In truth, a lot of things had brought her out here.

"I don't know what to do with my life," she said. "But it's not just that. I have friends and parents, but I feel so lost. Everything is out of my control and that frustrates me."

He nodded and put his camera down. "Do you have any ideas about what to do?"

"Yes, tons! I just don't know which ones to do and which ones will get me ridiculed. I'm so scared of what people think of me."

"That should be the least of your worries," he said forcefully. "Here, let's pretend I'm your mentor for a moment." He faced her. "What you are good at and what you want to do are what matters. There are a million and one ways to make money and a living. If what you love happens to do that, then good for you. If not and you still really want to avoid a lifetime of misery, then do it and find another way to make a living on the side. But not one that disturbs your life and happiness. If what you want has a good effect on you, it's the right thing." He smiled kindly. "And the right companion will join you. You'll support and love what they do, and they'll do the same for you. You won't be alone and lost forever. You are the author of your story."

She watched him flip through more photos, brow furrowed. "I get to pick my role in life?" she asked.

He met her eyes and nodded. "Perhaps not your circumstances. But who and what you are? Yes. Undoubtedly, yes."

CHAPTER 12
THE NORCAN AND THE WARRIOR

Friday evening, Celeste sat in her old car, looking into the partially destroyed park where she'd spent hours role playing. The sun hadn't set yet, so she could see through the trees enough to see the small wooden dock over-looking the lake. The water was low. She breathed steadily, convincing herself why she was here. To escape. To prove to herself and the people she'd met in that other world that she was a Planes Strider. That she knew her role. She picked up her D20 necklace and made her way into the woods.

I am a Planes Strider, she thought to herself. *I will be the hero they need. I'll find my role in that story.*

She came to the lake, looking down into the water. The bank was solid rock with a few loose areas she tried to avoid. She climbed up onto a rock jutting out over the water and looked across the lake to the higher perch.

She ran over the conversation with her teacher in her mind. What he'd suggested sounded like a lot of work to her. It made her wonder about that other world. What kinds of magic did Planes Striders have and how did it work? Were there any repercussions? It hardly mattered to her; she understood the role of a Planes Strider. To help those people. That place. To be a hero.

"I'll be a fighter," she said, turning the die over in her fingers. "Brave. Strong. A protector. The best hero that..." She stopped, thinking. What would she call that place? It had a name; she just had to hear it. Like she had heard Gwen's name. She smiled. "The best hero that Revary has ever seen."

Shoving the die under her shirt, she leapt onto the next outcropping. When she landed, the ground suddenly crumbled out from under her. She screamed as her arms flew up and her fingers stretched out to grab hold of anything to stop her fall. In a painful slide from the crumbling rocks, Celeste plummeted down into the icy water of the quarry basin.

She sank for a moment, her legs kicking as she tried to propel herself up. Then an undertow swept her legs away and turned her upside down, filling her nose with cold water.

Being shoved and tossed by the sudden rushing water, her head at last reached the surface and she gasped for air. It took a few more turns for her to right herself. Between the white water and the coughing, she found herself rushing down a roaring river in the middle of a wood. Movement on the shore just ahead made her survival instincts kick in and she waved her arms madly to get the attention of whoever was on the shore.

The sound of galloping hooves and deep, rough voices alerted her to a rush of running beasts. Thinking it may be the centaurs she had met, she called out again and screamed, "Help me!" while waving her arms.

Gasping, she sucked in icy water, filling her lungs as she toppled over again. Celeste thought she was done for when a strong rope like a lasso caught her wrist and heaved her out. The rope pulled her up onto shore and into strong arms. She coughed, spewing water all over the great chest of her savior as she clung to it, afraid to fall back in the water. Between coughing and blowing water from her nose, she could not see her rescuer.

She turned her face up to the strong body that had grabbed her. Large, yellow eyes in a dark green-skinned face met hers. The nose was slightly pointed and the cheekbones were high. But the strangest thing was the mouth full of large, sharp teeth. She realized she clutched a belt slung over a thick shoulder and the long black mane of a broad-shouldered humanoid. The creature strongly reminded her of the orcs in *Elderforge*.

Screaming, she leapt away from the creature and fell further than she expected, right onto her backside. The painful landing was not enough to make her hesitate and moan about her wounds. Everyone knew orcs were the villains. She scrambled to her feet, slipping on the wet river stones, and struggled a few paces away before dizziness made her fall over again. When she looked up, she faced a set of massive, black, shaggy horse's hooves.

Slowly, she stood. The horse was massive, but so was the being on top of it. Its entire frame was knotted with muscle, covered in earthen tones of skin. Black hair flowed from its head and small white tusks protruded from its snarling lips. Sparse leather armor closed around its massive frame, showing off the muscles. Dozens of similar creatures filled her sight. Some of them sat astride the great black horses and others were seated on massive wargs.

Celeste stared and backed away slowly only to find herself surrounded. Her hand went instinctively down to her hip and she found why she'd had a hard time swimming. She wore light but full armor over her torso, with plates of glittering metal strapped to her legs and arms. The sword at her side matched. She had turned into the fighter she wished to be.

"Do not, little human," the creature growled to her. This one, vastly ugly and covered in red warpaint and bone ornaments had to be the chief.

She lifted her hands above her head slowly. "My name is Celeste. I'm not from around here."

The one who had pulled her out of the river, the least ugly of the entire group, came forward and stood beside the chief. The creature leaned over and spoke softly. When the chief nodded, his hand still resting on his massive sword's hilt, the other monster turned to her and spoke.

"You speak our tongue?" her savior said gruffly.

"Oh, uh," Celeste stammered. Maybe she had? Was that part of the magic? Could she speak all the tongues of Revary? She hadn't thought about it before. "Yes?" she chanced.

The chief eyed her suspiciously. "No one speaks our tongue but the barbarians in the mountains. Or perhaps a foolish scholar from the city."

"I'm an adventurer," Celeste said simply, but fear still stiffened her limbs.

"We are the norcan, one of many clans in the west of this Plane, and this is our land. Where do you hail from, tiny human?"

"I hail from far away." She didn't know how the norcan felt about Planes Striders. "I am looking for Calimorden."

At the mention of Calimorden, the other norcan growled and some drew huge axes, war hammers, and long spears, growling intensely. The chief silenced them with a raised hand. He leaned over and spoke again to the one who saved her. They conversed quietly and the discussion became very passionate with hand gestures until both turned their gaze on her.

"Every human on this Plane knows where Calimorden lies," the chief growled. "How is it you do not?"

"I am here as a friend to all on this Plane," she tried. "I went to see Queen Zephyr to figure out what is destroying your Plane, but a dragon attacked. I want to know if my friends survived."

The norcan who'd saved her quickly faced the chief. "Father, it's as the seer said: a visitor from the Other World would come, able to save Mother." His yellow eyes scanned her. "Is it not our hour of need? Bring her to the tribe. If she cannot save Mother, we burn her on the pyre with the barbarian man from the north."

Celeste gulped, mouth falling open. Nothing like a life or death situation to see if she could muster up some other worldly magic powers. Before she could respond, the chief motioned for her hands to be bound behind her back, her sword and armor removed, and for her to be taken to the tribe. Seeing there was little to no way out, Celeste let herself be taken to the norcan's camp.

THE NORCAN MARCHED IN LONG, THUDDING STRIDES, making the journey—tossed over the muscled shoulder of her savior—a miserable one. Nausea overtook her and she begged to walk. The norcan let her, dragging her along on a leather leash like a dog, hands tied behind her back. She kept looking at the creature, trying to calm her nerves and thinking up ways to converse with him to maybe spare her in case she couldn't use the Planes Strider magic. She listened to her instincts and heard his name. It came to her like a whisper in her ear.

"Folkvar," she asked, "do you believe in the Planes Striders?"

He looked down at her, his lips turning down over small tusk-like teeth. "You know my name?"

She tried to look at ease. "It's something I've been able to do since I first came here. The names come to me like characters I read in a book long ago."

Folkvar turned his face toward the horizon, marching on. "I am a fool among my people for believing in people like you, with magic we cannot comprehend. The Eidolon came to me in a dream, telling me someone would come from beyond our world to aid us. I spoke to our seer and he had the same dream."

"The Eidolon came to you in a drunken stupor," the chief corrected with a grumble. "After his first hunt. Thought he was a great warrior. But you're still just an ignorant child."

Folkvar glared at his father's back. "The Eidolon is the ruler of Revary. He sits on the Glass Throne among the branches of the Golden Tree in the Astral Plane. Rarely does he appear to us, and never in physical form. He allows us to govern ourselves. But I saw him that night, after my first hunt. He told me to watch the prairies, that a champion would come to us. Save us from this darkness from beyond."

Celeste chewed the inside of her mouth a moment, thinking. "I've met the dragon. But what is happening to Revary that makes you all afraid?"

At this, Folkvar dropped his head. "You will see. Umbra's touch appears, bringing ailments we've never seen. Until the vanishing comes. The dragon is Umbra's dark harbinger and in its wake comes destruction and the vanishing."

The vanishing? The phrase sent a shiver down Celeste's spine. She didn't ask any more questions, curious to see what the norcan had been experiencing. The sparse trees gave way to open prairies. A few norcan warriors on huge horned and tusked beasts rode over the hills, calling to their tribe mates, coming back from a hunt. They headed to a tiny village made of animal skin tents. Behind the village, two dozen or so small pyramids dotted the prairie.

"Our fallen," Folkvar explained, seeing Celeste look curiously. "We move on, packing our homes and wandering the prairies. They stay."

She looked farther over the hills. At the base of a spine of purple mountains she spotted a small field of the pyramids. At this distance, they almost looked like flowers in the green, painted a faded yellow.

"Tonight, you may save two lives," the chief told Celeste as they entered the ring of giant tents. "If you are not who you claim to be, three lives will go to Umbra."

She didn't argue even though she had not claimed to be the Planes Strider yet. At least, not out loud. In games, whenever she was stuck—like really stuck—she just used a cheat code. She vaguely wondered if that was what it meant to be a Planes Strider in Revary as they neared the center of the norcan camp. Were there rules to what she could and could not do?

A huge communal fire burned in the midst of women and children norcan tanning hides, cooking, and building tools and weapons. A few looked up at the new human prisoner, but none seemed interested in her.

The chief roughly pulled open the animal-skin flap of his

tent and motioned Folkvar to bring her in. Folkvar grabbed her upper arm, his hand practically engulfing her whole limb, and shoved her forward.

"Wait," the chief said, looking behind them. He grabbed Celeste and whirled her around painfully. He pointed with a great gnarled finger between the tents. "Do you see that pyre on our borders?"

It wasn't far. She took in the crude dragon-shaped pyre and its kindling around the base. Tied to the center pole, a bare-chested young man about her age in animal hide boots and tanned leather hanging around his middle waited. His long golden-brown hair reminded her of Lance and she had to quickly rein in her thoughts as she took in his naked torso.

She cleared her throat. "Yeah, I see him."

"He awaits Greylheim, the dragon servant of Umbra," the chief explained. "You will perform your magic, save my chieftess, or see his suffering if you fail."

"You're giving him to the dragon like a sacrifice?" Celeste cried. "Queen Zephyr tried that. It didn't work," she reasoned as Folkvar marched her to the pyre and the bound man. The chief disappeared into his tent, no doubt to fetch his wife. "It didn't work, Folkvar," she tried again. "Umbra still came and attacked Calimorden. Don't let him die."

The norcan didn't reply as he pulled Celeste close enough to the pyre that she could see the green of the warrior's eyes. He looked down at her, weary and beaten. She wished she could break away and cut his bonds. But part of her, a part she hadn't known she had, also wanted to try to heal the chief's wife. To see if she was the champion Revary needed.

The chief approached, practically carrying a large and somehow beautiful norcan woman in his arms. Folkvar left Celeste to help support his mother. The closer the chieftess came, the more Celeste took in the pale gray of her skin. Her eyes were milky gray as well, unseeing, yet she wept.

"Her mind goes," the chief explained. "Umbra's vanishing takes their souls until they are hollow, empty vessels of hopelessness. A fate worse than death." Celeste felt bad for the chief as he at last showed emotion.

"We fight the same fight!" the warrior on the pyre cried out in desperation. "My people have been taken by this vanishing. I came seeking aid. Even now my mountain vanishes."

"Silence, human pig!" the chief shouted. He motioned to a norcan nearby who took up a flail. "Draw his blood so Greylheim smells our gift."

"Wait!" Celeste cried, trying to pull away from her bonds. "I'll do it. Just give me a second." She turned to Folkvar. "Untie me."

The younger norcan quickly moved behind her, untying her hands. She glanced at her sword on Folkvar's belt, but thought better of grabbing it and making an escape.

"Thank you," she sighed. She followed the chief as he laid his wife down in the long prairie grass. Celeste examined her. She had no idea what she was looking for. "What does this vanishing look like?" she asked, kneeling.

"Heal her!" the chief roared, signaling his guard to move in on the warrior.

The man on the pyre braced himself, eyes open as the first of several blows fell across his chest. Blood started to trickle down.

"I'm trying, I'm trying!" Celeste cried. "Folkvar," she ordered, "tell me."

The norcan glanced at his father and spoke, despite the chief's glare. "It is not something you can see. In our people, it is visible only like this. Then, they fade away from us. My mother has no memory of me or Father. Then, one day, she could not speak. She only weeps now."

Celeste's heart broke for the norcan, despite their monstrous forms. The chieftess lay still, her beautiful black hair losing its glow even as she looked on. Her green skin faded to an ashen gray. "I-I didn't pick the right role," she said sadly. "I'm a fighter, not a healer."

"Again!" the chief roared to his guard to start a fresh wave of lashes on the warrior. This time, he cried out as the flail tore his skin.

"Okay, okay!" Celeste shouted, laying her hands on the chieftess. "Cheat codes," she whispered. "Ephamor, I know your name. I, a Planes Strider, call upon my Other Worldly powers to heal you." She waited a moment, eyes shut tight.

When she clenched her eyes shut, something flashed into her dark vision: a humanoid form with red eyes. Black robes and cloak waved gently around the figure in tatters. It turned to look at her. Fiery eyes locking on to hers. When it did, a sudden spike of fear shot into her, forcing a terrified scream out of her. The dark figure knew her and where she was at that moment.

She fell backward, hitting Folkvar's massive shin. He knelt, bracing her. Celeste looked down at Ephamor. The color came back to the norcan woman's face and her chest rose and fell with a breath.

"She looks alive again," the chief whispered in awe.

Celeste looked up at the warrior. The guard had turned in wonder at the chieftess's sudden change in color. The warrior's eyes shone brave and stout, despite the torture.

"Let Galis go," she ordered the guard, naming the warrior. The guard dropped the flail and turned, cutting the bonds around the warrior, still in awe of the magic she had preformed. Celeste's stomach flipped as Ephamor's eyes fluttered open. She opened her mouth in a yawn that showed her own tusk-like teeth.

"My darling," she whispered, reaching up to the chief, "I am so thirsty."

Folkvar fell onto his mother, hugging her. The chief ran to get a pail of water. Celeste looked on, almost smiling. A gentle pride in using her Other Worldly magic filled her. Galis fell to his knees, holding his middle, which was still bleeding. Celeste turned to call for aid when something terrible caught her eye.

Far in the distance, near the base of the mountains, something black—like writhing tendrils—sprang up from the earth. The tendrils split an opening in mid-air, revealing a gaping darkness. One tendril spilled out and slithered along the ground silently, cracking the earth as it snaked toward the norcan camp.

Folkvar froze, seeing it, too. "The vanishing!" he cried, pointing.

But the silent, black crack reached the camp. Norcan warriors and children ran, screaming as a silent blackness grew from the tendril. It swallowed up entire bodies soundlessly, turning patches of the camp into solid black nothingness.

"Run!" Celeste cried, grabbing Folkvar's arm and pulling on him. But the norcan jerked against her, calling for his parents. "Look out!" she cried, running away from the camp and around the pyre.

She looked back to see Folkvar skirting around the vanishing camp, reaching for the chief as he, too, vanished. Where part of the vanishing touched the bottom of tents, it turned to nothing. But the bits that had not yet been touched still stood. A few norcan stopped, like zombies, and looked into the vanishing. When the chief and his wife disappeared, she caught Folkvar looking into the blackness.

"Don't look at it!" she cried. She grabbed him by his thick belt and towed him away as fast as she could. Once she had him turned, he ran with her. They zipped past the pyre where Galis crawled toward the ladder, trying to escape.

"Can you carry him?" she asked Folkvar.

The norcan hesitated, but gave in as the vanishing crept closer. He scooped up the human warrior in his thick arms and ran with Celeste.

She ran and ran, not wanting to look back. When her lungs seared and her legs went numb, she turned, gasping and holding her throat. One of the saber-toothed wargs the norcan road ran toward them, roaring in fright. She called to it, waving her hands to make it stop. When it did, she slung herself up onto it, Folkvar and Galis behind her. The three of them galloped away from the vanishing.

They moved quickly and Celeste looked back. The vanishing had stopped spreading. Pieces of the camp stuck out here and there, but for the most part, a large, black nothing now sat in the center of the prairie. She took several breaths, honing in on the black edge to make sure it was in fact not moving.

"It stopped," she gasped.

They slowed to a trot.

Folkvar slid off the warg and dropped Galis, letting the human warrior lean on him. The pair of them looked back.

"It came as if it were summoned," Galis said, pale and sweating.

"Or called," Folkvar added. He gave Celeste a sidelong glance.

"I-I didn't summon it," she stammered. Or had she? She held her hands up to look at them. She'd healed the norcan. Had her use of Planes Strider magic drawn the vanishing to the camp?

The black figure came to mind, too. It had seen her, had turned and looked directly at her when she'd used her magic.

"No way," she said flatly. "I'm supposed to use my magic. I'm a Planes Strider. That's not fair," she called back toward the vanishing. "I was supposed to know who I am in this world. I was supposed to use my magic."

A confused and devastating weight dropped in her gut. What had she done wrong?

CHAPTER 13
THE STAR

"Let us head for the shelter of the forest," Folkvar suggested solemnly.

Celeste and Galis remounted the saber-toothed warg and Folkvar led it at a slow pace to the tree-line. It took them several minutes to reach it and they let those minutes go by in silence.

Once in the trees, Celeste told Folkvar to stop so they could treat the barbarian's wounds. She expected him to hesitate again, but he didn't. They stopped and rested as he carefully cleaned the wounds and dressed them as best he could. The whole time, the barbarian winced and his face showed he wanted nothing more than to be away from the norcan. With the smell of the norcan fires far behind them, the cool, sweet smell of the forest filled her nose. She stepped away from the pair and finally got a closer look at her surroundings. The trees were so green they almost glowed. Their bark looked smooth and golden brown.

Looking up, she marveled at the spattering of bright stars

above. There were more stars in Revary than she had ever seen, except for in images taken from deep space telescopes. One star flickered so much it blinked out of sight then stuttered back to life. Wondering if the nomadic norcan knew anything about stars, Celeste asked why it flashed like it did.

"I do not watch the stars like the seers do," the gentle monster confessed. "We know nothing of them."

"And now you may never," Galis said sadly. He quickly added, "Not because of anything you've done. This is the time of year the centaurs make their pilgrimage to the Nether. Who knows what they will learn there?"

Celeste nodded. "I've seen them there." She frowned. "We had to use a gate, a portal, to get out of the Nether. Do all Planes have gate guardians?"

Galis shook his head. "The Nether can only be accessed by a gate. It's not a physical Plane like ours. More spiritual. Like the Astral Plane. But the guardian's don't let just anyone in or out."

"Like the centaurs," Celeste thought. "What did they find in the Nether?"

"They haven't returned." Galis's voice turned mellow. "They should have come back days ago with news, like they always do. Centaurs are never late."

"I was in the Nether," she said. The other two looked at her, impressed. "I came out with a centaur. I don't know what happened to her after Greylheim attacked."

"We've heard nothing," Galis informed her.

Celeste didn't reply, but something ominous lay in that truth. She'd always thought centaurs were strong, noble creatures, and if they were not returning despite their strength, then something darker than she had thought may have been present in the Nether. After seeing the vanishing appear as it had in the norcan camp, she started to comprehend the fear the people of Revary showed.

When Folkvar finished, Galis mumbled a genuine thanks.

As they walked further into a clearing among the trees to make camp, Celeste noticed the pulsing white star again. The light erupted soundlessly and spread over the sky in little twinkles, showering her vision with stardust.

"How beautiful," she whispered.

"And sorrowful," Folkvar said. "That star has died. See how the place where it vanished is only a black void now?"

All around the black space, other stars began to pulse and two more exploded in shimmery starlight far away.

"They would rather die than turn to dark stars," Folkvar added. "Beings of blackness, creatures of distortion and destruction."

"What is wrong with them?" Celeste asked. "Will all the stars go out? Turn to dark stars?"

"The stars are becoming corrupt," Folkvar explained gravely. "They cannot survive when they are so damaged, so they devolve into dark stars in the sky, sometimes taking other stars with them. That is the Celestial Plane. No beings from below that Plane ever travel there. To do so, we must ascend through the Arcane Plane. We cannot reach them, and they rarely come down to us. Before they vanished, the centaurs said Greylheim would be sent to devour the stars."

The stars can be eaten by a dragon? Celeste wondered. She took in the sky above, wondering now if the stars were living people, just like the humans in Calimorden. The waning moon glowed above. *How could I get up there to save them?* she wondered.

"A falling star!" Galis suddenly shouted, pointing over Celeste's head. "It fell just there."

"Go!" Celeste urged Folkvar. "I bet we can save it."

The norcan raced passed Celeste, leaving her behind. She swung herself up onto the warg, reaching down for Galis. Panting hard, she pushed toward where the starlight glowed on the ground. It pulsed in a perfect sphere of white light.

Folkvar gasped between breaths. "Never have I seen a star. Seldom do they come to this Plane."

"Only once have my brothers and I seen one," Galis said. "Mithra and Magnah came through our mountain halls earlier this spring on their way to visit Calimorden. They are amazing to behold."

Celeste looked up, repeating the names. They somehow sparked awe in her. "Who are they?"

"The sun and moon," Galis said. "Father and mother to all stars."

"What did they come for?"

"To warn Calimorden of the attacks they had suffered in the Celestial Plane," Galis recalled. "Little good it did them."

Celeste scanned the area, looking for the star. "Perhaps this one has come to escape such a fate."

She froze, spotting the star. As Celeste has suspected, she looked like a human, the most beautiful human she had ever seen. She had silver hair and eyes that glowed. A crown of starlight circled her head and her gown was made of moon-light. She lay in a crater, as if a meteor had struck the earth. To Celeste's great relief, the star sat up, put her hands to her head, and moaned. When she had shaken her head, she turned quickly back to the sky and reached her hand out with a sad cry.

"Mother!" she cried, and crystal tears fell down her face. "Why?"

Celeste and the other two reached her. The star turned to

face them and cried out in a mix of agony and relief. "Have you come to find me? Mother promised I'd be found."

She pushed herself up and ran out of the crater into Galis's arms. She wept, hugging him tight. Celeste was taken aback by her sweet and naive nature. She was quick to trust the strangers who'd watched her fall.

"I fell," the star wept. "Mother pushed me away."

The warrior awkwardly put his hand on her shoulder and gently stroked her hair. Her crown of pale starlight lit up his eyes.

"I saw the pulsing star," Celeste said. She took her cloak off and wrapped it around the shivering star. "Was that you?"

The star wiped her tears but held Galis tightly. "My brother. He became a dark star and Father smote him." She shivered, covering her face with her hands. "Mother told me to leave, to find the oracle. Then she threw me from my place in the sky."

"Oracle?" Celeste asked.

The star turned her moon-like eyes to the sky. "What stars are not corrupted now will only be devoured by Greylheim when he returns. Those who resisted the monster of darkness are doomed to be eaten by it. If we do not bend our light to Umbra, he will bleed my mother and we all will be devoured by Greylheim. Father is dying. We cannot save our Celestial Plane. Mother sent me away to find the oracle."

"Your father is the sun, right?" Celeste asked.

"Mithra, the golden sun," the star sighed, leaning her head onto Galis's chest, still enveloped in his arms. "He is old and took the brunt of Umbra's wrath." She closed her eyes sadly. "Mother said I must find the oracle. He will have answers."

"Star," Folkvar said, speaking for the first time in a while.

"This human you see before you is a Planes Strider. One from the Other World. She has proven her abilities, but it called up the vanishing, taking my tribe."

"I'm sorry," Celeste mumbled sadly. "I didn't know."

Folkvar nodded stoutly. "I understand. But we must know why it happened."

The star met Celeste's eyes, hope drowning them. "Umbra is of the Other World. Why did you call the vanishing?"

"I didn't mean to," Celeste said quickly. "I thought I was helping, but I guess I don't fully understand." She bit her lip. How could she help without causing more destruction? "Will the oracle be able to explain it?"

"The oracle is a questing myth," Galis added. "The people of my mountain speak of him like a legend to make ignorant warriors go on fruitless hunts."

"He is real!" the star insisted, pushing away to look Galis in the eyes. "My father, who is older than the mountains of the Surface Plane, saw the oracle when he walked the Surface. He was once a Planes Strider; the oracle will have answers. But now, he hides in the mountains. My mother gave me a map before she pushed me away."

"I cannot read star maps," Galis confessed.

"Nor I," Folkvar added.

"The oracle was a Planes Strider?" Celeste gasped. "What does that mean? Show me the map."

The star finally released Galis, sniffed, ran her hand under her nose, and said, "I am a guiding star. I will lead you there. But first..." She sighed heavily, partly shaking again. "May I rest? I am weary and overcome with mourning for my brothers and sisters." The star pressed her lips together as her eyes filled with tears. She was trying to be brave, to not weep.

Celeste looked up at Folkvar. "We could make camp,

right? This would be a good spot, away from the open prairies."

The norcan nodded. "I will hunt and Galis will build a fire."

CELESTE LAY AWAKE THAT NIGHT, HALF HER BODY freezing and the half facing the fire almost too hot. She tried to remember how time had flowed before. Sunrise in her world was sunset in Revary. But did it always work like that? She tried not to think about it too much, to not think about Lance, Oran, and Alice wondering where she was. Instead, she wondered where Gwen and the Nether elf were. Had they been hurt or killed when Greylheim attacked? If the elf had been killed, it would be her fault. She'd taken him up to the Surface.

"Are you a star?" the sweet, tinkling voice of the star asked Celeste.

Celeste turned to face the star where she sat between Folkvar and Galis. She shook her head. "I don't think so. I'm a fighter. This time, anyway. Why?"

"Only stars are awake at night," the girl said, laughing gently. Though she smiled, tears still filled her eyes in the firelight.

Celeste frowned gently. "Do you have night and day in the Celestial Plane?"

The star shook her head. "Our job is to light up your night. You should see the Celestial Plane. It's so bright, filled with glittering stars. Our palaces are made of light and stardust."

"Sounds confusing and beautiful," Celeste offered kindly.

"Not everything here will make sense to you, I imagine," the star said with the first semblance of a smile Celeste had seen on her pretty face. "And we have our own special powers."

The star gently put her hands on Galis's chest over the makeshift bandages Folkvar had supplied. A green, glittering light appeared under them. Her crown of starlight pulsed more brightly, then dimmed. Galis stirred and woke. The star gently removed the bandages.

"What are you—" he started, but then jerked into a sitting position. His hands went to his chest, feeling something Celeste couldn't see.

His wounds were completely healed. Scars remained, but the blood and marring had vanished.

"Whoa," Celeste mused. "Stars are healers?"

The star nodded. "Magic healers. Unlike others who must use the herbs the land offers. It is our one gift. I may not be able to hold a sword, nor am I strong enough to wield one, but I have my value."

Galis ran his hand over the new scars. "Thank you," he whispered to the star. He met her eyes and they held each others' gaze for a long time.

Celeste smiled, turned her back to them, and lay back down, willing sleep to help her make it through the cold night.

THE MORNING CAME AND THEY WERE OFF. GALIS AND Folkvar walked most of the way while Celeste and the star rode the warg. They marched all day, hardly stopping, following the star's guidance. After a bit of travel, they reached the edge of the hidden desert. In front of them, a vast, open range of bright orange sand spread wide. Hills and dunes of nothing but sand overtook the horizon.

"It's so sudden," Celeste mused.

"Created by the magic of sages from centuries ago," Folkvar supplied. "It was a mistake, but the people of the desert have made do."

Celeste led the way, stepping onto the shifting sands carefully. Something beneath their feet rumbled. "What is that?"

"Desert beasts, no doubt," Folkvar growled, scanning the sands. "They swim in the sand like fish in the sea. Keep walking."

The star studied the map, her light no longer visible in the bright desert sun. She rode upon the warg. Galis walked beside the mount, his hand resting protectively on the star's leg. Celeste's guard went up and she laid her hand on her sword, just in case something appeared. They marched on for several more hours, seeing very few living animals. She wondered when they would run into a village or a caravan of desert nomads.

Just behind them, a fountain of sand erupted into the sky, blinding them with hot grit. In the midst of the spout, a long creature covered in a brown exoskeleton with a stinger on its tail shot up. It had hundreds of long, spindly legs, and the two nearest its head were armed with thin pincers.

Celeste screamed. She didn't want to, but the thing looked exactly like a giant scorpion-centipede with pincers. She clutched the sword Folkvar had given her and stood back-to-back with the barbarian and his bigger sword.

The creature, which Celeste decided to call a sandpede,

dived headfirst into the sand and went under like a diver into water. The sand bubbled up ferociously as the sandpede advanced toward them rapidly under the ground. They backed up a few steps, then the barbarian lunged forward and thrust his sword down. Brown goo bubbled up from the sand, as well as the shriek of the creature. It lurched, then arched its long neck up, taking the barbarian with it.

Celeste leapt up onto the warg with the star and dashed a few yards away while her companion did battle on the head.

Galis grasped the spines, no doubt just hairs to the beast, and plunged his sword down a second time only to be deflected by the strong exoskeleton. The sandpede shook its head, tired of the pest atop it.

"Hold on, Galis!" Celeste called.

Galis was forced to drop his sword and use both hands to hold on while the sandpede bucked and dived into the earth again. As it burrowed into the ground, Galis let go and ran along its insect spine and off the back, leaping over the stinger as it swiped at him before entering the sand. But just as the tail went under, the head appeared behind him with a high-pitched scream. Sprinting to pick up his sword, Galis charged the beast, leapt higher, and swung his sword across its underbelly. It screamed again. He took hold of the shell before he began his descent and swung onto its back again.

"Look out!" Celeste called.

The stinger arched and jabbed at Galis. It missed him by a few feet as the sandpede realized it was about to stab itself.

It swiped at him from the side and Galis dodged the stinger a second time by dashing up the monster's spine to its head. The sandpede was not prepared to play that game and began to shake its head back and forth.

Galis slashed, making it shriek. With its mouth open, he

held onto its lower jaw and swung up underneath it, pushing his sword up into its soft throat. The thing bucked again and thrust its chin against the sand. Galis dodged by spinning around onto its back again. He leapt down in an arching flip, aiming with his sword at the back of the sandpede's head. As he arched over, he thrust his sword underneath the insect shell and into its head at last.

The sandpede lurched forward. Folkvar charged, his claymore posed to strike. Celeste stood up on the warg's back and raised her sword above its head. As the sandpede's head came down—Galis clinging to his sword as it fell—Folkvar used one stroke to sever the head. Celeste leapt up and with one strong swing also severed the stinging tail as it aimed a final blow at Galis.

The force of her jump carried Celeste behind the thing and Folkvar and Galis fell to the sand in front of it. They all paused and breathed. The star gazed at Galis in pure admiration, her large green eyes glittering brighter than before.

"That was amazing!" Celeste shrieked, spinning her sword triumphantly and placing her other hand on her hip. "I had no idea I had it in me."

"Nor I." Galis coughed as he tried to catch his breath. "A fighter indeed."

"That monster was sent here to ensure no one reaches the oracle," the star said. "It is little wonder no one has made it past."

"Yeah," Celeste laughed. She would remember this moment for the rest of her life. "But we did it."

They sheathed their weapons and walked a few more minutes before they reached a strange black monolith jutting out in the middle of the desert, large enough to be a tower. The dark stone was smooth and pointed at the top. In the center of the tower, a yawning archway opened and a set of stairs led into darkness.

"I suppose we go in?" Celeste said. "This looks like a place an oracle might be hidden."

The star nodded, consulting her map. "Be careful."

The stairs led down until all sunlight vanished. None of them had any fire or other light sources, but the star's crown glowed as bright as the moon in the dark, twisting stairwell.

Farther down than Celeste thought she could handle going, the passage soon opened up into a cavern with dark water below. The stairs ran along the walls of the cave for several more yards before they ended on a flat rocky ground. The shore of the underground lake was narrow and led to another doorway on the left.

Celeste took the lead with the star at her side for light. The cave was dark and cool compared to the desert above. Down there, one would never know if it was day or night.

CHAPTER 14
THE ORACLE

High plinking noises kept everyone on high alert until they realized water dripped from the ceiling. Celeste and Folkvar sensed something else in the cave. A steady wind picked up and dropped away every so often in perfect rhythm, as though the surrounding area breathed.

Once they went through the next door, more rocky tunnels and trickling water loomed ahead of them. To their right in the next cavern, a small set of rocks tumbled down and skittered to their feet. Something had to have moved above them. They stared at the dark shadows hard, frozen in mid-step, weapons at the ready.

At last, they heard a waterfall. A strange blue glow came from a protruding shelf above them. The waterfall noise came from there as well. Looking around, no obvious way to the ledge showed itself. Folkvar stepped back, handed Galis his claymore, and tensed his legs.

With a burst of speed and a mighty leap, his fingers found purchase on the edge and he hoisted himself up with a grunt.

"Well done!" Celeste called. "Can you see another way up?"

Folkvar walked out of sight above them, examining the terrain underneath. "This other side might be rough enough to climb."

Celeste went to the side of the cavern near the ledge and began to climb, the star and Galis right behind her. It was not an easy climb, and her fingers and forearms ached by the time they made it to the top. Celeste helped the other two up as best she could before turning to the sight before them.

The waterfall fell from several yards above and landed on the ledge in front of them, but did not splash out or overflow. It simply fell through the solid stone floor. Glowing in the center of the water, still as a stone, a silvery white and blue human head hovered. It was not attached to anything. There was only a neck and hair, coming from respective ends. The eyes were closed and the face rested, placid and peaceful.

"Is this the oracle?" Galis asked. A strange kind of fear and confusion filled his voice.

"It is," the star said. "I know his face, but…"

"Where is the rest of him?" Folkvar asked with a grunt.

Celeste stepped forward with her hand out and touched the water. In an instant, the eyes popped open and lavender irises focused on her. She squealed and withdrew her hand.

"I am rather frightening," the head said in a hollow, echoing voice. "But I am still who I was. Mostly."

"Are you the oracle?" Celeste asked, still cringing away.

"I was not, but then I was, and now I am," it said as if giving the most tragic news it had. "My body is probably long gone by now."

"I'm sorry to hear that," Celeste tried, wincing. "Can you tell us anything about Umbra and how to stop it?"

"I could tell you anything," the oracle said. "But that would be useless. Why say anything when I could say something?"

Confused and getting a little impatient, Celeste frowned at the floating head. "Stop talking like that. Tell me what I want to know."

"You want to know too much," the oracle sighed. "I bet you're like this at home, too."

Celeste crossed her arms and stuck her hip out to the side. "Answer my question and don't lie."

"I do not lie."

"At all?" she asked, raising a brow.

"Could be lying now," Folkvar grumbled. "What is this thing that speaks in such confusing ways? Shall I cleave it with my blade?" He lifted his great sword.

The oracle's face fell a little. "Damn. The norcan are worse than the barbarians on the mountain. I was like you once, sword-girl. Going on adventures and meeting new people."

Celeste blanched. "What does that mean?"

"He was a Planes Strider, remember?" the star said, clasping her hands. "He stayed in our world. That's how my father tells it."

Now Celeste looked at the obnoxious floating head quizzically and a little fearfully. This head was once a Planes Strider? What had happened to it, and would it happen to her at some point? "What happened to you? Are you trapped here? Where are you from?"

The oracle smiled and rolled his eyes to look away. "I don't really want to tell you. Mystery is so much more fun."

"That doesn't help me," Celeste sighed. "I'm a Planes

Strider, Oracle. If you are, too, then you know I'm here for a reason. Someone called me here to save Revary."

The oracle's eyes widened and he smiled sardonically. "My, my, my, quite the pompous oaf, aren't you, sword-girl? So proud and sure that you're the hero Revary needs."

Celeste dropped her hands from her hips where she'd planted them in exasperation. She quickly glanced at her companions. "Well, I am a Planes Strider. I've used Other Worldly magic. I've heard their names."

"Oh, I am sure you *are* a Planes Strider," the oracle assured her. "No doubt. That doesn't make you a hero, sword-girl."

"No one is a hero until they have acted with valor," Galis said like he was quoting some mountain proverb. "This is the time for such acts."

"The vanishing has taken my tribe," Folkvar said. "Even Calimorden has begun to fall. The Nether is taken. We must stop Umbra here on the Surface."

"Ah," the oracle sighed, his face turning down. "And here I thought my sacrifice would keep that monster at bay."

"It has," the star assured the floating head. "My father, Mithra, has seen many Planes Striders push back a darkness."

"Ah, Mithra!" the oracle cried in delight. "He was a boy when I came to Revary. So long ago."

"Now he fades," Galis said. "Umbra is weakening him, sending his servant Greylheim to the Celestial Plane to devour the stars." His hand slowly went to the star's shoulder. "She came to find help, like myself and Folkvar. We searched for a Planes Strider to lead us against the vanishing. We found one."

"My mother said you'd help us," the star begged. "We've come a long way."

The oracle finally looked serious. "Listen, sword-girl. I bet you think coming here is a lark, fun and games."

Celeste shifted a little.

"I was a Planes Strider from the Other World, like you," he went on. "Revary is more apart of our world than you know. It's linked through you. You are the tie that binds. If that tie is weak, both worlds could sunder. Our world won't look any different, but Revary could be destroyed."

"I-I'm not weak," Celeste stammered. She took in the armor she wore and the sword at her side.

"Alone, most people are weak," the oracle sighed. "That was the mistake I made. I had to stay here in Revary to close the portal through which Umbra came. But before that, it followed me back and forth between our world and Revary. It follows you even now, infecting both worlds."

The conversation she'd had with Mr. Granger came back to her. He'd said as much, saying most people were not meant to be alone. That they were stronger together. "How did you stay?" she asked.

The oracle swirled his head a little. "I chose to. When Planes Striders stay in Revary, we become oracles. Useless lumps of information. We lose our power, turn into a creature of fantasy. But when a creature from Revary goes to our world..." He shivered.

"They can come to our world?" Celeste asked, suddenly excited.

"You wouldn't know them there," the oracle cut in sharply. "This big beast would not be who he is here." He nodded toward Folkvar. "Here, he is the creation of hope, stories that inspire bravery. In our world, such stories are something else, something far less valorous, as this barbarian says. It is a fate worse than death."

"And if I stay," Celeste asked, "I become a story?"

"Part of Revary," the oracle said, nodding.

"So, how is Revary tied to our world?" she asked.

"The very existence of Revary is based on our world," the oracle replied. "That is why they quested for you." He looked to Folkvar, the star, and Galis. "They are desperate to remain alive. To exist."

"And I can save them?" she asked.

"Alone, perhaps." The oracle eyed her. "But with more people, definitely."

Celeste finally understood. The oracle wanted her to bring more Planes Striders across into Revary. To join her in their roles. To take away from her glory as Revary's hero. She didn't reply right away, not sure how she would even tell the others about Revary. Or if she wanted to. She liked coming over alone. Being the sole hero.

"I think I can do it on my own," she said.

The oracle sighed. "I must take you to him, then, if you will not listen to me."

A little annoyed that the oracle didn't believe her, she asked, "To who? Where?"

Folkvar, Galis, and the star all started at once.

"The Astral Plane?" the star asked, star-light eyes going wide with joy.

"To the Eidolon?" Folkvar added, suddenly hesitant.

The oracle smiled. "To the Astral Plane. To the Eidolon."

Celeste looked around the cave. "How do we get there? Couldn't that be days of travel? I don't have days. I have to go home at some point."

"We'd have to pass through the Arcane Plane," Galis said. "We cannot reach it, not even from the highest mountain. Nor the Celestial Plane."

Swiveling around, the oracle faced the soundless waterfall. "Step through. You'll take us there."

"No!" Celeste cried. "I used magic to heal Folkvar's mother and it must have pinpointed where I was because this black nothingness appeared and overtook the tribe. I don't understand how I can be a Planes Strider, have special abilities, but not be allowed to use them without blowing up like a beacon."

"This isn't your magic," the oracle corrected her. "This is the Eidolon's magic. Now, have faith and step through. All of you."

"This fountain will just take us there?" Galis asked quizzically, wary of mysterious magic.

The oracle rolled his eyes and puffed out his cheeks. "I am the oracle. I will take you there using the power of the fountain. This isn't just a magic gateway, but I will make it so. It is one of the few pieces of magic I have left. Now, step through. We don't have much time. And take me with you."

Celeste cringed away from the head, but Galis reached out and easily grasped it by its hair, holding it aloft in his hand.

"Now," the oracle said, "step through."

THE WATER DIDN'T SPLASH OVER HER HEAD AS SHE stepped into the silent stream. Celeste closed her eyes, wishing to not drown, to not fall through some portal back into her own world. Once she stepped all the way through the waterfall, warm, golden sunlight beamed onto her face. Slightly afraid, though she didn't know why, she opened her eyes. The sight before her took her breath away.

A green meadow sprawled out before her. The long, soft grass waved like an ocean, slow and rolling. But it didn't grow out of dirt; soft white sand waited under the grass. The sky blazed such a bright, golden yellow that she couldn't see beyond something huge right in front of her. And soon she realized it was because the light came from the very thing towering over her.

A tree made of silver and gold rose up, thick as buildings. The bark was smooth like silk, but silvery gray. The leaves, though they spun in the slightest wind, were made of gold. The light came from between the branches of the tree. But the tree wasn't the size of a normal tree, not even the giant red woods she'd seen pictures of. It stood taller and wider than any skyscraper she'd seen. She shielded her eyes to look up at it, but it hurt to do so. The air was the perfect tempera-ture, neither hot nor cold. Somewhere, the rolling roar of an ocean rose and fell. The others appeared behind her, coming out of a beautiful waterfall.

Two guards in golden armor with angelic wings gently flapping behind them approached the quartet. Celeste had the weird urge to stand tall, drop her shoulders, and raise her chin.

"Who is this who can travel by the Eidolon's own foun-tain?" one of them asked. His face was covered by a golden helmet.

The oracle spoke up from where he still hung from Galis's hand. "The oracle. Tell the Eidolon I have brought a Planes Strider."

The guard's shining head snapped to Celeste. "Can it be? Have you not heard, oracle?"

"I don't hear much in the cave where I've been stewing,"

the oracle mumbled. "Waiting for questers to come and find me."

The guard ignored the remark. "The Eidolon is weakening. All his strength goes to Revary, trying to hold off Umbra and its servants."

"What is the Eidolon?" Celeste asked. "Like a god?"

"More of an icon, a guardian," Folkvar supplied. "He rules over Revary from a distance. His life is Revary's life."

"He is the heart of Revary," the star said. "Beating, radiant, and just. It is rare that we see him." She smiled excitedly.

Now they were getting somewhere. Hopefully the Eidolon would be more helpful than the oracle had been. "Yes," Celeste said stoutly. "I am a Planes Strider. I want to save Revary so I can see it thriving and well. I'd love to see it without this darkness destroying it. May I speak with the Eidolon?"

The guards exchanged glances then summoned over six beautiful white gryphons. "We will take you. Know that we will fell you more swiftly than even the wings of our mounts if you move to harm the Eidolon."

The gryphons stood so much taller than Celeste that Folkvar had to lift her onto one. Their feathers were the softest she'd ever felt. "I'm not going to harm him. I promise. I'm here to help."

"Don't mind the winged folk from the Arcane Plane," the star said to Celeste when Galis lifted her onto a gryphon. "They are a proud people. They never descend to the Surface."

She glanced at the guards and their magnificent wings. She half-wished she had wings like they did when the gryphon shot off from the ground. Celeste screamed and dived onto the creature's neck, holding on with her legs and a handful of feathers. The gryphons flew up and around the golden tree. As they rose, Celeste spotted many strange people of Revary lining the branches and structures in the tree.

"It's like a whole village in the tree!" she called to the others.

"It is," the guard replied. "The Eidolon allows all to come to him for help, for council. Many are here now from the Arcane and Celestial Planes, afraid of the vanishing."

"And he can't just magic it away?" Celeste asked.

The guard turned his faceless helmet to her. She felt like he was judging her. "The Eidolon *is* Revary. The vanishing takes its toll on him with every new cloud of darkness. If Revary is devoured by this vanishing, the Eidolon will be destroyed as well."

Above them, many branches supported a beautiful glass balcony. A small tower, also made of glass, rested at the very top of the tree. The guards landed there, leading them over the glass floor. Their metal boots made a delightful clinking noise with every step. They ascended a set of oval steps to an open throne room. The guards bowed, folded their wings, and approached a throne in the middle of the room. Whatever was in the throne cast light like the sun. The entire room glowed white and gold, the glass glittering from the bright sun-like light on the throne.

As they neared it, Celeste made out the form that sat in it. Swathed in white, long white hair falling over his shoulders, the Eidolon sat. He wore no crown or gaudy clothing, just simple white garments. Celeste was shocked to find he was shockingly handsome and must have been about her age. He sat tall and had all the mannerisms of regality, but there was a slight bend to his shoulders, like a long walk bearing a great burden had tired him.

The Eidolon smiled at Celeste as they approached. "I was wondering when you'd come," he said. "Do you remember me?" His voice echoed as if it came to her from the end of a long tunnel. He spoke slowly, but had the most beautiful voice Celeste had ever heard.

At first, she panicked, wondering if she'd met him before. But then she remembered her vision. "I saw you, but only for a moment," she said, recalling it. "When Greylheim attacked Calimorden. I couldn't stop the dragon. I'm sorry."

His face glowed almost gold when he smiled again at her apology. His skin seemed to glitter. "No need to apologize, Planes Strider. I see much from my Glass Throne." He rose, a little shaky, to better present himself. "Have you decided to save Revary?"

"Yes!" Celeste cried, hand over her heart. "More than anything, I want to save it."

"And these are your companions?" he asked, motioning to Folkvar, Galis, and the star.

"Yes," she answered. "They sought me out. But please, tell me what I need to do."

"I already told you," the oracle mumbled.

The Eidolon's face broke into a beautiful surprised grin. "My old friend! I thought I'd never see you again. And least of all so little of you."

"Long story," the oracle mumbled, rolling his eyes. "I told her she needed to be strong, to understand her role in Revary. But she wouldn't listen."

Celeste scoffed indignantly. "I can do that."

"So I've seen," the Eidolon said, his face at last turning somber. "You have tried to use the power you have as a Planes

Strider in Revary, but you have not decided who you are. This lack of a decision has made you a beacon to Umbra and his servants. Using Planes Strider power told Umbra one has arrived in Revary."

"Then how do I do it?" Celeste asked. "How do I save Revary as a Planes Strider if I can't use my magic?"

The Eidolon tilted his head gently. "Do you not have friends? Ones who may give you council?"

Frustrated, she used all her strength to hold in a growl. "You won't tell me, either?"

Sadly, the Eidolon shook his head. "I can't tell you. I am part of Revary. You are the only one who knows how to save us." He gasped softly, pressing his hand to his chest. In silent pain, he shut his eyes and breathed raggedly. "It worsens," he moaned. "Celeste, don't do this alone."

She looked away, thinking. "I might have friends who would come. But would they believe me?"

"Is that important?" the Eidolon asked. "You can lead them here. Then they will see."

Again Celeste felt as if her role was being diminished. Did she really need to bring the others over? It could be fun. But the oracle had mocked her for such thoughts.

"Why do you do such battle within yourself?" the glowing boy asked. "Is there not one you can think of to bring with you, to strengthen your power, to help you find your role in this story? A bond so strong that they would follow you?"

She half-nodded. Alice, Lance, and Oran would follow her. They'd think she was crazy, but they might come. "Stella!" Celeste suddenly gasped. "My best friend. But we've been fighting recently." An adventure in Revary would be sure to bring them closer together. "But I need to go back to talk to her. It's been so long."

The Eidolon nodded. "I must send you back, then. You must go back to your world and find the answer."

Her heart ached to see the Eidolon struggling to stand, and ached even more when she thought about this fantastic world vanishing before she'd even gotten to experience it. Fighting sudden tears, she nodded. "All right. I'll come back. I promise." She turned to the others. "Look for me. I don't know where I'll appear next. Just please look for me."

Folkvar and Galis nodded sternly. The star jumped at Celeste, hugging her tight.

"Wish on a star, Celeste," she whispered. "They'll guide you back."

She wrapped her arms around the star and hugged her tight. She felt her body jerk as she started to disappear. "Wait!" she cried, but her vision was already blurring. "Find Gwen! The prince of Calimorden. I don't know where he is, but find him! I need him—"

But the ground dropped out from under her, and everything went dark as she fell.

CHAPTER 15
REVELATIONS

C eleste didn't sleep the night before she and the party were to meet up at the old arcade. She'd forgotten the entire point was to hang out and try to rekindle their strong bond through nostalgia. She clutched her blankets all night, going over what she'd say to the others. Trying to think of every possible outcome so she'd not be taken off guard, she ran through the scenario: they'd call her crazy, leave her, not be her friend anymore.

Or they'll ask you to show them, she thought to herself. *What if they believe you?*

"Oh, shit," she gasped, sitting up. "What if they believe me?" The street light outside flickered off. The morning had come and she didn't know the answer. She was putting her trust in an obnoxious severed head from another world. He'd told her to get council, ask for advice.

Lying back down, she glanced at her clock. Seven in the morning. She had four hours to figure out how to tell her friends about Revary, and then ask for their advice on how to save that place. Maybe once she saved it, they could all go there. They'd all choose roles and go on a great quest. Like real life *Sun Age*. She smiled, wondering what that might look like.

LANCE PICKED UP ORAN AND ALICE AND DROVE THEM to the arcade at the back end of town. The other two talked the entire way about times they'd spent there. Not together, since Alice was new to the group like him, but they had the same interests. Lance had never been. He'd hardly picked up a game controller, let alone voluntarily gone to an arcade. He didn't chime in to their conversation and Oran noticed.

"What's your favorite?" he asked Lance as they parked.

Awkwardly, he tried to think of a name of a game he might have heard, but none came to him. Oran was his best friend now. He wouldn't judge. "You'll have to show me your favorite," he said nervously. "I, uh, never went to the arcade in middle school like you guys."

Alice smiled kindly. "Aw, I'm glad you told us and didn't lie, making up some story. It's always so obvious."

Oran beamed. "You will love *House of the Dead*. It's one of the most satisfying games to ever exist. Especially when you're good at it."

"Are you?" Lance asked, knowing the answer already.

Oran nodded, smiling. He pushed through the door with such enthusiasm, Lance had to catch it as it bounced back before it clobbered Oran. Alice shoved past, running to Celeste, who stood in front of an arcade cabinet, already shouting with the anxiety that only comes from gaming.

Justin stood by Celeste, pointing to the screen like he was coaching her.

The arcade smelled like pizza and cotton candy. The bright neon lights and space-themed carpet made Lance's eyes burn. Glowing light from other games, claw machines, pinball, and a dozen other electronic beasts of entertainment he didn't recognize sent a thrill through him. He spotted a game with a basketball hoop but opted to skip it. This was his chance to try to get closer with the group.

Instead, he followed Oran to the game he'd mentioned before, which happened to be right beside the one Celeste was playing. He placed himself between them, across from Justin, who kept telling Celeste how to play. Alice stood behind Celeste, cheering her on. It looked like some kind of racing game to Lance. The way Alice chanted the times at the top of the screen told him she was about to break a record of some kind. He could hardly take in the old graphics and the turning without feeling ill.

"No!" Justin screamed as the screen read "Game Over" in big red letters just seconds later. "I told you not to use the break on that last turn. It slows you down just before the finish line."

Celeste sighed, puffing her cheeks out, smiling despite the loss. "I'm going to try again, calm down. But I want a drink first."

"You could have won there," Justin insisted. "Then you'd be finished and we could talk. Why don't you ever listen to me?"

Lance caught Celeste roll her eyes before she turned.

"Oh!" she gasped, almost running into him. "Didn't see you there." She giggled and her cheeks turned red. She didn't move, looking up at him through her long lashes. "Want to grab a drink before we really dive in?"

Lance glanced at Oran, who watched him carefully, expressionless. "Uh, yeah," he replied. "Tell me what's good."

She led him through the crowded floor to the small fast food restaurant near the back. "Red slushies are the best, of course," she said. "It's the traditional drink of all-day gamers."

"Thanks for telling me," he replied, ordering three. He dug for his wallet. "I'd hate to look like a poser."

She tilted her head up at him. "Poser? Never. You're one of us." Her face turned a little serious. "Don't you have friends on the team?"

He stammered a little and looked away, paying the cashier.

As if reading his mind, she shrugged energetically. "I'm just glad you're not one of those meatheads who bullies us." She tilted her head. "If I may ask, how did you and Oran become such close friends? Don't get me wrong, I'm really glad you are. I worry about him." With a groan, Celeste reached for the slushy the worker had placed too far back on the strangely wide countertop. She couldn't reach it.

Lance reached across the counter, towering over Celeste, and grabbed it for her. He couldn't stop the inner smile he got at reaching over her head, leaning close, to get her the drink. He handed it to her and she thanked him.

"He was in a tough spot one day," he said as easily as he could. He didn't want to boast, but he knew Oran and Celeste were close. She'd like to hear how he'd helped her friend, right? "I stepped in, but we didn't click then. It wasn't until later. But I'm not sure he wants me telling that story. I'm just glad he gave me a chance," he said after some reflection.

Celeste nodded. "He's a really soft guy." She took a long

sip, turning her lips red. "You're not how I thought you'd be." She bashfully looked up at him.

His mouth turned dry and he had to bite his bottom lip to stop the mad grin from appearing on his face. "I'm glad," he replied. "Hope we can be friends for a long time."

"Me too," she laughed, rejoining the others.

They sat down at a round table with red chipped paint. Alice and Justin were in a deep discussion about universities with Kiyoshi listening half-heartedly. Oran had his eyes on them as they sat down. Lance handed him the third drink.

"Celeste," Justin said, turning from Alice mid-sentence, "did you apply to Midwestern like I told you to? I sent you that link weeks ago."

"No," Celeste said simply. She glanced over at Lance. "I was actually looking at Houston. It has more of what I'm looking for."

Lance perked up. "I used to live around there. Always thought I'd end up playing for the Cougars."

As he spoke, he was keenly aware of Justin taking in the slushies and Lance putting away his wallet. The other boy's face fell before morphing into harsh sarcasm.

"What happened to, 'I don't let men pay for my food'?" Justin quipped.

Celeste blushed, choking on the ice, but didn't reply to the question. "I can find my own applications, Justin."

"Out of curiosity, Lance," Justin said, his tone turning nasty, "where are you applying to school?"

"I told you," he said easily. "Whoever scouts me."

"Houston was at the game last Friday, huh?" he pressed.

Alice dropped her face into her palm on the other side of the table.

"Don't," Kiyoshi said quietly.

"No, I will," Justin snapped. "Celeste is just waiting to be handed a future. Well, that won't happen. You have to be pro-active, Celeste. Stop waiting around for someone else to make your decisions for you."

"But *you* are," Celeste shot back. She stood up. "I'm going to go break my record now." She marched back to the game she'd been on before. Justin followed her.

Kiyoshi sighed and brushed large chunks of salt off a soft pretzel he'd bought. "Justin thinks he's the author of all our lives."

"I want to say he's just trying to be supportive," Alice added, "but from what I've seen in the few weeks we've all hung out, it's not support." She dropped her chin into her palm, leaning on the table. "Why hasn't he asked her out if he's so keen?"

Oran's head shot up. "Maybe he's scared she'll say no."

Lance agreed inwardly. It was terrifying asking girls out.

"Maybe he thinks she already belongs to him," Alice mumbled, rolling her eyes.

The conversation put Lance on edge. It was impossible to ask a girl out. If he did it wrong, he was a jerk for thinking a girl would go out with him. But if he didn't ask, they wondered why he wasn't man enough to step up. How could he win? Then there was Oran. He knew now that Oran had feelings for Celeste, and he didn't want to destroy the friend-ship he and Oran had.

"Hey," Kiyoshi said, looking around. "Where's Stella?"

Just then, Celeste shouted, but not at the game.

"Justin, leave me alone, please!" she cried.

She moved to shove him away from the controls of the game. Retaliating, Justin shoved her. She grunted, tripping on the corner of the cabinet and falling hard onto the ground.

Lance jumped up, exclaiming, and ran to the pair of them. "What the hell?" he growled at Justin, putting himself between him and Celeste.

"She fell," Justin said hotly. His face glowed red and he looked nervous.

"Get away from me!" Celeste cried, holding her knee and cringing in pain.

Lance reached down to Celeste and pulled her up, holding her hand when she made a pained sound after putting weight on the leg she'd been clutching. Justin glowered like he might eat Lance whole.

"Why are you trying so hard to wedge your way into our party, Lance?" Justin snapped, finally asking the question Lance had been dreading.

His eyes shot from one face to another. A dozen truthful answers fought to escape his lips, but he forced them back. They wouldn't believe him if he admitted he hardly had any real friends on the football team. It would sound weak if he said he thought they were cool. If he tried to explain that he had never really played the RPGs before and liked them, they'd think he was a poser. The words "I'm sorry," shot up like vomit but he held those back, too. Instead, he spit something far worse out.

"For the nerds of the school, you guys sure are assholes." Fire burned his face and he glared at them. To his surprise, none of them looked shocked at his words. In fact, most of them turned to look at Justin, waiting for his reply.

"Stop being a dick," Oran shot to Justin, safely tucked behind Lance.

Kiyoshi spoke, looking more resolute than Lance had ever seen the quiet boy. "Justin, I think you should go. Just for now."

"You serious?" Justin gaped, looking at them all. When none of them replied, he cursed, flipped them off, turned, and marched away. Kiyoshi sighed and jogged after him, both vanishing out the door into the bright light of day.

"I'll get ice," Oran said and ran to the counter.

Lance helped Celeste back to the table and propped her leg up on the bench. He sat in front of her while she rolled up her jeans. She looked utterly defeated. Her eyes started to sparkle as tears filled them.

"I guess I really screwed up everything, huh?" Lance started.

Celeste cut him off. "No, it's not you." She looked uncomfortable. Her eyes darted around the arcade and she took a deep breath. "I trust you, Lance," she whispered. "I'm sorry Justin came after you."

He met her eyes. She looked nervous.

"I have to tell you guys something," Celeste sighed when Alice came to sit behind her and Oran returned with a small bag of ice.

"You can tell me anything," Lance said.

THE OPEN, CARING FACES OF THREE OF HER FRIENDS made Celeste believe she really could tell them anything. Lance's brown eyes almost begged her to let him in on her secrets. If this wasn't the perfect time to tell them about Revary, there wasn't going to be one. She took a deep breath.

"Have you guys ever thought about other worlds?" she said steadily.

"Like Mars?" Alice asked.

"No, like the worlds in science fiction and fantasy books. Entirely different realities. Like the world of *Runes and Empires*?"

Lance nodded. "Isn't that what we do? We think about them all the time."

"Not like that," she sighed. Her chest constricted and her face burned. "Please, don't laugh at me. But I have to tell someone because I'm supposed to get council or something."

Alice smiled. "We won't laugh." Celeste clamped her lips closed and raised her eyebrows, scared. "We won't laugh. Right, Lance?" Alice repeated.

"We dress in fake leather and animal skins to run around half-naked on the weekends. We won't laugh," he promised.

Oran waited, quiet.

"Okay," Celeste said. She focused on a drying piece of gum on the metal leg of the table. "I've been to another world. A magical one."

She didn't look up. Neither Alice nor Lance spoke. She didn't want to see their faces.

"Remember that night when you all found me in the woods?" she went on, finding herself whispering. "I had literally fallen into another world called Revary. I met an elf and a prince that I rescued. I thought I was dreaming it up, but I went again. I got attacked by this dragon and I met their ruler called the Eidolon and this oracle said to seek council from friends." She gulped and looked up.

Despite the hope Celeste had for telling her friends about the world and the hope she had that they'd understand, Lance and Alice exchanged frowns masquerading as concern. She held her breath to stop herself from screaming at them. Lance looked more confused and Alice looked worried.

"Do you mean when we were LARPing that weekend?"

Alice adopted an authoritative tone that made Celeste's hackles rise. "We were playing, right?"

"During that," she hissed as a group of young kids passed by. She pressed the bag of ice hard onto her leg. She started to shake from the cold, fear, and excitement. It all twisted her stomach. "When I fell, I woke up in a place I'd only seen in dreams, I swear. I thought I was dreaming, but I wasn't. It's some kind of world that's being destroyed and the people there are looking for a champion to save them. They called me a Planes Strider. I have some kind of power there, but I can't figure out how to use it. They told me you guys could help."

"Is this something you guys do?" Lance asked, looking honestly confused. "Talk about LARPing outside of the camp? Because I thought that was kind of against the rules."

"It is," Alice sighed. "Celeste, if you want to tell us something, if something is wrong, just spit it out. We won't judge you."

"But you are." Celeste slid her legs around to face the table with the rest of them, the ice falling to the floor. Oran's mask of emotionlessness didn't help.

"Think about it realistically, Celeste," Alice said in her tone again. "Do you hear what you're saying?"

All her hope inside cracked. A sudden feeling of stupidity crashed into her. Why had she done this? *For Revary,* she reminded herself. Because she wanted to save it, bring them there, and have the wildest adventure any of them had ever had. Together.

She looked at Alice's unchanged face, then at Lance.

"Maybe if you showed us?" he tried.

"Have some faith in me, Alice. Not everything can be

learned in a textbook. You are smarter than that." She emphasized every word.

Alice looked away.

Lance leaned in, picking up the ice bag off the floor. He gently placed it onto her knee again. His fingers were so long they covered the bag and touched her bare skin. Another jolt of emotion shot through her.

"I want to see what you're talking about," he said steadily. Oran shot Lance a look. "Color me intrigued at the very least."

Celeste's heart leapt. "You mean it?" she gasped, trying to not grab his hand. Not with Oran looking the way he did. Lance nodded, making the butterflies in her stomach take flight. He trusted her. Or at least, he wasn't saying she was crazy right away. His willingness to see made her smile, and for a moment she was lost in his eyes.

Alice turned to face Celeste. "Can you show us?" Her voice was cautious. "Tell us everything."

Beams of light shot up inside Celeste. She hadn't called her crazy. She hadn't questioned her. She just wanted to see. It was like a miracle.

"I don't know how to get there," she confessed. "It always happens by accident."

"Just take us to where you have crossed over," Lance suggested.

Nothing could have prepared Celeste for the joy and relief she felt when Lance and Alice looked at her eagerly. Either they wanted to prove her wrong and calm her down, or they honestly wanted to look into it. They weren't convinced, but the fact they had decided to take a chance on her was more than she could have asked for. Oran's face was still impassive, impossible to read.

"When?" Alice asked.

Celeste pressed her lips to one side, thinking. She looked around. "Where's Stella?"

Alice shrugged.

Celeste's shoulders drooped as some of the excitement left her. She needed to patch things up with Stella first. "I'll tell you when. But not yet."

CELESTE WAS SO BRIGHTENED UP BY ALICE AND Lance's acceptance of her confession that Justin's remarks didn't bother her anymore. They passed a few more hours in the arcade, Kiyoshi coming back looking disgruntled, before they split up to head home later in the afternoon.

Celeste was halfway out of the parking lot when Oran called to her.

"I was wondering if you could give me a ride?" he asked shyly.

"Didn't Lance bring you?"

Oran nodded. "But he has to talk to his dad on the phone on the way back. That makes me feel awkward."

"Gotcha. Yeah," she said happily, reaching over and opening the passenger side door. When Oran got in, she said, "I have a question to ask you." Oran waited, his blue eyes eager and wide. "What would you name a misunderstood Nether elf?"

"Does this have to do with Revary?" he asked flatly.

Celeste half-shrugged, biting her lip sadly. "Yeah. The names come to me, but his didn't. Yet." A sudden thought hit her. The oracle had told her to get council. That several

Planes Striders were better than one. What if the elf wasn't hers to name? She frowned, even more confused than before.

"I'd call him Yilith," Oran said into the silence. He met Celeste's eyes and shrugged shyly. "Just sounds right to me."

Celeste nodded and trained her eyes ahead on the dimming sun. "I like it. Yilith it is."

The street lights were coming on as they passed into Oran's neighborhood.

"I wish you would have told me," he whispered. His voice hitched like he might cry.

She gripped the steering wheel. "Do you believe me?" She glanced sideways at him.

Oran sighed, forehead pressed against the window. His gentle breath fogged up the glass. "Celeste, if you've found a way to escape this world, this life, I want to find it, too." He cleared his throat and she swore she heard tears in his voice. "Why'd you say I was clinging to Lance the other day?"

She slowed down. His street was close and this sounded like a whole new conversation. "What are you talking about?"

He cleared his throat, his tone still broken. "On chat the other day when I was hanging out with Lance."

"I didn't?" she said, stopping fully at a stop sign. "In chat? What day?"

Oran turned to face her and her heart broke when she saw the devastation there. Something else had hurt him, besides whatever she was meant to have said. "Well, then someone using your account did."

Celeste thought back. She hadn't been in the chat room for a week. She'd logged in just before the awful dinner to see if anyone was around. Stella had been with her. She'd tried to mend their harsh words from before.

It hit her.

"Damn it, Stella," she whispered. The car behind them honked for them to get going. She did, slowly. "Oran, that was Stella." She scoffed dryly. "Why is she so angry? What did I do?"

Oran turned away, sighing again. "I don't know. But make it right."

She didn't press Oran about apologizing for words she hadn't said. But his silence, his melancholy, stung. Like she'd done something to upset him and not known it.

He got out and she watched him to make sure he got into his house. Once he did, she decided it was Stella she should have told about Revary. She'd make it right. She'd save their friendship.

CHAPTER 16
TRUE FRIENDS

I n the game store, Oran helped Lance run a fun campaign that was strong in story and role play. Oran had said action was good, but story was better with action. He had been chanting circular definitions like this as though they were spells for Lance to learn.

After an hour of working through a beginner game with some younger children, Lance had to work behind the counter with customers and the registers. Here, in this store, they could talk openly about Celeste's confession and no one would think twice, assuming they were talking about a game of some kind.

"Do you think Celeste can take others across with her?" Oran asked, leaning over the tall cabinet with trading cards in them. He was short enough to have to heave himself up a little so his feet dangled. "I'd love to have an adventure like that."

Lance kept his face neutral as he once again sorted the

messy dice bins. The manager, Donny, seemed to have picked up that Lance didn't mind it and always had him do it now. Lance took out a green D20 and rolled it between his finger and thumb. "Let's pretend like she's telling the truth, okay?"

Oran nodded, picking up a black die with fake blood splatters on it to examine it.

"She mentioned how she was urged to seek council," Lance went on, thinking. "That—what did she call them?— Planes Striders were stronger in numbers. So maybe she was trying to tell us so that we'd want to come with her." He waited for Oran to reply. Lance would give anything a try with Celeste. It sounded crazy, yeah, but he wanted to be part of it.

Oran dropped back down to the floor with a thud. "What if she never came back? What if she died there? What if she decided one day that that world was better than this one and never returned? Could that happen?"

Sensing his fear, Lance said cheerfully, "This is Celeste we're talking about. She's crazy tough, right? She won't let anything happen to her." But Lance saw something else for the briefest moment behind Oran's eyes. Something dark and hopeful. It made him stop his menial task and look Oran in the eyes. "She wouldn't. She knows there are people here who love her and care about her. People who would support her. People who would miss her."

Oran nodded, but looked away from Lance's hard gaze. "Revary was right to choose her. If I had to pick a hero, I'd pick her."

Lance heard Oran loud and clear. He dropped the dice he was sorting and pressed his palms into the glass cabinet, dropping his head while he sighed. Oran was so hung up on

Celeste. Like Stella was on Oran. Lance realized he had walked in on a group of long-pining friends who had somehow developed feelings for each other over high school. They all had such a history. He had planned to ask Celeste out, but Oran was right; she had a way of making him nervous she'd say no.

"High school sure as hell isn't middle school," he said at length. "You tend to see people in a different light, am I right? Oran, ask her out. Just do it, for shit's sake."

Shaking his head and putting it down so his black and multicolored hair obscured his face, Oran sighed. "If she turned down Mr. I-Got-Into-College-and-Have-a-Life-Plan, then what chance do I have?"

Oran had a point. Lance had wondered the same thing. Justin was everything any girl should want to attach herself to. The guy was a breeze: all lined up for school, knew exactly where he was going, and what he wanted. That wasn't a bad thing. In fact, Lance was rather jealous of Justin's life plans. "He's got everything together, that's for sure," Lance mumbled, grabbing a box of new figures to put into the display case.

"Don't you?" Oran asked, reaching into the box to pull out an elf wizard figure. "Thought that scout came and talked to you after the last game."

Lance looked up, frowning playfully. "How did you know he spoke to me?"

"I'm a nerd, Lance. I'm not stupid. I know when some old fart in a red and white overpriced jacket comes to a high school football game with a thick folder and pen, and talks to the head coach, he's not here to volunteer for the car wash."

To Lance's surprise, Oran went from proud and happy for him to doleful as he spoke. "What is it?" he asked.

Oran sighed and dropped the wizard he'd picked up, dropping his chin into his palm. He looked away from Lance. "I've never gotten along with Justin. Kiyoshi is so quiet. And the troll has never been anyone's friend. I've never..." He refused to look Lance in the eye.

Lance didn't make Oran say it. He understood. "I'll aways be your friend, Oran. I've never had a friend like you." As he said it, he realized it was true. "You're easy to be around. I don't have to put on an act for you. You have a way of seeing past my bullshit exterior and..." He trailed off, thinking. "You don't judge me for trying to join a group where I don't belong."

Oran narrowed his eyes. "Is this a trap?"

Lance shook his head and grinned. "But, as your friend, I have to encourage you go for it."

Oran went pale. "Go for what?"

It hurt him a little to say it, but he had to. He honestly liked Oran too much to horn in on Celeste. "She's not into Justin," he said stoutly. "I'm just saying, she could be into anyone who shows interest and doesn't try to force her to be something she's not. You'd let her find herself."

Oran bit the inside of his cheek and nodded once slowly, his frail happiness drifting away.

"And," Lance offered his downtrodden friend, "you're not a dick, so you do have that up on Justin."

A little smile crept up on Oran's face through his melancholy. He changed the subject, clearly uncomfortable. "If Revary is a magic world, do you think we get to be, like, wizards or something?"

Intrigued, Lance hummed. "I'd be a warrior. Or some fighting class."

"Of course," Oran laughed. "I'd be an arcanist or some

kind of channeling wizard. You know how in *Runes and Empires* you have to have an artifact to channel your magic through? That's what I'd want. I'd have a big-ass spellbook on my side and a cloak with a deep hood."

Lance couldn't stop the genuine smile taking over his face. True or not, showing interest in Revary would play in Oran's favor when he broke his lifetime of silence and asked Celeste out.

WHEN CELESTE GOT HOME FROM WORK, THE STREET lights flickering, someone was waiting outside Stella's house across the street, leaning against the garden wall. When her eyes adjusted to the darkness outside her car, she saw it was Stella herself. She wore a man's oversized jacket against the cold and was texting madly on her cell phone. She wiped away tears. The best friend instinct kicked in and Celeste dashed across the street to her side.

"Stell, what's up?" she asked.

Shutting her phone quickly and dropping it in the pocket of the jacket, Stella shook her head and wiped her tears away. "It's nothing. Just crappy people." She sighed and shook her head. "I just had to talk to someone."

What about me? Celeste thought. "What happened?"

Stella didn't answer and Celeste knew she wouldn't. Instead of pressing her friend for an explanation, she slipped her arm around Stella's and laid her head on her shoulder, waiting. When Stella was ready to talk, she would. They had always confided in each other for years and that wouldn't change.

But Stella had pretended to be Celeste in the chat room the other day and had said some awful things to Oran. She'd get to that. Right now, something had upset Stella and Celeste didn't want to push her away further.

"We missed you last weekend at the arcade," Celeste whispered. "I was hoping you'd hang out." She sighed. "Stell, I have something I want to ask you."

Unexpectedly, Stella straightened up and laughed dryly.

"What?" Celeste smiled nervously at her friend's sudden change in attitude.

"Why can't you all agree with Justin?" Her voice changed to a sarcastic plea. "He's right, okay? Just wise up and see what's before you and deal with it. Stop running away to your fantasy worlds, stop reading stupid books, stop wearing black and coloring your hair, and face the real world. We have to survive and just live. Society demands we have cars, houses, kids, and careers. You'll be happy if you just give in."

Celeste stepped back. Stella had shoved off from the house and paced while she ranted, her voice growing louder and louder.

"Why will he not man up and help me?"

"Stop," Celeste hissed, hearing a dog bark in the distance. "What on earth are you talking about? You mean Oran?"

"Yes! Always Oran!" she screamed in reply. "He's so immature, but he'd be perfect if he'd drop the act and face reality. He's smart. He could be an engineer, an accountant, or anything! I'm trying to fix him, but he's so stubborn."

Aside from all the talk about society and appearances, Celeste understood. "You really really like him," she said breathlessly. "I thought he was just a crush or something."

A kind of agonized, roaring groan escaped Stella's throat. "No, I like him, but he's not right yet."

"Yet?" Celeste spat the word. "Stella, I don't know what's going to happen out there in this 'real world' you and Justin keep mentioning. But from my experience, I am in the real world now and it's just fine. I'm just fine and so is Oran. This is high school, the best years before the real struggle begins. Why can't we enjoy that a little bit longer?" She stopped and raised her hand, holding herself steady. "Oran doesn't need to be fixed. He knows what you're trying to do and he doesn't want it. That's what everyone tries to do to him. It's not affectionate, Stella. It's controlling and he's not interested in being controlled. Not since his dad died."

"Don't make excuses for him," Stella spat. "He's moped around long enough."

"Long enough? It's been six months. He lost his dad, Stell. It's really been hard for him. Don't you see how he's struggling?"

Stella turned rabid. She laughed harshly. "You don't see what I do, Celeste. You don't see how he's hurting."

"Trust me, I do," she shot back.

Stella's black-lined eyes slowly turned on Celeste, like she might strike like a snake. "Then why aren't you trying to help him? Why are you letting him fall deeper and deeper into this pit of despair he's dug ever since his dad?"

Celeste stammered, shaking her head. "I'm letting him grieve. I-I don't know what you mean. I'm here for him. That's the best I can do."

Stella sniffed and turned away, heading to the front door. "You refuse to see anything bad, Celeste. You are so stuck in keeping things the way they are. Let me give you a piece of advice: it won't happen. We're all going to split up and leave and go our own ways. And you know what?"

Celeste waited, tears filling her eyes in the cold.

"It's a good thing," Stella finished. "Change is good. Sometimes, we have to make hard choices, make people angry at us —to save them." She took a deep breath.

"You want to break everyone up?" Celeste whispered.

Stella snarled. "I want you to face reality. I want this fantasy world you live in to shatter. To break. Refusing to see the real world isn't cute. It hurts those of us who live in the real world. You've ignored me since that stupid meathead joined our group. You have no idea what I'm going through. You don't know anything, Celeste!"

Then she sighed deeply.

"After Halloween, I quit. I can't handle this anymore. I'm deleting my online profiles, tossing my tabletops, and selling my consoles. I'm tired of pretending to be your best friend when you won't even talk to me anymore, choosing to ignore the change going on around you."

Her friend turned to the door to leave. There was only one way Celeste knew she could try to change her friend's mind. Something drastic to save what she had with Stella. She could give up all that other stuff Stella had mentioned, but not Stella herself.

"Wait, Stell." Courage flooded Celeste as Stella halted on the last step. "What if I show you something? Something so very special. Something bigger than anything we could ever plan for. Will you agree to wait and talk to us then?"

"More magic and sorcery?" Stella mocked. Her tone cut Celeste's heart. "What is it?"

Celeste didn't back down. Her heart was set. "The best kind of magic ever. I promise."

"Tch." Stella laughed sardonically again.

"It will be worth it. Meet me at the quarry a couple miles from here. Thursday evening. Bring your costume."

"Why?"

"There's a world beyond ours." Celeste gulped as the truth spilled out of her. "A place where you can choose who you are, how strong you are, what you can do. I think I did it wrong before. I chose the wrong role." She frowned. "I chose the wrong role," she repeated, thinking. "I don't know who I'm supposed to be in that world. I know what I'm supposed to do, I think. Heal? Protect? But I was a fighter and that wasn't right." She sighed, still not sure. "But when you cross over, you become someone the people there need. A hero."

Stella finally met Celeste's eyes. Something in her frown told Celeste she believed her. "You went to this world in the woods?"

Excited, Celeste nodded. "I don't understand all the rules, but it's amazing. I promise, Stell, if I can take you there, you'll see." Without stopping for a reaction, Celeste told Stella everything she had told Oran, Lance, and Alice. She expressed her hope for meeting Yilith and Gwen again, told her about Folkvar and Galis and the weird oracle. She told her about Greylheim, Umbra, and how everyone feared it, but she had no idea who or what it was.

"There is a kind of magic in this world that helps me get there," she ended. "I want to show you. I know you've felt left out, like I've been ignoring you, and I'm sorry. We're better friends than that."

Stella remained quiet for a while before asking, "You choose what you are when you cross over?"

Taken aback by Stella's willingness to listen, Celeste nodded. "I think so."

"And we—well, you—had power over that place?"

"Revary. And yes."

"You want to save it from destruction?"

Celeste nodded.

Stella's eyes glassed over and she hummed in thought. "Fine, whatever." With dark, narrow eyes and a sarcastic shaking of her head, Stella sighed. "This is the last time, Celeste. Remember, I quit."

CHAPTER 17
THE OREAD PROPHECY

N ear the northern reaches of Revary, Galis, Folkvar, and the star waited for the Planes Strider to return. But their time wasn't spent idly.

Galis let go of the monster's head and it fell forward with a hard grunt. The beast was a bonkor. It was much like a bear, only bigger and with horns and teeth that best resembled a python's. A large clawed paw had slashed a three-trailed path across his chest, but that was the only wound. The monster had lost its head. He panted, wiping the blood off his skin, and turned to face Folkvar, who had lost his footing on the craggy mountain and slipped. He reached down and hauled the towering norcan to his feet.

"You barbarians are beyond my comprehension!" the oracle screamed from where he hung on Galis's belt. "I said not to enter that narrow pass. Did you listen to me? No! You'll never find the Planes Strider if you do not listen to me."

"Is there no way to shut him up?" Folkvar asked as the star came out from her hiding place and called to the warg, which had fled. Folkvar slung his bow around his shoulders and crossed his muscular arms over his chest against the rising cold.

"He is right," the star breathed. "That was reckless. But it is your way." She said this to Galis, her cheeks pink. "Is it safe to pass through now?"

Galis heaved his sword onto his back and led the way into the narrow path. "Yes. Bayla, the current queen of the Oreads, will have her shaman with her and be near Sapphire Caldera. Winter is on the way, and they will be looking for visions in the blue water. They will be able to give us counsel."

The Silver Ice Mountains crawled over Revary's most remote realm with jagged, unforgiving edges and drop-offs. Galis led the party over the labyrinthian pathways. Deep calderas and sharp peaks cut off most of their vision. They'd not had an easy journey since the Planes Strider had vanished. She'd begged them to find her again. With no leads, Galis had counseled that they speak with the queen of his people. The Oreads were a fierce people and their queen could cast for visions.

Folkvar led the warg with the star riding on top, shivering in the quickening wind. He'd given her his cloak, but it did little against the sharp fingers of the wind.

Galis hoped they weren't too late to meet the Oreads. As giants of the mountain, the mythical people did not interact with his tribe often. And his tribe feared them, bending their heads to their leadership.

The path tilted up for another half mile before it opened up onto a great overlook. White clouds dimmed the sun to a soft glow, nearly matching the gray color of the mountains that touched them. A few evergreens dotted the lower parts of the distant peaks. A lush emerald field of thick grass below surrounded the Sapphire Caldera. The lake would have glittered if the sun had been out. Even without its warm rays, the water was a deep, clear blue.

"I see them," the star gasped, pointing down the trail. "They are so tall."

Galis followed her finger and found what he sought, his heart lightening in his chest. The Oread queen, tall, imposing with wild yellow hair and animal-skin adornments dripping from her arms, a silver circlet around her head, stood near the blue water with her shaman. The shaman, dressed in little more than a few animal-skin wrappings, stood with her arms outstretched to the sky. She made wild, wobbling animal-like calls like a song.

Galis turned to the others. "Do not speak unless spoken to. I am not sure the Oread queen will take kindly to a lowly mountain tribesman like myself interrupting their visions."

Folkvar and the star shared worried glances, but followed their companion down the path. By the time they neared the pair of Oreads, they had stopped their calls and stood together, gazing into the water. The gravel shore crunched under Galis's boot, alerting the blind shaman to his presence. The shaman turned to face them and waited as they approached. The wreath of trees here at the base of the caldera made it more secluded than it felt from above. The wind blew less.

"Adventurers, I am Availa, shaman to the queen," the shaman said to them, her lips black and stone stiff. "In a vision, I saw you coming. Brave warriors, friends of the Planes Strider. It is dangerous to be upon the queen's mountain this time of year." Her blind face turned enough to let Galis know she was looking toward the star. "You've come far." Her brows furrowed. "You seek a champion." She turned to the queen. "Bayla, they come seeking counsel about the lost prince of Calimorden."

Bayla, the queen of the Oreads, had been kneeling by the sapphire water. She stood, easily over seven feet tall, and looked down her pale, straight nose at the group. "Has the vanishing gone so far?" Her voice was deep and rich, like the roots of a mountain.

"Yes," the star replied quickly. "My mother sent me away as my brothers and sisters were destroyed. Umbra has a servant, a great dragon, that has the power to devour even us."

The Oreads glanced at one another, faces serious.

"I have seen this," Availa whispered, touching her bound eyes. "I thought the visions of a dragon devouring the moon were a sign. Not reality."

"There is a blackness in the midst of the prairies as well," Folkvar added. "It is spreading toward Calimorden where Queen Zephyr waits to be destroyed."

Bayla suddenly gripped Availa's arm. "The golden crown," she said, clearly reminding Availa of something. "Not two days ago, we saw it together. We witnessed a golden circle over the mountains, near the Guardian River, in a vision."

Folkvar moaned at this. The Guardian River cut off a long-cursed portion of Revary, a place where the snow never ceased and the sun hardly shone.

"You think it was Prince Gwen?" the star asked, standing up excitedly in the stirrups. "The one Celeste mentioned. From Calimorden?"

Availa nodded, her strange ornaments waving gently. "But the crown was followed by a crawling blackness in the vision. Something else seeks the prince."

Above them, a dull roar of thunder rolled over the clouds. The shaman looked up, but Bayla held their gaze. "We have been casting for visions all morning. We saw you coming. But we also saw the Planes Strider. Is what Availa says true? Have you met a Planes Strider?"

"Yes," Galis answered quickly. "She healed this norcan's mother and freed me from them."

Availa slowly turned her head down from the sky. She smiled a little. "Only a Planes Strider could unite a norcan and a warrior from the mountain. In times such as these..." She looked back up at the sky and didn't go on.

"We have trust in the Planes Strider," Galis countered. "She promised to return to Revary. We cannot let Umbra get a foothold like it did in Calimorden. Queen Zephyr gave in too quickly."

"So she has," Bayla sighed. "We have been searching for a champion. For answers. But we cannot leave our mountain. We must see to our people as the vanishing crawls down from the heavens and ascends from the plains."

"If you must go, then go east," Availa said. "There you will meet the prince and the elf. But I see only destruction if you start this journey alone. Where the Mirror lies, the truth of our world lies. Only a Planes Strider can use it properly. I shudder to think what will happen if one of you goes there."

"Mirror?" Galis asked.

"I have seen a Mirror," Availa said. "It is very far and guarded by invisible enemies. Men have screamed in terror or dashed away or killed themselves as they neared it. I have seen them swing their swords at unseen foes and lose battles to ghosts."

Galis raised his head. "I am not afraid of invisible enemies."

"Stupid barbarian," the oracle sighed. He would have shaken his head had it not been the only bit of him left, dangling from Galis's belt.

Availa turned her head down to look at the oracle. "One who stayed," she mused. "You know the power of mirrors. You understand what I have seen."

Folkvar waved his hand at the oracle when he didn't reply right away. "What does this mean, dead man?"

The oracle mumbled and rolled his eyes. "It means, someone is going back and forth between Revary and the Other World. Not like Umbra. Not like your Celeste. Someone has found a way to open a door to Revary. Mirrors are doorways between worlds. It had to have been created."

Galis felt a cold stone drop into his gut. Somehow, this didn't sound like good news. Just then, another roll of thunder ambled across the sky, trailing to the east. As it did, a purple streak cut slowly across the sky then burned bright as it landed on the other side of the mountain.

"What was that?" Galis asked.

Availa sighed darkly.

"A dark star," the star replied. Her eyes were wide and full of fear. "Falling to the earth. It is the not the first I have seen in these last few days."

Bayla's powerful shoulders drooped. "So it has come to this. Corrupted stars have fallen to the Surface Plane. Adventurers, hurry. Find the prince. Find the Planes Strider."

THE VAST GUARDIAN RIVER, COVERED IN MIST, stretched out before them. The water in it moved at the pace of funeral marchers and was the color of sable. No wave broke the surface and no sound issued from it. It appeared to flow endlessly to the left and right. They could vaguely see the banks on the other side through the fog.

Folkvar lifted a branch and touched it to the water's surface. When the green leaves brushed the black waters, they immediately lost their color, turned to a bleak gray, and shriveled up. The decay began to travel up the branch toward the norcan's hand. Folkvar quickly dropped the branch into the water. The splash sounded strange, as though it came from the far end of a stone tunnel.

"Corrupted water," the oracle said in a way that made him sound like a fascinated teacher. "Nasty stuff. The nyads must have fallen to the corruption."

"Can we cross?" the star asked.

"Sure, swim it," the oracle said. When Galis took one step closer, the oracle screamed, "No, foolish bonehead! I didn't mean it."

"I'm only looking." Galis frowned as he gazed into the river. He had no reflection in it. The sun was the only thing reflected in the black water. Galis's brow furrowed more as he saw something was not right with the sun. He whirled around in terror and pointed. "Look at the sun!" he cried.

The others turned and the star cried out, covering her mouth in shock with both of her delicate hands. The sun glowed and was larger than it had been the day before. The edges of it were a darkened orange, growing more orange as they gaped up at its yellow face. But the most terrifying sight was a large, black crack, which started in the upper righthand side, wide and dark, then narrowed and splintered into smaller fissures about halfway down toward the center.

"My father," the star said at last. "This is why my mother

sent me away!" She put her face in her hands and fell to her knees, weeping.

Galis knelt next to her, placing his hand on her shoulder. He had no words. He didn't even know if his tribe still lived. It had been too long since his capture. The mountains had been silent as they'd passed through. The courage—let alone the time—to go off trail and investigate his tribe had left him. He understood her pain.

"A boat!" the oracle called. "Let us cross and return as speedily as we can."

Gliding across the waveless waters was a gray decaying boat with a high prow. In it stood one bipedal creature with sickly blue skin and webbed hands. His eyes were white and blind.

"One more, I think, is all," the boatman said in an old, whispery voice. He repeated it over and over as his ferry came closer.

"One more what?" Galis asked as the boat hit the shore.

"One more time is all it can handle, then down it goes, I think. It's nothing." The boatman pushed the boat with a long wooden pole. The boatman's arms were large and muscled from pushing the ferry along.

"Can you take us across?" Folkvar asked.

"Oh yes, to be sure. It is what I do. One more time, I think, is all."

Galis gave Folkvar a quick glance. They both thought the same thing: the boatman had lost his mind.

Carefully, they climbed in, leading the warg cautiously onto the ferry, and were soon out in the midst of the black water. The corruption slowly snaked its way up the wooden pole the water-man used to push them along. He didn't seem to notice. No sound came out of the water.

"Where are the others?" Galis asked. "This river should be full of your kith. They use this river for fishing and selling among other things."

"Gone under, is all. It's nothing," the water-man said, grunting while he pushed. He shivered as the finny spine on his back turned pale then gray before their eyes. "I'll see them soon. We always stick together, us river folk."

"You should leave the boat and come with us," Folkvar said. "I do not like to see a creature give up so easily. It is not an honorable way to die."

The water-man gave a kind of bubbly laugh. "Not giving up, just going to see them, is all."

The star looked at the gray color of the boat and gathered up her skirts into her hands.

"Will the water harm you?" she asked.

"Probably so. Just take away my essence, I think, is all. And that's nothing."

"Is that what this decay does?" Folkvar asked.

The water-man's face fell as they landed on the next shore. "No. Makes you heartless, gone, and empty. Dead but walking, decaying, nothing, and all of the above, is all. It's nothing."

After they got out, he waved to them. "It happens to us all one day or another. This is my last ride. No point. I'm finished. Why wait?"

Galis opened his mouth to ask the water-man what he meant, but the humanoid slapped his hands together, took a deep breath, and dived gracefully into the black water. Hardly a ripple lapped out from his entry and no sound splashed up. The star stared in horror at the spot where the water-man had vanished. She reached out as if to pull him back, but Folkvar took her hand and drew her closer to him, away from the tainted river.

"To die this way," the norcan sighed. "There is no glory in it."

"And I wonder about glory in battle," the star countered. "Is it a good fight if we cannot know what victory will bring? Can we heal from this, even if we do find the Planes Strider?"

Galis said, "I am a warrior and would rather die fighting."

The star met his eyes. "It is your way." She turned and faced the white land before them. "My gift is to heal. And if finding the Planes Strider is the only way to heal Revary, I will do it." She stepped into the torrents of thick, swirling snow.

CHAPTER 18
UNLIKELY FRIENDS

T he other side of the river was like a new world. Snow and wind whipped and lashed at them the moment they took five steps inland. A thick layer of ice covered the trees like glass. Huge stalactites of ice hung from the bows of the trees in blue and white spears. Bushes covered in ice and snow had turned to massive, hard boulders. From the depths of the blizzard came the calls and howls of wolves with thick, pure white fur. Even their claws and noses were white. Their angled eyes glowed crystal blue.

Also ducking and hiding, playing a fierce game of chase, were a snow fox with his two bushy tails, and a winter hare. In the branches, perched with strong silver talons, a pair of snow hawks and winter crows with black eyes watched them pass. Upside down in a tree, shielding her young in her wings, hung a large white bat. She opened her red eyes as the small group passed, but did not dare move for fear of her young being exposed to the cold wind.

Galis shivered first. His animal-skin garb was not meant for such weather. Folkvar braced himself against the wind.

They marched only a half mile into the woods when Galis stopped and Folkvar lifted his hand for silence. His nose twitched as he sniffed the air. He flicked his hand down and they all crouched low.

"One is human," Folkvar said. "I do not know the other."

Galis raised his head just above the snow mound they were hidden behind and looked. Perfectly visible in the white world was a Nether elf in black robes. Galis had seen only one Nether elf in his life, and it had been speared on his father's pike. They did not leave their lower Plane often. He could only think of one reason a Nether elf would be above the lower Plane. This might have been the elf Celeste had mentioned, but he could not be sure.

Folkvar opened his mouth to ask Galis what he had seen when a voice cried out in authority, "Do not move. We have you surrounded!"

Galis ducked all the way down and answered back, "Who? You and your Nether elf? Who are you?"

Stepping out from behind a tree a safe distance from them was a young man in a silver tunic and chainmail. His long blue-black hair whipped around his face under a golden circlet.

"Are you Prince Gwen?" the star asked, poking her head over the bush. A pale pink blush colored her white face.

When he saw her gentle frame and her glowing hair, he lowered the point of his sword. "Yes?"

She gave a gleeful cry and ran to him, throwing her arms around his neck and weeping for joy.

"Celeste sent us to find you. I am bursting with joy at this meeting!"

Galis ran to catch up with the star. Sword still poised, he and Folkvar came up behind her while she embraced the tall human man. His broad shoulders were covered in a thick black fur cloak. A small bundled black mass stood beside him.

Gwen met Galis's eyes over the star's glowing head. "Who are you?" His eyes snapped to Folkvar, momentarily flashing in shock.

"Galis of the Stone Peak," he replied as the star finally released the prince. "This is Folkvar, son of a prairie chief and lone survivor of his tribe."

"The vanishing?" Gwen asked.

Folkvar nodded silently.

Gwen exchanged a look with the short black-clad elf at his side. "I am Prince Gwen, last heir of Calimorden. This is Yilith, exile of the Nether. We were both saved by the Planes Strider some time ago and have been looking for her ever since."

"Celeste," Galis supplied. "Yes. Availa, the Oread shaman, told us you would be here. Why are you on this side of the river?"

The Nether elf pulled his hood tighter over his head. "I saw a dark star. It fell on this side of the mountains. I believe it landed in Sylvan Murk."

"The home of the sorceress?" Galis asked, his fear beginning to rise.

"Let us not stand in this wind and ice," Folkvar grunted. "Let's hide from the elements before we freeze and continue our discussion then."

Soon they were all seated around a fire that crackled in a circle of stones in a cave of ice. The star sat wrapped in one of Gwen's fur cloaks. She sat close to Gwen, soaking up his heat.

"Any chance I could snuggle up in there with you, star girl?" the oracle said with a leering smile. "It's so cold out here."

"Can we not cast him into the fire?" Galis moaned, tearing the head from his belt.

"I cannot believe you found the oracle," Gwen mused. "My mother searched for him for years. I was raised on tales of his powers and magic. Can he really tell the future and look into other dimensions?"

"Not that we've seen," Folkvar sighed. "I have seen his usefulness and have more patience than Galis, but I under-stand his desire to cast him into the flames."

"Hey," the oracle pouted. "I'm right here. You don't have to talk about me like I'm a lamp on a stand. Not that any of you know what that is... And I got you here, didn't I?"

The Nether elf—Yilith, he'd said his name was—handed out rabbit meat he'd cooked over the fire.

More suspicion set into Folkvar's eyes. "You seem relaxed around this Nether elf, human. I would not have thought that kind of prejudice easily dismissed from one such as you."

Gwen caught the full meaning of the remark and set his face, determined to not let emotion rise out of him in anger.

"A lot has changed since the Planes Strider," Gwen said evenly. "Celeste rescued me from the Nether. I may have become a servant of Umbra if I had stayed there. I owe her my life. So, I must suffer certain company for that."

Galis saw Folkvar's jaw twitch, understanding the human prince's meaning.

They chewed the meat in silence for a while and all huddled closer to the fire as what little sun there was shone down.

"Have you seen the sun?" Folkvar asked when they were all finished. "The cracks and darkness?"

"Corruption," the elf said softly.

"It has reached the Celestial Plane, of course," the star put in. "That is why I was sent away. To escape it."

"Where are you headed now?" Gwen asked.

"The Oread shaman told us to go east and find a Mirror," Folkvar began. He shook his head. "She said it was a portal, a doorway for the Other World."

Yilith looked up, his black eyes reflecting the licking flames of the fire. "Does that mean that's where Umbra came from?"

"I think," Galis said, poking at the fire to keep his hands busy, "it means we might be able to call up the Planes Strider. Or that another could come. I'm not sure."

"There's too much we don't know. We should return to Calimorden," Gwen said. "Inform the queen of what we find. She can send out messengers to all the corners of the Surface Plane, sharing what we've learned." He didn't meet any of their eyes and blinked as a shallow frown touched his brows.

Galis saw the expression. "What troubles you, prince?"

Gwen took a slow breath. "I'm not sure I can trust my mother anymore. But who else do I have? Calimorden's reach will be unmatched."

Folkvar shook his head. "Your messengers would be dead before they reached the prairies. We should go there after we find the Mirror. I'd trust whatever we find in the hands of my people over the delicate hands of a submissive queen."

Gwen drew his cloak tighter around himself. "Calimorden

is also defensible. Umbra's darkness has changed the people of Revary. If they do not become harbingers of more vanishing, they'll become empty monsters, attacking the Surface dwellers. The servants of Umbra rally them. They are mobilizing as entire armies to spread the vanishing. Cities are falling. I will take the oracle to the queen. He may have council for her."

"The queen shall not lay hands on the oracle." Folkvar's voice rose. "He has deep secrets. Already your mother has made a deal with Umbra. Why do you think she will change her mind now?"

"She is not yet corrupt," Gwen begged. "Yes, she made a mistake—"

"Throwing her only son into the Nether to satisfy a master of darkness like Umbra is not a simple mistake," Galis pointed out.

"A human who sacrifices her own son?" Folkvar inquired. "Not even my father would do such a thing. There is no honor in sending another to die, no matter the reason."

"Yes, a war chief who devours his victims on the battlefield," Gwen spat back. "I am heir to that throne and will do what I think best for my kingdom."

The star gently placed her hand on Gwen's arm to calm him and smiled at his new hope and courage.

Folkvar stood to his full height and glared down at Gwen. "I am a warrior's son and will not be commanded by a human princeling. I will not allow you to take the oracle."

"Make them shut up," the oracle said, wincing.

The star stood up between them. She turned her sparkling eyes to Gwen and clasped her hands over her heart.

"Please, hold your temper." She turned to Folkvar. "I know the agonies you suffer, having abandoned your people.

You are a great leader among your people and to follow another puts you ever so low. But for the sake of finding the Planes Strider again, follow Gwen. Let us go to the Mirror in peace, and return to one of the last bastions against Umbra: Calimorden."

It took a few breaths for the prince and the norcan to calm themselves enough to sit back down. Both of their strong hands resting on the pommels of their swords was noted by Galis and Yilith. Galis met the elf's eyes and saw they understood each other: they had to work together if they wanted to find the Planes Strider.

THE JOURNEY THROUGH THE SNOW AND ICE WAS never silent and pushed the party's endurance to their limits. The wind continued to howl louder and louder. The star remained bundled up. Gwen had a long pelt of fur he lent to Galis to keep his body warm, which he tied around his shoulders with leather. At first, the Nether elf walked in pace with Galis, keeping up easily. But soon his short legs wore out, no match for the snow. The star helped him up onto the warg's back to join her. Folkvar stepped over the snow easily with his long, powerful legs.

Soon, the howling grew too loud and deep.

"That's not the wind," Galis called to his companions, stopping the march.

In the darkness ahead of them loomed the purple eyes of an alpha snow wolf and two sets of blue-eyed followers.

Gwen stopped and placed himself between the wolves

and the others. "Folkvar, take the star to safety! Galis and the elf, with me."

For a terrible moment, Folkvar hesitated after the elf leapt down to Galis's side. He even unslung his bow, but the star put her hand on his shoulder in fear. With a roar spurred by the rage of not participating in what was sure to be a glorious battle, he turned and galloped up a hill to take her to safety.

The alpha wolf slowly lowered down onto the snow to sit, his eyes still flaring and his teeth still barred. His minions would do the fighting for him. With a deep bark, the others leapt at the warriors.

Gwen dived to the side and summersaulted back up onto his feet just in time to raise his blade to shove aside a dagger-toothed maw. Behind him, the elf drew his bow, nocked an arrow to it and disappeared into the underbrush.

Galis caught the full weight of the wolf that launched at him and sank into the snow from the force of the leap. It immediately tore at its victim with long teeth and white claws. The jaws closed down around his forearm, but did not pierce the skin protected by the ornamented metal greaves tied at his wrists. The metal pushed in, bent by the wolven jaws. Pain cracked through Galis's bones. With a cry, he angled his massive sword and plunged it into the wolf's shoulder. He missed his mark, but it caused the animal to reel and leap away.

With a swift, arching slice, Gwen cut his opponent across the face, taking one eye. It only whined once before launching another attack. The wolf circled around him, flicking its tail and watching for an opening. Gwen took his sword in both hands, knowing he'd need it against the massive beast's weight. Suddenly, the wolf whined and clawed at its own face as though some little monster plucked at its eyes. A small arrow from the elf's bow stuck out of its left eye.

"Gwen, behind you!" the elf called from where he had been hiding.

The prince turned quickly, and a huge open jaw clamped down around his entire shoulder. The alpha tackled him, cracking his bones and pulling him to the ground. Fueled by a rage only wild dogs know, the alpha whipped his head back and forth, shaking Gwen like a dead rabbit. His sword flew out of his hand as blood spattered the snow.

Galis saw the elf leap down from his perch and hesitate as his eyes went from Gwen to him. He had been caught by the other wolf by the ankle and reached desperately for his sword, which still stuck out of the wolf's shoulder. Gwen had stopped screaming, and was no doubt passed out now. Making up his mind, the elf dashed toward Galis as he shot one arrow over his shoulder at the wolf that had Gwen in its maw. The monster howled as the arrow hit its shoulder and it dropped the prince.

The little elf leapt with all his strength over the last wolf, which clutched Galis in its jaw, aimed, and shot a small black arrow right through the base of its skull. The wolf fell dead, its fangs still firmly clamped on the barbarian's leg.

The alpha scanned the scene before suddenly dashing away into the darkness.

Knowing Galis had the strength to pry his leg free, the elf ran to the fallen prince and helped him to stand. His shoulder was mangled and needed a lot of care.

With the wolves gone, they gathered together to tend their wounds. Folkvar came back, the star in tow upon the warg's back.

"This way," Folkvar said. "We found a cave to rest in. Out of the wind."

Galis slowly trudged to Gwen and helped him up, supporting him as they all slowly marched to the shelter.

"I can heal you," the star said, sliding off the warg and kneeling before Gwen once they were all safely inside. She held her hands out and a soft glow from her crown of starlight illuminated the cave.

Galis watched her as her face pinched in concentration. Suddenly she gasped and fell back onto her heels. "What is it?" he asked, concerned for her.

"I... I can't," she gasped. "My magic is weak. I can't reach it. Like the source in the Celestial Plane is weakened. Or empty."

"The weakening of the sun," the oracle whispered in thought. "You are losing your powers as Umbra grows."

Galis winced as the pain from his own wounds mounted. "What does that mean?"

The oracle pressed his black lips to one side. "It means we need to find that Planes Strider. Who knows what other creatures have also lost their magic?"

The star sighed. "I'm so sorry. I cannot help you."

Gwen moaned and gripped his bleeding wounds.

"I can," the elf whispered somberly. He moved to Gwen and raised his hands. "Please, let me."

The prince glared in silence but didn't fight when the elf removed his cloak and tunic. Using his nimble fingers, the elf went to work on Gwen's wounds.

Folkvar remained dissatisfied. "You should have let me fight," he grunted. "Perhaps you would not have been so hurt. We have many miles to go and now we will be even slower."

Gwen would not be able to lift his sword for some days

with the injuries he'd sustained. The elf bound his neatly stitched shoulder and tied a sling around his neck for support. Then he went to Galis, removed his fur boots, and began cleaning his gnawed leg and foot.

A windless silence fell at last. The storm subsided with the disappearance of the alpha wolf. The star quivered, quiet as she watched the elf work.

"You are different than your kin," she said in her sweet, soft voice. "I did not know your kind knew the healing arts, especially as well as you do."

The elf scrubbed away the last of the blood from Galis's foot and gently applied healing ointment from his pack. Her comment made his cheeks redden. He looked up into Galis's eyes to apologize when he touched a particularly tender spot, making the warrior hiss and cringe.

"Sorry," he whispered, half-flinching, waiting for a blow of annoyance to fall.

Despite the pain, Galis smiled kindly down at the elf. "I've had worse. But I've never felt gentler hands. You have a gift."

The Nether elf swallowed, calculating his response. "It was a sin among my people. To heal, I mean. If one of our number is wounded, we send them out to die. The concept of healing is punishable." He pressed his lips together, having spoken too much. "That and my faith in the Planes Strider is what got me exiled."

Gwen looked up at this. Now he understood the nature of his meeting with the elf. "That's how we met you," he said. "You were wounded. Did your people leave you?"

The elf sighed as he worked. "I shouldn't speak of it."

"You can," Galis offered. "You may always speak among us. And to me."

The elf looked up at his companions, lost for words. At

length, he said, "I was a healer among my people. Not magically, like a star. I studied the herbs and their healing properties. In secret. I did not want my kinsfolk to die like they had for so long. But some of our number learned of my healing and set a trap so I would be wounded and could be cast out. To suffer with none to save me. I did not want my people to submit to Umbra. I left to find aid. They let me go, hoping I'd perish."

Galis said, "The ways of your people sadden me. My tribe puts its people first. We know that to survive, we must band together. Brothers, sisters, mentors, fathers, and mothers; our first concern is each other."

"I wish I was among your people," the elf said without looking up.

Galis smiled. "We can be war brothers. No tighter bond than that exists."

The firelight reflected perfectly in the elf's all-black eyes. His face took on a strange expression as his white lips parted to reveal his pointed teeth in a true smile.

"After all, we're all we have," Galis added to include everyone. "Sent to hunt for a way to save our people, or sent away from our people. We'll make our own tribe."

The star giggled and clapped her hands. "I like that idea," she said.

Folkvar shook his head. "What a strange tribe we shall be."

CHAPTER 19
THE DARK STAR

Galis led the party over the flat snowy surface the next morning. More than once they stopped to let Yilith catch up until Galis convinced him to ride the warg with the star. He pressed his head down into the wind, as did the others, until his boot hit hard, snowless black rock. Shaken, he looked up.

Before him, something more terrifying than the cursed winter land met his gaze. What might have been mountains and a forest were now blasted back. A deep black chasm arched up from a place of impact. Trees were shoved back, most fallen. Some had been charred black by fire spreading out from the center of the meteoric impact. In the middle rose a shape. It looked like the earth, having been melted to liquid by the impact of the falling meteor, had splashed up and then become solid again. Like fulgurite sticking out of the earth, only it rose several stories into the air.

"It's like a castle pulled from the earth," Yilith mused. "See the windows and the portcullis at the base?"

The others came up alongside Galis. Folkvar cursed softly.

"If I had to describe a curse, this would be it," the monster mused.

"Is it a palace?" Gwen asked. "Did the falling star do this?"

"Dark star," the star corrected, shaking. "It was black and purple. Corrupted."

Galis glanced at the star then back at the destruction. "This is where Availa said the Mirror would be. We must find it and call to Celeste."

"And if we run into the dark star?" Gwen asked.

The warrior glanced sideways at the prince. "A norcan, a mountain warrior, a Nether elf, the heir of Calimorden, and a star from the Celestial Plane. If we cannot take one star, we are not fit to be Revary's saviors."

Folkvar hummed in agreement and took the first step onto the rocky ground. He stopped, exclaiming when he did. "It's like there is a wall between the snow and the black rock," he said.

Galis stepped onto the rocky path to see what Folkvar meant. To his surprise, the howling wind was cut off immediately and his skin burned hot from the warmer air. A heat wave came off the place of impact, thawing his bones. "When the dark star landed," he thought out loud, "it blasted away the winter curse." He swallowed hard. "It must be a powerful star."

"Courage, Galis," Folkvar growled, pulling his sword from its great sheath. He led the way into the crater, eyes sharp and keen. "There is a sort of barrier around the palace. I feel it. The winter curse does not touch this land."

They reached the base of the fulgurite tower and looked up. The air whispered, quiet and still. Galis traced the strange curves and crevices of the structure up and down before stepping through the open portcullis. Inside, only empty halls of stone rounded out before them. Stairs to the right showed the way up.

"Single file," Yilith suggested. "If more than one of us falls, run."

"Agreed," Galis said.

"We are to be heroes for Revary and the Planes Strider," Gwen added. "Not one another."

Folkvar gave Galis a knowing brow raise at this, but took the lead anyway. Yilith came behind him, then the star, then Galis and Gwen. In the utter darkness of the winding stairway, the star's green crown of light glowed brightly. It guided them up the black steps until they heard voices.

A young woman's voice called out, shouting, growling, then exclaiming in joy. The party stopped for just a moment to arm themselves before continuing up. Galis stopped Folkvar when the bright archway at the top beamed light onto the stairs. He took the lead now and motioned for the others to wait. Galis pressed himself against the wall and ascended the last two steps to look into the great round space at the top.

Like the top of a tower, the fulgurite palace opened up into what he imagined a wizard's stargazing room might look like. The floor was open, save for a few menacing spikes jutting out to the side. The surface area was larger than he'd thought it would be, perhaps twenty-five feet across. In the center stood a sharp piece of glass like it had stabbed up from the ground. It was black, yet reflected back the space around it.

Before it stood a young woman. She wore a simple black silk dress with no decorations or markings upon it. Just long, to her feet, with wide, elegant sleeves. She also wore a crown like the star, only hers was made of black light, with a mysterious purple glow. Around the surface of her skin, the air bent, distorting what he could see behind her. A simple black mask obscured her entire face.

"I've done it!" The dark star laughed, gripping the sides of the Mirror. Her voice was deep, distorted and unnatural. "Now, what should I do? Will you come?"

Galis's blood ran cold when he heard a strange, rumbling crackle from inside the Mirror.

The dark star shook her head. "What are you talking about? Who has come…" She stopped. In a second, she snapped around and met Galis's eyes. Her eyes were wide behind her mask. She hummed in that strange, distorted way.

Seeing his cover blown, Galis marched out, flanked by the other four. The dark star stammered and wrung her hands. "I don't know what to do. Help me!" she shouted to the Mirror.

Again, that vile sound replied to her. Her eyes flicked to Yilith. The elf planted his feet and drew his straight blades.

"Have you fallen to Umbra, sister?" the star asked sadly. She held her hands out straight at her sides, palms glowing. "Our power is healing. What you've brought is destruction."

The dark star's eyes ran over the party before her. "It's you. All of you," she whispered, almost in awe. "You've come, just like it said you would. You're looking for her, aren't you?"

Galis put himself before the others, shielding them. "You're a corrupted star. What have you done to the Mirror?"

"This is my Mirror," the dark star shot back. "I opened this portal to Revary myself."

"Are you a Planes Strider?" Galis asked, confused. Fear mounted in him. Planes Striders were powerful. One in league with the darkness would be the death of Revary.

"I am whatever I want to be," the dark star jeered, her

voice strange and warbling. She smiled darkly. "You've come to use the Mirror to call her up, but you won't have it."

The dark star narrowed her eyes in what looked like disgust. She positioned herself in front of the Mirror.

"I came prepared." She raised her hands as well, black light pulsating from them. She thrust her hands forward and black tendrils and shadows shot out of the Mirror at the party. Galis slid to the side to avoid the first onslaught of dark winged creatures and whipping limbs that burst from the Mirror. He hacked a few, trying to clear a path to the dark star and the Mirror.

Behind him, Gwen grunted, getting surged by a flock of the monsters. Folkvar hacked and slashed his way toward Gwen to help defend him. Galis put himself in front of the star and Yilith. Yilith, being small, slid around the soulless army, severing wings and bits of the tendrils with fierce screams. The dark star stuttered backward to hide behind the Mirror, calling on the thing within for aid. Galis tried to follow her, but moved slowly, making sure the star was safe.

The dark star peeked around the Mirror. She smiled and pressed her hand to the front of it, calling up the darkness within. From where her hand pressed into the Mirror, what looked like the vanishing spread out and down from it. It crawled across the floor, forcing Galis back.

"Don't let it touch you," he ordered the others. He leapt over the initial corruption and charged at the dark star. She screamed and dodged away, turning into a purple beam of light to shoot across the space to safety. He advanced on the dark star, determined to stop her.

Behind him, Folkvar's cry of rage made him turn. He'd been cut deep on the shoulder by a winged fiend. With the great fighter distracted, the tendrils had wrapped themselves around Gwen, pulling him into submission.

"You'll do," the dark star snarled, seeing the captive prince. "The power of corruption will be on full display!"

Galis lunged back as the dark star ripped her hand toward the Mirror. Gwen cried out as the darkness pulled him into the Mirror by some invisible force. Galis flung his hand out and seized the prince's, dropping his sword to hold on tighter. He grunted as the fiends went for his eyes, trying to get him to let go. The star leapt up, blasting a wave of white, hot light into the tower room. The fiends shrieked and were blinded. But the dark star pulled once more. Gwen was wrenched from Galis's hand and vanished, screaming, into the Mirror.

Horrified, Galis fell backward and gaped into the black Mirror. Behind him, Folkvar roared as the fiends drove him near the edge. The fiends wouldn't die, like they were immortal monsters from another world.

A thought struck Galis as he picked himself up and rounded on the dark star. Her eyes widened in terror from behind the mask when he glowered at her.

"Help me!" she shouted to the bodiless voice in the Mirror. No sooner had she asked and Galis advanced on her again than the Mirror shook and the surface shattered in a rain of painful, sharp glass.

Being close to it, the glass cut Galis across his chest and face. He winced and turned away, but saw that the Mirror was still whole. Something had soared out of it. A beast twice the size of a man, though shaped like a man, with great, bat-like wings and a whipping, spiked tale shot out at him. It caught him and flew to shove him over the edge. Folkvar hauled himself up just in time and slashed at the monster, saving

Galis. The norcan's blade cut the beast across the face but did not deter it.

Behind them, Yilith defended the star until Galis heard the dark star say, "You! You are the one I want." Galis couldn't stop the dark star from attacking the elf and the star now. The star watched the dark star advance toward Yilith. She put herself between them and shoved at the dark star with white light.

"You're a healer!" the star begged as the dark star easily overcame her. "Don't bring this darkness to us."

The dark star shot black light at her, knocking her to the ground. "Healers are weak roles," the dark star shot back. "No one wants to play a healer."

Yes... the voice in the Mirror agreed with a menacing laugh.

Galis realized the closer he got to the Mirror, the less he heard of the area around it and the more he could hear the thing inside.

This is a star of Revary, the voice praised the dark star. *You are a dark star of another world. You are powerful. Strong. Capable of destruction! Kill them!*

With one hand, the dark star shoved the star out of the way. Commanding her tendrils, they shot out and grappled Yilith even as he struggled.

Galis roared and tried to fight off the beast, shoving it away. Somehow, this single dark star was overpowering them. Like she had strength they did not...otherworldly powers.

"Yes," the dark star cried. "I want *her* to come to me!"

A moment of silence came before the dark voice in the Mirror hissed, *Then take the elf. You see what you desire in him.*

The dark star's eyes flashed, locking on to Yilith as he struggled.

Yilith's black eyes went wide and he leapt, dashing away with a cry.

"Don't touch him!" Galis cried, locked in combat with the beast. But he couldn't stop her.

The dark star pointed at the Mirror, purple magic snapping around her wrist and fingers, then she lunged, shoving her order toward Yilith. A forest of black tendrils shot out, seizing the elf easily. Yilith fought madly, cutting the arms, shouting as he struggled to wiggle free.

"I see why you're her favorite," the dark star said, black tracks dripping from around her eyes. "She will come to save you." She jerked her arms back in a wave, the tendrils whipping Yilith toward her and the Mirror.

Galis shouted against his combatants, desperate to reach Yilith and the retreating dark star. She slammed the Nether elf against a fulgurite spike, binding him there. Yilith writhed and fought with all his strength but could not loosen himself.

He met Galis's eyes. They were filled with fear. "Don't leave me!" he cried.

Galis hesitated. He waited just long enough for the dark star to shoot a string of snapping lightning at the star. It hit her and she screamed. She fell to the ground, writhing and twitching against her will. Galis ducked as the beast's tale whipped toward him, the monster still locked in combat with the norcan. The star's pained screams filled his head, driving him mad with worry. Yilith cried to be saved. Galis felt helpless.

Kill them now, the voice rumbled to the dark star.

"No," she replied, smiling at seeing Galis paralyzed. "I want them to live. I want her to come and rescue them."

Galis sensed the thing in the Mirror was not pleased with this as a soft rumble shook the fulgurite tower.

The dark star smiled viciously and swung her arm in a great circle. Behind Folkvar, a black and purple portal opened. "Will this do?" she asked the voice. "I'll send him away. To fight my new beast."

The voice replied with a dark laugh.

Galis spun to see Folkvar and the beast tip into the dark star's portal. Beyond, what he thought must be the Sylvan Murk Forest wavered into view. The norcan roared in rage as he fell through, grappling with the beast as he did. The mountain warrior cried his name as he tried to reach out and grab his friend back. But they vanished into the portal. In a snap, the fiends exploded into black smoke, filling the area. Galis turned to face the dark star. She stood before the Mirror, smiling.

"I know you," she said, her black lips parting. "You are all creations of the girl you call Planes Strider." She lifted her hands and the black limbs shot toward him, binding his arms behind him and holding his legs to the ground. Galis grunted and twisted but couldn't throw off the dark binding. The dark star stepped over the other star. She lay on the ground, whimpering in pain. Behind the dark star, Yilith writhed against his bonds.

The dark star stood before Galis, looking up at him. She smiled and reached up to touch his chest. He recoiled but her power held him still. The dark star sighed and shook her head. "The things I could do in this world." She met Galis's eyes. "And she wanted to keep it all for herself."

He took a ragged breath. "Are you...a Planes Strider?" He prayed it wasn't true. They'd come to call a champion to Revary, and instead, this dark star had fallen into their world.

The dark star shrugged, tracing his muscles with her eyes and biting her lower lip. "I have no idea. I heard a voice, it called me, I came. Now I have magic and strength I never thought I would. I've imagined such things." She narrowed her eyes, doing battle within herself. "I want to do bad things to you, but I also want your Planes Strider to suffer." She smiled up at him. "Lucky you. But him," she pointed to Yilith, "I'm keeping. I need him. And this..." She pulled the oracle from Galis's belt. "This is going to keep an eye on wherever the great Umbra wants."

"What do you mean?" Galis growled, trying once again to break free of the bonds. They didn't budge.

"Celeste is not used to equal competition," the dark star went on. "She's a cheater. She uses abilities she shouldn't have, claiming it's all in the name of fun and the game. Well, I'm the game master here, too. Let's see what she does next time she comes over." She smiled. "I'm sending you to an ally of mine who will hold you until she comes back and finds you. And if she doesn't, well..." The dark star shrugged. "If you're lucky, Folkvar will find you. Assuming he can overcome that beast."

She drew a circle with her arm again and with a scream, the star fell into the same portal Folkvar and the beast had vanished into. Galis cried out and the dark star pressed her palm to his mouth, shushing him.

"Galis," Yilith called desperately from where he remained bound. "Find her. Come back."

"I won't leave you behind," he growled.

The dark star smiled again. "You don't have a choice." She raised her hand and a beaming purple light burst forth, blinding him, making his mind ring in utter numbness until he blacked out.

CHAPTER 20
SYLVAN MURK

Celeste waited by the quarry, turning her favorite green D20 over and over in her fingers. *I'm doing the right thing,* she told herself. *The Eidolon said to bring over more Planes Striders. We'll be stronger that way. I took council and decided she should come.*

But she also knew, deep inside, she hoped this would bring Stella back. Make them friends again. It was what had worked as kids: tell them a secret and friends would stick around. Right?

"I'm here. What now?" Stella said, slightly winded from walking up the terrain to the top of the quarry.

Celeste stood up and turned to see Stella in her simplest black robe and dress with flowing sleeves.

From the distance, the loon called. Celeste smiled and turned toward it. "Do you hear that?" she asked. "He's calling for his other half. Isn't it a beautiful sound?"

"Is that a wolf?" Stella asked, a little nervous.

Celeste laughed. "No, it's a loon. A king of ducks."

A little light returned to Stella's face. "Oh, that's kind of cool." She waited a minute. "Is that why you dragged me out here on a school night?"

Celeste shook her head. "No. I want to take you to my very special world. I've told some of the others about it. It's pretty wild."

An exasperated sigh pulled Stella to the ground. She crossed her legs and her arms. "Don't try this trick with me, Celeste. I'm not five, you know?" Her voice mocked Celeste's as she said, "Let's go on an adventure and see how imagination can take you to wonderful worlds of discovery and fun!" She frowned. "No."

Celeste wouldn't give up. She plopped down next to Stella and took her hands, holding them tight. She looked Stella right in her dark eyes. "I went to another world. I want to show you. Take you with me."

A buzzing from Stella's pocket interrupted her. Her cellphone vibrated.

"Ignore it and get on with your voodoo," Stella sighed.

Unhappy at the interruption and her friend's words, Celeste said, "You want to go? You don't think I'm crazy or don't believe me? Lance and Alice were pretty skeptical."

"You told Lance?" Stella snapped.

Her sudden outburst shocked Celeste so much she leaned back, away from her long-time friend. "He's my friend, Stell. Of course I did. And Alice. Oran was a little more open." She smiled.

Stella's face dropped. "I bet he was." She sighed and took Celeste's die from her. She held it up, catching the setting sun, and turned it over in her fingers, taking in the inner glitter. "Let's get on with your magic. How do you intend to send us over? Do you need a conduit or something? Like a mirror?"

Celeste shook her head and laughed nervously. "I usually fall. But with two of us, I thought'd we'd just hold hands and close our eyes. It'd be nice to cross over gently for a change."

Stella held her hands out, her face saying she thought this was a waste of time. Reminding herself that at least Stella was here, Celeste took her hands and they closed their eyes. She clenched them tight, the die sharp in their hands.

Take me back, she begged. *I'm coming and I brought help.*

She'd go over as a fighter again. Someone strong. "Stella, think of a role you want to play. Like in *Runes and Empires*."

"Does it have to be from *Runes and Empires*?" Stella asked.

Celeste made a small humming sound. "No. I just use it like a guide. Know what you want to be?"

"Uh," Stella stammered. "Yeah, sure. A sorceress, I guess." Celeste head her mumble something else under her breath.

They waited.

The night bugs suddenly went quiet, but Celeste kept her eyes closed. She took a deep breath and tasted the wet earth on the air. Then, just as quickly as they'd vanished, the night bugs started to sing again. This time, they sounded strange. Like creatures she'd never heard before. A small sensation flitted through her stomach. Like falling, but less so.

When they opened their eyes, it looked like the same place, only the rocks glittered and had intricate, ornate knots and swirls carved in them. In the woods, tiny little orbs of light circled the trees like large glowing fireflies in broad daylight.

Stella gasped and stood. "What have you done?" she cried.

Celeste leapt up and called into the woods. "This is it, Stell," she squealed in joy. "This is the place!"

Even with the fairy woods in front of her and the

sparkling rocks with their magic symbols, Stella shook her head. She looked unimpressed.

"So, this is it?" she asked.

Celeste nodded, a little let down. "I wonder where everyone is." She wandered closer to the woods, peering past some trees. This place was a side of Revary she could love easily. No dragons trying to kill her. No sandpedes attacking from under the ground. Just little fairies bobbing in and out of the sylvan shadows. But it was also oddly dark. And quiet.

"Hey there," she said to one of the swirling wisps. "Where are we? Is Calimorden close?"

The wisp stopped moving around the tree in its elegant, flowing dance and looked up at Celeste with huge orb-like green eyes. It looked like one of those slim little green aliens she'd seen in cartoons. Only this one had tall, pointy bat-like ears and iridescent wings at its back, buzzing like a bee's.

"The sorceress is just there," the wisp said excitedly, pointing into the trees. "The castle, too, as a matter of fact. All is well with Zealnis the sorceress, as a matter of fact. She's looking for the one who forged the Mirror. That's not a fact."

Celeste smiled at the cute thing as it rubbed its face on the tree again and again. "Can you lead us there?"

"I cannot, as a matter of fact," it squeaked. "But maybe I could. If she doesn't know, she cannot beat us into jelly. Yes, perhaps I could, as a matter of fact."

"Who's going to beat you into jelly?"

"No one, of course!" it laughed in a rather tiny, maniacal way. "I'll lead you right to her, as a matter of fact."

"Celeste!" Stella growled as she followed the fairy. "There is no way I am following some freakish little glowing thing into a strange wood."

"This is the place." Celeste spun around to face Stella,

walking backward after the wisp. "My magical world. It's called Revary."

Stella continued to glare until Celeste stopped and walked back toward her. "Swear you haven't drugged me or used one of those hoodoo spells from that freaky shop you work in?" She sounded only half-concerned.

Celeste wrinkled her face and arched her eyebrow. "I would never, Stell." She took one cautious step. "Give it a try, most powerful sorceress." She looked Stella up and down. Her dress had turned to one of black and purple, and a crown hovered around her head made of strange black light. "You almost look like the star I met," she mused. "But more... sorceress-y." Celeste frowned. "Actually, you look just like her. You sure you're a sorceress?"

Stella grunted in reply, stepping over some moss-covered rocks. "So, this is Sylvan Murk then?"

Celeste made a face, showing she wasn't sure. "Does that feel like the name to you? If it's right, the names will come to you. Like a name you've forgotten but sounds so familiar."

Stella mumbled for a minute, then said, "Yeah. I've heard of it before. Does that mean I have Planes Strider magic?"

Smiling, Celeste nodded.

Sighing, her shoulders falling, Stella nodded. "Whatever. I guess I can't do anything else now that I'm here but follow you."

Celeste didn't want it that way. Her heart sank a little. Revary gave her everything she wanted: an escape where she acquired the power to do anything, to become anything. She was in control. She wanted to share that with Stella.

"Am I powerful?" Stella asked.

Celeste shrugged. "I don't have magic. I'm a fighter." She

looked down at her outfit and noticed she had everything she'd had before: the armor, the sword, the boots.

A thoughtful frown creased Stella's face then. Seeing her contemplate sent a thrill through Celeste.

"Maybe here I have magic because I chose to be a star?" Stella only half-inquired as she rubbed her hands slowly together.

Celeste smiled. "So you *are* a star! I thought you wanted to be a sorceress."

Stella sighed. "Maybe Revary knows best. So. Magic?"

"Well, that's what I've theorized, anyway," Celeste said. She looked Stella up and down. "You make a great star. I suppose I wouldn't have spells like a star because I'm a fighter, right? They don't get spells. But Planes Strider powers, whatever those are, seem to be rather vague. I haven't tried to use them too much since the norcan tribe. It's like it called Umbra to my location, sending up a flare. Not sure why. I thought I was supposed to use magic to help Revary, but it backfired."

Stella smiled condescendingly at Celeste. "What magic did you do?"

"Magic healing." She glanced ahead, making sure they still followed the wisp. They walked deeper into the fairy forest.

"You were a fighter," Stella said with confidence. "Not a magic healer. It wasn't your role. It's like you cheated."

"What?" Celeste gasped, looking up at her friend. Then she stopped. "Well, that kind of makes sense, I guess... I didn't mean to cheat. How can I cheat in Revary?" she said louder.

Stella said stoutly, "Pick a role, Celeste. You may be all

powerful, but you have to play within this world's rules. You have to know who you are, too."

Celeste stopped, mouth agape at her friend's words. It stung to be called a cheater.

"I guess you're right," Celeste said cautiously. She glanced sideways at Stella. Her nails had turned black and a kind of purple sheen glittered over her skin. "What made you pick a star? How did you know that was even a thing here in Revary?"

Stella shrugged with one shoulder. "I think you must have mentioned it when you told me the story."

As they walked through the forest trying to keep their eyes on the wisp, Stella eventually grew wonderfully curious about the place. It was like they were tromping through the woods behind school again, as they had done as little girls, looking for unicorns.

For hours they wandered around the forest into bogs, smelly droppings, patches of mosquitoes, bushes with thorns and mud. Every time one of them slipped or groaned or cried out in pain or disgust, the wisp chuckled.

"Enough!" Stella shouted, stopping all of a sudden. "You're taking us around in circles, you little imp."

"Not imp!" the wisp chuckled, turning over in the air in delight. "Wisp."

"How do you know, Stella?" Celeste asked.

"In circles and squares and some zig-zags, as a matter of fact," it piped happily. "Or maybe just circles."

"I know you have," Stella snapped. "I have a great sense of direction right now. I've felt it for about twenty minutes, but I wanted to be sure."

"And you're positive?" Celeste asked for clarification. She

reached up and snatched the wisp out of the air, holding it tight. "I guess stars know directions?"

Stella stammered. "Uh, yeah, I guess, maybe."

"Damn, I should have been a ranger." She glared at the wisp. "You're leading us in circles."

"I am not, as a matter of fact!" it screamed, wiggling out of her fingers and rushing up to her face in a green fury, its wings making a zinging kind of buzz.

"You lied. You said you'd take us to the castle."

"Calimorden? That castle? I can take you there, as a matter of fact." It turned to buzz away again.

"Stop saying 'as a matter of fact,' " Celeste mocked at its back.

"He can't help it," a smooth, amused voice said from behind a tree. A purple hand reached out from the shadow of a tree and snagged the wisp's wings between two fingers. "It's waspish for 'I lie.' "

"Come out of the shadows," Celeste ordered, her hand going to her sword hilt.

Seeing her do this, Stella widened her stance and held her hand up. A sort of soft, wispy crackle of lightning danced between her fingers and her crown of spiking light glowed.

The being behind the tree didn't step out. It hovered into view. It was a tall, spritely boy with black hair sticking out from his head every which way, like he'd just gotten off a rollercoaster. His eyes and brows angled up in a permanent snobbish look. His purple skin contrasted with his sparkling black clothing. Iridescent purple wings with black veins spidering through them jutted up from his back. He smiled, emphasizing high cheek bones. Celeste thought he looked exactly like the kind of dark court fairy Stella would make up.

"Already the fairy realm is buzzing with talk of you and

your brave warriors," the fairy said in that smooth, lazy voice. "Even the great Umbra is aware of your meddling in its affairs of the Nether. Its power grows even more over this land now. How I hate that." He pouted and gripped the struggling wisp in his fist harder as it nearly slipped out.

"Are you a fairy?" Stella asked, smiling. "You look like goth Peter Pan."

The dark fairy smiled with a mouth full of teeth, every one of them pointed and glistening.

"I am not, as a matter of fact."

"So that means yes?" Celeste asked. The fairy blinked at her as it squished the wisp a little more. "You said that when he said 'as a matter of fact,' that meant 'I lie.' So, you are a fairy? But not like that one."

The fairy spun on his toes and made a bow that somehow felt like he was mocking them. "I like you. So astute. Jinx is the name. Serving the sorceress Zealnis through forced servitude is the game."

Celeste noted he didn't tack on the annoying phrase to the end of the sentence. Did he need to be saved, released from this sorceress? Concerned, she frowned a little. "Are you one of those fairies that can turn small like a pixie and then…" She waved her hand at him, "Turn full-sized?"

Jinx pretended to blanch at her badly-phrased question. "Absolutely not, as a matter of fact," he said. "I am never captured by Zealnis and put into a jar with no opening for air and shaken like an elixir in need of mixing, as a matter of fact."

"Oh." Celeste winced. But after the annoying interaction with the wisp, she didn't think this sorceress was in the wrong. She wanted to smash the wisp into jelly herself.

The wisp squeaked in fear as Jinx's fist squeezed again.

"Put it down, you weirdo," Celeste ordered. To her delight, he did. She met Stella's matching glare. She hated the riddling, lying characters in the games they played. But she knew how to get a little control over him. She glowered at the spritely fairy. "Listen, Jinx. Where is Calimorden? And where are my warriors?"

Jinx clenched his hands and grimaced when she said his name. "So, you are the Planes Strider. They are not far. One came to Sylvan Murk, they did. Seeking you." His purple eyes flicked between them rapidly three times. "You should meet the sorceress. She's powerful. Can help."

Celeste waited for the telling phrase, but it never came. "Okay, Jinx. Take us to Zealnis the sorceress."

Jinx hissed through his sharp fangs. He growled and clutched his throat, his eyes popping wide as he coughed. "I have spoken too much. Come to the castle. I will lead you."

"This guy is nuts," Stella whispered. "I like him."

CHAPTER 21
THE SORCERESS

W hen they broke through the woods, a stone village appeared ahead of them. Elaborate statues of warriors with flowing robes of marble stood on pedestals. Towers pierced up from every building. In the center of the stone city, a great pointed and cruel-looking castle with many spires and slender turrets clawed towards the sky.

Celeste slowed to a cautious walk, taking in the people as they crossed from the dirt road to a cobbled path. The people in the village wore only bits and scraps of graying clothes. Hoods and more wrappings obscured their faces. Their limbs almost looked like mummies, all wrapped up. The only way they could tell a person moved underneath was by the shape the tatters took. Like zombies, these people trudged about, pushing carts and shambling along the road without a desti-nation. Not one of them spoke as the group neared. When Jinx approached a cluster of them as he led them into the city, the people made a ghostly moaning sound and rushed away from him.

"Even the sky is gray," Stella mused, looking up. "No clouds, but...it's gray."

When Celeste passed them, wrapped hands went up to shield their invisible faces and they cowered beneath her as if she were a bright fire.

"Creepy," she mused. "Are they...people?"

"They are all creatures." Jinx smiled wickedly. "This is the fate of Calimorden and all of this world. Umbra's power grows. They shrink away from you because they fear that which is not like them. Not empty. Not vanished. Underneath, they are mere husks of dust."

Celeste looked around in horror. She teared up at the thought of the beautiful kingdom of Calimorden becoming like this. Great Queen Zephyr and even Prince Gwen, cowering on the ground in rags. The scene made her shudder. She could not imagine Galis or even Folkvar like this.

"Does the sorceress here know about this?" Celeste asked.

"You shall meet her," Jinx whispered.

Soon, they arrived outside the great black gates of the spired, twisted castle.

A guard in rusting armor led them through the gates and into the castle. The foyer was huge and circular with a decaying red carpet leading up a set of stairs to two more sets of stairs on either side of the room. At the top, between where they branched off, loomed a huge door. The rusty armor pointed to it.

"I don't know about this," Celeste whispered as they ascended the stairs.

"This is what we've come here for," Stella said. "Haven't you been going mad to know about this Umbra? We have to help them. Remember, you have powers here you don't have in our world."

Celeste thought for a moment, then nodded. She wanted this, wanted Stella to join her and for them to go to Revary together. To save it together. "All right."

The doors, huge steel things on massive hinges, opened wide to admit them. In the center of the large stone room was a revolving bed covered in acid green cushions. A tall, pale woman perched on it. Her seat rotated to face them.

Her eyebrows arched powerfully over long, thick, dark lashes. She wore a dress of glittering satin blue, and her hair was the same acid green as the cushions. Something in her skin sparkled. A faint blue tint hovered around the skin near her eyes and scalp that matched her dress. She held up a perfectly round glass ball in her hand.

"I saw you coming," she said in a sing-song voice. She stood up with a deep, labored sigh, the glass ball still hovering where she had left it, and took a few steps down from her throne toward them. "Dear Celeste, I have wanted to meet you. Word of your appearance has traveled far."

Celeste stammered, holding her ground as the tall, beautiful woman walked toward her. "You know me?"

The woman nodded, eyes sparkling. "I've been waiting for you. My servant has finally redeemed himself and brought you to me."

Zealnis turned her eyes to Jinx and they narrowed to golden slits. She pushed her clawed hand out to the fairy and with a magical force, propelled him into a cage that quickly snapped shut. His head hit the bars, purple-red blood trickling down from his scalp. He tried to yell back at her, but with a swift snap of her wrist, she struck him mute.

Stella covered her mouth to stifle the gasp of shock she almost let out.

"He has betrayed me for the last time," the sorceress said, pressing her hand to her forehead. "Celeste, trust no one here. With the powers in this world, you can never know who is friend and who is foe."

Celeste took a couple cautious steps forward. "Have you seen your city? It's falling apart because of Umbra. What can I do to help you?"

The woman smiled and laughed beautifully. "Do not listen to the fae, my dear," she said. "Every word they say is a lie. It is their way." She walked down to meet the two girls. "Is what they say true? Are you Planes Striders?" Her eyes went to Stella then Celeste. "You look like a warrior of Calimorden and a..." Zealnis tapped her chin, eyes narrowing. "A kind of star, perhaps?"

Celeste watched Stella as she finally dropped her hands.

"Sorceress," Stella said, cautiously taking a step toward the mute fairy. "May I heal him?"

Seeing her friend show a softness warmed Celeste inside. She eyed Zealnis, wondering if she would allow it.

Zealnis looked interested more than angry. "By all means, Planes Strider." She waved her hand slowly toward her captive.

"Wait," Celeste whispered, walking with Stella to the captured fairy. "Last time I used healing magic, it drew the vanishing to me. It appeared so fast..." The sight of the norcan being taken by the impenetrable darkness still haunted her.

Stella knelt by Jinx and motioned him forward. He cautiously came to her, his eyes locked on Zealnis, thinking she'd make a sudden move. "I told you, Celeste," Stella said with no doubt in her tone, "play by the rules. Do what your role dictates. I am a star. They heal. They protect."

She slipped her pale fingers into Jinx's hair and touched his scalp. A black and purple glow grew under Stella's palm for just a moment, then went out. She gently brushed his hair aside to look at where the damage had been. To Celeste's shock, the cut in the fairy's scalp was gone. She braced herself and looked around. Nothing came. No rumbling, no darkness.

"How did you know?" Celeste said, letting out her breath in relief. "How did you know stars heal?"

Stella didn't miss a beat and said quickly, "You told me stars are healers."

Celeste opened her mouth, but didn't speak. Had she? She didn't remember saying that. "But you said—"

"Planes Strider," Zealnis said loudly, cutting into the conversation. Celeste turned. "Would you like to see your warriors?"

"Galis? Folkvar?" she gasped. Zealnis nodded. "Yes! Are they here?"

Zealnis smiled. "I will show you."

The sorceress ordered two chariots to the front of her castle; one for her and Stella, the other for Celeste and a shackled Jinx.

Celeste eyed the gloomy fairy. "Why are you bringing him?" she asked.

Zealnis held her head high as they mounted the chariots. "He is a traitor to me and the magic people. I will not let him out of my sight. We go below."

The halls outside the main rooms of Zealnis's castle teamed with the wrapped people, who still wandered around with no goals or actions in mind. Some even bumped into walls or other villagers.

"Why do your people go around all bound up?" Celeste asked.

"Because they are no more," Zealnis said. "My people have vanished. These are their echoes. The shadows of my land. Mere shades of what once was. They are empty. Vanished."

She reached out a pale hand and pulled the hood off a passing man, wrapped up and carrying a broken sword loosely in his hand. When the hood pulled away, the man hissed and cowered under the eyes of the strangers. There was nothing under the wrapping but the vaguest shadow in the shape of a man's head. If someone did lurk beneath to give the rags shape, they were invisible.

"Without these wrappings," Zealnis said, "I have no people. As they vanished, turned to echos and shadows, they bound themselves while they still had a mind, to be able to see each other. But that is useless even now. The vanishing came slowly, taking them away piece by piece. Same as my city. It was worse than if it had all fallen at once."

THE DUNGEON BELOW WAS DANK AND WET, AS SUCH places often were. More wraiths acted as Zealnis's guards at every gate and window. After walking past cells of norcan, unicorns, other fairies, a few caged corpses, and even one that held a large tank with a mermaid in it, they finally arrived at the one Celeste was looking for. Inside, shackled to the wall and slumped over, was Galis. The oracle no longer hung on Galis's belt.

Celeste smiled at the sight of the fearless barbarian she had longed to speak to again. But her heart broke at seeing the wounds on his body.

"Release them," Celeste said, half-begging and half-ordering the sorceress.

When the woman didn't move to comply, Celeste's hand went to her sword. "Release them," she said again. She felt a sudden shift in the air as Zealnis's brows went up slowly and she smiled.

"You are the Planes Strider," Zealnis said simply. "I know you are. Jinx, my ears in the fairy world, has told me of the Planes Strider. But I never expected her to be this trusting. This naive. These prisoners were brought to me." Her green and blue eyes twinkled. "And now, you've come willingly into my prison."

"Stella, stand back. I'll get her," Celeste cried as she drew her sword, kiting away a few steps.

"No, I got this." Stella lifted her hands and a black, terrifying orb appeared. The room bent around it, pulling Zealnis toward it.

Celeste only gaped at the strange magic for a second before quickly smashing the lock with the hilt of her sword, arms strong, and dashed in to release her friend. Waking Galis with a few firm slaps, she quickly untied his arms.

"You returned!" the warrior exclaimed. "We were searching for you. We—"

"I've come with help," Celeste said, cutting him off. They could talk later.

"Folkvar was sent away through a portal," Galis panted. "He was alive last I saw him."

Stella tossed her a sword from outside the cell and Celeste handed it to Galis. "Hurry up. We have to run."

She turned back to face Zealnis. "Are you a servant of Umbra?" she asked as the sorceress struggled against Stella's strange and terrifying magic. "Did you give it this city like Queen Zephyr gave her son before I came here?"

Zealnis's beautiful face twisted into a hideous, toothy grin and a malicious laugh escaped her. "You stupid Planes Strider," she snarled. "I invited Umbra here. The more Revary is touched by his corruption, the more your world feels it. This wasn't my plan, but after what I've been shown…" Her eyes widened. "You know nothing of your own world, Planes Strider. Whatever you do here will take a toll in your world. There is darkness there, too." She smiled. "I was promised a new kingdom if I complied. A new world to reign over."

"It's all lies." Celeste didn't understand, but the impulse to run overcame her desire to ask questions. "Galis, go!" she shouted. "Stella and I will take care of her."

Galis hesitated for a moment, then ran. "Meet me outside," he called back.

"Guards," Zealnis shouted, "do not let them escape!"

Immediately, all the statues of gargoyles, wyverns, and smaller versions of spider-lizards on the wall broke free of their stone prisons and ran after Galis.

"Greylheim!" the sorceress called. "Greylheim, hear me and come to me. I have the Planes Strider."

"Stella, run!" Celeste cried as the earth shook and trembled.

Stella didn't move. "She'll get away."

"*We* need to get away," Celeste urged, taking her friend's arm. "The dragon is coming."

The earth split again, and fire spewed out in hot, rushing

torrents. Remembering what had happened the last time the giant dragon appeared, Celeste dragged Stella behind her and dashed back down the cell block, not wanting to fall and reappear in her own world just yet.

Cantering down the hall almost didn't save them. The earth and stone crumbled beneath them as Zealnis screamed behind them, "Fly, master of the wind! Stop the Planes Striders!"

The walls began to collapse around them and little gargoyles grabbed at their feet as they crawled down the walls only to fall into the ever-expanding fiery pit. With a scream, Stella tumbled as the floor dropped out from beneath her. Celeste turned and dropped to her knees, grasping her friend's hand. Beneath them, shining out from the smoke and ash in the craggy fissure, came Greylheim's orange eyes and the silhouettes of his fangs over his burning throat.

Stella took one look down and screamed in utter horror. "Celeste!" she cried.

Celeste gasped. The heat made her hands slick, and her arms burned from holding her friend up.

"Stella," a gravelly voice whispered over the debris and fire. "Come back to me and I will keep you safe."

Across the widening fissure, Zealnis floated slowly toward the struggling girls. Her green hair and blue dress snapped and waved in the hot wind from Greylheim's breath. "Listen to it, Stella. You are more powerful than her. You are a queen among Planes Striders. You understood your role. You knew how to respect Revary. Your name is a sign of your might! You are not just a star, Stella. Your role in this story is far greater than you think."

"I can't hold you!" Celeste called over the soothing voice.

Stella craned around to look at Zealnis, her tempting

colors flitting around her, her arms outstretched to her. She slowly met Celeste's gaze again. Celeste instantly saw her decision.

"No!" she grunted as Stella's hands slipped farther down.

In that instant, a huge black arrow zoomed past Celeste's ear and plunged with a jerking thud below Zealnis's chest, where her heart would be. She screamed and tumbled back to the ground. Craning her head around, sweat dripping into her eyes, Celeste saw Folkvar with a huge crossbow, coming to her aid. He charged down the corridor on a massive black warg and swept up Stella with one hand. Gripping his arm as she had seen heroes do in movies, she swung herself up. Both of them in safety, he galloped down the line of cells, covering her and their retreat from the monsters.

"Folkvar!" Celeste cried in joy. "You weren't captured?"

"Later," the norcan growled to her, focusing on the battle and the escape.

"Run, then!" Zealnis screamed from behind them. The rest of the ground broke and the walls shattered as Greylheim burst out with a deafening roar and a spew of fire.

Celeste took a crossbow Folkvar handed her and turned. She aimed up at Greylheim, who gained on them fast. Stella ducked down and clung to Folkvar's side. The huge dragon did not shrink away from the large norcan crossbow or the small Planes Strider girl wielding it.

"Stella," Celeste called, "help me!"

Stella reached up and shot blinding starlight onto the tip of the mighty arrow. Immediately it glowed and the tip extended with a black, glowing point. Celeste released the arrow then and as it flew, the star magic grew and expanded until the arrow became the size of a spear. It soared toward the unsuspecting beast.

When Greylheim opened his fiery maw to blow his infernal breath, the spear sped with Celeste's excellent aim and plunged through the back of his throat. Not expecting the hit, the dragon jerked back, its wings propelling in the opposite direction. With a strangled cry, its claws clutching at its pierced neck, Greylheim flapped and crashed to the ground with a huge thud.

Ahead, they met up with Galis, who had rounded up the warg.

"Is it dead?" Stella asked.

"I doubt it," Celeste answered. She leapt onto the warg, clicking her tongue to flee as the others followed her. "Folkvar, we need to get to Calimorden."

"What, why?" Stella asked.

Celeste felt tears well up in her eyes. "It's the only place I know here. They might know where the others are; might have heard something. We have to start somewhere."

CHAPTER 22
A FINAL COUNCIL

They fled Sylvan Murk quickly and found themselves alone once they reached the main road. The dirt path bent around the hills and forests until they reached the outskirts of the human city. Celeste looked sadly around the city of Calimorden as they passed through. The city had been devastated. Small patches of black vanished areas lurked in the oddest places, taking Celeste by surprise. Lines of the people ambled aimlessly toward the west.

"What happened?" Celeste asked, half to her companions and half in reference to the city.

Galis sighed, his breath shaking. "We lost Yilith, the oracle, the star, and Gwen."

Celeste pulled the warg up alongside him. Her heart sank and tears prickled in the corners of her eyes. "Tell me."

With a sorrowful glance at Folkvar, Galis recounted the battle they'd had with the dark star, their journey to find a way to call her back, the Mirror. Folkvar interrupted every now and then to add a detail or an exclamation of rage.

"We failed you, Planes Strider," he said at length. "Gwen fell to the vanishing. It took him into the Mirror." He dropped his great, brutish head and closed his eyes.

"The star was wounded," Galis said. "I don't know what happened to her after I was sent to Zealnis by the dark star. She took Yilith hostage."

"She spoke as you do," Folkvar went on. "Only a Planes Strider can open a portal for the vanishing as she did. We called for a Planes Strider and she came." The norcan looked confused, betrayed. "She threw me and that beast through a portal. I landed in Sylvan Murk and battled the thing for hours. Finally, it left, called home by the dark star. I wandered for days before I gathered from Zealnis's spies what had happened to Galis. I knew I had to come back and save him. Fortunately, you were there as well."

"I can't believe you lived," Stella said flatly to Folkvar.

"By the grace of the Eidolon," the norcan replied gravely.

"Gwen?" Celeste gasped. A frightened pause stole her voice. "He's gone?"

Neither Folkvar nor Galis said anything.

"And Yilith...she took him? Another Planes Strider?" she whispered in shock. "But, the dark star, she used a mirror to open a portal to Umbra?"

"So it seemed," Galis replied. "Celeste, we cannot stand up to a Planes Strider. Their power is infinite if they learn to wield it. The oracle warned us this might happen. I..." The warrior shared Folkvar's look of betrayal and hurt. "I never thought a Planes Strider would harm Revary. Attack us."

"No kidding," Celeste exhaled, still in shock. "Maybe this is what the Eidolon knew would happen. That's why he urged me to bring more over. More Planes Striders. My friends." She glanced at Stella. "You'll help me, right?"

Stella didn't meet her eyes. "I like this place. Of course I'll help. We'll go see the queen of Calimorden?"

"Right now," Celeste said, nodding to the palace gate.

The white castle was still partly in shambles from Greylheim's attack. The inside lay dark with no torches lit. Even the throne room was filled with melancholy when they entered it. A single brazier of fire flickered in the center of the hall. On the throne hunched Zephyr, her back bent and her head bowed. Beside her on a little round table hovered the oracle in his blue light.

"Celeste and company, I see," the oracle said. "Come for another round, have you, Planes Strider?"

"How did you get here?" Galis asked the oracle. "Last we saw you, you were a captive of the dark star?"

Celeste looked from the queen to the oracle. "Queen Zephyr, have you been talking to the servants of Umbra? How did you get the oracle?"

"Celeste," Queen Zephyr droned from her throne, interrupting them. "Why have you come back? You did no good last time. What makes you think you will make a difference now?" She raised her head and looked at the company before her. "A barbarian and a norcan. And who is this glowing star I see before me?" Her eyes latched onto Stella. "Why have you returned so soon? Where is my son? Was he not part of your ragged party?"

Celeste stepped forward. "As I recall, I saved him from the Nether Plane. You sent him there to Umbra to save your city. I've just come from Zealnis's realm. The place is all but destroyed. Is that what would've happened to Calimorden if you had not sacrificed Gwen?" Her voice cracked as she held back the knowledge that Gwen had been taken by the vanishing in the Mirror. He was gone despite her effort to save him.

The queen drew herself up a little more. "You speak to me as an authority? You are just a child."

This hit Celeste like a slap, making her cheeks redden. Just a child. Everyone—her parents, Justin—treated her like a child. Talked down to her. Tried to tell her what to do. Not here, not in Revary.

"I have the power to save you," Celeste said dangerously. "I am trying. I have friends who can help me." She'd wanted to bring Stella to Revary to repair their friendship, but the magical world was falling into destruction quickly. "We have a way."

"Then why are you not doing it?" Zephyr snapped.

Celeste tried to form the right words. If she explained that she had to bring her friends over, that they had to leave first to get them—Zephyr would fall into more despair.

"We have to return to our world," Stella said with so much power and authority, Celeste almost didn't recognize her voice. "Can you send us home?" Stella asked the oracle.

"Yes." It smiled in its blue light. "You've stepped into your role, haven't you? Look how powerful you are. I don't think this land is good for you, Stella." The dark mirth still twisted his voice. "You don't want to be here, but isn't that power fun?"

"Stop it," Celeste snapped. "If she wants to go home, she can. Please take her back."

"Leave?" Zephyr asked as Galis and Folkvar made grunts of concern.

The oracle swiveled its head to Celeste now. "Why do you want to abandon your friend so badly?"

"I don't," Celeste said. "I just want her safe. She'll help me bring the others. Right?"

"Of course," Stella replied.

"Very well. I'll send her home right now," the oracle said.

"Thanks." Celeste turned to Stella, but she was gone. "Where is she?" she screamed.

"I sent her home," the oracle said, false hurt in his voice. "Like you said to. Now we can really get down to business."

"That's not what I wanted!" she cried. "I wanted to explain to Stella what we needed to do first."

"She is not your friend, Celeste," the oracle warned.

She had more to say to Stella, to explain. "I wanted to share an adventure with her. To repair our friendship."

"Are you sure?" the oracle asked. "You're sure you didn't want her gone so you alone could be the hero?"

"No," she snapped, glaring at the infernal head. "I just haven't figured out how to be a hero yet. You seem to have all the answers. Tell me what to do."

A small smile spread across the oracle's face. "I cannot tell you. That's like cheating."

"So cheat," Celeste commanded.

"I can't do that," it giggled. "Remember, the magic knows when you cheat, when you don't play by the rules."

Celeste glowered at the head. Why did so many people accuse her of cheating?

"Remember the norcan tribe," the oracle murmured.

Zephyr moaned and leaned her head back into her throne, eyes closed. "This talk about the Other World means nothing to us, Planes Strider. Look at your companions. Think of them. Think of my son." She gasped to stop a sob that rose in her throat. "There is a Mirror on our Plane now, created by a

Planes Strider. An opening for Umbra to come and go as he pleases."

"The Mirror," Celeste said. "Where is it? What does that do?" She turned to Folkvar and Galis.

The warrior went slightly pale as the memory etched a fresh sorrow onto his face. "The dark star used it to bring the vanishing into the Surface Plane. There were fiends, shadows, monsters. The beast came from the Mirror and attacked us. She spoke to it."

"Mirrors," the oracle said, glaring at Zephyr as she ran her hand through his aged, brittle hair, "are portals, Celeste. Some of the oldest magic there is. A Planes Strider could use one to cross over from the Other World to Revary, or any other world filled with magic."

"There are more?" Celeste gasped.

"There are...an infinite number," the oracle said seriously. "And you—a Planes Strider—may reach any of them. But you found Revary. This thing we call Umbra is from that Other World. I don't know what it wants here or why it is making our world vanish."

"Can finding the Mirror help?" Celeste asked. She turned to face Galis and Folkvar. Her eyes caught their wounds, scars, and the weariness that tensed their muscles.

"It's far," Galis replied. "Hidden behind the cursed winter lands."

"The Planes Strider who made it can move it," the oracle interrupted. "And I think the dark star will. Especially now that her location has been discovered."

Celeste let her eyes roam around the partially destroyed throne room. With Gwen gone, she half-wanted to let Calimorden succumb to its fate. To let Zephyr have the end she clearly wanted. But the hopelessness was too much to bear. She had to save them. Even the empty, hopeless queen. She needed to make sure she understood. That if there were any risks involved, she could calculate those in. She'd told four of her friends about Revary, and Stella had come over with her. That was a good start. They could build a party, cover each others' weaknesses, and build on each others' strengths.

"Oracle," she asked, "what will it mean if Revary is destroyed?"

The queen moaned languidly and turned her head to look at the oracle, waiting for his reply.

"Ah," the head sighed, his eyes cast to the floor. "That's a complicated answer, Celeste. Revary is many things."

"What are the risks of bringing my friends over?" She didn't want to endanger them. This was her world to save.

"Only that which they do," the oracle replied cryptically. "Staying is another matter."

"Staying?" she asked, shocked. "We could...stay?"

Galis and Folkvar gave each other a quick glance.

"You could..." the oracle whispered. His old, decaying face suddenly turned distant, sorrowful. "But it changes you in ways Planes Striders are not meant to be changed. It changes the Other World, too. Celeste." He sighed so heavily she thought he might weep. "Don't stay. Don't even think about it. I mean, look at me. You don't want this."

The empty, destroyed throne hall suddenly took on an ominous aura. She could hear Folkvar's hard breathing in the silence that followed.

"All right," she said at length. "This dark star took Yilith and we don't know why. The Mirror seems to be some kind of portal for Umbra. And this dark star, this other Planes Strider, is helping Umbra bring this vanishing over in full force. I want to see Revary as it was meant to be. I will save you." She left out the part about not being sure how to do it. But she had friends who were clever and creative. She couldn't do this alone, just as the Eidolon had advised. They'd be just what she needed. "I have to go back. I have to talk to my party. But I swear, I won't let you down. I won't let you all be destroyed. They'll know what to do." She turned to face Folkvar and Galis. "Stay together. Watch for me."

Folkvar's yellow eyes firmed in fortitude and he nodded. Galis's blue eyes shone with hope.

"Trust me. I'll be back," she said.

CHAPTER 23
BREAKING POINT

T he time between her last visit to Revary and the week of Halloween, Celeste saw little of Stella. Or rather, made little eye-contact with her. They were at school together and in the same classes, but Stella spent most of her time with her eyes glued to her cellphone, sending messages to some unknown person. Taking Stella to Revary hadn't worked. It had pushed her even farther away.

"I tried talking to her," Alice whispered as Ms. Vanders handed back her tests over *A Midsummer Night's Dream*. "She either ignores me or says I have no idea what's going on in her life. And," Alice went on, examining her near-perfect score with a critical eye, "Kiyoshi wants to know why you haven't told Justin. Don't you think it may help if you tell him?"

Celeste scoffed. "What can I tell him? I mean, really."

"The same thing you told Lance and me," Alice said firmly. "Just let it come."

Not Justin. He'd never understand.

"I'll think about it," she said.

Celeste groaned and hitched her backpack higher up onto her shoulders. Alice followed her to their free period, keeping quiet. Celeste was about to suggest they all meet up in the old library when a loud voice announced, "Make way for the troll king!"

Alice made a disgusted sound and turned to walk the other way down the hall. "Garzier is on a rampage," she mumbled. "Handing out special invites to his stupid Halloween party."

Celeste stopped, turned, and faced the troll and his entourage.

"What are you doing?" Alice hissed. "I don't want to talk to him. He's my lab partner already and that's enough time with this guy."

"His dad's house is in Sunnybrook," Celeste whispered back, mentally preparing herself for coming face-to-face with the insufferable troll. "He may break our rules, do things outside the boundaries of *Sun Age*, but he throws the best damn parties in that oversized shanty of his."

"You can't be serious," Alice asked, deadpan. She gripped the straps of her backpack hard and winced. "Why would you want to go all the way up to Sunnybrook to hang out with this..." Her voice trailed off as Lance and Oran spilled into the hall with a class. "Do you all normally go?" she asked, suddenly casual.

Celeste nodded. "I'd love it if you came. And of course Lance." She laughed nervously.

"Good grief." Alice smiled. She shook her head. "Okay, I get it. I see. Fine, fine, I'll go. I'm nothing if not a good wingman."

"What's that?" Celeste asked over the din of the bells and shuffling students. "I can't hear you."

"I said 'I want some wings, man,' " Alice said quickly. "You know, sports bar wings."

Celeste smiled, confused.

Garzier approached them, his head held so high he looked down his nose at the girls. He was flanked by four other guys, two from the basketball team he used to play on. "Peasants," he said, his brown eyes sneering. "I normally wouldn't deign to speak to lowly vermin such as you."

"Shut up, Garzier. You invite me every year." Celeste held her hand out for the invitation.

The troll held it up, balancing it on the corners between two long fingers. "Perchance this year I won't?"

"Perchance I will tie you to a street lamp," Alice shot back, mocking him.

Garzier clicked his tongue. "That is no way for a lady to speak. A gentleman like myself wouldn't stoop to such base company."

"I will base the shit outta you," Alice growled. "Give up the invite or scram, twerp."

Garzier arched a black brow. "You might treat with me more civilly if you knew I hadn't yet extended an invite to that barbaric companion of yours, Celeste."

Stammering, Celeste glared at Alice. "I didn't say anything, Garz. You didn't invite Lance?"

"Not yet."

Alice groaned loudly and rolled her eyes. "I'm finished. Meet me in the old library."

Glaring hard at the troll king, Celeste proffered her hand again. "Come on, troll, I know you're inviting me. You need me for your campaign." Garzier often ran a horror one-shot campaign during his massive parties in his rich parents' house and Celeste often ran the games.

"Do I sense some discord among your party?" Garzier asked, holding the invite out of her reach. He smiled.

With a final sigh, Celeste snatched the green, gossamer paper and shoved passed him. The halls emptied out as the other classes started to fill, so she found the door to the old library without too many eyes asking what she was up to. The old library was a part of the school sectioned off behind a few very old, easy to lockpick, thick wooden doors. Students were not allowed in the area, so that made it prime turf for hanging out in peace. One door with a foggy glass square window in the middle opened onto a set of very old, creaky wooden steps that took them into the old library.

Alice was coming back down the stairs when Celeste opened the door.

"Where are you going?" Celeste asked, watching Alice.

"Someone up there wants a word," Alice replied. "I'll be right here. Don't worry."

Curious, Celeste pushed open the door. The old library was a beautiful place. Bookshelves formed perfect rows, floor to ceiling. Large, gothic windows lined the eastern wall, letting in a lot of sunlight. Dust drifted through the air, and no lights in the place worked, giving it an old, mysterious appearance. Ladders on wheels leaned against bars on top of the shelves, and Celeste had always wanted to climb one.

In a chair on the far side of the big wooden table that took up the majority of the entryway sat Justin. Celeste tried to hide the look of disappointment on her face. She started to wind her way through the stacks of books on the floor toward him.

"What are you doing up here?" she asked.

"We always hang out up here," Justin replied. He fiddled with an old battle mat and miniatures they'd left up here just in case they ever needed an escape. He looked uncomfortable. "Remember when we slew the Prime Warlock of Gesterburg up here?" He picked up a D6 and twirled it around his fingers.

Celeste stood behind him now, looking over his shoulder. He had a notebook out in front of him absolutely covered in handwriting. She could see through the pages from the way the sun hit it, and almost every page had been filled with writing.

"Yeah," she replied. "That was the first time I heard Oran exclaim in excitement. He'd been so quiet all freshman year."

Justin sighed and leaned back in the chair, despondently dropping the die. That clearly wasn't what he wanted to hear. She turned her attention to the notebook.

"Oh, what do we have here?" she asked, smiling. "A new campaign?" She faced him, leaning against the table and teasingly flipping the pages.

Justine grabbed her wrist and held it. She giggled and tried to pull away, but he held on tight.

"What's up?" she asked, her cheerful facade slipping.

Justin stood, moving in front of her so she was stuck between him and the table. "Celeste, I'm going to try this one more time."

She pulled on her arm, but he squeezed her, making her stop. "Hey, cut it out." She tried to smile and make light of his force.

"You cut it out," he shot back. He leaned onto her, making the edge of the table press uncomfortably into her. "Celeste, this is the last time I'm going to try to convince you."

"Of what?" she grunted, trying again to pull away. "You're freaking me out."

Justin sighed and held her hand down at her side, pressing it into the table. He grabbed her other hand and looked her dead in the eye. "I need you to listen for five minutes, that's all."

She gulped but nodded.

He took a deep breath. "We are out of here sooner than you think. I've applied for a big school down south and…" He smiled, so proud. "I got in. You can, too. Celeste, if we work hard and keep our heads down, we can graduate in four years."

Confused and having no idea what he was going on about, she shook her head and frowned.

"No, listen," he snapped, crushing her hands. "This is the only way I can get you to stop for a second and hear me out. Stop struggling!" he barked when she pulled again.

"Okay, Justin, what the hell?" she asked, her voice breaking. "You don't have to interrogate me like I'm a prisoner of Dunbar. I'm listening."

"You don't. You never do," he replied. "It's harder than ever now with that bitch-boy athlete hanging around."

"Lance?" she gasped.

"Celeste," Justin began again. "Come with me. Apply. You'll get scholarships. You can apply for grants. We can get this done and get started on our lives."

"*Our* lives?" she asked for clarification. "Justin, our lives are not connected after high school."

"You sure?" he whispered dangerously. "Because I see you trying your damndest to keep us together. I know what you're feeling, I get it."

"Oh, no, no," she stammered. "I just mean the friend

group. Justin, we've been friends forever. I don't want that to change."

"I do," he said, leaning closer to her. "I want us to be more than friends. You're so smart, creative, driven. You just need someone to guide that ambition. To control that wild spirit."

One word in that sentence set her heart hammering in fright. "I don't need anyone to control me," she said. "I can figure out what to do on my own."

"You do, though." He pressed himself into her again. "You go after things that you can't take down. Like in *Elderforge* during the summer. You took on more opponents than you could handle and had to cheat to win. You even went up against me. I can help you. Let me lead you to victory, Celeste."

Below, Lance, Oran, and Kiyoshi's voices rose up to them. Stella's came in a grumble as the stairs creaked with the others ascending. Alice stopped them halfway up the steps and muffled conversation could be heard. Celeste got the sudden urge to call for them to come up.

"So," Justin went on. He was so close to her. Her cheeks flushed and she turned her face away. "Stop waiting for someone to hand you a plan for life, because they won't. Join mine. Support me and I'll support you. If you won't choose what you want to do in life, let me choose for you."

"And then?" she whispered, clenching her eyes shut as he was so close now his nose almost rubbed her cheek. *Don't make me hate you now*, she begged. They were old friends. Why was he doing this? Changing their dynamic?

"We start a life together," he said.

"Justin," she gasped, opening her eyes. "I don't like you like that. Please, back up." She shoved against him, but that had been the wrong thing to do.

Justin growled and shoved her back hard so she bent backward over the table, falling onto it. She cried out and scrambled to get up, but he blocked her way, trapping her between the table and him.

"Stop!" she cried, trying to jerk her hands away.

"Calm down. I just want to talk," he said over her. "You're making this way worse than it is. Listen, okay?" He let her up, but didn't let her flee.

Below, the voices had stopped.

"I'm doing you a favor!" Justin growled. "You're lucky I decided on you. I could have anyone."

"Then take anyone," she shot back. "You're ruining years of friendship."

"*You* are!" he snapped back. "This is the natural next step. Why are you fighting it?"

She held still, locking her eyes onto him. "I don't like you like that. Why can't we stay friends?" Tears filled her eyes. No, they couldn't be friends after this.

"I never saw you as a friend," Justin confessed. His hand snapped to her face, gripping her chin so hard her cheeks were crushed into her mouth. "I've waited our entire lives for you, Celeste. Waited for you to find yourself and realize your potential."

She fought to speak around his iron grip, her lips smashing together into what she knew was a forced pucker. "You wasted your time, then."

"You'll change your mind."

She shoved Justin off and fell, crawling over a mountain of books.

"Get away from me!" she screamed, hurrying toward the door on all fours.

Justin grabbed for her, to pull her back, but the door burst open.

"Justin, stop!" Lance shouted, shoving Justin away from Celeste.

Instinct kicked in and all sense flew out of Justin's head. He cocked his fist back and swung with all his might. He stepped into the swing and turned at his middle. The might of the punch staggered her, but hit Lance square in the eye.

Lance gasped, more in shock than anything else, and stumbled back. Stella and Alice shrieked and leapt out of the way as Lance tripped over a pile of dusty old books. The books more than the punch made him lose his footing and he fell hard. His head cracked against a leg of the huge wooden table.

Oran made a loud cry and rushed to his side, stammering and asking if he was all right. A black and purple bruise already bloomed around Lance's face. A tear dripped down his cheek, purely pulled just from the impact. Lance wiped at it savagely, teeth bared up at Justin.

"Lance," Oran started, but Lance shoved him off and stood. Oran stumbled and fell. Celeste took in Oran's shocked and wounded expression.

"Get out," Lance said measuredly. He towered over Justin, chest heaving in controlled gasps.

Celeste shook, partly from fear, partly from the tension that coursed through her. Her cheeks burned and she swore she could still feel his fingers crushing them. Justin met her eyes. He took one step toward her, hand up, lips parted to speak, but Lance and Alice each took a threatening step forward.

"Really, guys?" Justin snapped. "You going to team up on me?"

"We don't have to," Oran said from the ground where he'd fallen.

"I think it's best you go," Alice whispered softly.

A tense ten seconds of silence filled the old library before Justin spat, mumbled obscenities, and turned. He knocked over every pile of books on his way out and shoved Kiyoshi down as he passed him. He slammed the door. A man outside the door swore as Justin blazed past him.

"Kiyoshi, are you okay?" Celeste asked, helping her friend up.

The meek boy nodded. "Never seen him like that. That was scary." He moved to start lovingly picking up the books and re-stacking them with care.

Lance turned to Oran and pulled him up, giving him a quick one-sided hug. "Sorry. I just had to—"

"I know," Oran cut in, his face reddening. "I figured after. Someone had to step up to him."

Alice agreed, slapping Lance affectionately on the shoulder before bending down to help Kiyoshi stack the books. Celeste watched Lance as he let Oran inspect his growing bruise. He'd been brave. She'd thought she could handle Justin, but he'd hurt her. She wrapped her arms around herself and let Alice put a bracing arm around her. If Lance hand't been there, if the others hadn't come in when they had, she didn't know what she would have done.

"Actually," Stella cut in, pocketing her phone. "You didn't have to do that, Lance."

Celeste looked up, shocked. "What are you talking about? Justin's lost it, Stell. He's got no grip on reality anymore."

Stella's black brows shot up. "Really, Celeste? This coming from you? You're so unhinged that you've gone off and escaped into your own little fantasy world, leaving the rest of us behind. So much for wanting the group of friends to stay together." She began to walk toward the door. "I heard you in there. I saw you."

The others all stood still as stone, watching Celeste. Her mouth went dry and she couldn't swallow.

"But, Stell," she stammered, "I took you over. I showed you. I need you all."

Stella clipped her hard with her shoulder, shoving past. "Focus on your world, Celeste. And I'll focus on mine."

Completely at a loss, Celeste watched Stella vanish out the door, slamming it. Oran appeared at her side, close behind her. She felt his desire to hold her hand so she gave in. She turned, wrapping her arms around his neck and buried her face in his shoulder. His dyed hair was soft against her cheek and smelled like he'd just freshened the color last night. A hand, strong with long fingers, rested on her back and gently patted her. She knew it was Lance.

Why was everything falling apart? Why could she not fix everything and keep all her friendships in tact? Keep them together? Things were moving fast and she couldn't get a grip on them, keep them strong. It felt like a losing battle. Like the others didn't care they were drifting apart. Of course they'd made new friends and that kind of thing always strained old relationships, but Celeste couldn't see how adding two new players could divide them that much. And Lance and Alice were amazing people, bringing strengths they didn't have.

They were a well-balanced party.

Oran gently pulled her arms from around his neck and slowly turned her toward Lance. She let him, wrapping her arms around Lance's middle and sniffling away her emotion.

"Thank you," she said to him. She knew Justin wouldn't

have hurt her, but what he'd done had ruined any chance of keeping him as a friend.

Lance put one arm around her neck and one hand on the back of her head to shelter her. She loved his warm fingers in her hair. In that moment, she knew she had to bring them to Revary. All of them, if she could. They would help her save Revary and stay strong together.

CHAPTER 24
HALLOWEEN

L ance suggested they all meet up at the game store before Garzier's Halloween party so they could drive up together. He busily managed a large group of freshmen and young kids at a table in the middle of the store. The owner of the store, hearing school had let out, called him in almost instantly to work, since he was free. Oran told Lance that Garzier the troll king would be hosting his massively popular Halloween party at his parents' house. They lived in one of the richest neighborhoods and basically allowed the troll to do whatever he wanted. Oran told Lance the group went purely for the fantastic house and the unbeat-able snacks and drinks his mom served. His parties, despite who he was in real life and *Sun Age*, were the best. His mom had been some big-shot actress in the Middle East and his dad had been a wealthy producer before they'd moved to the country. The parties were lavish, and if Lance was being honest with himself, he was excited to see the troll's house.

"It's his parents' house," Oran offered as he helped one of

the younger players do the math on his character sheet. "He lives in that big neighborhood behind the country club. They put him in the public school to make sure he turns out normal. So much for that."

"Must be a humbling experience," Lance mused, thinking of the troll in their very normal high school.

"I think that's the point," Oran agreed, handing the pen back to a little Korean boy.

Lance looked back at his table of adoring ten year olds. "Got it figured out, Hans?"

"I killed you for forty!" the boy called across the table to Lance. "Your orc is dead and I won. You lose."

"No, Hans," Oran explained. Lance sighed in frustration as the small child once again derailed his campaign.

"There is no winning in *Runes and Empires*," Lance shouted back playfully.

"I can win!" the boy cried back. "You lose."

Confused and genuinely baffled, Lance picked up the guidebook. "It says right here that the point is to play the adventure, Hans. I'm the game master. I don't get to win."

"Which means you lose!" Hans insisted.

Oran stepped in. "Your wizard moved forward and that stone is a trap. You activated the poisoned darts in the wall. You can either roll a saving throw or try to roll to get out of that hallway. Either way, you killed your elf friend behind you."

"What?" a girl exclaimed as she realized her friend had led her into a trap. "Did you not see the crack? That can mean there's a trap. Use your seeing-eye spell!"

"Okay, kids," Lance sighed, pulling his hair up into a ponytail. "I am out now and Donny will be here in five minutes to finish up the campaign. Take a break and no cheating."

"Winning is not cheating," Hans quipped.

"Hans, there's no winning in—" Lance bit his tongue. "Never mind. You want to win? You win."

"I will." The boy smiled.

The bell rang on the front door just as Lance and Oran reemerged into the front of the store. Celeste, Alice, and Kiyoshi came in, taking a table near the front. Celeste smiled up at him as he came and joined their table, with Oran close behind him. Kiyoshi opened his laptop and plugged in to the internet quickly.

"Sorry," he apologized as the others pulled out their table top equipment. "There's a raid in *Elderforge* for a sword I've been wanting."

"The Blade of Amaronath?" Oran asked. "I got it last week. It's amazing."

Celeste looked up, her face bemused. "I tried to get it last month when it first dropped, but I couldn't. How did you?"

"We're fighters," Lance offered. "The sword is class-based."

"Classist," Alice grumbled in good humor.

"Oh," Celeste said. She dropped her hands onto the table for a moment, looking despondent.

"If you want," Lance cut in quickly, "you can start a new character, and I'll grind with you." He felt Oran's eyes flick to him without moving his head. "I need to grind anyway."

Oran's pale fingers spun a D4 anxiously. Guilt filled Lance right away, knowing how Oran felt about Celeste.

"We can all go," he added, nudging Oran with his elbow.

"Won't that split the XP too much?" Celeste asked.

"Actually, no," Lance replied with a smile. "The caves, the ones with that purple stuff I keep calling jello. Oran?"

Oran's dark eyes lit up. "Oh, yeah, the Caves of Moridium. It will get really boring, but the creatures in there give triple XP."

Celeste smiled across the table at Oran and Lance. "You'd do that? Just so I can have the sword?"

"Sure," Oran said, looking far more at ease. "We could just talk while we destroy some little purple goblins."

They set up their battle map and Kiyoshi joined them moments later, having acquired the sword. Lance led them through a little bit of role play before they started a dungeon crawl he'd been planning for weeks. They had a few random encounters to get some potions and random loot before he led them into the darker, more twisted parts.

"I cannot believe you're going to the troll's party," Alice said to the whole group once they were well underway. "I have never been and I really don't want to start now."

"I need you to come," Celeste said, having her character loot the items that dropped from their recent battle while Alice was distracted. "I have something to ask you all and I just feel like I could do it better after a huge party."

"At the house of our enemy," Oran added sadly, moping through his black bangs.

Lance slung his muscled arm around Oran's narrow shoulders. "Think about it this way. We go to his place, where he is king, ignore him to his face, eat his food, drink his wine, dance, party, and he can't stop us." He finished by roughly ruffling Oran's hair, leaving it uncharacteristically messy. "Alice, from where you're standing, you see a dark hallway."

"That makes sense," Alice laughed. "Hey, let's go loot this mysterious dark hallway I just found. I guess I could do that."

She switched back and forth between game-talk and reality flawlessly. "Do we have to use these costumes, though?" She had been disgusted at buying an in-a-plastic-bag costume from the super store down the street.

"The rules are no *Sun Age* costumes," Kiyoshi reminded her.

The group fell strangely quiet as they made their way through the in-game cave. Normally they'd be packing and getting ready for a weekend of *Sun Age*. But not now. Celeste hadn't sent out any messages about it since Stella had turned distant. They had waited on her to give the all clear so they could let their clans know, but she hadn't said anything about it. Not with Stella gone and after the incident with Justin.

Lance looked up from his game master screen and studied each of them as they did some light role play with an NPC he'd dropped in for flavor. Despite not wanting to break up the party, he was witnessing the demise of years of friendships. Had he come in just at the end to leave after graduation, losing the new friendships?

He caught Celeste chance a look up and noticed no one looked at her for an answer or a prompt for the puzzle they'd encountered. Except Oran. His black-rimmed eyes met hers for what felt like the first time in forever. Surrounded by their blackness, they seemed bluer than before. Rounder and more inquisitive. He tried to ask her something with his eyes, but she didn't seem to notice. Lance felt for Oran. He made up his mind then to try to get Oran to ask Celeste out at the party. He'd give her up if it meant everyone could still be friends.

"Okay then," Lance said loudly after a few hours of *Runes and Empires*. "Let's terrorize some trolls tonight."

THERE WAS NO DENYING THE GRANDEUR OF THE party. The troll king's neighborhood was rich and full of every kind of Halloween party. Other houses on his road vibrated and thudded with similar parties. His house was the most decorated. Black and orange glitter and party decorations covered the facade of the house. The entire front lawn had been turned into a realistic-looking graveyard complete with animatronic zombies, skeletons, and fog. His mother had really outdone herself on entertainment as well. The huge backyard had been converted into a dance floor where a DJ had what must have been their entire class dancing. A trio of gothic dancers in shimmery black costumes had even been hired to get the party started. Somehow, the lights in the gigantic pool glowed purple and soft. Round orbs the size of softballs floated on the surface. Garzier's mother floated around, talking energetically with a few kids, showing them pictures on her phone of her "back in the day." She was a tall woman with beautiful brown eyes and black hair to rival a fairy tale princess. But it was all straightened and gelled to stick up in a shape that reminded Celeste of a dandelion. She wore a black dress with a plunging neckline.

Celeste felt awkward at first because she didn't even know the hostess's name. "Mrs. Halabi," the troll's mom said happily, adjusting her Elvira wig. "But you can call me Farasha." No one remembered Garzier's name, either. He had gone by Garzier or troll king for so long, they had all forgotten his last name. Mrs. Halabi had drunk just enough that she let cascades of high school kids cross her threshold and took their coats and bags before announcing that she'd "go upstairs and leave you kids alone."

After a few rounds of walking alone through the party, Celeste spotted Stella alone with her phone. She wasn't dressed up—just wore jeans and a black camisole with a lacy bolero shrug. Her face turned down into a genuine pout. Celeste made her way cautiously to her friend's side and tapped her on the shoulder.

Stella turned, clearly expecting someone else. Her face fell like a rockslide. "Oh. You."

"Stell, can we talk?" Celeste begged.

"About what?" Stella quipped. "How you let Justin and Lance get into a literal fistfight over you? Which is pathetic and gross, by the way. Or how it looks like Donny stood me up? Or how you want to transport your friends over to a magical world so you can live out some hero fantasy? Thanks for sending me ahead, by the way, so you could stay behind."

The last one took Celeste by surprise. Her mind whipped back through everything Stella had just said. She went for the most normal one first. "Donny? The guy who works at the game shop? We don't even know him."

Stella gave her a sardonic smirk. "I do. We've been talking for a while now. Since you won't talk to me."

Celeste stammered, the words refusing to leave her throat. "I want to talk to you. I want to know what the hell is going on and why you're so upset."

This seemed to be the wrong thing to say. Stella's sad eyes fell even more. "If I have to explain it to you, Celeste, you will never get it."

"Could you try, please? I thought if I shared Revary with you, you'd understand. I thought we were best friends."

Stella made a guttural scoff that almost sounded like a

snicker. "We were never best friends, Celeste. You're lonely and pathetic. I'm the only one who put up with your whining and moaning all these years. And your weird fantasy escapism." She raised her brows. "You suck in real life, and you suck in Revary. You can't figure out how to grab ahold of your potential. But, oh, maybe that's because you have none."

Stella pushed past her and grunted loudly.

The words struck Celeste so hard, she lost her voice. Her legs went numb.

"And another thing," Stella said, whipping around to face her. "Tell Oran you're not interested before he wastes his life pining over you. You're pathetic and not worth it. Stop pretending like you don't know how he feels about you so you can play innocent when he finally snaps."

"I-I don't even— What are you—"

"Exactly," Stella interrupted. "You have him on hold while you go over scenarios of you and Lance. That's why you always talked me out of making my move on Oran."

"No," Celeste growled, pointing a strained finger at Stella. "I talked you out of hitting on Oran because you wanted to posses him. And he wasn't interested."

"At least I liked him and let him know."

"Like Justin let me know?"

Stella's eyes bulged and tears instantly fell from both of them, making black lines down her cheeks.

"You don't understand, Stella," Celeste tried again, reeling in her malice.

"Understand what? That friendship is magic and I need to believe in it, let you run all over me, tell me what to do? It's not that simple."

Baffled, Celeste watched Stella leave out the front door. She followed at a trot and saw her greet the guy, Donny, from the game store. If she remembered correctly, Donny was a junior. Despite that, he sat astride a motorcycle and handed Stella a helmet before she climbed on and they sped off into the night.

"That's cool, I guess," she sighed. Donny had done nothing to her personally, but she loathed him now for taking Stella away. She stood outside and was taking in the troll's magnificent front yard when a voice interrupted her.

"The troll wants to do his one shot," Oran said meekly behind her. She turned, happy to see him. "He said you have to come or he'll kick you out."

Celeste rolled her eyes and wiped at them quickly, realizing a tear had appeared. She slung her arm around Oran and went back inside. "Well, I'd hate to get thrown out. Especially since I think I saw a cheese fondue fountain inside."

The party thumped around them. A minion of Garzier's came down a long winding staircase and ordered Celeste and Oran up "to the master's chambers."

"Gross," Oran mumbled. "Don't phrase it like that."

The upper level of the house seemed to belong entirely to Garzier and his obsession with *Runes and Empires*, *Elderforge*, and live action role play. The walls had murals of fields and castles painted on them. The lighting glowed dim and wavered like a fire somehow. A huge round table sat in the center with throne-like chairs around it. Celeste spotted the others already sitting around it.

"Ah, Celeste, the master of all," Garzier said in a bizarre accent. "We are pleased you have joined our table."

"Oh, yes, kind wench, fetch me some juice," Alice replied in a nasally accent. She held a goblet with her pinky out to the side.

Celeste let a small smile brighten her face, but the gloom

✕ 289 ✕

from the lashing Stella had given her lingered. Oran guided her to a seat between him and Lance. Kiyoshi, looking oddly satisfied, sat next to Garzier with a bowl of cheese sauce and a bag of chips.

"Welcome to Brightonhold, the realm of the most powerful half-orc kingdom," Garzier began, handing them all character sheets already filled out. "Today you are tasked with investigating a portal that has appeared in a nearby village. Monsters and ghosts have come through it, terrorizing your orcish kingdom. You must find a way inside, discover the source of the power behind the attacks, and make it back alive. The only way to it is through a haunted realm known as The Harrowing Spine."

Lance hummed, looking surprised. "Not bad, troll."

Garzier smirked. "Nothing I do is bad, nor mediocre, for I am a master of my craft. And the blade," he added, giving what he must have thought was a dangerous look around the table.

Kiyoshi rolled his eyes so hard Celeste expected them to stay in the back of his head.

Alice picked up a dice tray and took a bag Garzier offered them. She hummed in delight when she dumped out a set of emerald and gold dice. "So, let's say—for example—we go inside this portal world."

Alice looked up quickly, meeting Celeste's eyes before turning back to the table. Celeste's heart jumped.

"How do we get back?" Alice asked.

Garzier smiled. "You are standing outside the portal when a man with blue skin approaches you."

"No," Kiyoshi moaned, leaning his head back. "Not another main character NPC, troll. Let *us* play the damn game."

The troll glared, keeping eye contact as he placed a miniature on the battle mat. "This is a one shot. I have to have some control. And my mom wants you out of here by three in the morning, so..."

"Just go on," Oran said.

Garzier did. "The stranger tells you that one must stay behind as an anchor, to bring the others back."

Celeste's heart jumped into her chest. "An anchor. So, there is a chance we won't come back?"

The troll looked up, clearly surprised by her taking an actual interest in his game. But it wasn't his game she wanted to know about. *There are rules,* she told herself. *I have to know what they are and follow them.*

"Yeah," she started, studying the miniatures before her. "We all were given roles, right? Alice is a warrior. I'm..." Her heart dropped a little and she sighed. "I'm a healer."

"That's a noble role," Oran tried. "Without a healer and someone to buff us, we'd never win fights."

True, she thought. *But I'd rather hack and slash. No one wants to stand back and throw spells. But this was the role I was given...*

The star was a healer. But she was gone now. The dark star Galis had mentioned must have been the opposite of that: destructive. That was why the darkness had swallowed up the norcan camp: she'd used a healing spell when she wasn't a star. Umbra must have felt it and known immediately that a Planes Strider had appeared. Celeste finally understood.

Lance added, "And I'm an arcane fighter. I have tons of ways to shield and protect you."

Celeste blushed. "But would you mind being the healer?" she teased.

To her surprise, Lance shrugged. "No. That's what team-work is."

She sat back, quiet. Did Revary really have a role for her to play that she just had to accept?

No, she thought to herself. *That's who I've always been. I tried to mediate at home. I tried other ways of keeping our friend group together. I'm a healer. That's who I am.*

"Right," Garzier went on. "You have been given roles. How you use those roles is up to you. This is Brightonhold after all. The possibilities are endless."

"Is this a world you made?" Lance asked.

Garzier nodded.

"Can I respec?" Celeste asked.

The troll didn't take her bait. He smirked. "Why? So you can dump all your stats into strength and try to change to a fighter? No. Respecing is cheating at this point."

No cheating, she thought. Why did so many people accuse her of cheating?

Then it hit her.

She *had* cheated in *Elderforge.* She didn't cheat in Sun Age, but that was because it was her game. She was the game master. She didn't have to cheat. If she didn't like how a story went, she could guide the players to a new outcome. She made the rules. She never cheated in *Runes and Empires,* despite what Justin thought. But she never played a different role. Always the paladin, the warrior, the fighter. Never a tank to protect her team. Never a healer to keep them strong and buff them. She always had to be in control. That was the role she'd given herself. Revary had a different role for her. She needed to play the part Revary needed. She had to give up what she wanted in order to save it.

"Damn," she whispered, sinking into the chair. Her spirits

fell a little. Stella had been right; she wanted to be the hero for Revary. It was the only place she'd felt in control. But the more she fought to be in control, the more she destroyed Revary. "I won't cheat," she sighed, sitting up. She met each of her friends' eyes. "I'll play by the rules, even if I cannot make the rules."

"You can't," Garzier said simply. "This is my table. My rules."

She nodded. "Got it, Troll King."

Kiyoshi shrugged. "You still get to make your own story. There's always ways to min/max, even within certain parameters. You just have to figure out how."

Celeste looked at Alice. "If you could be any role you wanted in real life, what would it be?"

Alice hummed, tapping her chin and smiling. "Well, since I'm going first, I can pick whatever I want. You guys have to build a team around me."

Lance chuckled. "Just tell us."

"A fighter," Alice said easily. "I'm strong. Tall. Always looking out for others. Even if it annoys them." She smiled. "Oran?"

Celeste looked at him next. He paled a little and stammered until Lance gently nudged him.

"It's not glamorous, but I'd be a fallen arcane sorcerer," he said.

Garzier spit a laugh. "Not an edgy rogue?"

Oran shook his head. "Lance?"

"I like arcane, too," he started, running his hands through his hair. Celeste loved how his shiny brown hair caught the fake torchlight. "But I'd be an arcane paladin. Like, a warrior with magic, but with lots of points in strength."

"A little too much book learning for you, jock," Garzier shot. They ignored him.

Celeste froze as they all turned to look at her. "Well," she sighed, "if that's the party, we don't have a healer."

"I can change," Alice offered.

"No, don't," Celeste cut in. "I need to learn other roles anyway. If I don't try other things, how will I know what I truly am? I'll be a healer. Someone who can help, fix things. Protect the group. Kiyoshi?"

On the other side of the table, Kiyoshi looked up, thinking. "I've never been one for action. I don't like conflict. From here, it's okay, because I'm safe around a table."

"You could be our anchor," Alice suggested. "Safe, but helpful."

Kiyoshi smiled. "I could do that."

"I'd be a paladin," Garzier said, holding his head up high. They ignored him.

Celeste smiled, knowing why her friends had indulged her side conversation like they had. Her heart warmed and tears filled her eyes.

"Well, damn, if you're going to cry about being a healer, you can change," Garzier shouted, planting his palms firmly on the table.

"No," she said, sniffling. "I'll be a healer. I know who I am now."

CHAPTER 25
THE ARCANE PLANE

L ance drove to the park an hour before Celeste had said to meet there. He left his car in the lot near the entrance where it branched off toward either the lake or deeper into the woods. Knowing she would go to their great hall, what they called the big shelter with the huge fireplace, he went to the lake. They'd agreed to meet early in the morning, so the dew still clung to the grass and a mist hung over the water. He leaned over the railing of a tiny deck, looking down into the water. It was so clear he could see an old set of stairs leading down. It looked like an underwater dungeon they might crawl in *Runes and Empires*.

The conversation on Halloween played over in his head. He'd been the one, later, to suggest they all cross into Celeste's world together.

"You're early," a soft voice said behind him.

He turned to find Celeste walking toward him. She wore jeans that hugged her thighs and a green hoodie. She looked tired. "I wanted to mentally prepare," he joked. He had also been hoping she'd show up. She joined him, her elbow close to his as they both leaned over the lake together.

"So," he asked cautiously, "how does this work?"

Celeste smiled dolefully. "I'm just figuring it out. But I used this last time." She pulled a string out from under her shirt. On the end hung a glittering green D20. "I, uh, got you one, too." Shyly, she reached into her pocket and pulled out a similar necklace. The D20 on the end was white and pearly, with gold lettering. "For a paladin, I thought."

A genuine smile broke the worried furrow on Lance's brow. "Thanks, Celeste." He took the necklace and slipped it over his head. "Feels right."

Celeste blushed madly, smiling and trying to hide her face. "To cross over, I've learned that we have to pick a role. Decide who we are. But we have to stick to what we've chosen to be." She chewed the inside of her cheek and looked up at him. He loved her crystal clear green eyes. "I was a fighter, because I wanted to be strong. But then I tried to magically heal. Because Planes Striders—us—we have any power we want there. But we can't abuse it. We can't... become gods." She leaned back, arching her back and closing her eyes. "It hurt the people there, brought this darkness to the place and devoured them."

"Holy shit," Lance murmured. "Like a beacon. Like using our powers outside the parameters of what you chose signaled to it that you were there."

She nodded. "Sticking to arcane paladin?"

He looked down at her. She was so much shorter than him. Something in her eyes waited for his answer, hoped for a certain reply. "Yeah, like I said the other night. Strong, magic wielder, wings. So I could…" He stopped himself. Was it too embarrassing to say?

"So you could watch my back," she supplied, not using the words he had initially wanted to say. But close enough. "Because I'll be a healer."

"Yeah." The reply came whispered. His eyes traveled down her face to her small pink mouth. His throat went dry as the sand in summer. He wanted to lean down to her. To kiss her. To let her know that he'd protect her no matter what. She made him want to be brave.

"Hey, guys," Alice called, waving from just beyond the bend in the gravel path. "We're here. Should we head to the shelter?"

"So," Kiyoshi said when they all stood in a circle around him in the shelter, "the theory is that I'll act as an anchor. I'll focus on you and maybe some memories we have together. Something to ground you here."

"Will that work?" Alice asked.

"We're just trying for now," Oran said. He stood between Lance and Celeste. "If we are Planes Striders, maybe we can send ourselves back?"

"Maybe," Celeste offered. "I've never tried. I wonder if it will open up a portal for more of this Umbra to come through, though."

"We'll all be there," Alice said, taking Celeste's hand in hers. "We'll be strong together. We can figure it out."

She nodded and Lance met her eyes.

"Close your eyes," Celeste whispered. "I think the magic doesn't like to be witnessed. Let it take us all at once."

Lance heard her breathing hard, whispering, "Revary, open up to me. Someone is calling. They have to be."

He tried the same thoughts, adding how they wanted to help. To save that place. "What do we do once we get there?" he asked softly.

Celeste hummed. "The Eidolon said to bring you over. I'll take you to him."

Lance nodded.

"Do you feel that wind?" Oran asked beside him.

"Yeah," Lance breathed. "It's cold. And something is coming in on the wind."

"Like mist," Oran replied.

Lance touched the D20 necklace. *Send us to Revary,* he thought.

A million sensations overtook Lance at once. His stomach flipped like he had missed a step in the dark. Powerful muscles he'd never felt before flexed on his back, jerking him upward. Like Oran had pointed out, something like mist filled his lungs when he breathed. Beside him, Oran dropped away and screamed like he'd been killed.

The terrified shout forced Lance's eyes open. Sun blinded him, like he was on the same level as the fiery orb. Clouds engulfed him and strong winds battered against his body. But something—coming from the powerful muscles on his back —held him still against the wind. Oran's dark form vanished into the clouds, his desperate scream fading.

Cursing, Lance reached for Oran, diving through the clouds on instinct. A powerful beat behind him was quickly followed by the flashing of bright, white feathery wings at his sides. They were his, attached to his back and thrusting him down while angling into the wind to hold him aloft.

Propelled by gravity and his magnificent new wings, Lance reached Oran and snatched him up, shooting back up through the clouds. Unused to the strength of the wings, Lance rocketed himself and Oran higher than before. They burst through a thick cloud into a magnificent airship-filled village.

Oran gasped, clutching Lance hard. "Get us down," he begged.

"Where?" Lance asked, seeing mostly clouds, rope bridges, and strange piers beneath them.

"Literally anywhere," Oran pleaded.

Lance felt a strange pain as Oran's grasping fingers found the short, sensitive feathers at the base of his wings near his back. Oran had wrapped his arms around him and scrambled for anything to hold on to. Under his own fingers, he felt rough feathers on Oran's back, too.

Spotting an actual hard surface, Lance aimed for where the airship docks turned into a village. He noticed every being, human in shape, had wings. Some walked along the ground, which was covered in clouds, and some flew or hovered, catching the drafts. He tried to land gently but his knees buckled when he hit the ground too hard. Oran flew from his arms, rolling over the ground and he soon joined him in a heap of limbs and wings.

When he sat up, Lance took in the place they'd fallen into. Clouds covered almost everything in thick white blankets. But the village shone: everything was made of either brass, gold, or shiny gems. Every structure—house or shop—had a huge telescope sticking out the top. They'd landed in a small manicured garden outside what looked like a gem-encrusted observatory. The sky above opened up, utterly cloudless.

Struck mute, Lance rose and helped Oran up. He looked down to take in his new clothing. A white wide-sleeved coat, tight breaches, and shiny boots covered his body, and what he would call a pirate hat topped it off. A fall of feathers fluttered from the brim. He laughed and looked down at himself. On his right arm, a kind of arcane-powered metallic glove glowed with gems and soft wisps of purple puffed out.

"What's that do?" Oran asked.

Lance laughed when he saw his friend in similar—though black—attire.

"I think we're arcanists?" Lance said. "I think that's what that symbol means." He pointed to a pendent around Oran's neck. "Like a mix between arcane magic and tech or something."

"Arcana-tech is what Celeste called it once," Oran offered. His eyes drifted to the magnificent wings on Lance's back, folded gently. "Damn, that's kind of cool."

Lance craned his neck around to take them in. He tried to unfurl them, but didn't know which muscle to flex. The instinct hit him and the right wing unfurled, arching forward. He touched the feathers and marveled at the sturdiness. "This is weird," he said, smiling, eyes wide. He looked at Oran. "You have wings too, but…"

He walked behind Oran and touched the broken, brittle feathers on his black wings. They hung weakly down his back like a cloak.

"Figures," Oran sighed. "I would have broken wings."

"The price of dark Arcana-tech," a strong female voice said behind them. They whirled around to see a tall woman in a nautical hat and coat clomp toward them in thigh-high leather boots. She had messy, long chestnut hair and wings like Lance's folded behind her. She wore a saber on her hip and a smug expression on her face. "A true arcanist and a rogue arcanist together?" she asked. "Unnatural."

"We don't want any trouble," Lance said quickly. He suddenly felt the weight of a weapon at his side, too. He glanced down to see a long, straight, one-sided blade with a revolver for a handle.

"Don't even think about it, boy," the woman said, seeing him eye his weapon. "If you don't want any trouble, why did you crash into my observatory mere moments before take off? Are you here to track the beast and take it before us?"

He saw now that a dock, high up on the building, supported a medium-sized ship with sails furled, some off to the side like wings.

"And with a rogue arcanist?" She clicked her tongue and sauntered toward them. "Perhaps you are here to stop our hunt for some bounty?"

Lance shook his head and put himself between the woman and Oran. "You're bounty hunters?"

The woman smiled, shrugged, and quickly glanced at her ship above them. "You looking for work? A ship is the safest way to the Surface Plane. We don't typically frequent it, but it's so full of Nether scum these days that the urge to slaughter has me mad with desire."

So they were killers. Lance met her eyes carefully. "Surface Plane?"

The woman narrowed her eyes. "Yes," she said measuredly. "This is the Arcane Plane. City in the clouds. The center of Arcana-tech."

"Is Calimorden on the Surface?" Oran cut in.

The woman nodded. Her eyes lingered on Lance's face a

little too long, making him uncomfortable. The woman suddenly smiled. "I can take you down. I'm going there, anyway. I should tell you now that though I am beautiful, I have a will of iron and cannot be swayed by your pretty face. And I advise you not to try anything on my decks. You, rogue arcanist, better not pull anything funny with that spell book I see you have tucked away under your coat. I've rarely met one of your kind and I never like them, save what they can do for my ship, and a fine ship she is. Same goes for you, captain pretty. No trying anything with that Arcane hand of yours."

Lance blinked before he found his voice. "I don't know how to use it," he said honestly.

"You'll figure it out. Men always do." She smiled, showing beautiful teeth. "Now quick, up the stairs to my vessel. We must catch these winds to carry us down." Before they could reply, she kept speaking, hauling them up the stairs. "I'm Captain Anastasia, or Stasi, if you're my father, but you're not. This great piece of wood and Arcane-powered machinery is *The Sun Piercer*, once my father's and now under my command."

The captain smiled again and waved her arm for them to inspect the deck of her airship.

"Hunting rogue Nether creatures like vampires, elves, and monsters are the game in my family, but that's not all. We also vanquished the great wolf of Dunmar, killed the beast of a Thousand Souls, and dispelled the Great Haunting many years ago." Her smile widened at the looks on the boys' faces.

The ship was made of wood, brass, and gold, like the rest of the city they had landed in. Other winged Arcane beings moved about, preparing the ship to sail.

"No funny business, rogue," she said, pointing at Oran and wiggling her finger.

Frowning in confusion, Oran opened the yards of fabric that made up his coat and found a spell book there. It was made of black and purple fabric on the outside, bound closed with a belt.

Oran pulled out the book, the word "Arcanum" written across it, and began to flip through it. It was full of levitation spells, healing potions, elemental attacks, and other things. He closed it and looked up at Lance.

"I guess I have some reading to do. Can you do magic?"

Lance looked at the gauntlet on his hand. "I bet that book is what makes you a rogue. You don't need something to channel like this."

The ship jerked as the captain shouted for the cleats to be released. The machine swiftly ascended before leveling out and moving on the winds. Anastasia captained the ship down, breaking through the first line of clouds. Lance turned and looked back up, realizing they were actually in the sky. The city looked to be built on a huge brass and gold saucer flying in the sky.

"Marvelous, isn't she?" the captained called to him, seeing his expression. "Not many of us travel down. We haven't had need since our ascension to the Arcane Plane a millennia ago. We use our magic to advance our technology, or weapons of war." She smiled at him as if he shared this worldly view. He supposed she must have thought he did since he was supposed to be from the Arcane Plane.

Lance shook his head, thinking the captain seemed slightly unhinged. Oran was pressed up against the main mast, steadying himself and flipping through the pages of the Arcanum. Lance was about to ask what'd he found when the sky darkened. It happened so fast, Lance looked up, expecting to see a solar eclipse. Lightning cracked out from a particularly dark cloud.

"Lieutenant!" Anastasia screamed from her helm. "What is this weather?"

A man with glasses, a fine mustache, and high boots ran to her side with a compass and a map, which tried to fly out of his hands.

"I don't know, Captain. One moment it was peaceful sailing and the next, this storm rose up from the ground."

Lightning cracked overhead and thunder rolled under them.

"Bring in the sails at once," the captain yelled over the wind. "Boson, man the helm."

She ran to the edge, followed by Oran and Lance, to look over. Dark clouds surrounded them like guard dogs.

"Arcanist, dissipate this storm at once," she ordered Oran.

"I don't know if I can," Oran called back. He opened the Arcanum again and began to flip through it.

From the clouds burst an ear-splitting roar. Flying out from a lumpy clump of grayness came a huge beast on dark wings. Its dark blue body was hard to see against the darkening sky.

"There it is!" the captain screamed. "The beast we are hunting. To the cannons at once!"

But the cannons were almost no use. The beast ducked and dodged the flying orbs easily. It screamed and tore at the sail when it dared to get close to the flying ship.

"Take up arms," Captain Anastasia called to her men. "You as well," she said to the Planes Striders.

Lance pulled his gun-blade out excitedly, ignoring the fact he had no idea how to use it. He held it in his left hand to leave his lightning arm free and spun the barrel. He smiled down at Oran, who rolled his eyes and flipped to a page that read "Storm Spells."

The beast landed with a heavy crash on the deck, splintering some of the wood. It dived into the fray of men that came charging at it and easily clawed them aside.

Lance leapt down, landed, aimed, and shot with his new weapon. He hit the beast right in its shoulder. He noticed that the shoulder was already damaged by something else and the beast howled as the bullet hit.

With it reeling, Lance thrust his armored hand out and lightening sprang from his fingertips into the beast's chest. In a moment of pained rage, the beast charged again, biting and clawing men. Suddenly the wind blew cold and rain began to pour.

"Oran," Lance yelled. "Not rain!"

"Sorry!" he cried from the deck. "That wasn't supposed to happen."

Tossing his feathery hat aside, Lance engaged in combat with the beast now. His blade was sharp and cut at the beast's flesh easily. He went in for a strike, then leapt back and fired the trigger. He found he was amazingly agile in this world and could leap back out of reach of the attacks with supreme ease. It would have been easier if the other crew members had not been getting in the way and angering the beast with weak attacks. Soon, the beast had bitten nearly every one of them and Lance saw that its fangs dripped with poison.

"Oran, on three," Lance called, holding up his right hand.

Oran counted and on three, they both hurled lighting at the beast while Lance fired his last shot. That was enough. Screaming a gargoyle roar, the beast leapt up and over the side and plunged below.

The ones who had been bitten rolled on the deck, holding

their wounds and moaning. The first already stood back up. Lance focused on the crewman and noticed his eyes had vanished. Not turned invisible, but where his eyes should have been, there was black nothing. Like shadows spreading over his face. His wings dropped and he stood still. Slowly, his mouth started to fall open. The same kind of blackness showed inside his lips.

"What's that?" Lance called to Anastasia.

"Boson," Captain Anastasia called. "Take us down. We have a deposit for the Surface Plane."

CHAPTER 26
CAPTAIN OF THE SUN PIERCER

T *he Sun Piercer* jerked as they broke beneath the clouds. Behind Lance and Oran, Anastasia cursed violently.

"They're all vanishing!" she cried. "Help me get us down safely."

Lance ran, flapping his huge wings twice, to reach the rudder of the ship at the back and hold it steady while Anastasia grasped the helm. The airship tilted dangerously as the sails flapped, no longer maintained. The Surface below came into view. A sort of castle-topped city, crawling up a great hill that spanned miles, came into view. The large stone city sprawled out, eventually turning into farm homes with crops and livestock, where the city no doubt got its supplies from. The hill melted into the ocean on the western side, where a fishing village lay.

"Ah, Seahold," Anastasia called. "We will drop our vanished there."

"Into the city?" Lance asked, horrified. "It looks like this black stuff spreads. You could destroy the whole place."

"Tragic," Anastasia called back. "Better the Surface than the Arcane Plane. They cannot reach us and we never come down to them. Without reason like this, anyway. It's the perfect place to dump the infected."

Oran gave Lance a look that begged him not to fight the eclectic bounty hunter.

"If you don't like my choice, then you can join them," she added.

Lance faced her, about to quip back that she needed them to help her pilot the craft when something hit the hull with a cracking thud. Oran toppled down, rolling over the deck as the ship tilted. He screamed, hands flying out to grasp anything to save himself from a fall. Anastasia was tossed from her grip on the helm and crashed into the mainmast, having fallen over the upper deck railing. Lance stayed still, having jumped off the deck and used his wings to grab the wind currents, staying steady.

He shot down toward Oran as something ripped at the ship again.

"It's that beast!" Anastasia cried. She pulled out her gun and fired a blackpowder shot into one of her crewmen, who mindlessly reached toward her.

Lance seized Oran and flew up to perch on the upper deck. "Find a spell like you did before," he instructed before diving over the side, Oran calling after him.

He scanned the side, getting a handle on how to angle his large feathery wings to drift and sway. A large three-clawed trail raked the side of the ship, showing where the beast had clawed the hull. But the creature wasn't visible. Careful to watch his back, knowing the monster could fly, he drew his saber and reloaded it with rounds from his belt. He prepared to rebound when Oran's cry of warning shot up from the ship.

Lance spun in the air only to have his foot seized in a grip so hard, he felt bruises appear on his skin under the leather of the boot. His joints strained as the beast pulled on him. He shot his eyes down and took in the blue and black monstrous form of the creature. He kicked at it, but missed, since the beast held him at arm's length. Panicking, he tried to fly, flapping his wings in a staccato rhythm. Snarling, the beast reached up and grasped the long feathers at the end of his wing as it beat down.

The pull on the soft feathers shot pain through Lance he never thought he'd experienced. It shot up the wing, into his shoulder muscles, and then down his spine. He gasped and then shouted in pain. With one wing held, only the beast kept them aloft. The monster shot up over the airship. Lance thought it would take him away to its lair when a sparking, purple bolt of lightning struck the beast. Roaring, the thing dropped him. It careened down toward the ever-approaching Seahold.

Lance let himself crash onto the deck of *The Sun Piercer* and rolled to find Oran running to him.

"Nice shooting," Lance praised.

"Doesn't matter," Oran cried. "We're going to crash."

"I can't hold her!" Anastasia screamed as the airship careened into the ground with a jolt.

Lance wrapped his arms and legs around Oran in an instant and shot into the air. The crash below exploded loudly as timber ground against the stone streets. The sails collapsed in on joints designed for such an emergency landing, saving them, but gravity rocked everything else on board. Anastasia went tumbling down, crying out in horror. The city structures rose up around them, blocking their view of the villages beyond. Lance watched as the ship slowed and eventually came to a stop in a huge palace square. Oran clung hard to him, craning his neck to look down.

"Where is everyone?" he asked.

Lance drifted down, curious as well. A white drawbridge spanned a moat just outside the square, leading into the wide-open city. "I think I saw few people run into the castle. They were running from people who were walking like the people who got bitten." He glanced at the castle. "Let's go inside here. Someone has to be home. We can get information."

"But the captain?" Oran asked as Lance set him down on the palace steps.

"I have a hard time caring if she got banged up in the crash landing," he said sternly. "She brought that vanishing stuff here on purpose." He folded his wings down behind him and marched inside. Oran jogged up behind him to catch up with his long strides.

The inside of the palace was dark. No torches or candles burned. The air felt cold. Lance followed a red and gold carpet deeper in, wondering if it led to where they might be able to find some kind of living being and get some directions.

"Where are the others?" Oran asked softly. "Do you think they're okay? I mean, I thought that thing was going to eat us alive."

Lance's worry revved up. "I hope they are. I hope they're with Celeste. She knows this place. Knows what to do.

Oran's face pinched. "Do you think they're okay? Why'd we get separated? We all left at the same time."

Lance shrugged, but his heart twinged. He hoped they

were all right. Wherever they were. "We'll find them," he added with conviction he didn't feel.

"Hey, look," he said. A hall to the right led into a great library. A massive round table stood in the center under a dark chandelier. Swords, books, chairs tipped over, and other things indicated that people had left in a hurry.

"Creepy," Oran whispered. "Hey, a map!" he shouted, running to the table.

Lance leaned over his head to look. The map, hand-scrawled on yellow parchment, showed what looked like a globe, but divided into five layers. "How cool is this?" he said to Oran, smiling. "The Nether." He pointed to a dark black and red area and the label next to it. "Oh. Surface. I see what she meant now. Look, this is us. And here's Seahold." He pointed to the eastern side of the Surface Plane. The ocean spread out inwardly, dividing Seahold on the east from Calimorden on the west. "Damn, we're far away," he said sadly. "That's the one place I remember her mentioning. She'd probably go there. Right?"

A few miles of prairie with black Xs scrawled over them made up the middle before leading out into forested spaces and mountains. Revary wasn't massive, but large enough to give Lance pause.

Oran climbed up onto the table to look at more of the map. "Astral Plane," he murmured. "There's nothing on it but this weird gold tree and the word 'Eidolon.'"

"Maybe they're Astral monkeys," Lance joked, making Oran laugh. He stepped onto the table to join him, standing over him. He tilted his head. "Glass Throne," he read. The phrase was written over the top of the golden tree. "Must be a king or something."

Behind them, out in the hall, something clanged. Like a

long metal spear or pipe had fallen and hit the stone floors. Lance shot two feet into the air, wings out and saber drawn. The metal rolled, then stopped when it clinked against another solid object.

Oran shuffled behind Lance, pulling out the Arcanum. "Do you think it's Anastasia?"

Beyond a shadow of a doubt, he did not. "Go out that back door," he instructed. "We'll circle back and get on *The Sun Piercer*. We should leave now that we know where Calimorden is. We can fly the ship there."

Oran hopped off the table and opened the back door. "It leads into a servants' exit," he called back to Lance.

"Go," Lance whispered, following him.

The pair hurried down the stone alley, ducking low and moving as quietly as they could. The hallway towered above them into utter darkness. Lance squinted into the palace's darkness.

"Wait," he said, grabbing the collar of Oran's dark coat. The blackness at the end of the hall didn't look right. He watched it carefully, holding his breath.

At first, it simply looked dark, since no torches lit the way. But then he saw it: the black shadow crept ever so slowly toward them. Lance pulled Oran back to him fully now, holding him in place. He watched as the darkness overtook a pillar. The sconce that would have held a torch fell to the floor with a clatter and rolled until it hit the wall on the other side of the hall.

"Is that what we heard?" Oran asked.

"Shit. Run!" Lance called. He turned and dashed back into the map room. "Go out the front, back to the ship!"

Lance, having trained and played football his whole life, ran much faster than Oran. He left him yards behind in a matter of minutes before stopping. "Come here," he called, holding his arms out.

"Oh, no," Oran panted. "You are not bridle carrying me like a puny little NPC."

The door to the map room, which they'd just reentered, fell from one vanished hinge, cracking and thundering to the floor. "Like hell I am," Lance growled. He reached back, scooping Oran up into his arms and using his wings to help propel them back out into the daylight. Oran cried out in protest until they exited the palace. Only then did Lance set his feet on the ground.

"Sorry," he panted, leading the way back to the square. "I couldn't risk that stuff getting to—"

A huge black and blue leathery blur tackled Lance harder than he'd ever been hit in his life. It hit him so hard in the chest that he lost all his breath and choked. The beast's scaly, black-clawed fingers dug hard into his sides as it grabbed him. Together, they rose into the air as the beast started to flap its great wings.

"Screw you!" Lance shouted, struggling against it. He pulled his saber out and shot it in the shoulder.

The beast reeled, dropping him, and turned in the air to dart back to Oran. Lance landed hard on his back, which once again winded him. His eyes watered as he watched the monster bear down on Oran, who ran, flinging purple lightning after the thing. Lance growled, shooting toward them. He gripped his saber, ready to fire.

"No!" a voice called from seemingly nowhere. It was a girl's voice, one he thought he recognized. "Not him, monster."

The beast stopped pursuing Oran and turned on Lance.

"Yes," the voice said with a dark giggle. "Him, you can maim."

Lance flung his wings wide, stopping his chase and turning to flee as the beast turned back on him. Someone was controlling the beast. Just as he turned, he swore he spotted a girl in a black dress, wreathed in purple light with a glowing crown, hovering above them, watching. This must be the one who controlled the beast. She raised her hand, what looked like a comet glowing and growing in her hand.

Lance cursed and cut around a corner, unable to get enough wind under his wings to propel himself higher. The beast rocketed around the corner, catching up to him. It tackled him hard, the pair rolling down the city street. His wings, spread out when the beast grappled him, felt like the joints sprained as they rolled. His saber flew from his hand, clattering several yards away.

The monster pinned him to the ground and glowered down at him. It had a humanoid frame with fangs and large, twisted black horns. Its bat-like wings arced overhead while a bifurcated tail whipped and snapped in joy at having caught its prey.

"Take his wings," the girl ordered, her voice echoing from all ends of the street.

The beast gripped Lance by his neck and flipped him onto his stomach, holding him down with one arm. He shouted, pushing into the street and kicking his legs madly. The beast gripped his soft wing at the base of his shoulder. Unsure what this pain would feel like, Lance screamed, thrashing madly. Sweat poured from his scalp and his long hair stuck to his face.

Suddenly the beast lurched, snarling in pain. It turned, roaring behind it. Still pinned under the monster's massive frame, Lance couldn't see, but he heard Oran's grunts of effort as he hurled dark Arcane magic at the monster.

"Oran!" Lance cried desperately, flailing against his captor. He reached his right hand out, stretching his fingers toward his saber.

Oran must have seen it, because a second later, the saber, propelled by invisible hands, flew into his grasp. Shouting in effort, Lance twisted as much as he could to aim at the beast. Seeing this, the beast growled and gripped his throat again. Lance fired.

The monster reeled back, shouting, black blood spattering out. The force of the shot ripped its claws from Lance's neck, tearing his skin. His own blood leaked from his neck. Panicking, he pressed his hand into the wound and fired again at the beast as it fled. Lance looked around, but the floating girl had vanished. The beast followed suit, fleeing.

"Shit, you're bleeding," Oran gasped, terrified when he saw the state Lance was in. He pulled Lance's hand away from his neck only to gasp and shove it back harder.

"That bad?" Lance croaked. His head felt light. "D-don't suppose there's any h-healing in that book of yours?"

Oran shook his head, trembling. "Let's get to the ship. The captain has to have medical supplies."

Lance nodded, but his stomach turned. Unable to stop himself, he swooned, falling hard onto his knees against the stone street. "I think I'm just f-freaking out," he panted. "I've not lost that much blood."

"Okay, okay," Oran said calmly. He pulled Lance up and supported him. "Breathe slowly and deliberately. Don't make yourself dizzy. You're okay."

Lance couldn't stop his panting, spinning his head even more.

"Stop," Oran pleaded. "You're going to make yourself pass out."

So much of his blood splashed down his front. He gasped, but no air seemed to be getting to his brain.

"Lance, stop!" Oran shouted. "I can't do this on my own. You're too freaking huge for me to carry, you big dumb jock."

He forced himself to exhale and take shallow, slow, shuddering breaths. Oran was right. He wouldn't be able to help if he didn't get control of himself.

"Okay," he whispered, the world slowing its spin. "Let's go."

When they reached the ship, it was empty. The crew and Anastasia were gone. Oran helped him up the rope ladder and leaned him against the mainmast.

"How are we going to get this thing going?" Lance asked. "I guess it's not too bashed up."

Oran glanced around, then patted Lance's shoulder and smiled. "You'll figure it out, captain."

CHAPTER 27
PARTY ASSEMBLED

The wind rushed passed Celeste's ears so loudly it deafened her. The sensation of the air shooting around her told her she was falling. Plummeting. One second, she stood in the woods with the others, the next, she and Alice were screaming as they flipped over and over in the air. Clouds swooshed past them until the blue of the ocean zoomed up to her, smacking her hard against the surface.

The water was cool and swallowed her whole, into the dark. Green rays of light penetrated in from the top. Remembering to pull her elbows in, she shot beneath the waves and slowed to a stop. Just as she opened her eyes, preparing to kick toward the surface, something shot by her. Something with a huge fin and a spear.

Grunting and panicking, she spun her arms and kicked furiously. Her panic mounted. A clawed, webbed hand shot out and grabbed her ankle. Screaming into the water, bubbles bursting before her face, she spotted a pod of mermen swirling around her and Alice. That was when she saw Alice was dressed like a warrior, scimitar in her hand, fending off the mermen. Celeste saw she wore a silky dress, like the star from before, only hers was golden and bright.

Thrusting her hands out and calling on her star magic, a comet of gold and white light burst from her hands. The mermen hissed and cringed away like they'd been burned. Calling on the magic again, she shoved the watery attackers further away. Alice swam to her, face and lips blue, and together they broke the surface.

Celeste gasped. Never had she loved air so much. She splashed, keeping her head above the water and looking around. Perhaps a mile off, the shore bobbed to her right. Alice sprang up, gasping and still splashing.

"Behind you!" Alice called as she cut a determined merman on the face with her curved knife. "They just don't stop!" She panted as one pulled her under the water again like lightning.

"Alice!" Celeste screamed from where a rolling wave threatened to push her under. If only the waves would stop for a moment, she could get her head above water.

A cold, strong hand seized her ankle again and plunged her deep under the blue water. She screamed, but was cut off as her head submerged under the rolling wave. Blinded by the folds of her skirt, she screamed again, sending another blast of starlight into the water. Her would-be captor fled again, hissing.

Alice struggled nearby. She had been grabbed by two mermen and one tried to take her short dagger from her. Alice swung, cutting the scaly skin for what Celeste saw must have been the dozenth time.

The water pressure became too much and her lungs burned as she continued to struggle toward the top. She made one last escape attempt when a long harpoon broke the surface and hit her captor right in the shoulder. They both looked up at the same time to see the shadow of a huge wooden ship cross over the broken sun.

Alice had already swum away from the mermen who had abducted her, who now had large-shafted arrows sticking into their sides. Another harpoon launched from the boat, warning off the last of them.

A huge, thick net dropped in and scooped up Celeste and Alice. They hung on to the ropes and made loud, dramatic gasps as they broke the surface again. Seeing each other safe, they rolled across the net to each other and hugged tightly, not about to let go.

As they were brought up out of the water, Celeste saw the vessel resembled an old Viking ship. The figurehead was a dragon with fishy frills on its head, and wings made up the sides of the boat. When they rose up over the rail, she came face-to-face with a beaming Galis and a very sea-sick Folkvar. He looked far more green than normal and did not smile at all.

"Galis!" Celeste leapt out of the net and into his arms with a gleeful shriek. She turned and hugged Folkvar around his middle. "I'm so glad to see you both again," she said. "How— I mean, did you know we would be here?"

The warrior helped the girls to the middle of the boat, where they leaned up against the few provisions the two Revarians had lashed to the mast. "When you left Calimorden, the Oreads arrived," he said.

Celeste took the offered fur blanket from Galis. "The

Oreads came to the human city?" For some reason, she hadn't thought they would.

Galis nodded. "Availa said you'd come like a star, falling into the ocean between Calimorden and Seahold. And so you have." His eyes went to the crown of light on her head, then turned sad. "We set out right away to wait for you."

"I've brought more Planes Striders," Celeste offered. "They will help me figure out what we should do." She glared into the bright sun reflecting off the ocean. "There should be two more. Two boys."

Folkvar, hand over his stomach, replied, "We saw only you two. Even Availa said only two would fall into the ocean." He stopped, his hand clapping over his mouth, and closed his eyes.

Celeste frowned, meeting Alice's just as concerned face. "Maybe they landed inland," she suggested.

Galis gathered drink and food for them as Celeste introduced Alice to them. Both Revarians looked oddly uncomfortable when Alice excitedly shook their hands as though they were celebrities.

Folkvar didn't touch the food and only sipped at his tankard. He was very nauseated from being at sea.

Celeste understood. "Your kind have probably never set foot on a boat in all their generations, huh?"

"I am the first of my kind to set sail," Folkvar moaned, "and I can guarantee I will be the last. The sooner we return to land, the better."

"Indeed," Galis agreed. "The sky is looking more foreboding as we speak. The darkness from Seahold concerns me. I think it has fallen to the vanishing."

Alice agreed. "The others may be on land. And you said

the oracle claimed the more Planes Striders, the better. We should all shack up together."

Celeste agreed as well. With the oracle out of their reach and Celeste having no desire to confront Queen Zephyr, she had only one last idea: meeting the Eidolon again. If what Galis had guessed about the darkness was true, perhaps they could get some answers and clues about how to destroy Umbra. He had told her to bring more Planes Striders, and she had. Maybe now he'd have some advice.

"How can we get to the Astral Plane?" she asked as they turned the sail to catch the wind and head toward the shore. "Can we get there without the power of the oracle?"

"You'd need to find a way to the Arcane Plane first," Galis informed them. "Near impossible task unless you can fly. Or climb the highest mountain and wait for when they pass over."

Celeste hummed in disappointed thought. "I wonder about that Mirror, too. That seems to be a portal for things like this beast to come through. Like whoever opened it is using it to transport the monsters of Umbra here. We need to destroy it. And they took Yilith?"

Galis's face fell and his shoulders slumped in shame. "I failed him."

Folkvar put his hand on Galis's shoulder. "Don't. It was up to me as well. The dark star was too strong for us."

Celeste hoped that Yilith's life could be saved, too. She had already lost Gwen.

"And the star?" Celeste asked.

Galis shook his head. "I don't know."

They had to find Oran and Lance. Surely they weren't far. They had all come over together. Why hadn't they landed at the same time, in the same place?

"Not long now," Galis said. He pointed into the distance. "There is a dock between Seahold and Calimorden."

They sailed on for some time before Seahold became more visible. Celeste stood at the railing and looked over into the ocean before focusing onto the city before them. As Galis had said, the sea separated Calimorden from Seahold in a wide blue plain.

Celeste faced the expanse between the two cities and spotted something strange. She frowned, shielding the sun from her eyes with her hand. "Is that...an airship coming out of Seahold?" she cried.

"LANCE!" ORAN SHOUTED FROM HIS PERCH ON THE rail. He had been tempting fate with a levitation spell he had found in the Arcanum. "I see Celeste! She's near the ocean's edge. She's with Alice, and they have company."

Lance leaned up against the rail, still faint from his battle with the beast. With joy at last, he called over the edge to her and waved his arms. She heard him and looked up, surprise and joy on her face. Celeste jumped up and down, pointing toward them. They heard her and Alice squeal with delight.

Hovering the ship a few dozen feet above the ground, Lance kicked down the ladder from *The Sun Piercer* for Oran. He stumbled over the side, flaring his wings to the catch the sea breeze and float down onto the dock. Celeste's mouth dropped and her eyes went wide. The two Lance didn't recognize stood back, shock on their faces as well.

"Holy paladin," Celeste gasped when Lance's boots hit the ground. "Wow."

Her awe made him suddenly self-conscious and he fought to press down the redness that rushed to his face. His legs, weak, crumpled under him and he crashed to the ground in a feathery heap.

"You're hurt!" Celeste cried out, kneeling next to him. "What happened?"

If he had been in a better state, he would have loved the feel of her hands holding him, gently lifting his chin to see the wound on his neck.

Oran ran up behind him and quickly explained what had happened.

Celeste reached out and took one of the feathers of his wings in her hands. To his surprise, he felt her fingers trail down the wing. It gave him a strange tingling feeling. "Holy shit, Lance, I'm so sorry," she said once Oran finished. She hugged him around his neck, letting him lean on her.

"People in the Arcane Plane have wings," he offered with a shrug. "Oran got the raw end of the deal, though. He can't fly."

She smiled weakly at Oran, then looked back at him. "I'm a star now. I can heal. Here."

Celeste re-adjusted herself under him, cradling him in one arm, his wings splayed out on the ground. She touched her other hand to the wound on his neck and a soft glow emanated from her hand. A weird tingling crawled over Lance's neck as his flesh knitted back together and a surge of energy shot through him. He gasped and shivered.

"Better?" Celeste asked.

"A lot." He smiled and sat up, folding his wings behind him. He stood, then offered her his hand. She took it, blushing as he pulled her up.

Chattering and disjointed storytelling began to ensue until

they were all gasping and in awe of each other's adventures. Celeste began the long narrative of the Revarian's adventures to fill them in on the Mirror and the beast and the predicament they now found themselves in.

"It's like Revary knew," Celeste said, winded from the excitement. "It put you on the Arcane Plane so we could have a way to reach the Eidolon."

Galis left Folkvar at the edge of the docks, where he lurched, doubling over, and finally heaved over the side. "First, the Mirror," he said. "I want to show you what we're dealing with on the Surface Plane."

"Mirror?" Oran asked.

Celeste sighed heavily. "Another Planes Strider has crossed over and opened a portal for the darkness that's eating Revary."

"We saw it," Lance grunted, remembering the ever-encroaching darkness in the castle in Seahold. "Does that mean we're up against someone from our world?"

This made Celeste frown in thought. "I've heard Umbra is of our world. But I think this Planes Strider is helping it. That Mirror was acting as a portal." She nodded, having come to a decision. "Show us the Mirror. If we can sneak a peek before we go to the Eidolon, we should. Just so we know exactly what we're dealing with."

"Did she look concerned?" Lance whispered to Oran as they piloted *The Sun Piercer* in the direction Galis indicated.

"What?" Oran snapped back with a hiss.

"When Celeste saw I was all banged up, maybe dying." He smiled. "Did she look worried?"

"God damn it, Lance." Oran shook his head and looked forward.

Lance immediately regretted his childish prodding. He knew how Oran felt about Celeste. But, he reasoned with himself, he had almost died, surely. He'd lost a lot of blood. Had almost had his new wings ripped from his body. Reimagining the situation made the reality sink in.

"We're really here," he said more gently. He touched the scar on his neck. "This really happened. Oran, we have to be careful."

"We will," he promised. "You've got my back, right?"

He nodded, giving him a confident half-smile.

"There!" Folkvar shouted, gripping a rope near the front of the ship. "See it amongst the mountains?"

Lance and the others joined him in looking over the edge. A range of steely mountains cut off a glittering forest from a dark, brown expanse of dead earth.

"The winter land is gone," Galis mused, frowning. "Like it was plucked from the very earth."

Celeste pushed past the others and squinted at the dark castle jutting out from the mountains. A dark haze covered it, but she could still count the spires and see the tall tower, partially destroyed. Something inside glinted sharply every second or two.

"That's the tower with the Mirror?" she asked.

Galis nodded.

"I…" Celeste frowned, eyeing the castle carefully. "I know that castle. Where have I seen it before?"

Oran joined her at the railing, putting his hand dangerously close to hers, Lance noted. He scanned the wicked spires and towers as well. Even he thought he recognized it. "Is it from *Elderforge*?" he asked.

Celeste gasped. "No, it's Stella's! Stella's castle from our campaign." Her hand flew to her mouth, gaping. "Guys... It's Stella. She's the dark star."

CHAPTER 28
THE EIDOLON

"Lance," Celeste said flatly, "take us away. I don't want to try to get in there. I just…I can't."

"It looks abandoned," Lance said offhandedly. "No lights or movement." But Celeste shook her head.

"A friend of yours?" Galis asked Celeste.

Celeste zoned out, looking over the side at the castle as it got smaller and smaller. Lance piloted the airship up and away from the earth. Soon, the clouds covered it and she lost sight of it.

"Yes," she whispered, still lost in thought. Alice appeared by her side and hovered close by, giving silent support.

"We didn't know," Galis said. "When we faced her, she wore a mask that covered her face. Her voice was distorted and odd."

"We should have known," Folkvar growled. "We were blinded by our faith in the Planes Striders."

Celeste gasped and looked up. "Don't say that. I swear, I'll stop her."

"How?" Galis asked.

Celeste looked to Alice, then to Lance and Oran, who stood by the helm. "There are more of us. And we'll ask the Eidolon for guidance. I did as he said. Now I want to know what I'm supposed to do."

"We don't have the oracle this time. You'll have to get past the guardian to the Astral Plane," Folkvar reminded her. "A dragon like a comet. He is the sole watcher of the Astral Plane and the stars. As more stars fall, the more he has failed in his one task."

Celeste thought back to the one gate guardian she'd already encountered. "I got past the guardian of the Nether Plane. I'm sure this one will not be so different." She gripped the rail hard, looking up into the oncoming stars. "We can get that high with the ship. Where is the guardian?"

"Mount Margon," Galis offered. "Nearly impossible to scale as the air disappears. One cannot breathe that high. At least, not for long. And it is cold."

"Tell Lance how to get there," Celeste said. "We'll take our chances. We have to get to the Astral Plane. The Eidolon said to bring more Planes Striders over and I have. He must have advice for me now. I need to know what to do."

Galis nodded and moved across the deck to stand by Lance, guiding him. Celeste glanced to where Lance and Oran stood, managing the flying vessel.

"I see that look," Alice said with a light smile. "But I don't know which one you're looking at."

Celeste rolled her eyes. "Why do I feel like I've cheated on all my friends?"

Alice's smile faltered. "Because you're trying to make choices that involve everyone. Focus on yourself in our world. But for now, let's think about what we need to do here. Like, how strong am I, for instance?" Alice raised her fist and flexed her arm, inspecting her muscles.

This made Celeste laugh a little. "Pretty strong. When I was a fighter, I felt very mighty."

"Very mighty," Alice echoed with a grin. Then she stopped. She yawned, her mouth opening wide. "Oh, no. I feel it."

"We're ascending?" Celeste called back to Lance.

Lance nodded. "Mount Margon is close."

"How do we travel to the Celestial Plane without the oracle?" Folkvar asked as the party convened near the helm.

Galis said, "The guardian of the gate, Syderial, will open it for us. I don't see that he will have much choice."

"I can open the gates," Celeste said. "I did it in the Nether and I'll do it again if I have to."

A sudden freezing wind cut through Celeste's thin dress. She shivered and crossed her arms. She caught Lance look at Oran and flick his head in her direction. Her cheeks burned red hot when Oran stepped forward and offered her his huge black coat. She took it without complaint. Oran blushed as she did.

"Watch for the peaks coming out of the clouds," Galis warned Lance.

No sooner had he said this than the mountain came into view. Parts of it rose up higher still into the darkening blue of the sky. The rest already loomed far below them. A stone tower, hewn from the very mountain, stood atop Mount Margon.

"Sometimes my tribe would try to make a pilgrimage to the top of Mount Margon," Galis said.

"Fools," Folkvar grumbled. "How many made it?"

Galis half-shrugged. "A few Oreads claim to have seen the top. It is from them we know that the guardian waits here."

Celeste gasped, the air thinning quickly. Above them, the sky had turned a dark navy blue. Colorful specs glittered above them. "Is that the Celestial Plane?" she asked.

Folkvar nodded. "The home of the stars. And above that, the golden tree and the home of the Eidolon."

"Are there portals there like the one we found?" she asked.

"Sometimes," Galis replied. "Or so they say in the songs."

The airship crested the mountain top and they were greeted with the wide opening of the tower. It was larger than Celeste had thought, opening with no doors to cut off the inside from the wind. A single stone with a giant sword pierced into it waited inside. Lance, Galis, Alice, and Folkvar heaved ropes with metal hooks on the end over the side and pulled the airship close to the mountain. Everyone was gasping for air. Lance heaved the gangplank down and led the party off toward the tower.

They crossed the massive stony threshold into the room with the sword, but no celestial dragon greeted them.

"Hello?" Celeste called. "Syderial?"

Lightning cut across the sky and they turned to a stone archway that led out into the abyss. A dragon, much like the ones Celeste had seen in Chinese legend, appeared from the lightning and flew toward them in huge, undulating waves. His long whiskers trailed behind him.

"A Planes Strider," he mused in a deep voice that sounded like it came from the inside of a massive, empty stairwell. "I heard your call."

Celeste gulped. "We, uh…" She found herself stuttering in

the presence of the dragon. "We need to cross into the Astral Plane."

"So you do," Syderial replied. He landed gracefully, his sheer size still shaking the tower, and walked to them. "I have...failed my role, Planes Strider." He bowed his head and his voice turned sorrowful.

Celeste shifted her feet and glanced around nervously. Was the dragon bowing to her? "Um," she stammered. "What do you mean?"

"Greylheim torments the Celestials," Syderial said. "It is my job to protect them. But he comes as I do, as he wishes."

"Don't feel like you've failed," Celeste said. "I've seen the stars falling. But Greylheim has been sent by someone like us. Umbra is from our world, I've been told. So his power is beyond you. But we're here in number to stop him."

Syderial gave a huge sigh. "It may be too late. The Eidolon is very weak."

"Then let us through," Celeste begged. "Let us go to him. I need his council."

Syderial blinked slowly, taking in the party before her. "You are our only hope."

He stood up on his hind legs and gripped the sword in the stone with his front legs. With a grunt, he turned it like a key. A blinding golden light erupted in the stone archway and then expanded like a door opening. Through it, Celeste saw the familiar golden tree.

"Thank you, Syderial. I won't let you down."

Celeste marched with conviction, the others following her, through the portal and to the golden tree.

THE SENSE OF WONDER FROM THE ASTRAL PLANE
filled Celeste, just as it had done the time before. The winged
guardians came down and helped them mount the gryphons
again. Together, the party soared up to the upper levels of the
golden tree. They passed the one where Celeste remembered
the Glass Throne to be and went up another level. The
balcony they landed on led into a wide open room that
Celeste immediately knew to be a bedroom. The room was
filled with plants of many colors and singing birds dancing in
the rays of the ever-shining sun, but a huge white bed filled
the center. The gauzy sheets and curtains around it were
rumpled, as if someone had just left the bed.

Standing amidst the plants, almost glowing, was the
Eidolon. He ran his hands up and down the trunk of a small,
potted tree. He moved almost lovingly amongst the plants,
whispering to them. Celeste led the party closer at the guards'
behest and looked into the Eidolon's handsome face. Dark
shadows surrounded his eyes now and his skin was so pale it
looked white as ivory. One hand, which he ran down a long
leaf of what looked like a palm, shook slightly. The other
hand was wrapped around a book with a white and gold
cover. He turned when they got close and smiled weakly.

"Ah, so the Planes Striders have returned," he said with as
much glee as he could muster. "I am glad."

Celeste made an awkward bow. "I promised I'd come back."

"And with reinforcements." The Eidolon motioned to the
others. "And two from Revary. But only two." His shoulders
fell. "There is little of Revary left by now. Follow me."

He moved farther into the garden to a golden pool set in
the floor.

"Do not touch the water," he instructed. "Just look."

Celeste and the others leaned over just enough to gaze into the mirror-like surface of the water. Slowly, a map appeared.

"That's Revary," Oran said, pointing. "Lance and I found a map of it in Seahold." He tilted his head. "So much of it is blacked out."

"The vanishing," the Eidolon said sadly. "Umbra takes more and more of my land every day. Corrupting them."

Celeste studied the map. "What happens when that darkness takes hold? Where do they go?"

"To your world."

They all looked up, shocked. Alice made a small, confused sound and Folkvar grunted.

"How can we go to their world?" the giant asked.

"You are not meant for their world," the Eidolon replied. "When you go there, you will change shape, not be as you are here."

"And us?" Celeste asked, suddenly slightly afraid. "What are we here?"

"Whatever you choose to be." The Eidolon smiled. "As you are. The only rule is that you play the part you have chosen, as you know."

A slight frown creased Celeste's brow. "How do you know about that?"

Though weary and ill-looking, the Eidolon smiled. "I am Revary and Revary is me. I know all that goes on in my land. And Revary is dying, being taken piece by piece."

Celeste gulped and looked back at the map as even more parts turned dark. "And when Revary is gone?"

The Eidolon's golden eyes shone with tears. "I will be, too." He looked up.

"How do I stop it?" Celeste begged. She looked at the others and they all nodded.

"Have a grand adventure," the Eidolon said.

"What?" Celeste said, confused.

The young man took a slow breath like it pained him. "Celeste, Revary is just a story you tell yourself. You decide what happens. Planes Strider," he added with a smile. "Just as you read stories of other worlds, so others read your story, becoming a part of you and you a part of them."

This made the room go quiet. Celeste felt fear fill her, but also wonder. "I'm so confused," she stammered. "What do you mean, I'm a story?" She pressed her hand into her chest. "I'm real."

"Very real," the Eidolon said with a smile. "To the people who read your stories, you are more real than they are. When they read your story, you will become a part of them, just as those in Revary are a part of you. The way to save Revary is to go out and do what you must."

Lance shook his head. "You're making less and less sense."

The Eidolon tilted his head and half-shrugged. "Perhaps. But it is what you must do."

"What must I do?" Celeste burst. "Please, help me."

"What can I tell you?"

Celeste looked from Oran to Lance to Alice. "Well, in *stories*, or the games we play, someone gives us a quest and we go and complete that quest. That's how the story progresses. It's the only way I know how to make a story."

The Eidolon laughed weakly but in genuine delight. He coughed, the exertions hurting him. "Is that why you always start in a tavern?" he asked. "So someone can come and find you? Give you a quest? Perhaps there are marauders or goblins harassing the town?"

Oran's mouth dropped open. "Actually, yeah."

Celeste faced the Eidolon full on. "Fine then. Give me a quest."

At this, the Eidolon raised his head up as best he could. "Help me to my bed," he said.

Celeste moved forward to his proffered arm. He shook so much she was shocked he was standing. She guided him to his bed where he sank down, almost being swallowed up by the fine bed clothes.

"Your quest is not easy," the Eidolon said. "It involves one of your own, one who can make Revary and unmake Revary."

"Stella?" Celeste asked.

The Eidolon nodded. "Planes Striders are the only ones who can bring in the vanishing darkness like she has. She is helping Umbra destroy Revary."

"But why?" Celeste asked.

"Only you can answer that."

She looked away. "I... I don't know."

"Then you cannot defeat her."

Celeste frowned down at the Eidolon. "I'll figure it out. She's my best friend. I don't know why she'd do this. But I'll stop her, I swear."

"Then stop the servants of Umbra," the Eidolon went on. "Defeat Greylheim and then defeat Umbra's hold on Revary."

"Can we defeat him?" Oran asked.

The Eidolon shook his head. "That is beyond even your power. But you can free Revary of his grasp."

Celeste turned to face the others. "There is one other thing we might need." The others waited for her to go on.

"The oracle," she said. "He's a Planes Strider too and has helped us before. He might be useful."

Lance nodded in agreement, looking her in the eyes. "You know best."

She went on, "We're a pretty balanced party. I guess we just dive right in. We all have our special talents."

Lance nodded. "Let's go get the oracle and take down the dark star."

CHAPTER 29
A TOUCH OF CORRUPTION

Celeste looked over the railing of *The Sun Piercer* down at Calimorden. Parts of the land had fallen away, crumbling from places that were mere blotches of blackness. When they landed in the square of the palace, no one came out to greet them. In fact, no movement drew her eyes to the dark corners of the desolate palace. Walls had fallen down and crumbled inward, trees were scorched, and shadows of people lay smeared out on the remaining walls and pavements.

"It looks like the shadows of people after a nuclear blast," Oran whispered. "Like that picture in our history books."

Celeste shivered. "What happened, do you think?"

"Stella," Alice said, her teeth gnashed. "Looks like a star exploded in here, killing everything."

Celeste's heart broke. Alice was right.

"The Planes Strider did this?" Folkvar asked, gripping his sword hilt tight.

"So it would seem," Celeste whispered. She didn't want to

believe it. "How could Stella do this?" she asked, almost crying. "The people of Revary didn't do anything to her."

"But *you* did," Lance reminded her. "She thinks you betrayed your friendship. I can't help but feel slightly responsible."

"No way," Oran cut in. "You had nothing to do with her going psycho."

Celeste led the way over the bridge and through the gates to the massive stairs that led up into the palace's main halls. Everything was the same there, too. Destruction and desolation tore at the walls and had blasted the ceilings away. The doors to the throne room hung open at an odd angle. The inside looked cold and dark. She pushed past some fallen debris and looked inside.

To her surprise, slumped in the throne sat Queen Zephyr. Her whole frame had shrunk to a mere skeleton and her once regal clothes hung tattered, moth-eaten and decaying on her frame. Her hair lay lank and brittle and was falling out. She was dirty and breathing loudly through a parched throat.

"Your majesty?" Celeste called from a few steps away.

Clutched in her hand, the oracle head glowed. His eyes were bound shut with a rag and the queen's scabby, rotting hand was clamped over his mouth to stop him from talking. At the sound of Celeste's voice, her zombie head shot up and faced them.

Alice and Celeste shrieked as the queen's eyeless sockets glared in their direction. Oran shuddered.

"Is that the Planes Strider child I hear?" the queen said in a squelching tone. Her voice struggled to make it past all the grime that had accumulated in her throat.

Celeste swallowed her fear and nodded. "Yeah," she whispered. "We've come for the oracle."

"Come to take my power?" She clutched at the head more tightly. "You cannot have it. It will save my son. Bring Gwen home now. My dear boy."

Her head dropped and dry sobs escaped her throat.

Celeste motioned the others forward while she took a few more cautious steps.

"Let me take the oracle and I'll find Gwen." She knew this was a lie. Gwen was dead, but she would have preferred the queen just handed over the oracle.

"You cannot have it!" screamed the zombie queen.

She leapt forward and reached a decaying hand out for Celeste, but Alice's curved scimitar was there first. With a cry and a gargling shriek, the queen dropped the oracle and clutched at her severed limb. It didn't appear to be blood, but something dark and rank splattered across the ground from the wound.

"Stay away!" Alice warned. She gasped, losing her breath over the shock of what she'd just done.

"Holy shit," Lance cursed behind them.

"Guards!" the queen shouted. From behind the throne, a small host of men and women warriors appeared. They looked just as soulless and hallow as Zephyr. "The dark star has commanded me," she murmured.

"Stella?" Celeste asked, taking a cautious step back. She had no sword. No way to defend herself. She had to rely on the others. "What did she do, Zephyr?"

The queen, moaning and holding her bloody stump, sat back into the chair. "Took everything," she groaned. "Killed them all. But what does it matter? I don't even care. Gwen is gone. My kingdom is destroyed. Umbra comes closer every day. I cannot stand up to the Planes Strider."

"What about us?" Celeste shot back. "You knew I was coming back. Why didn't you wait for me?"

"Wait!" Zephyr lurched forward, holding onto the arm of her throne with her one good hand. "Wait for you is all I've done since you brought Gwen back to me. I waited, Planes Strider. And you brought another here who would destroy us. We are alive by her will alone." She motioned to her black sockets. "By her will alone. I was told—" She stood and took one step down the stairs from her throne, "—to simply touch you."

Like a viper, she threw her one hand out and grasped Folkvar's arm. The norcan roared and threw her off, but not before black tendrils trailed from the queen's fingers onto his flesh, then vanished. With the queen's cry, the guards leapt forward. Lance drew his saber, Galis his blade, and Alice hers. Celeste ran away, raising her hands as they glowed with starlight.

"I must do the bidding of the dark star!" Zephyr cried. She threw her hand out and blackness, a void, shot from it toward Folkvar.

Celeste gasped and threw a shield of starlight out, blocking it. The norcan turned to thank her, but quickly became engaged with one of the guards.

"Oran," Celeste called. "Get the oracle! He might be able to help us."

Oran moved, shooting purple lightning from his finger-tips. He angled himself closer to the oracle. Galis cried out as one of the guards cut his ribs. Celeste ran in his direction, her hand outstretched. Something like glittering, bright smoke issued from her fingers and touched his side. The blood didn't vanish, but the wound healed. With that pain gone, Galis shoved the guard off and killed him.

"No!" Zephyr shouted when Oran snatched up the oracle. "The dark star gave him to me for my fealty."

"You don't even know what I am!" the oracle shouted when Oran tore the gag off his mouth.

Folkvar dispatched a guard and ran toward the queen. She screamed and dropped to the throne room floor, cowering. "Don't!" she begged. "It's over anyway. You cannot stop her."

Lance sliced the last guard and stood still, sword dripping. He panted and looked around. His hand began to shake. Celeste wondered what was wrong, but didn't have time to ask.

"I'm just a tool now," the queen moaned. She collapsed against the throne and wept.

Celeste walked up to Lance's side and gently touched his arm. She wanted to embrace him, but now wasn't the time. She looked at the carnage around them. She realized now why he shook. She took his hand in hers and held it tight. "We will stop Stella, Queen Zephyr. I wish you'd have waited for me." She held her head up high. "Is she here? In her castle?"

"No," Zephyr sighed deeply, sinking into herself. "She fled her castle on Umbra's orders to hide. She moved to another place. In Sylvan Murk. She's taken over Zealnis's palace. Probably killed the sorceress."

"I know it." Celeste nodded. "Let's go."

"I SEE IT," ALICE SAID FROM BEHIND A TELESCOPE. "That's a castle Stella would choose for sure. All black and spiky. It's in a valley between two dark mountain ranges."

Celeste met her at the railing and squinted out into the growing darkness in the direction Alice looked. "We'll land about a mile out and walk in. See if we can sneak in, maybe."

Oran's face had been placid and emotionless for a while now. His blue eyes had dulled with a constant sheen of worry. But now they looked up. "Look." He pointed out over the mountains. "The dragon."

Celeste turned to follow Oran's gesture and spotted it. Flying high above the mountains, undulating and roaring, came Greylheim. Behind him, a darkness began to spread, blotting out the sky. The moon, hardly visible in the setting sun, had a crack running down its middle. A star fell from behind it, shooting toward the earth. Greylheim spotted it and charged at it, his wings beating quickly.

"Oh, no!" Celeste cried.

The dragon opened his maw and swallowed up the star. Celeste swore she heard it scream as it died in his belly. She watched Greylheim flap his huge wings and ascend, vanishing into the Celestial Plane. "Can he reach the Astral Plane and the Eidolon?" she asked the oracle where it hung once again on Galis's belt. He and Folkvar joined them at the rail.

"No," the oracle replied somberly. "But he doesn't have to reach the Eidolon to hurt him. You saw him. He is ill, weak. The more Revary dies, the more it hurts him."

"We are running out of time," Folkvar whispered. Celeste looked up at the giant warrior and noticed a dark shadow around his eyes. His breathing was labored. Her eyes tracked down him to the place on his arm where the queen had touched him. She thought she saw a hand-shaped mark on his dark skin, but couldn't be sure.

"Let's hurry, then," Celeste said. "I want to save Revary

and return it to its full glory." Then she wanted to stay, just for a bit. To see it as it was meant to be experienced. Alive and well.

They disembarked and made sure they had everything they needed. Then they started their trek toward Stella's palace.

"She knows we're coming," Oran said to Celeste, pulling her back to speak with her alone. Alice and Lance took the lead while Galis fell behind to walk beside Folkvar. "We won't be able to sneak up on her."

"You seem pretty sure," she said, stepping high over rocks. Everything around them was quiet. Like all the sound had been sucked out of the environment.

"I know her, and so do you." Oran didn't make eye contact. "You know she's counting on it. We don't know what she has planned, except that she's ready for us."

"It's not as hopeless as all that," Celeste tried. "We'll get in there, stop whatever she's doing, and get her back to the Other World."

Oran waited a moment before he spoke. "What happens if one of us stays here?"

Celeste thought before she answered. "The oracle said it wouldn't be good. That we'd become part of Revary."

"Would that be so bad?" Oran asked.

She didn't stop walking, but she heard something in Oran's voice she didn't like. "What about our world? The people there who love us?"

Oran didn't reply, just kept his head down. Celeste glanced sideways at him. Was he saying what she thought he meant? She didn't want to believe it. She'd just never addressed his desperation. Or his darker thoughts. She really had been a bad friend.

Behind them, something heavy crashed to the ground. They both spun around to see Galis gripping Folkvar, who lay on the ground.

"Help me!" Galis called to Celeste. "It's the darkness."

Gasping, Celeste ran back. Folkvar groaned and rolled over onto his back, holding his arm where Zephyr had touched him. Celeste fell to her knees and picked up Folkvar's head, cradling it in her lap. Dark shadows spread from Folkvar's eyes.

"I...feel it," the great warrior whispered. "Taking me. The vanishing."

Celeste spread her fingers and touched the mark on his arm, summoning her healing powers. The light glowed, but nothing happened. "I can't heal him!" she cried. "What's happening?"

"Umbra," the oracle said from where he hung. "The vanishing cannot be healed, Celeste."

"Then how do I stop it?" she asked, panic making her shake. She looked up at the others. Lance looked just as lost as her. "How?" she shot to the oracle.

"Do as the Eidolon says," the oracle snapped. "You wanted a quest. You have one."

"But Folkvar," she wept. The norcan panted in her arms.

"Don't...let it...take me," he pleaded. "Let me go like a warrior, with a blade between my ribs."

"No." Celeste sniffled, wiping a tear from her eyes. "I can stop it. I know I can. I just..." But she didn't know. She sobbed.

"Galis," Folkvar asked, his breath rasping now. "You understand. Don't let me become an empty vessel. Don't let it take me." He swallowed hard. "Do it."

"But, Folkvar!" Celeste wailed. "Is dying worse than being taken to our world?"

"Celeste," the oracle said somberly. "It's not like you think. The won't come over to our world as they are. They'll be monstrous things. Dark and terrible things. They won't be as they are. Yes, death is preferable."

"I trust you," the norcan interrupted. "I know you will save my world. It just won't have me in it."

Celeste sobbed when Lance reached down and gripped her under her arms, hauling her up. He wrapped his arms around her and steered her away.

"I'm sorry!" Celeste screamed. "I'm so sorry, Folkvar." She wailed, clutching onto Lance as the others left Galis and Folkvar to carry out the brutal act. She knew in her heart that it was the right thing, but that didn't make it easier. Or make her feel like less of a failure.

"We'll find a way to save them," Lance whispered. "We'll do everything we can to stop this."

CHAPTER 30
BLACK HOLE

As the party drew closer, something appeared above one of the many turrets of the black castle. In a blast of purple and black light, a huge, gaping black hole appeared in the sky. The edges blurred and distorted as a halo of purple light swirled around it. Above them and to the north, Greylheim continued his destruction of the stars. Celeste wondered what had happened to the star, but didn't want to ask. Not now. Galis had said Stella had taken her and Yilith, and she didn't know what her old friend would have done to them.

"No guards," Alice mused as they entered the tall, thin castle. "This whole castle is more tower than palace."

Lance looked up, his wings unfurling slightly.

"No," Celeste said, guessing his intent. "We don't know what she's doing up there or what her powers might be."

He looked a little let down, but nodded. "Then we take the stairs?" he asked.

Celeste trotted up the first few flights and was winded by

the time they found the steps that branched off and led up into the tower where the black hole waited above it. The others panted too, but looked determined. Celeste looked around as she shoved opened the door at the foot of the stairs. No guards again. It was like Stella wanted to be found.

Then I guess I'll give her what she wants, Celeste thought. She squared up and marched up the steps, Oran, Lance, Alice, and Galis behind her.

"Be wary," the oracle warned in an annoyingly high voice. "Planes Striders are powerful beings."

"I know," Celeste said, her jaw set. "That's why I'm not afraid."

"Be afraid," the oracle advised. "She's your friend. You know her rage, her anger. Be very afraid."

Unsure what the warning was supposed to mean, Celeste took a deep breath and charged up the last few steps. She broke from the stone floor up into the open air chamber at the top of the tower. Four cruel spikes jutted up from the tower. In the center of them, the black hole swirled, sucking in the air around them, creating a harsh, cold wind. Below the black hole were two pillars. Chained to one was a big blue beast. It lay on its back, chest heaving as something white, like glowing and glittering smoke, was pulled from its eyes and mouth. The thing looked like it hung on the very edge of death.

"That's the thing that attacked Oran and me," Lance said softly.

On the second pillar was someone that made Celeste's heart stop. A small, black-clad figure hung by his wrists, head tilted back in unconsciousness.

"Yilith!" Celeste cried, unable to stop herself. She almost ran forward, then caught sight of a huge black-framed Mirror and a young woman standing before it. Stella gazed into the Mirror, though it was almost blacked out. Something—not her reflection—moved on the other side. "Stella," Celeste whispered, taking a few cautious steps forward.

"Don't come any closer," Stella warned. She raised her hand and a host of cloaked men appeared from black smoke. "Or my vampire army will have to deal with you."

Celeste looked around and scoffed through her nose. "This is so like you, Stell. A tower, sucking the life essence out of helpless victims." She glanced at Yilith. "Is he alive?"

"For now," Stella replied. She turned and faced Celeste. "I was hoping you wouldn't find me here. I knew the others would meet up with you again and I thought they'd take you to my other castle. I guess I underestimated you."

Celeste couldn't help but think how beautiful Stella was. With her black silk dress, her long hair with shots of purple in it, and her glittering, violet eyes. Celeste ran her hands over her own simple gold silk dress before meeting Stella's eyes. "What are you doing, Stell?" she asked quietly. "Why Yilith?"

Stella's eyes went cold as ice. "Because I know he's your creation."

Celeste frowned. "What do you mean?"

The dark star grinned. "I know exactly how Revary works. The dragon, servant of Umbra, told me." She shook her head. "You don't know. Celeste, I want Yilith because I know he's your character. You made them all when you came over the first time. This is your world. And you brought me to it. So I took him. And I will use his life essence to power this black hole. And you know what it will do?"

Celeste didn't move, waiting.

"Bring the vanishing here. It will swallow up this entire

region of your Revary." Stella gestured with a grand wave of her arm to the world beyond the tower.

"Why?" Celeste begged, tears threatening to fill her eyes.

Stella glared at her, clearly disgusted. "Because this is *your* world, Celeste. You made it, and I hate you."

"What did I do, Stell?"

Stella's eyes flitted from Celeste to Oran, then to Lance. "You destroyed what we had," she whispered. "You brought him in." She jabbed a finger at Lance. "And you took Oran from me."

"What are you talking about?" Oran interjected.

"You don't know because she is obsessed with Lance," Stella called to him.

Celeste went bright red.

"You don't know what you're talking about," Lance said. He drew his gun-blade. "I didn't hurt anyone."

A harsh, cold laugh bubbled up from Stella's throat. "It's ironic, since Celeste was the one who wanted everything to stay as it was. But she was the one who changed everything."

"Stella, stop," Celeste begged. "You don't know what you're saying. I didn't do anything. Lance didn't hurt anyone. And Oran was never yours."

"He would have been if you'd stopped leading him on!" Stella screamed.

An unknown guilt filled Celeste. She looked back quickly at Oran. His brow wasn't furrowed in denial. He looked hurt.

"I... I didn't know," Celeste tried. "Stella, please, you have to believe me. Oran," she turned back to him. "I'm sorry. You never..."

"I know," he said flatly. He gave her a weak smile.

"And you should hate Lance," Stella shot to Oran. "He came in and took Celeste's attention from you. He made

Justin angry. He tore us all apart by trying to weasel his friendship in."

"Lance was the only one who listened to me," Oran spat. "The only one who stood up for me. I don't hate him."

"Ugh!" Stella roared. She raised her hand, a black light glowing in her palm.

"Stell, wait!" Celeste cried, raising her hands. To her surprise, Stella halted. She went on, "I'm so sorry. I'm sorry I wasn't there for you. I'm sorry I've been so distracted. I'm sorry we haven't taken on the new challenges in life together. You're right; I've been a terrible friend. I admit that. I see that now. I swear I'll do better. I've been trying to do better. That's why I brought you here. I wanted to share it with you. I wanted us to stay friends."

Stella blinked. "I'm finished with this." She raised her hand and shot a bolt of black starlight into the black hole. When she did, the beast gasped, then exhaled a final breath.

Confused at why Stella would use the beast like that, Celeste blinked and watched it die. No sooner had it breathed its last than it transformed. The beast melted away to reveal a young man in princely garb. He had blue-black hair and a golden circlet around his brow.

"Gwen!" Celeste screamed. "How?"

"The vanishing," Stella smirked. "I transformed him once the darkness touched him. Rather than take him, I mutated him to do my bidding. A gift to me from Umbra."

A weak, "No," escaped Celeste's lips before she could stop it. She looked hard at Gwen, begging to see him breathing. But his handsome face remained impassive and unmoving. He was gone. Her eyes cut to Yilith, whose essence was also draining.

"Once the little elf is gone," Stella jeered, "Umbra will

have a dark portal strong enough to come through." She pointed to the black hole. "Soon."

"No!" Celeste screamed. She launched herself at Stella and tackled her to the ground. As she did, the vampires screeched and dived at the others. A sudden and brutal fight broke out around the two struggling stars.

"Where is she?" Celeste growled as she and Stella grappled with one another. "Where's the star?"

"Dead," Stella grunted back. "I killed her first."

Celeste screamed, a ray of light blasting from her palms. Stella toppled head over heels, protecting herself with a purple barrier of dark light.

"Yes, fight me!" Stella crowed. "No dice this time, Celeste. Just you and me."

Celeste spread her fingers and conjured a small shooting star in her palm. "Oran, get Yilith," she commanded with a shout. Then she hurled the small comet at Stella. The dark star blasted the comet to pieces before it hit her. Celeste took the second Stella was distracted to run to the other side of the tower. Stella's voice cried after her. Celeste turned to take in the battle raging around her in the small and cramped space.

Oran ran toward Yilith but a vampire stopped him, blocking his path. Oran used lightning to try to blast the monster away, but it dodged and knocked him over. The thing gripped Oran's hair and pulled his head back, mouth popping open.

"Don't bite him!" Celeste shouted, raising her hand to blast the vampire with starlight. Before she could, Stella sent a small meteorite pelting toward Celeste. She had to dive out of the way and crashed hard against the ground. When she looked up, the vampire had bitten Oran and had started to drink his blood.

Just as she shoved herself up, a shot rang out. Lance had aimed and fired his gun-blade at the vampire, hitting it square in the head. The thing jerked and tumbled off Oran.

Celeste stood up. "Oran!" she cried. He didn't move much, shaking and trying to rise. Lance ran to his side to defend him against another attack.

Just as Celeste got up, someone screamed. She looked to see Alice diving toward the edge, hands scrambling to catch Galis's outstretched fingers as he tumbled off the tower. She caught him and grunted loudly as she hauled him back up.

Celeste turned back to face Stella. Over Stella's shoulder, the unmistakable outline of a dragon undulated toward them.

"You can't win this fight," Stella said, giggling. "I have powerful allies, and you have only puny party members." She laughed again and held her hands up. A ball of black starlight began to grow in her palms.

"Shit!" Celeste cursed and ran around the perimeter of the tower. Above, the black hole pulled so hard she felt herself slip. Something inside rumbled and she swore she saw eyes looking out at her.

Stella screamed and hurled her ball of black light at Celeste. Taking a chance, Celeste stopped running and raised her hands, making a barrier of bright white light. The black light glanced off it and ricocheted toward Greylheim. The huge dragon couldn't move in time and took the black light straight to his chest. Hot, orange blood spurted out from the dragon and it roared.

"You idiot!" Stella screeched. She turned to watch Greylheim flip in the air, turn, and glide down to the earth.

Celeste's eyes went wide. *So that's why he was destroying the Celestial Plane. Starlight hurts him.* She panted, wondering how wounded the dragon was. Behind her, Stella grunted.

She turned to see her old friend circling her arm to make another black hole. The pull instantly hit Celeste and she jerked, sliding over the smooth tower floor in the direction of the pull. She grunted and tried to fight it, but there was nothing to hold on to. Making a guess, she conjured up an orb of starlight and hurled it into the black hole. When the orb hit the black hole, the thing crackled and fizzed out.

I have an idea! she screamed in her head. She checked that everyone was still fighting the vampires. Oran was still down and Lance was doing his best to defend him. Celeste took four huge steps away from Stella and focused inward. A growing sense of power rose inside her.

"What are you doing?" Stella sneered. "You look like an idiot, standing with your hands like that."

But Celeste didn't care. With a shout, she pulsed out the growing light within with every bit of strength she had. A bright white light burst from her in a ring of glittering starlight. When the wave hit the vampires, they ignited in flames and burst like human-sized bombs. Ashes filled the air. The light vanished and Celeste felt every bit of air leave her lungs. She gasped and fell forward onto her knees, wheezing.

Alice made a sudden lunge and growled. When Celeste looked up, she saw Alice had grappled Stella. "Don't even think about it," Alice hissed in Stella's ear from behind her.

"You bitch," Stella growled, her teeth clenched. "You think you can stop anything that's already set in motion?"

Celeste got to her feet with Galis bracing her. Lance helped Oran rise. "We're going to try, Stell," Celeste panted. "Something you never did. You gave up."

The animosity in Stella's eyes only grew. "No, I didn't. I just came here to take away your precious magic world."

"You don't understand," the oracle said. "What you do here has very real repercussions in your world."

"So do it," Stella grunted, trying only once, weakly, to throw Alice off. "Just get it over with, Celeste."

"What?" Celeste gasped. "No way. I can't do that. How did you? Did...?" She sniffled. "Did you really kill the star?"

Stella laughed coldly. "Fed her to the dragon like in the story books. Things are different here, Celeste. I don't have the qualms I did in our world. Here, I am powerful."

Celeste sobbed quietly. "And Gwen." She looked up, glaring through her tears. "How could you?"

"I told you: I wanted to destroy what was yours. What you made. Umbra told me to ignore my inhibitions, and I have. It wasn't easy, but here I am."

Alice tightened her grip, making Stella wince. "What should we do?" Alice asked.

Celeste looked at Lance and Oran. Oran was pale and shivering. "Don't do anything you'll regret," Lance said softly. "Don't..." But he didn't go on.

Celeste took a deep breath. "Alice, take her back."

"No!" Stella shrieked. Then she smiled. "You can't stop it, Celeste. Umbra is nearly here. Even if you take me and close the black hole, it will come. You cannot stop it. I was just expediting the vanishing. The destruction."

A glare creased Celeste's face. "I can't believe you did this."

"Well, I did." Stella smirked.

Alice met Celeste's eyes over Stella's shoulder. "Let me take her. Mirrors are portals. We'll go home. She can't hurt you there."

"Actually," the oracle said through partially closed lips. "She can. Revary is a reflection of our world."

"Then how do I stop it?" Celeste begged.

Just then, something cracked. The sound of splitting rock crackled through the air like lightning. They all spun to look. The huge gray mountains around them turned into black nothingness. Because of that, some of the base cracked and fell away, causing a huge avalanche below. The sky was perfectly black, all the stars and sun gone.

"Oh, my God," Celeste whispered. "It's really here."

"You have to hurry," Alice said, her tone turning urgent. "We'll go. You stay."

"But what do I do?" Celeste begged.

Alice shrugged, defeated. "I don't know. But we have to take her away through the Mirror."

"That will work for sure?" Celeste asked.

"Yes," the oracle confirmed, rolling his eyes. "Mirrors are gateways."

Alice nodded in resolution. Dragging Stella, who kicked and grunted, she made her way back toward the black Mirror. She stopped just before it. "You all be safe. And come back."

"Careful, Alice," Lance called to his cousin. "We'll see you soon."

Alice nodded then leaned into the Mirror. Stella screamed in protest as they tipped into the glass. The smooth surface rippled and swallowed them up like water. Celeste gasped at the strange magic. She waited, but nothing came back through. She hoped they landed safely in the Other World.

She turned to Lance and Oran. "If either of you want—"

"No," Lance cut in. "We're staying. And..." He glanced over the edge. "I have an idea of who we can ask about how to save Revary."

Celeste only wondered for a moment. If he wasn't dead, Greylheim was wounded and lying just below.

Above them, the black hole crackled and vanished. Celeste looked up, then her eyes snapped to the pillars where Gwen's body lay, and Yilith.

"Yilith!" she screamed, running to him. She landed on her knees and lifted the elf into her arms. "I'm so sorry. Are... Are you...?" But she couldn't go on. She didn't need to. His breath came shallow and his body felt frail in her arms. "I'm so sorry," she whispered again. She lay her forehead against his.

"It's all right," the elf whispered. "I believe in you. I will see Revary again." His voice was so weak and soft, she had to lean in close to hear him. "Just do that, Planes Strider. Save Revary. Bring it back." He shuddered in her arms. "My mission was to find a Planes Strider, and I did. Now it's up to you."

Celeste nodded. "I couldn't save you. I couldn't save Folkvar. Or Gwen."

"Enough," Yilith hissed. "Do it now. While you have time."

"But—" she started again.

Yilith raised his hand and placed his cold fingers over her mouth, silencing her. "Go to the dragon. Slay it."

His hand fell away and his eyes closed. He still breathed, but Celeste knew the breaths were numbered. She nodded, sniffling. "All right. I'll go slay the dragon."

CHAPTER 31
A DRAGON OF MANY WORLDS

Celeste led the way down Stella's tower and out into what remained of Revary. The stillness almost sucked the air out of her lungs as she looked around for the fallen dragon. She spotted it lying near the base of the tower, head down as it struggled to stand. The mountains behind them splintered again and another avalanche overtook a small town near the base. The tops of the mountains vanished into blackness, leaving nothing behind.

"What do we do to stop that?" Lance asked. "What if it touches us?"

Celeste gulped. "I'm not sure."

"I've seen what it does to us," Galis replied, gripping his long sword hard as they approached the dragon. "I won't fall so easily."

As they neared the dragon, it didn't strike a defensive pose. Greylheim let out a great sigh and flopped to the ground with shivering repercussions. The earth trembled again.

Laying its head down between its forelegs, its great orange eyes met each of them.

"Our battle is not one to fight," he said in a slow, deep voice. Hot red dragon's blood covered the ground beneath him from where Celeste had redirected Stella's attack. "We are all going to die here and now. Umbra is coming. Its corruption is here now. Look around you. See the mountains fall, the surface collapse, the sky in tatters like a ripped flag, the sun's last embers falling. This is the world of the Planes Striders' imagination. Revary is only here because of your dreams, stories. But all you have done is dream, Planes Strider. You do not take action; you do not act on your passion."

Celeste met her friends' eyes. They didn't understand either. "Are these your last words, dragon?" she asked.

"Strike me down now and Revary will perish!" Greylheim snarled back. "Don't you want to know how to save your precious world?"

"You'll tell us?" Oran asked. He'd backed up and raised one hand, ready to sling his arcane magic should the dragon attack.

Greylheim took a deep breath and let it out, blowing hot breath over them. "There is no reason for me not to now. I am dying. I know that. But so is Revary." He raised his head and looked around. "This is the last plot of earth left. Everything is gone, even the Celestial Plane. The Astral Plane is sundering and that boy king is dying."

Celeste glared hard. "Then tell me, dragon. We're running out of time. Tell me and I might even save you."

Greylheim chuckled deep in his throat. "It is a hard truth, Planes Strider. When you hope for a great future, Revary's borders are expanded. When you act on those dreams, they

^X 358 ^X

become real in your world and in Revary. When you just dream them up and never do anything about those thoughts, they die. When you push those dreams, half-created, out into the world without taking care to see they are the best they can be, those are weak pieces of this land. Corrupted ones."

"But Planes Striders have ideas all the time. They dream all the time," Lance said. "Why is Revary being destroyed, then?"

"Have you not seen what you do?" Greylheim asked. "Even I am disgusted at the Planes Striders when I venture there. You do not use your minds to create fantastic dreams anymore. You do not use your hearts to hope. You do not put into action that which you hope to achieve. You are corrupted and so are your dreams! You only wish. Wishes are not good enough anymore. You must *do*." His eyes turned to Celeste. "You wait for dreams to come true rather than make them a reality. You cheat to satiate your lack of victory."

Guilt burned Celeste's cheeks.

Oran said, "I still don't quite understand who you are, then. Are you someone's dream?"

Greylheim growled again, his face twisting in offense. "I am no Revarian! I am not of this world. I am not of any world you can ever know now. To understand me is to know my greatest enemy, and I cannot allow you to do that. I like ignorant beings. I make Planes Striders hopeless. I make them crave things that will destroy that which gives them the ability to think for themselves. I prefer your weak aspirations. I want you wishing, never acting. Wish, wish, wish, little dreamer! Wait for the wishes to come true and hope. There is no power in only wishing."

Celeste thought about the dragon's words. In a strange, unreal way, they were beginning to make sense. She had to let her mind free of its constraints to think, and that wasn't easy. She had to realize that the material world, of gravity, substance, and physical touch that she knew, was not the only world.

"Our world, then, and us," she motioned to Oran and Lance. "Who are we? The Eidolon was not clear on that."

The dragon smiled. "Why should I tell you?"

"Because you're dying as well," Oran pointed out. "You're tired. The corruption has you, too. I thought it wouldn't affect you."

The orange eyes narrowed on Oran. "I am a great servant of Umbra, not its master. It takes who it pleases. I give myself willingly to further its cause." He sighed again. "You are right, however. The vanishing is in me already. But I go joyfully. With my sacrifice, I was able to take two of your friends. I took their hopes and dreams and made them vessels of empty ambition."

"Justin?" Lance said as Celeste said, "Stella?"

"Yes." The dragon grinned. "You see it now. They are alive and prosperous for Umbra! Wanting things that do not really make them happy, working themselves to death for a world they hate. They see no way out and are trapped by my ideas. Umbra is rooted deep in their minds. When they lose all hope, they will be loyal servants, like myself, preaching my sermons to your world. They will have no purpose in life. People with no purpose are easily corrupted; vessels of vanishing. They are all mindless action with no wishes and no dreams."

"What do you want with a world full of Planes Striders?" Celeste demanded.

"It is they who create all things in another universe." He smiled mysteriously. "Like your story. If your story were to be shared, I would lose my battle. Your adventure has been a good one, for you have grown in strength and wisdom. If others were to know of your quest, they might join you. Stories like yours cause Planes Striders to think mostly good thoughts, gives them desires to find purpose. That is what I loathe. Humans who understand their purpose are impossible to control."

"We just have to tell our story to stop you in our world?" Oran asked. "That's it?"

"Wrong!" Greylheim snarled. "You must act, Planes Strider. You must do with purpose that which you were made to do."

Oran's face suddenly dawned with understanding. But it also fell. He looked like he'd suddenly learned some terrible news.

"That doesn't help us here," Lance said. "How do we stop this?"

As he spoke, lightning cracked across the sky so loud it shook the earth. The thunder followed it, rumbling in their very chests. More came in an endless string of crackles and thunder. Greylheim looked up.

"We are out of time. If we must go, I will take you. Goodbye, Planes Striders." The dragon launched itself at Celeste and the others.

"Watch out!" Lance cried as they stumbled back into the now thunder- and lightning-filled darkness. "Don't touch it."

Greylheim spun on the spot and turned to glare at the little humans he'd missed in his leap. "Revary is only a small patch of life now."

Celeste looked around as the darkness inched closer. "What do we do?" she shrieked.

"Come, dragon!" Galis shouted. He ran the perimeter of

what was left of the ground, toward the tower. Greylheim watched with a hunter's glint in his orange eyes.

"What are you doing?" Celeste cried.

"Go, Planes Strider," Galis said, planting his feet and spinning his sword in his grip. With his other hand, he flicked his fingers, summoning Greylheim.

The dragon turned and bounded at the mountain warrior. Celeste screamed, but Lance gripped her shoulder, his wings unfurling.

"Protect me," he gasped. With a powerful gust from his wings, he leapt into the air and soared over the head of the dragon as it dived. "Oran, give me some power," he said. He held his gun-blade up and a bolt of purple lightning spidered out from Oran's hand to the blade.

Celeste flexed her fingers and created a starlight barrier around Lance as he flew up. The dragon tried to use its tail to swat at Lance, but it bounced off the barrier. Ignoring Lance, Greylheim finished his dive onto Galis, catching him in his maw. Galis groaned in agony as the dragon bit down on him, but he'd positioned his sword well. As the dragon bit down, the blade pierced him up through the top of his mouth. Greylheim growled and thrashed as Lance came down from above. He stabbed the dragon through the top of his skull and fired a shot.

With a jolt, the dragon lurched, then stopped moving. A moment later, Greylhiem teetered on his feet and fell.

"Get down!" Celeste shouted, seeing the head of the dragon would fall into the wildly snapping and roaring darkness.

Lance leapt up, his wings beating, and gently hovered to the ground. Both panting, Celeste flew into his arms, hugging him tight. Greylheim fell, and his long neck took his head and Galis into the darkness. It didn't move.

"Good barrier," Lance gasped. Celeste sniffled, and nodded. "Oran." Lance turned, looking.

"Galis!" Celeste called, not daring to get close to the darkness. No one answered back. "Galis," she said again weakly. "Lance, I've failed. They're all gone. Every last one of the people I met. They were looking for me, hoped I would save them, and I failed!"

Lance petted her head, but still looked around. "Where's Oran?"

Celeste looked up, still hugging him around the middle tight. "He was just right here." Fear gripped her and she pushed away from Lance. "No way the darkness got him." She looked around. "Oran!" she screamed.

Together, they both called into the ever-encroaching darkness. Celeste ran into Lance's arms again, holding him tight. "What's about to happen?" she gasped.

Lance looked around. Then he stopped, looking above. "Look," he cried.

Celeste looked up and immediately spotted what he saw in the darkness. A single golden, glowing tree. It was so far away, it looked to be the size of a thimble. She focused on it. "Do you think...?" she asked, not daring to hope. "Do you think the Eidolon is still alive?"

"Let's find out." Lance gripped her hard, pulling her up so he carried her in his arms. She slipped her hands around his neck and held on tight.

"Lance," she started. "If... If we die before we get there..."

"Don't," he interrupted. "Don't say anything you'll regret once we're home and all this is a memory."

They both glanced down to see they stood on the last,

smallest patch of grass. Lance looked up, bent his legs, and launched himself into the air. Celeste's stomach flipped as they shot up. The darkness surrounded them and the lightning and wind picked up so strongly that she thought it might rip her from Lance's arms. She clutched him tight, burying her face in his chest.

A few times, Lance tilted dangerously to the left and right, buffeted by powerful gusts. But he held the course, taking them through the vanishing and up closer to the golden tree. The closer they got, the larger it became. Lance angled hard against a strong current and soared to the outstretched branches. He kicked his feet forward and landed hard, almost dropping Celeste. She slid down and looked up into the branches of the golden tree.

"I see a light coming from one room," she whispered. "I hope that's him."

Together, they ascended a partially broken set of steps and headed up to find out if they were indeed too late to save Revary.

CHAPTER 32
DREAMS OF CREATION

A light inside the doorway was so bright that Celeste's eyes watered as she entered. She blinked, rubbing them, and then squinted into the room.

"Wait a minute," she said. She glanced around as Lance came in behind her.

The room was not the large, glowing bedroom the Eidolon had been sitting in when she'd seen him last. Instead, the setup from her own basement greeted her eyes. But it wasn't her whole basement. The light hung above the gaming table, which was covered in dice, miniatures, maps, pens, and other paraphernalia and evidence of their games. The chairs even sat around the table. But that was all that was familiar. No walls surrounded the gaming table, and the light simply hung from the air. Around them grew trees filled with birds softly singing, like they were far away. Sunlight burst through the leaves and branches, splashing over them. To the left of the game table, a pool of water waited, reflecting back the trees and sunlight like a perfect mirror.

Celeste looked down, feeling the weight of her silken dress gone. She stood in her green t-shirt and leggings. She snapped around and saw Lance wore jeans and a hoodie now, his wings and gun-blade gone. They were normal again. She looked around, confused. Behind a few trees, a glass archway reached up to the sky before curving elegantly back down into the ground. The earth was a strange mixture of the carpet in her basement and grass.

"What's happening?" Celeste asked.

"This is your basement, isn't it?" Lance asked, looking around. "I mean, sort of."

She nodded. She swore she heard music coming from somewhere, but couldn't pinpoint where. Both of them spun on the spot, looking around. Celeste leaned over the gazing pool and looked at the reflection there. As she leaned over, she noticed her own face didn't look back at her.

"It's not a mirror," a smooth, smiling voice said. Celeste whipped around to the glass archway. Standing there, robed in white, his yellow hair aglow under a glass circlet, stood the Eidolon. He stepped through as if coming back to them after having broken off conversation. "The gazing pool shows other places."

Celeste looked back, calming from her initial jump. "But it looks like here. The trees, the sun."

"It *is* here," the Eidolon said. "But in another place. Just as this is your basement in your own home in your world. But also not. It's your home in another place."

Lance and Celeste shared a quick glance with one another.

The Eidolon smiled and laughed lightly.

Lance faced him. "You look better. Stronger. How is that possible, since Revary was destroyed?"

The Eidolon nodded and came around the table, admiring the miniatures. "Destroyed, but not gone. You carry it in here." He tapped his chest. "It's ready to be reborn, I think. Just as you are."

"Us?" Lance asked. He suddenly took a defensive pose. "What's going on?"

"Wait, Lance," Celeste said softly, taking his arm in her hands. "Don't get scared and combative." She looked at the Eidolon. "What do you mean?"

The Eidolon picked up a miniature Celeste knew all too well: it was her fighter. He spun it in his fingers by the base, admiring it. Then he smiled and gave a laugh. "The vanishing took you. You no longer exist in Revary. If you wait too long, you won't exist in your world, either."

"Can we go back?" Lance asked.

"Of course. But do you want to leave Revary?"

"No!" Celeste cried. "I tried to save it. I really did! But I failed." She dropped her head in shame and a tear came to her eye.

"You shouldn't worry so much," the Eidolon said. "You have the power of creation. Make Revary again. Make it how you always imagined it to be." He smiled coyly. "I know you wanted to see it before Umbra. This is your chance."

"Umbra!" Celeste said. "We couldn't defeat it. I never even saw it."

The Eidolon's face fell a little. "There is more to Umbra than simply being the villain in this story, Celeste. Umbra exists in your world, too. Has the same devastating effects. There are many infected with the vanishing. They have no purpose. Or don't know their purpose. Like you: they don't know their role in life. But Umbra is more than that. It comes in many shapes and forms, some harder to see than others."

"Can I save them?" she asked. "If I don't know my role..."

"Perhaps." He set her miniature down. "There are those around you who know their purpose."

"Justin?" Celeste asked. "Even Greylheim said he was corrupted."

The Eidolon smiled and shook his head. "One among you has learned to be brave. Learned who he is inside and has embraced his role." His eyes flitted to Lance.

Lance shifted his feet and looked uncomfortable. "I have? I don't feel like it."

"And you won't always." The Eidolon smiled kindly. "But you have. You have faith in yourself. You have learned bravery and kindness. You are ready."

Celeste felt left out now. She glanced at Lance and saw him looking a little more at ease. Would she be ready?

The Eidolon picked up a D20. "Magic exists in these little rocks?"

Lance and Celeste glanced at one another again. "I suppose," Celeste answered. "But can we focus on getting us back?"

"Whatever you want, Celeste. It's your story."

She shifted her feet at that, not sure what to say or think. "The vanishing took us," she repeated. "So, where are we?"

"Somewhere in-between," the Eidolon replied, his face finally turning serious. "If you stay here, Revary will be gone forever, as will you."

"Then how are we here?" Lance asked. "If we got taken?"

"Because there are others sharing your story." The Eidolon smiled. "They are keeping you alive right now."

"Kiyoshi?" Lance asked. "The anchor?"

The Eidolon didn't reply.

Celeste gulped and looked around. "What do we have to do?"

"Why don't you start with remaking Revary?" the Eidolon asked. "What do you want it to look like?"

Celeste took a deep breath and looked into the gazing pool. "Well, I want Calimorden back. I want it clean and full of warriors with valor in their hearts. I want it to be a place adventurers can go to find quests and have a good time at the tavern."

"Sounds amazing." The Eidolon looked into the pool.

Celeste and Lance followed his gaze and saw the pool turn dark. Then, something like a sunrise brightened every corner of it. The sun splashed over a white palace with grand walls and many colorful flags and standards outside it. Green fields sprawled out around it and a sparkling blue moat surrounded it.

"That's it!" Celeste squealed in joy. She grabbed Lance's arm and jumped up and down. "That's Calimorden." She looked up. "And Gwen's there. He's coming back from a hunt and is alive and well."

"So it shall be." The Eidolon smiled and nodded. "What else?"

"The norcan," Lance suggested, pointing to the green fields. "Great warriors and violent monsters at the same time. They're defending their borders from—"

"Goblins!" Celeste burst, grinning broadly. "But a rogue posse of bandits are coming back for revenge on the goblins for raiding their camp."

"The warriors in the north are there, too," Lance said. "They're about to celebrate the coming of a twin-tailed comet that brightens up the whole sky. Their shamans will read the stars and make prophecies that will send them and their descendants on quests for generations to come."

"Marvelous." The Eidolon beamed. He looked down and they watched everything they'd said come to life in the gazing pool.

Celeste's heart leapt into her throat as she watched everything spring up, new and fresh. "They're all alive," she said, her nose tingling with emotion. "Galis, Yilith, Folkvar and the star. I want it all to be as it should be."

A burst of starlight filled the gazing pool as the Celestial Plane came back into existence. Celeste watched in wonder and could only imagine what the world looked like outside the golden tree now.

"Can I see them?" she asked.

The Eidolon looked up, his face sad. "This isn't your story anymore, Celeste. Your chapter in Revary is coming to an end. Don't interfere with their new lives. Let them live them out. Let them be. Give them adventures, yes, but don't insert yourself into someone else's story."

"But," she started, tears filling her eyes. "But if all this is true, they're okay. They're back. Don't they remember me?"

Lance placed his hand on her shoulder.

"No," the Eidolon said sadly. "To reenter their lives now would be to take away that which you have just given them. Remake Revary, save yourself. And be satisfied."

Celeste sniffled and looked up at Lance. "We've done our part," he said as calmly as he could.

"And you, Celeste?" the Eidolon asked. "Do you know your role?"

She took a deep breath and watched the sun rise over Calimorden. "No. But that doesn't scare me. I think I'll figure it out. I have to try. I have to turn my wishes into actions. And I will. I know what to do."

The Eidolon beamed at her. "What will you do first?"

Celeste couldn't tear her eyes away from the pool, watching Revary be birthed anew. "I'll investigate my future. See what I want to do. Then...I'll apply to colleges. I have to set myself up for success. I can't wait around for the world to tell me who I am. I have to find out for myself and commit."

"Well spoken."

"But where's Oran? He was with us," Lance asked.

"Oh, Oran!" Celeste burst, spinning back around to look the Eidolon in the eye.

The boy raised his head, then looked down at the floor, avoiding their eyes. "I spoke with Oran before you came to me," he said. "The vanishing...didn't take him."

"What?" Lance asked. "Then where did he go?"

"Into the vanishing. But he went of his own accord."

Celeste didn't believe that. "No, he wouldn't."

"He did. It is a sad choice, but it was his to make, no matter how wrong it was."

"It *was* the wrong choice," Lance said. "Where is he? What happened to him?"

The Eidolon clasped his hands behind his back and still didn't look them in the eyes. "When a Revarian crosses over into your world, they become something terrible. A lie, a voice whispering darkness in your ear. Here, they are good stories. In your world, they become corrupt and turn into bad stories. A Planes Strider is little different. They can stay behind in Revary. But they become memories—stories or dreams—in your world. Ones that eventually fade. He will be forgotten, and perhaps that will be the best thing."

Celeste felt Lance tense up beside her. She looked up into

his face and saw him swallow hard, his eyes betraying his worry.

"Oran wants to stay," the Eidolon said sadly. "It is not the right choice, but it is too late now. He is part of Revary and cannot go back."

"No way," Lance said stiffly, his voice thick. "He wouldn't..." But he stopped. "No. I know better. He would."

"But why?" Celeste sobbed. "What about his mother? Us?"

Tears even filled the Eidolon's eyes at this. He finally met their gazes, his golden eyes shimmering with tears. "As I said, it was a bad choice. A selfish one, perhaps. I shouldn't allow it, but perhaps he will speak with you?"

"Please," Lance said. "Can you find him?"

The Eidolon nodded and turned to the glass archway. He stepped through it and vanished.

Alone, Celeste turned to Lance. "Why'd he do that? What do you know?"

Lance shook his head. "It's not for me to tell. We've had conversations, though. Ones that worried me. But I thought... I thought I could save him."

"Save him?" Celeste asked.

A bright flash indicated that the Eidolon had returned. Behind him came Oran. He looked pale and wore black garb that reminded Celeste of warlocks in *Elderforge*. His face fell when he spotted them.

"Oran!" Celeste cried. She ran to him, throwing her arms around his neck. "Why? What did we do wrong?"

He stood stiff at first, not reciprocating the embrace. Then, after meeting Lance's eyes, he gave in and hugged her. "You didn't do anything."

"But I should have!" she sobbed. "I should have known

you were having these thoughts. You're one of my best friends. This is my fault. I wasn't watching out for you."

"No, it's not your fault," Oran said, pulling her off him. "I made this choice."

"You shouldn't have had to make it," Lance cut in, coming up behind Celeste. "Why didn't you talk to me more?"

Oran swallowed and shrugged. "I didn't know what to say. You'd worry no matter how I said what I was feeling."

"No shit," Lance shot back. "This is all my fault." He turned to the Eidolon. "Is there anything we can do?"

The Eidolon shook his golden head. "He is part of Revary now. If he crossed over to your world, you would not know him there. He wouldn't be as he is even now."

"But, Oran," Celeste begged. "Please, tell me why?"

Oran's face twisted in sadness. "It's too hard to explain, Celeste. All you'll do is blame yourself." He eyed Lance. "It's no one's fault but my own."

"But it's wrong!" she sobbed. "You're a Planes Strider. What about your mother?"

Oran nodded. "She'll eventually forget me."

"And until then," Lance said, "we, what, mourn you?" He sniffled and looked away to wipe his hands across his eyes.

"You will all forget," the Eidolon said. "Like a story you once read, he will fade from your mind."

"Oran," Celeste said, tears thickening her voice. "How can you make us hurt like this?"

He didn't reply. He looked down into the gazing pool and remained silent.

Lance lunged forward, engulfing Oran in his arms in a tight embrace. Once again, Oran didn't reciprocate until a moment later, his arms wrapping around Lance's middle.

"Take care of her," he whispered, but Celeste heard. "Please, Lance."

"I will," he promised, burying his face in Oran's dark hair. He held him tight a moment longer before letting go. The three of them looked at one another.

"Oran has failed his quest, I am sorry to say," the Eidolon said at length. "That is what has happened."

Oran didn't look at the Eidolon, accepting his verdict.

The Eidolon stepped forward. "It is time for you all to leave," he said. "You have done what you were meant to do, and now your chapter in Revary must come to a close."

"What do you mean?" Celeste asked.

"I mean, you shall not return to Revary."

"Oh, no," Celeste sobbed, dropping her face into her hands. "I wanted to see it."

"And one day you may." The Eidolon put his hand on her shoulder. "But not as you have. You will never walk these Planes again. Now you must find your purpose in *your* world. Save your story there just as you have here. Do you understand? That is what you must do."

She nodded. Lance stepped away from Oran and reached for her hand. She took it and they both faced the Eidolon.

"Then go," he said, smiling. "Go back to your world."

The light grew brighter, blinding them.

"Oran," Lance called beside her. "I'll never forget you. I refuse. Got that? I'll never forget you."

The white light grew until it was too bright and they had to close their eyes. Celeste gripped Lance's hand hard, desperate to not let go of him.

CELESTE BLINKED, HER EYES WATERING AGAIN. SHE looked up into the branches of the trees where the sunlight— or whatever the light was—blinded her. Her hand moved around at her side, searching for Lance. He wasn't there.

"Lance!" she cried out. Then, when the thought hit her, she weakly called, "Oran?"

When her eyes adjusted, she saw she stood in the center of a wood. Cool air touched her cheek, and the sun shone warmly down. Her nose twitched, catching a familiar, musty, woody scent. She knew these woods.

"Guys?" she called, spinning on the spot. Some birds called back, and the day bugs sang louder. The leaves above turned to gold and orange, a few splashing bright red among them. Autumn was in full swing. She gasped. What time was it? Glancing down at her watch, she saw it was five in the evening on a Saturday.

Once the shock of being back in her world wore off, she trudged down the hill to where she knew the parking lot, the ranger station, and a phone waited. The soft dirt path turned to gravel under her feet. To her left, she passed what they often called the town hall: the shelter with a firepit where they had held many of their meetings about *Sun Age* and had written many campaigns. Soon, this little spot would be the only bit of the park left. She could hear the construction close by.

She jogged down the gravel path to the resting place where a few more shelters and the ranger station waited. No one was on duty as it was Saturday, but she could still access the payphone on the side. Begging there to be change, she checked the change return and found a quarter. Thanking the Eidolon, she put it in and dialed her home. Her mother answered, worried sick about her, and raged for a solid ten seconds before Celeste asked to be picked up. When she asked how long she'd been gone, her mother said all day.

"Only a day?" she whispered, which earned her another earful. She hung up and wished she knew Lance's number by heart. She waited, arms wrapped tight around herself until her mother appeared in their old minivan. Apologizing for running off without leaving word, she remained quiet for the rest of the trip back as her mother gave her another lecture about running off. She was swiftly grounded from all social events, but Celeste didn't care.

Once back in her room, she dashed to her computer and fired it up, hoping the others were near theirs. She jumped into their chat room and immediately typed:

I'm home. Please tell me someone is here.

She waited about ten seconds before Alice typed, *Here. Alive and well. You have to tell us what happened.*

What happened to Stella?

She ran off. You?

Long story. Lance?

He's home. Told me a few things, but not everything I'm guessing.

Celeste sighed in relief and collapsed into her computer chair. She looked at the list of her online friends and saw Oran's name hovering in gray. Her heart snapped in two all over again. She dropped her face into her hands and cried.

Her computer chimed and chimed again. Someone was typing to her. She looked up to see Kiyoshi on.

I had wild visions while you guys were gone, he typed. *Glad you made it back. Where's Oran?*

She froze. *We need to meet up,* she typed after a moment. *My house, after dinner.*

THE BASEMENT WAS DARK. THE ONLY LIGHT COMING from the one above the table. Everyone sat around it, watching and listening to her. Celeste had been talking for what felt like hours by the time she came to the end where she and Lance had stood alone in the Eidolon's weird room that was a cross between her basement and the woods. But she couldn't stop. She went on and on, Lance interjecting every now and then. Alice's eyes were huge, and Kiyoshi sat stoic and unmoving. Once she got to the part about Oran, she stopped. She couldn't go on. Lance took charge then and bravely finished the story, explaining how Oran wanted to stay.

"How...why?" Alice asked, sputtering.

Lance looked away from them then, fiddling with a miniature on the table. "He'd been talking like that for a long time," he said softly. "I thought if I stayed close, was his friend, he'd change his mind. It's better than..." He couldn't say it. "You know?"

Kiyoshi clasped his hands under his chin, frowning in thought. "We can't blame ourselves. That will just lead to unbearable guilt. And I suppose it is better. This way, we'll forget him. He'll be a memory we can't quite grasp. There will be no pain later."

"And us?" Alice asked. "What now? Stella ran away from me when we came back."

Celeste looked up through her tears. "Where did you land?"

"In her room, in front of that big mirror," Alice explained. "She shoved me hard and ran. Her mom wasn't home, so I just let myself out. I was just glad to be home." She shook her head. "I don't know how you crossed over so many times, Celeste. It's not for me. I want to stay here. Make adventures here. Live this life." She licked her lips, thinking before she finished with, "You're brave to keep going back. It was too scary for me."

"Well," Celeste said, "we won't be going back. The Eidolon said so." She sighed, done crying and exhausted.

"You want to go back?" Kiyoshi asked, a little shock showing in his voice finally. "After everything that happened?"

Celeste looked at Lance. "Sort of. I understand that place. Better than here."

"Don't," he cut in. "Find out how this world works. Play *this* game."

She sniffled again. "But I don't want to do it. This world is so lonely. And complicated."

"Uh, hello?" Alice said, pointing to herself and then the other two. "We're here. We're a party. We're not lone adventurers. We all have trials and quests to complete. Let's do it together."

Kiyoshi nodded, a small smile finally breaking his stoic face. "And let's try to not forget what's happened. None of it."

"Together?" Celeste asked.

"Together," Lance said, taking her hand.

From above, Celeste's mother shouted that they'd better be studying and not playing games. Celeste smiled at her friends and shouted back, "We're ready for anything. Don't worry."

CHAPTER 33
FALLOUT

Celeste braced herself outside Stella's house. She hadn't reached out the night before when they'd all gotten back. She thought maybe Stella needed some space. But she couldn't wait any longer. Besides, it was only a matter of time before the real fallout began. That morning, Oran's mother had called them, asking where he was. He hadn't come home the night before. Celeste said she didn't know. They all left the park in separate cars.

She knocked hard on Stella's front door. She held her breath. What was she going to say? She didn't have a plan. She just knew she had to say something. Stella had been her best friend since first grade and Celeste wanted to know if they were ever going to be friends again. She doubted it. How could she after all Stella had done? Tried to do? But she had to at least talk to her.

"What do you want?"

The door opened enough for Celeste to see Stella's mom's face behind the crack and golden chain that locked the door.

"Oh, uh, Mrs. Blackwell," Celeste stammered. She twisted her fingers together in nervousness, forcing herself to make eye contact. "Is Stella home?"

The woman sneered through the crack in the door. "She is. She doesn't want to talk to you. She told me what you said about her at school."

"Huh?" Celeste burst. "I didn't say anything about her at school. This has nothing to do with school."

Mrs. Blackwell scoffed, wrinkling her nose. "You're no longer welcome here, Celeste. Stella doesn't want to see you."

"But, Mrs. Blackwell, please! I need to talk to her. I need to..." She sighed inwardly. "I want to apologize." What had Stella said she'd said? Whatever it was, it was a lie.

"It's too late for that, Celeste," the woman said. Her eyes dulled. She wasn't going to hear anything Celeste had to say now. She was closing her out. "The damage has been done. There's nothing you can do to take it back. I'm disappointed in you."

Celeste melted into the pavement. "Me, too, Mrs. Blackwell. I'm sorry to have bothered you."

The door slammed shut and Celeste heard her turn the lock. She looked at the purple paint on the door and tears welled in her eyes. She used to love seeing that purple door. Stella usually came out of it. Now it was just a locked door.

Celeste brushed a tear away and walked down the steps onto the sidewalk. She looked back at the house and up at the window she knew was the one in Stella's room. She gasped. Stella stood in the window, looking down at her. Celeste waved and then motioned for her to come down. Stella only glared down at her and then turned away from the window without so much as blinking.

Now Celeste wanted to shout. To yell. To demand that

Stella take back whatever she said about her. But what was the use? And besides, she still loved Stella. At least she had tried.

Try again? she wondered to herself. *Another day?* Would it matter? Or was Stella done with her for good? *I didn't do anything wrong!* Celeste thought as she dashed back across the road to her house. But was that the issue? Stella had been hurting and she hadn't asked why. She hadn't even noticed.

Yeah, she thought. *This is my fault.*

She ran into her own house and up to her room where she opened her chat rooms to see who was on. No one was except Justin. She looked at his avatar and wondered what he was up to. She thought about kicking him from the chat room, but then thought better of it. Maybe he'd leave of his own accord? Did she need to speak to him?

Then, the alert sound beeped, telling her Justin had sent her a message.

Oran's mom called me, he wrote. *He didn't come home last night. Know anything?*

Celeste hummed in thought. Did Justin care enough to ask? That seemed strange. She poised her hands over the keyboard and thought. Should she say anything? What if she sounded guilty?

His mom called the cops, Justin typed again. *If I were you, I'd get ready.*

Celeste went pale. The cops? Would they come around asking questions? She swallowed and blinked, but didn't reply. Downstairs, someone knocked on the door. She waited, listening, and holding her breath.

"Celeste," her mom called up after a few moments. "Someone here to see you."

She didn't move, eyes wide. What was she supposed to say

to the cops? She froze, hands still over the keyboard. Someone knocked on her bedroom door.

"Celeste, it's Lance," her mom said, her voice muffled through the door.

"Lance?" Celeste asked. She bolted up and ran to the door. She swung it open.

Before her stood her concerned-looking mother and Lance. His brown hair was a little messy, but fell in front of his deep brown eyes. She liked that.

"Hey," Lance said, hands deep in his pockets. "I need to talk to you."

"Talk?" her mom asked, raising one brow.

"I swear, just talk," Lance said respectfully.

Her mom nodded and turned to head back down the stairs. Celeste motioned Lance into her room and then closed the door. Lance came in, looking awkward. She liked that he wasn't completely at ease like he usually was. It made him cute.

"So what's up?" she asked. She sat on the edge of her bed and motioned for Lance to sit in her computer chair, but he paced instead.

Lance didn't take his hands out of his pockets and turned away from her. "Yesterday was, I mean..." He sighed and turned to face her. "That was crazy, right? I can't stop thinking about it. About everything we did. About Oran." He stopped then, his eyes suddenly bright with tears.

Celeste shot up and went to him, putting her arm around his middle. She hugged him and her cheeks suddenly flared and her heart hammered. She almost held her breath, but then breathed in his cologne. It was something woodsy and almost like amber.

This was the first time she'd touched him like this. Her

skin seared where it touched him. She laid her face against his chest and held him tight.

"I know," she whispered. "It's all a lot."

Lance slowly put his hands on her back and hugged her in return. He dropped his head and pressed his cheek into the top of her head.

"The nightmare I had last night was terrifying," he said. "I kept seeing that monster, feeling it grab wings that aren't there. Every time I close my eyes, I see something from Revary. And it scares me."

Celeste tightened her hold on Lance. "I know. I'm so sorry. I don't know how to make it all go away."

They waited a moment before Lance slowly pushed her away. He looked into her eyes a moment and then nodded. "I don't want it to go away," he said. "I just want to know that it all was worth it."

Celeste licked her lips and tried to think of a reply. Worth it? What would make it worth it? She sat onto her bed and looked into the middle distance, thinking.

"Celeste," Lance said softly. He sat in the computer chair and pulled it up close to her. "I promised Oran I'd watch out for you. And I mean to follow through on that promise."

She looked up into his deep brown eyes and saw something there she never thought to see in Lance's eyes; pleading. Was he about to ask her something? She scooted forward on the bed and took his hand.

"Go on," she whispered.

Lance took a shuddering breath and nodded. "I don't know how to ask this. Considering everything we've gone through."

Celeste couldn't stop the smile that spread her lips. Tears prickled in the corners of her eyes. "You don't have to ask. I understand. Lance, you came to Revary with me. You believed me. You were so brave. I can't say no."

His eyes lit up a little and a shy smile cracked his face. "It feels wrong to ask you out after all that's happened."

"After all that's happened, you have to ask me out," she countered. "After all that's happened, how can I say no? You risked your life for me. You were there when Oran left. They're all leaving. But not you."

Lance shrugged with one shoulder, his grin widening. "So it's okay to ask you to go out with me?"

Celeste nodded. "Mhm. And I'd love to." She stood up and hugged him again, this time throwing her arms around his neck. She buried her face in his neck and squeezed when she felt his arms around her middle.

"I can't leave you behind after all that, I just can't," she said and a small sob rose in her throat. "Say you'll stay with me for as long as you can."

Lance stood up, lifting her into the air in his strong embrace. "As long as you need me. I swear."

"Me, too," Celeste sobbed, her toes reaching for the floor beneath her. "Me, too."

"Don't ever leave me," Lance said. "Don't leave me behind in any of your adventures."

Celeste slid down, her arms still around his neck. She looked up into his eyes. "Never," she promised.

Lance closed his eyes, a tear leaking out from under his dark lashes. He pressed his forehead to Celeste's and waited. She let him rest his head on hers, closing her eyes, too. She loved the feeling of him leaning on her. She wanted this. The sadness. The love. The promises. She wanted it all. And now they had each other, as well. They'd face the world and their adventures together.

CHAPTER 34
EXPERIENCE

L ance's eyes burned and watered. He hadn't blinked in over a minute, staring speechless at the picture of Oran in the newspaper. His chest hurt so bad he wanted to groan, but he was paralyzed. The photo was black and white, but showed Oran's distant, sad face clearly. His eyes looked up forlornly at the camera through his black bangs. It was his senior picture from school. The paragraphs under the picture were a plea from Oran's mother to anyone who had any information about her son. They had all already been questioned by the police a day or so after they all had come home.

It had been late at night. When the police car showed up, Mom had freaked out. He'd told the police they had all split up after playing in the woods. He'd said that was the last time he saw Oran. When asked why he didn't report him missing before, Lance insisted they'd parted ways at the park, and he thought Oran had gone home from the park. When they'd said Oran had gone missing, Mom had hugged him tight.

Lance had gone numb as he'd spoken to the police. It had been a terrible weekend.

It was a lie, though. Oran wasn't going to be found.

That Monday at school, Lance walked with Celeste down the hall and out to his truck after class. She was perkier than he'd thought she'd be. She smiled at him as they entered his truck, practically glowing.

"What is it?" he asked, his own spirits still down from seeing the picture in the newspaper.

Her face fell a little. "Are you okay? You've been distant all day."

He looked away, out the front window. He spotted Alice talking to a girl and smiling brightly. They appeared to be flirting with one another.

"Oran's picture came out in the newspaper this morning," he said in a low tone.

Celeste reached over the center console of the car and took his hand. "I saw. I know you must be blaming yourself."

"I am," he interjected quickly. "I couldn't... I couldn't save him. He's gone."

"He's alive, Lance," Celeste said quickly. "He's not dead. He's just not with us." Her lips turned down a little at this. "He's in Revary now. And that's what he wanted."

Lance swallowed hard and nodded. He wanted Oran to be in their world, though. Emotion welled up in him, breaking the dam he had built up inside. "I want him here," he burst. He pulled his hand away and gripped the steering wheel, refusing to face Celeste as his eyes watered. "I tried to tell him that I'd be here for him. He said he'd be here for *me*. He lied to me, and he left me."

He couldn't stop the sob that erupted from his throat then. Celeste quickly leaned over the center console and wrapped her arms around his neck. He let her hug him while he calmed down. He knew Oran was alive and probably just fine. But he had left him. Somehow, in the short time they'd known one another, he'd grown attached to Oran.

Celeste ran her lithe fingers through his hair, hitting a few tangles on the way down. She sighed and he heard her smile as she hummed out a breath.

"He was shy, but brave, you know?" she whispered. "He was always there for me. I think I took him for granted. I think he wanted us to know what it means to miss someone. Like he did. We understand him more now that he's gone."

Lance pulled away and wiped at his eyes, turning away from Celeste. "I didn't need to know. I already understood."

She waited a beat before saying, "I didn't. I've never lost anyone. This is a wake-up call for me, Lance. To not waste my life. To pick a role and play the game. To learn the rules. To gain some experience. Partings are part of life, and we don't always get to pick when we lose someone. I know that now. I know that I should have been there for him more—like you were. But I can't change that. I *can* learn from it, though. That way, his sacrifice isn't in vain. We have to move on. For him. Do you see?"

He took a shuddering breath and looked out the window to his left. He nodded. "We don't always get to pick the lessons we learn. We just have to learn. Play the game."

"And try to win," she added with a grin.

Finally, he turned to face her. "I can try."

"Not alone," she reminded him. She leaned forward and gave him a quick kiss on his cheek.

Lance cleared his throat and sighed. "You wanted to tell me something. What was it?"

Celeste pressed her lips together, trying not to smile, and

sat back in the passenger seat. "I applied to the University of Houston."

Lance's face lit up. He'd been scouted by them just a few weeks before and had been offered a massive scholarship. He'd accepted, of course. Thinking of moving back home had brightened his otherwise bleak end of the year. "And?" he asked.

Celeste couldn't stop the smile that broke her face now. "I got in!" she crowed. She pulled a letter from her pocket and unfolded it for him to see. "The school of business accepted my application and offered me some scholarships. The rest is covered by grants. Lance," she breathed, getting up on her knees to be on eye level with him. "We can go together. You won't be alone."

He'd been worried they'd have to break up. Ever since coming back from Revary, they'd been going out, and he was afraid they'd have to part ways once they entered university. "Business school?" he asked.

She nodded. "I want to do something on my own. Entrepreneurial stuff, you know? What about you?"

He laughed nervously. "We won't have any classes together."

She tilted her head, waiting.

"I went into English. Creative writing." He paled in embarrassment.

"How..." Celeste stammered, trying not to ruin the moment. "How did that happen?"

"The campaign I was running?" he said. "I had Kiyoshi help me write it into a manuscript. I submitted it as my application to the school of English. They liked it. I'm minoring in literature so I can teach."

"Teach?" Celeste burst. "This is so... So weird! You as a teacher?"

"Well, college professor. I want to get my master's and teach at a university."

"Holy crap," Celeste giggled. "We really had a bad influence on you, didn't we?"

Lance shrugged, smiling shyly. "The best way to preserve our memories is to write them down. I want to show others the power we discovered. I felt that was the best way."

"And what about football?"

"I need a major area of study. I need something to have my degree in. Football is happening on the side. If I get drafted, that will be awesome. But if I don't, I know what I want to do."

"Wow," she breathed. She sat back and smiled. "I'm surprised. You're right. We won't have any classes together. But that's okay. Right?"

"Totally," he agreed.

She nodded, eyes forward. "We'll be the only ones staying together."

"We have our chatroom," he reasoned. "We'll still be playing *Elderforge* every night or so. We won't leave anyone behind. We'll all be together even though we're apart."

"But not us." She smiled and took his hand again. "We'll be together forever."

CELESTE LOOKED AROUND THE TABLE FROM BEHIND her dungeon master screen and surveyed the group. Kiyoshi hummed and picked up his character, tapping the base in thought. The game had been quiet for some time while they did battle with a horde of vampires in a cave. The chair beside him was empty. Oran's chair. Kiyoshi glanced at it before looking up.

"I can't do this," he sighed. "We need to go see his mom and tell her what happened."

Alice winced and shook her head. "Not if you want to remain on the outside of an asylum."

Celeste sighed sadly and looked across the table at Lance. "We went and saw her yesterday."

Kiyoshi looked up. "And?"

"She's messed up," Celeste said as diplomatically as she could. "She begged us to tell her something we might not have told the cops. She... She thinks he's dead. I had to roll with that. We're all invited to his memorial service in a few months."

"It's only been a few months," Alice said, aghast. "She's giving up?"

"I think she's trying to heal," Celeste offered. "She's getting counseling. Like we all should."

"I am," Lance said softly. "I go once a week now. It's helping."

Alice tilted her head sympathetically at her cousin. "I didn't know that."

"I didn't tell you," he said. "Was too embarrassed."

"Don't be," Celeste interjected. "That's a good thing."

A moment of silence passed as they all stared despondently down at the battle mat. Suddenly, Kiyoshi smiled and laughed lightly.

"Oran would try to befriend the vampires if he were here," he said. "Remember during the *Curse of Stormridge* when he tried to convert the big bad vampire to our side?"

At this, Celeste smiled and nodded. She told Lance, "Right before you joined our group. We were playing this horror campaign and Oran tried to save every last vampire in the entire story."

"He said they were just spawn and innocent," Kiyoshi put in. "That they didn't deserve to die." He shook his head. "He always saw the good in the darkest of people."

Celeste's chest tightened at the memory, but she smiled. In the privacy of her own mind, she tried to imagine what Oran would become in Revary. What would he choose to be? She took a deep breath to calm herself as the emotion rose in her. He was safe, she told herself. He was happy.

A small tinge of melancholy touched her heart as she remembered the Eidolon's words: she'd never go back to Revary. With Oran there to protect it, she doubted she needed to.

She smiled. "Alice, it's your turn."

EPILOGUE
MANY YEARS LATER

S un spilled through the gothic windows of the old classroom of the University of Northminster. It made the dust particles in the air look like fairies. It also warmed up the stacks of books on the opposite wall, making the entire classroom smell like old books. The sun was a rarity in this part of England.

Lance tucked his hair behind his ear before answering the student who had asked him a question. "It's not really supposed to make sense like that, Morgan," he said evenly. "We know the windmills are just that: windmills. But what we know isn't important. It's how the main character sees them. We're meant to experience this through his eyes, even though we know the truth."

"But I don't get it," Morgan moaned. "Why does he think they're giants?"

Lance shoved his hands in his pockets. Class had ended a few minutes before, but the girl wouldn't stop asking questions. He liked that about her. "Listen, Morgan, come talk to me. The rest of you, get moving before you're late for your next class."

His class quickly picked up their book bags and rushed out, chattering the whole way. Morgan approached his desk. Lance looked around the classroom, loving the dust he caught floating in the sun beams shining through the gothic windows. The place was old, and he liked it that way. Made it feel like a magical school.

"Professor," Morgan said, holding her books to her chest. "Besides windmills, I was wondering why you're here. You seemed really into travel literature early this semester, and it got me and Bri talking. Wondering why an American came to teach at Northminster."

Lance leaned against the big wooden desk, crossing his arms. "My wife and I were running away from some windmills of our own. If that makes any sense."

"Not really," Morgan sighed. "I still don't get the windmills."

"Giants, Morgan," Lance said patiently. "Big, huge monsters that want to hurt us."

Morgan's eyes went wide. "What were you running from? You and your wife?"

Lance sighed. "The past. It's complicated. But I'm here now, a professor at the University of Northminster, and I'm still waiting on your short assignment to be turned in." He raised his brows at her.

"Oh, I'm sorry!" Morgan fumbled in her book bag and pulled out a single piece of paper. "I actually did have it done on time, but I wanted to make sure it was perfect."

He took it and smiled down at it. "So long as you are having some sort of discussion about the literature, you did fine."

"That's all?" Morgan asked. "Just discussion? Even though the story didn't make much sense?"

Lance nodded. "If you walk away with more questions than you had before reading it, then the piece did its job. Stories might not make sense, but they're not supposed to be perfect copies of reality. They're not supposed to replicate the world around us. They're supposed to improve it, to show something the author sees."

Morgan made a sour face. "So the point of all this old literature is to confuse us?"

Lance laughed. "Something like that."

THE CITY OF NORTHMINSTER BUZZED LOUDLY FOR A small English city. Lance jogged to the little cafe where Celeste waited with a stroller with their two children inside it. She had her face buried in a large novel with a fantastic cover: a warrior facing a dragon over a spine of mountains.

"What are you reading?" Lance asked, sliding into a seat next to her. He leaned over and kissed her.

"Kiyoshi's new book," she said simply. "It's pretty good. Very dark, though." She sighed and closed it, setting it down. The title beamed up at them, red text on a mostly white cover.

"*Arbiter of the Vampire Lord,*" Lance read the title out loud. He hummed and tilted his head to take in the cover better. "Does the main character on the cover look familiar?"

It must have been a vampire character of some kind. Fierce blue eyes looked out from behind a fringe of black hair. Lance swore he knew that face. It triggered something deep in his memory he couldn't place. The harder he tried to remember, the more evasive the familiarity became.

Lance pulled himself out of his reverie and looked up at his wife. "Kiyoshi. Wow. Haven't heard from any of the old crowd in years." He thought back to those days. Their senior year. "Heard from anyone else?"

Celeste shook her head, pressing her lips together. He guessed she didn't want to talk about it.

"You missed it," Celeste said, bringing him back to the present. "Story said her first words, and Arial quickly told her to shut up."

Lance laughed and leaned over the stroller to look at his one-year-old baby girl and their three-year-old son. "That so, Arial?" he asked. The boy didn't reply, choosing instead to play with a toy in the bottom of the seat.

"He won't talk for me yet," Lance sighed sadly. "What did Story say that made him upset?" He ordered a coffee when the waitress walked past.

"She said she wanted his car." Celeste smiled proudly. "And Arial loudly declared no and told her to find her own car."

"Ah, that's my girl," Lance beamed, leaning over to kiss Story on the top of her head. "Maybe she'll grow up to be a mechanic."

"Lance, no," Celeste laughed. She cleared her throat and leaned back to look at him. "How was class? Your students still adore you?"

He smiled and laughed lightly through his nose. "Sometimes. One of them asked me today why we came to Northminster. She asked what we were running from." He eyed her carefully, knowing she hated this conversation. Moving continents had been her idea. She'd wanted to leave not just the

Midwest, but the U.S. all together. She'd wanted to run far after Story was born.

"Please don't start," Celeste begged. "We have a good life here. I love it."

"And I love you." He checked the table and saw her calendar open. "How's business?"

"Booming," she smiled. "I have a meeting this evening with a potential client who happens to be a member of parliament."

"Fancy," Lance said sarcastically.

Celeste giggled and slapped his arm playfully. "It's really good money. She may be a little bit of a handful to work with, but I think I can really make her place shine."

Lance shook his head. "Who would have thought interior decorating would be your thing?"

She pressed her lips to the side, giving him a look. "It's more than that. It's my business. I own it. It's mine. I made it all on my own, you know? I chose this."

"I'm hurt. I helped. I was there for you through it all."

"Yes, you were. My own little Shakespeare."

Lance leaned over the table and kissed Celeste hard on her lips again. She giggled into his mouth and kissed him back.

"I love you, too, Lance."

He broke the kiss and smiled at the three of them. "So, what's on the docket for today?" he said, slapping his knees.

Celeste shrugged and blushed. "Normal life things. Arial has his checkup in an hour, and we need to go grocery shopping. How's that sound?"

Lance closed his eyes, soaking up the rare sunshine. "Sounds amazing and perfect."

Abi works part-time as a free-lance ghostwriter, editor, audio-book narrator, and is one half of the partnership that owns Altered Reality Magazine. She hopes to one day make these passions her full-time job while she hunts for the next bohemian adventure.

She has published works of fiction, poetry, academia, and even won awards for her short stories in science fiction and horror. Her novel, *The Trial of Two*, was named an Honorable Mention in the Writer's Digest 2021 self-publishing awards and won first place in the dark fantasy category in The Book-Fest Awards. Abi is also a proud mom of two ferrets. She currently resides in Kansas.

Abi is one of nine children--all who share the creative spark.

Find Abi online at: www.abigaillinhardt.com

ALSO BY ABIGAIL LINHARDT

Season of the Runer Book I: The Trial of Two

Season of the Runer Book II: Sojourn

Season of the Runer Book III: The Eldritch Hunt

Season of the Runer IV: The Father of Monsters

Season of the Runer Book V: A Cure for Fate

Prince of MidWest

Why They Killed: A Waksha Virus Novelette

These Darker Streets

Writing as A.J. Morgenstern

DarkFront Witness: Haunted

DarkFront Witness: Hunted

DarkFront Witness: Free

www.ingramcontent.com/pod-product-compliance
Lightning Source LLC
Chambersburg PA
CBHW051935240626
47153CB00005B/1498